PRAISE FOR

CRASH INTO YOU

"Revved up and red-hot sexy, *Crash Into You* delivers a riveting romance!"

—Lorelei James, *New York Times* bestselling author of the Blacktop Cowboys series and the Rough Riders series

"Hot and romantic, with an edge of suspense that will keep you entertained."

—Shayla Black, USA Today bestselling author of *Mine to Hold*

"A sexy, sizzling tale that is sure to have readers begging for more! . . . I can't wait for Roni Loren's next tantalizing story!"

—Jo Davis, author of *I Spy a Dark Obsession*

"Sexy as hell, gutsy as all get out—*Crash Into You* has balls! Watch out. Roni Loren, just like the men in her books, knows how to keep you up all night. *Crash Into You* is sexy as hell and goes into the dark places other writers shy away from. Loren understands the dark beauty of D/s and treats her characters with respect even as she takes them to the very edge of what they and the reader can handle. I can sum this book up in one word: Damn!"

—Tiffany Reisz, author of *The Siren*

"This steamy, sexy yet emotionally gripping story has the right touch of humor and love to keep readers coming back for a second round."

—Julie Cross, author of *Tempest*

"A stunning first work. I read it straight through in one sitting, and I dare you to even attempt to put it down."

—Cassandra Carr, author of *Talk to Me*

Titles by Roni Loren

Fall into You

RONI LOREN

HEAT | NEW YORK

THE BERKLEY PUBLISHING GROUP
Published by the Penguin Group
Penguin Group (USA) Inc.
375 Hudson Street, New York, New York 10014, USA
Penguin Group (Canada), 90 Eglinton Avenue East, Suite 700, Toronto, Ontario M4P 2Y3, Canada (a division of Pearson Penguin Canada Inc.) • Penguin Books Ltd, 80 Strand, London WC2R 0RL, England • Penguin Ireland, 25 St Stephen's Green, Dublin 2, Ireland (a division of Penguin Books Ltd) • Penguin Group (Australia), 707 Collins Street, Melbourne, Victoria 3008, Australia (a division of Pearson Australia Group Pty Ltd) • Penguin Books India Pvt Ltd, 11 Community Centre, Panchsheel Park, New Delhi–110 017, India • Penguin Group (NZ), 67 Apollo Drive, Rosedale, Auckland 0632, New Zealand (a division of Pearson New Zealand Ltd) • Penguin Books, Rosebank Office Park, 181 Jan Smuts Avenue, Parktown North 2193, South Africa • Penguin China, B7 Jaiming Center, 27 East Third Ring Road North, Chaoyang District, Beijing 100020, China

Penguin Books Ltd., Registered Offices: 80 Strand, London WC2R 0RL, England

This book is an original publication of The Berkley Publishing Group.

PUBLISHING HISTORY
Heat trade paperback edition / January 2013

Library of Congress Cataloging-in-Publication Data

Loren, Roni.
Fall into you / Roni Loren.—Heat trade paperback ed.
p. cm.
ISBN 978-0-425-25991-7
1. Women sportswriters—Fiction. 2. Erotic fiction. I. Title.
PS3612.O764F35 2013
813'.6—dc23
2012031810

PRINTED IN THE UNITED STATES OF AMERICA

10 9 8 7 6 5 4 3 2 1

To my husband, Donnie, who once asked me in an airport,
"What if next time I don't have to leave?"
and then moved his whole life
to be with me. I'm glad you took the risk
on us all those years ago.
I love you, babe.

ACKNOWLEDGMENTS

First, a huge thanks to every reader who has picked up one of my books. You have given me the opportunity to follow my dream and tell stories for a living. And for that, I will be forever grateful. *hugs*

To my family, who is always there for me to celebrate the successes and to pick me up when things go awry. I love you more than I could ever put into words.

To my fantastic agent, Sara Megibow. You are always there with good advice, a sympathetic ear, and a barrel full of enthusiasm. And to my editor, Kate Seaver, thank you for loving my books and working hard to make them the best they can be.

To my writer buddies Jamie Wesley, Julie Cross, Dawn Alexander, and Genevieve Wilson. Thanks for making me laugh, listening to me vent, and for all the cheerleading. And to Taylor Lunsford, my fearless beta reader, for donating your time and for loving Grant.

ONE

Come on, baby, don't give up on me now. Charli Beaumonde gripped the steering wheel tighter as her eight-year-old Toyota's headlights flickered for the second time in ten minutes. She adjusted her rearview mirror, wondering, not for the first time, if she should've stopped in one of the small-town motels she'd passed thirty miles back. The deserted highway hadn't seemed quite so jeepers creepers this morning on her way out of the city as it did now.

But then again, those motels had looked more Norman Bates than bed-and-breakfast. She was probably better off taking her chances with her on-its-last-wheel car.

She hadn't planned to be out in boondocks Texas this late at night, but the chance to see who was coming and going from the family home of Dallas University's top quarterback recruit had been too good to pass up. Who knew so many men in suits had business in such a podunk Texas town?

She hadn't gathered enough damning evidence to put together a story for the station yet, but she was getting there. If she could get one of the players to slip up and talk, give her some names, she could blow the cheating scandal wide open and virtually secure her promotion to the on-air sidelines reporter for the Texas Sports Network.

Her boss had already told her she was one of the final candidates. Charli didn't know how many other people she was up against, but she knew that she could go toe-to-toe with anyone on sports knowledge. Plus, she felt like her screen test had gone well. All she needed now was the one big story under her belt to show that she had the reporter chops as well.

She smiled, picturing herself on the sidelines of the college football games—microphone in hand, the smell of fresh-cut grass and sweaty athletes, the deafening roar of the crowd cheering for their teams. She couldn't think of anything that would make her happier or any place she'd rather be. The years of working her ass off behind the scenes would finally pay off. She may even get enough of a salary boost to be able to spring for a new car.

She adjusted in her seat, but the faint flash of light in her rearview had her glancing in the mirror again. Distant headlights pierced the black vortex behind her. Her shoulders loosened a bit, her grip on the wheel easing. For some reason, knowing she wasn't the only person on this lonely road gave her a weird sense of comfort. She pressed a button on her radio to tune into her favorite sports talk station and settled in for the last hour of her drive back to Dallas.

But right when one of the hosts started bitching about the Cowboys offense, the glare of headlights became blinding in her rearview as the driver flashed his high beams on and off. Squinting, Charli grabbed the mirror and turned it away from her. "What the hell?"

She slowed down a bit, thinking the driver must have some emergency and wanted to get past her. But when she eased up on the gas, he didn't go around, he just got closer. *Flash. Flash. Flash.* The lights created a strobe effect in her car, disorienting her. She grabbed the steering wheel and jerked it to the left to move into the other lane, but the other car stayed on her rear as if it were tied to her bumper with rope.

"Shit." She tried again, going back to the right lane, but the car followed, nearly clipping her rear bumper. The creeping unease she'd been fighting since she'd pulled onto this highway morphed into a hot flood of panic.

Whoever was in the car wasn't trying to get past her—he was trying to get *to* her.

She slammed on her gas pedal in an attempt to put some distance between them and regain her vision, but her four-cylinder Toyota was no match for whatever was behind her. The rumble of a bigger, more powerful engine drowned out the quiet hum of her own.

She felt around for her cell phone, but the damn thing had tumbled to the floorboard when she'd made the hard lane change. Keeping her hands firmly on the wheel and knowing her speedometer was sliding into a zone it'd never ventured to, she tried to bump the phone closer with her left foot. Once it was within reach, she took one hand off the wheel and attempted to make a grab for the cell. *Come on, come on, just another inch.* But as soon as her fingers closed around her only lifeline, a hard jolt rocked the vehicle, knocking her head hard into the steering wheel and sending her world into a spin.

The sound of squealing tires was the last thing Charli heard before everything went black.

Grant liked the quiet cocoon of the night. His resort, The Ranch, didn't slow down until three A.M. most evenings. So after spending his time over there, supervising and making sure everything was running smoothly, he relished the walk over from the main resort area to his private cabin on the far corner of the property.

Not many things could match the calming effect of the breeze blowing through the fields of grapevine, the night bugs singing, and the kind of rich silence that could only be had this far out of the city. In fact, there was only one other thing that could trump it—having a beautiful woman fully surrendering under his hand.

That's what he'd really been hoping to find tonight—and every night for the last four months since he'd handed off his last trainee to her new dom. But even with The Ranch at his fingertips, finding a woman who appealed to him and his particular wants was proving near impossible. His tastes had grown refined, specific. He had no shortage of applicants for his monthlong immersion training. But the submissives he came across were either not ready for the level of commitment he required during training or were secretly hoping he'd take them on long term. And long term wasn't his game.

The one-off, uncommitted play sessions could sometimes meet his immediate needs in between trainees. But it was like a carnivore living on a vegetarian diet. He was never truly satisfied. He craved the intensity that could only be reached when a sub fully gave herself to him for weeks at a time.

So instead of clearing his mind with the all-encompassing experience of D/s, he was left to rely on the sound of the crickets and the blanket of the night to soften the edges of his thoughts. It was really the only time of the day when his brain would shut down and simply be.

But when he made the turn around the last bend in the path toward his home, a faint screeching sound sliced through the thick night air. He stilled, his ears and body going on full alert—a skill he'd never shaken from his years in the army and CIA. The distant sound of a revving engine followed the screech and then faded.

He frowned. Probably a driver stopping suddenly to avoid an animal in the road or something. The car had sounded like it had driven off, but Grant didn't want to assume everything was okay. The highway his ranch sat off of wasn't heavily traveled. So if someone had gotten in an accident, the coyotes and bobcats would probably find them before help did.

He jogged the rest of the way to his cabin and headed straight for his pickup truck. He pulled his keys from his pocket and his boot hit the gas before he'd even shut the door completely. The drive up to the main road only took a few minutes at a normal pace, but when Grant saw twin beams of light in the distance, he kicked into overdrive, his truck bouncing along the dirt road like an off-road racer.

By the time he got to the main gate, he could see the front end of a car peeking out of the ditch on the opposite side of the road. The soft whine of the dying horn filled his ears. "Shit."

He threw the gear into park and jumped out of the truck. The gate was chained with a padlock, but he didn't want to waste time getting it unfastened, so he planted a foot on one of the bars and vaulted over it.

"Hello?" he called out after landing with a thud on the other side. Only the fading horn and the smell of burnt rubber greeted him. He hurried across the road and peered down into what appeared to be a wrecked Toyota. The tail end had slid into the ditch, the runoff rainwater from yesterday's storm rushing past the back tires. Grant squinted, trying to see into the front seat. The headlights were the only illumination besides the moon, and all he could make out was the outline of a person in the front seat.

"Hello?" he called again. "If you can hear me, I'm here to help you."

No response.

Grant hurried around to the other side of the car and carefully worked his way down the muddy embankment to get closer to the driver. His boots hit the bottom of the gully and water sluiced over his feet. Even this close, it was still too dark to see much. He grabbed his cell phone out of his jeans pocket and hit the button to illuminate the screen, holding the phone out toward the closed driver's side window. The faint light from the phone spilled onto the profile of a woman, head slumped against the headrest, eyes closed.

His stomach flipped—a familiar sick feeling that never failed to show up no matter how much injury or death he'd seen in his life. *No. Come on. Be okay.* He wedged open the door, the soft earth only allowing him to get it halfway open, and leaned into the car to put fingers against the woman's neck. The strong *thump, thump, thump* of her pulse touched his fingers.

"Thank you, God." He touched her clammy cheek. "Ma'am, can you hear me? You've been in an accident. We're going to get you some help."

Though, with the nearest hospital forty-five minutes away, he wasn't exactly sure when said help might get there. He hit another button on his cell phone.

Marc, one of his managers, answered on the first ring. "Hey, Grant, what's up?"

"I need you to find Dr. Montgomery. I think he was playing with Janessa tonight in a cabin on the west side."

"You want me to interrupt a scene?" Marc asked, the surprise in his voice evident. "Is everything okay?"

Grant quickly explained what was going on and told him to also put in a call to 911 to get an ambulance headed this way. Once he'd given Marc his marching orders, Grant returned his focus to the woman in the car. He'd learned first-aid skills in the military so knew not to move her neck or try to get her out of the car. But he checked her breathing to make sure nothing was obstructed.

Her seat belt was on, so she'd had some protection in the crash. But based on the swelling knot on her forehead, she'd hit her head on something—most likely the steering wheel. With gentle fingers, he brushed her hair away from the tender spot to examine it closer and make sure it wasn't bleeding. He leaned in to get a better look, but a low moan made him halt.

He turned his head and the woman's eyelashes fluttered. Another garbled sound passed her lips.

"Shh, easy now," he soothed, using the tone he employed when dealing with skittish horses. "Try not to move, darlin'. We're going to get you some help."

Her entire body went rigid, and her lids flew open, her eyes going wide with fear.

He backed out of the car a bit, so as not to freak her out more, but put a hand on her shoulder. "It's okay. You're okay. You've been in an accident. I need you to stay still until the doctor gets here to check you."

She blinked, her lips parted as if to say something, but then she winced and her hand went to her head. "Dizzy."

"You've hit your head. Try to take some nice, slow breaths." Grant kept his voice coaxing as he watched her follow his directions. "Can you tell me your name, darlin'?"

She squeezed her eyes shut, continuing to take deep breaths. "Uh . . . Charlotte, no . . . Charli."

"Okay, good, Charli," Grant said, relieved to hear she still knew her name. "Do you know where you are or what happened to you?"

"I'm . . . I . . ." A crease appeared between her brows as if she were trying hard to locate the information. "I can't remember."

He squeezed her shoulder. "That's all right. We'll worry about that later."

The sucking sound of feet hitting wet earth drew Grant's attention back toward the ditch's embankment. Dr. Theo Montgomery was making his way down, wearing a pair of pajama bottoms and an open oxford shirt, and holding one of the well-stocked first-aid kits from The Ranch. Red marks, no doubt from Janessa's flogger, marked his bare chest.

"Status," Theo said, all business.

"Name is Charli. She just woke up. Breathing is fine. Probably concussed—can remember her name but nothing about what happened. Contusion on her forehead. I haven't moved her."

"Good." Theo moved in when Grant stepped out of the way. He introduced himself with the short, quick style of an ER doctor and started his examination. Charli would be in good hands.

An hour and a half later, the sun was starting to peek over the horizon as an EMT checked Charli over one last time and discussed the situation with Theo. Grant stood off to the side, watching as the beautiful redhead tried to stay focused on the conversation these people were having about her.

"Looks like it's only a mild concussion. We can bring her back to Graham Regional and keep her for observation," the EMT told Theo.

"I don't want to go to the hospital," Charli said, her voice low and hoarse. "I just want to go home and rest."

The young guy frowned down at her. "Ma'am, do you have someone at home who can keep an eye on you for the next twenty-four hours?"

She closed her eyes, rubbing the bridge of her nose, like it hurt to think. "Uh, Tom Brady."

The EMT's head tilted. "The quarterback?"

"My cat."

The ever-serious Theo smiled a bit at that. "Charli, I don't think your cat can call 911 if you go unconscious again."

"He's very smart," she said, not opening her eyes, but her mouth twitching at the corner. "Could probably . . . figure it out."

Her voice was fading a bit, her exhaustion evident.

"No, I think you'd better let them take you in," Theo said. "You need to have someone with you for a little while. And you can't drive home right now, anyway. It's not safe and your car is trashed."

She raised her gaze then, a flicker of fight-or-flight passing through those green eyes. "Please, don't make me. I hate hospitals."

The underlying quiver in her voice hit Grant square in the sternum. He prided himself on being able to read even the subtlest of clues in others. It had served him well when extracting information from people in his days in the CIA and made him quite the formidable dominant now. And what he was sensing was honest fear in this woman. It was more than not wanting the inconvenience of a hospital—she was genuinely freaked out at the thought.

Before he could think it through, he stepped forward. "If the lady doesn't object, she can stay here for the day. I have unoccupied cabins at my vineyard. She's more than welcome to use one, and I can check on her every few hours."

Charli's attention slid to him, her eyebrow lifting beneath the knot on her forehead. "You have a vineyard?"

He chuckled. No doubt his muddy jeans and plaid work shirt didn't scream that in addition to his covert side business, he ran one of the most successful wineries in Texas. He held out his hand. "Grant Waters, owner and operator of Water's Edge Wines."

She took his offered hand, and Grant felt the slight tremor go through her fingers, caught the quick-as-lightning glance at the open collar of his shirt, the slight hitch in her breathing. *Well, well.* His body warmed in a wholly inappropriate way at her subtle signs of interest. He quickly dropped the handshake and stepped back. *She's had a blow to the head, horn dog. Reel it in.*

Theo crossed his arms and nodded in Grant's direction. "I can vouch for Mr. Waters. I'm a guest at his . . . vineyard cabins all the time. You'll be comfortable and safe here."

"And I can drive you back to town tomorrow," Grant offered, trying not to sound as eager as he felt. "I have to go into Dallas for a business meeting anyway."

She smirked and the faint freckles on her nose twitched. "You're not some serial killer rapist, right? Because I've had a shitty enough night already."

The unexpected comment made him laugh. No, he wasn't a serial killer rapist. But the way she bit her lip after making that comment had his less-than-pure thoughts driving up to an NC-17 rating.

"Nope. Just a rancher and winemaker." And owner of the most elite BDSM resort this side of the Mason-Dixon. But that wasn't something she needed to know about him.

At least not while she was concussed.

But later . . . well, later was ripe with possibilities.

He'd always had a thing for freckles.

TWO

In the depths of Charli's sleep she felt warmth against her skin, a gentle caress, but it took her a few minutes to clear the cotton in her brain and fully awaken. When she finally opened her eyes, she was graced with the true reason Wranglers were invented bending over the small dresser on the far side of the bedroom. The soft, well-worn denim molded over Grant's backside as if the material was simply another layer of his skin.

Knowing he hadn't noticed she was awake yet, she took the moment to drink him in. And, my, what a big gulp he was. Six-six at least, maybe six-seven. Basketball height with a baseball player's body and the corded forearm muscles of someone who came by their strength the old-fashioned way. She felt the urge to have his hand against hers again—that big paw closing over her smaller one. His handshake had made her feel . . . dainty and delicate—something she damn sure never felt around most anyone.

He set down a plate of sandwiches and peeked over his shoulder, those killer blue eyes crinkling a bit at the corners when he noticed her looking back at him. "Well, look who's awake. I wasn't sure if you were going to crack an eye open before the sun went down."

She pushed up on her elbows, fighting past the slight wave of nausea the movement caused. "Have I been sleeping long?"

"It's almost six," he said, pushing an escaped lock of his wavy dark hair off his forehead. "I didn't want to wake you, but Doc said to check you every few hours by touching your arm to see if you moved. Plus, I thought you might be hungry."

So he had touched her. Even knowing that sent rosy warmth coursing through her veins, a warmth that seemed to be zeroing in on the juncture between her thighs. She shifted her weight in the bed, suddenly all too aware that she was only wearing panties and her T-shirt beneath the blanket. She tried, unsuccessfully, to fight off the blush that rose in her cheeks.

God, what was wrong with her? She'd just been in an accident and all she could focus on was the way this man got her hormones hopping. Maybe she'd done damage to her brain with the accident and had reverted to crushing on someone like a damn teenager. She should take his picture and hang it on her wall so she could draw hearts on it.

"I'm not sure I should eat. I still feel kind of queasy."

"Yeah, you're pale." He grabbed a few saltines off the plate and handed them to her. "Maybe try some crackers first. Might help to put something dry in your belly."

"Thanks." She didn't bother telling him she always looked pale—compliments of her mother's Irish genes, the only thing her mother had bothered to give her. She bit into one of the crackers and it crumbled, covering her and the bedcovers with crumbs. "Oops, sorry. Guess that's why crackers in bed are a bad idea."

He laughed, a deep tenor of a chuckle. "I promise I won't kick you out of my bed for that."

Her chewing paused, and a hot shiver went through her, drawing her nipples tight against her T-shirt. She couldn't tell if Mr.

Handsome Cowboy had intended that to come across as flirty as it sounded; his expression gave no indication either way. But her body sure wanted to take the comment down a certain path.

She almost laughed at the thought. Who was she kidding? Guys who looked like him didn't flirt with girls like her—especially considering she probably looked like a midnight mug shot with a lump on her head, her hair in a tangle, and no makeup—not that she ever bothered to wear makeup on a normal day anyway.

She needed to get her concussed head out of lusty la-la land and focus on getting back home. She had work to do. "What time do you plan to head to Dallas tomorrow?"

He leaned back against the dresser, crossing his ankles, and creating a nice frame for the healthy bulge in his jeans. His gaze flicked down briefly, no doubt noticing the now-hard points beneath her shirt. He wet his lips. "My appointment isn't until two, but I reckon we can head out a bit earlier so we can get you home."

She swallowed past the dryness in her throat, not sure if it was the saltines or the view making her mouth so arid. "Sounds good. I really appreciate this. I'll pay you whatever the fee for the cabin would've been for the night."

"You won't," he said with the simple authority of someone used to getting no argument. "You're my guest. Your money's no good here."

She sat up straighter, his tone pushing her least favorite button. "Then I'll pay for the gas to get back to Dallas."

He shoved off the dresser, rising to his full height, a smirk hiding beneath his five o'clock shadow. "And my grandmother would flip in her grave. Women in my world don't pay for anything."

Her hackles rose. "Well, now wa—"

He took her hand and rubbed a thumb across the top of it, his touch incinerating the thoughts in her brain. "You've had a rough twenty-four hours. I don't need your money. And you don't owe me anything. Though I do have one small request, Ms. . . ."

"Beaumonde."

"Beau— Wait a second," he said, cutting off whatever he'd been planning to ask her and dropping her hand like she'd become contagious. "Do you know Max Beaumonde?"

She frowned, trying to pull herself from the hypnotic state his touch had induced. "Yes. He's my older brother."

Grant tilted his head back and looked at the ceiling. "Ah, hell. Of course he is."

Charli had no idea if her head injury was messing with her focus, but she had trouble following the shift in Grant's demeanor and the conversation. "You know him?"

Grant sniffed. "Yeah, you could say that. He's got a bullet lodged in his shoulder that was meant for me."

Charli stared at him, the words taking a few moments to register. "You're Ice?"

A dark cloud seemed to cross over Grant's face. "Was. Gotta love those army nicknames."

Her brother had told her stories about his army buddy, Ice. Had told her the guy had gotten his name because nothing seemed to get to him or scare him. But when one of their missions had gone awry, Max had ended up being the one to protect Ice from a fatal shot. Her brother had gotten a medal for it, but no one in her family had ever met the guy Max had saved.

"Wow, Max will be thrilled to know you're only a state away. He lives in Baton Rouge."

Grant went to the tray of food, turning his back to her. He busied himself pouring a bottle of water into a glass. "He knows where I am. We've kept in touch. He's mentioned he had a sister a few times, but I assumed you were in Louisiana with the rest of his family."

The air in the room had changed directions—awkwardness replacing the electricity she'd felt moments before when he'd held her hand. She cleared her throat. "Uh, you were saying you had a request for me?"

He headed back her way and set the glass of water on the bedside table. "Never mind. Wasn't important. Now you rest up, and I'll check on you later tonight. My cell number is next to the phone if you need anything."

What she needed was him touching her again, but apparently that buzz of sexual energy had only been one-sided.

"Grant?"

He turned around in the doorway. "Yes, ma'am?"

"If you do talk to my brother anytime soon, don't mention this, okay? His heart's in the right place, but he's a little . . . overprotective." And bossy and overbearing. And thinks she can't handle the big, bad city alone.

"Yeah, sure, no problem." Grant's gaze traced down the length of her, lines of strain around his mouth. She thought she heard him mutter—*who could blame him?*—but he walked out before she could ask.

Grant shifted on the too-short couch, trying to find a comfortable position, but only ended up twisting his blanket into a knot around his thighs. With a groan, he yanked off the blanket and sat up. The clock had already crossed over to four A.M., so falling asleep had sort of lost its point anyway. He rolled his shoulders, trying to coax out the tension that had embedded there the moment he'd caught Charli looking at him with interest in her eyes.

Charli-*freaking*-Beaumonde. He'd been on the verge of asking her out—a stupid move in the first place because he didn't mess with women who weren't part of the scene. That was setting up disaster from step one. Nothing like springing on a vanilla person—*Hey, I'm a dominant and a sexual sadist. Oh, and I run a BDSM resort where I have submissives offering themselves to me daily.* Yeah, fun conversation.

But it would've been even worse if he had found out afterward that she was Max's sister. The guy had saved Grant's life and was a real friend—even if they didn't talk often these days. And Grant knew that Max's protective streak ran deep enough to rival his own.

That killer protective instinct was why Max had been there the day Grant had ended up walking right into a trap. Grant had wandered from camp, needing to be alone after realizing it was the one-year anniversary of something he couldn't bear to remember but couldn't ever forget. He'd been numb and honestly not caring if he lived or died—but Max had followed. Had watched Grant's back and, ultimately, had jumped in front of him when Grant had found himself on the bad end of an enemy soldier's gun.

Max had risked his life without hesitation to protect him. So Grant could only imagine how protective and not-cool-with-it Max would be if Grant had made a move on his baby sister.

No, Grant had to do the right thing. Even if that meant he'd gone to bed with a headache and a case of blue balls. He just needed to get Charli back to her own place and out of his line of sight. Then he needed to get over his picky tendencies and take up one of the submissives at The Ranch on her offer and indulge his starved libido.

He'd let himself go too long and had gotten to the point where he wasn't thinking straight—where he'd actually considered asking a girl on a date.

He didn't do dating. Or relationships. Or vanilla. What exactly had he thought he would do with a girl like Charli? Take her out for a movie and then what? The minute she found out how dark his cowboy hat could get, she'd hightail it like a jackrabbit running from a bobcat.

A muffled cry filtered through the quiet of the cabin, breaking Grant from his thoughts. In an instant, he was on his feet and heading to Charli's closed bedroom door. He'd checked her an hour or so before and she'd been in a sound sleep, but another whimper of distress had him rapping sharply on the door. "Charli, you okay?"

When she didn't answer, he turned the knob and pushed the door open. Charli was on her side, sheets tangled around her and one long leg exposed from ankle to hip. Resisting the urge to stare, he dragged his attention upward and crouched next to the side of the bed. Sweat soaked her hair, plastering strands to her forehead and the swollen knot.

He laid a hand on her shoulder to give her a gentle shake. "Charli, wake up, darlin'."

She moaned again, and her face twisted into a scowl. "No, stop, go around . . ."

But he could tell she wasn't talking to him. Some nightmare had taken hold. He jostled her a bit harder, calling her name. At that, she screamed and launched herself upward, knocking her head into his before he had the chance to back off.

Her eyes snapped open, wide with panic as she scanned the room.

"Shh, Charli. You're okay," he said, rubbing his own forehead. "You were having a bad dream."

She glanced over at him, blinked. The wildness in her eyes seemed to dissipate as she stared at him. "Grant?"

"The very one."

"Ow." She put her hand to her head, and he tried not to notice that she'd sweated right through the white T-shirt he'd let her borrow. The dark shadows of her nipples peeked through, sending a rush of his blood decidedly south. He forced his gaze upward. He couldn't get a hard-on right now. He was already enough of an asshole for thinking about her that way when she'd clearly woken up from a nightmare.

He cleared his throat. "You all right?"

"Yes. No." She shook her head slightly, like she was still trying to clear the cobwebs. "I think my memory is coming back."

"About the accident?"

She swung her legs over the side of the bed and stood, either unconcerned or unaware that she was only in a T-shirt and what looked to be grandma-sized panties. "I need to go home."

"Whoa," he said, stepping closer. "What's wrong? What do you remember?"

"I don't want to rehash it. I just—" She glanced down at her state of undress and even in the predawn light he could see her cheeks darken. "Shit. Where are my pants?"

"I washed everything and hung your stuff up in the bathroom."

She hurried past him, a bit unsteady on her feet, and went into the bathroom. The sink turned on and off. When she stepped out again, she had her jeans and her own shirt back on and had twisted her long locks into some kind of makeshift bun. "Since we're both up anyway, do you mind taking me now?"

"I don't mind, but I'd sure like to know why you're moving so fast all of a sudden. Tell me what's going on."

"It's not important," she said, grabbing her purse.

"The hell it isn't." He crossed his arms over his chest, squaring off with her. Her agitation wasn't simply a need to get home. She'd remembered something bad. He could almost taste her fear, like the air had been flavored with it. "Take a breath. I'll take you home. But tell me what's got you scared."

Those green eyes, the ones that had been so soft and inviting the day before, turned guarded. But if she thought the tough-girl face was hiding the anxiety he could feel vibrating off her, she was sadly mistaken. He'd spent too many years reading cues in people. She'd have to do better than that to fool him.

She took a deep breath. "Look, I appreciate the help you've given me. I do. But I just need to get home."

"If you're in some kind of trouble, Max would want—"

She raised a hand to him, halting his words. "If it were up to Max, I would still be living around the corner so he could make sure the wind didn't blow on me wrong. And everything is fine."

Sure it was. She hadn't even been able to keep the eye contact when telling the lie.

He had to stop himself from calling her on it or demanding honesty. She'd only put up more defenses, and that would get them nowhere.

Looked like the girl who he'd lain awake fantasizing about all night didn't respond well to his bossy side. Par for the course. "Fine. Wait out front, and I'll drive my truck around."

She gave him a curt, satisfied nod, thinking she had won. "Thank you."

He bit his tongue and headed out the door.

She wouldn't be thanking him later when she found out what he was about to do on the walk back to his cabin. In his personal life, he considered a woman's consent as sacred as religion. But when it came to someone's safety, he wasn't going to waste time asking for permission.

He was taking charge of this rodeo.

THREE

The ride back to Dallas was a quiet one. Grant made attempts at polite conversation with Charli, but she couldn't concentrate. All she could think about was the fact that she'd been purposely run off the road by someone—that she could've been killed.

She planned to call the cops when she got home and was out of Mr. Sexy Cowboy's earshot. But she knew that whatever small-town police force covered that stretch of country road probably couldn't do much without any witnesses or license plate numbers. She couldn't even give them the make or model of the car. The lights had been so bright. All she could figure was that it had been a truck or SUV of some sort. Something that was taller than her vehicle.

And most likely it had been a drunk driver or kids letting a prank get out of hand. At least she hoped that's what it'd been. The other possibilities were too frightening to consider.

"So you're really not going to tell me what happened, huh?" Grant asked, his tone light, but his expression tense beneath the brim of his cowboy hat. "Even if I ask all polite-like?"

She couldn't help but smile at that. With that low drawl and dimpled cheek, he could pretty much ask her anything, and she'd probably fold at some point. But she knew his type too well. Her brother Max was the same way. If Grant found out she could be in some kind of danger, he'd be calling her brother in an instant and treating her like she was ten. She definitely didn't need that. "You're not used to hearing no, are ya, cowboy?"

He smirked, deepening that dimple and confirming her allegation. "You must've given Max hell growing up."

She shrugged. "I grew up in a house of dudes who would've locked me in a protective tower if there'd been one available. It was grow some balls or perish."

"Eloquently put."

She turned away, trying to hide her cringe. God, why was she always doing that? Talking like she lived in a locker room. It was fine at work because working with the sports crew *was* like a locker room, but sometimes she forgot that most women in the world didn't go around talking about balls. "Sorry. They taught me how to throw a perfect spiral, but eloquence, not so much."

"No apology needed. I was just teasing." He took the ramp off I-30 and headed toward her neighborhood. "Remember, I was in the military. I can be disgustingly offensive in six different languages if necessary."

For some odd reason, that knowledge sent a little tingle through her. The thought of him talking dirty with that molasses-toned accent . . . oh, my. She rolled down her window a tick, hoping the blast of air would cool her suddenly warm skin and dissipate some of the enticing soap and fresh-cut-grass smell wafting off Grant. The man was downright intoxicating. She probably would never see Grant Waters again in her life, but he had sure as shit secured a starring role in her next sexual fantasy. "Take that next left. It's the fourth house on the right."

Grant followed her directions and some of the tightness in her shoulders loosened, knowing she was getting back to her own territory where things made sense. But as soon as they made the last turn, the blue-and-red flashing of police lights had her heartbeat rising. Was that car parked in front of *her* house?

Grant glanced her way, his frown lines deep. "Is that your place?"

She nodded, her tongue thick in her mouth.

He rolled to a stop in her driveway, and she was shoving the door open before Grant had even shifted into park. Her shoes hit the pavement, and she made a beeline toward the first officer she saw. His head was bent over his pad as he made notes.

"Excuse me? What's going on?"

He lifted his head. "You a neighbor?"

"No, I live here. I'm Charli Beaumonde."

He looked toward her little white house, his expression grave. "Sorry, ma'am. We tried to reach you on your cell phone, but couldn't get you."

"It's dead."

"Well, your neighbor called us early this morning to report suspicious noises and a man in your backyard. It was too dark to get a description, but she knew he didn't belong there. Said you never have men over."

Great, even her neighbors were keeping track of her piss-poor love life. She rubbed her arms, a chill beginning to work its way through her. "Did you find him?"

"By the time we got here, the perp had already left. Looks like he got in and stole some computer equipment. Your office is a mess, but nothing else looks to be disturbed."

The already steady pounding in her chest moved into her ears. Someone had broken into her office? With all her . . . *No.* She put her hand to her forehead.

Grant who'd stepped up behind her, put a hand on her shoulder and squeezed, as if sensing that she was near panic mode.

The officer looked up at him, then back to her. "Besides the desktop, did you have anything valuable in there?"

Valuable? Just all the research and notes she'd been busting her ass to collect on this story. She wet her lips, her throat trying to close up on her. "I had information about a news story I'm working on. Notes."

He jotted down something. "Anyone who'd want that information bad enough to break in?"

She rubbed her fingers over her brow bone, her head feeling as if it had a fissure splitting the middle of it. The list of people who could be involved in this scandal was long and unproven. Plus, how any of them could know what she was working on and where she kept her notes was a wonder. "Not really."

The cop shrugged. "Probably not connected. We've had a few break-ins in this neighborhood over the last couple of months. It's most likely kids looking to score some electronics."

After another round of questions from the other officer and a tour of the damage, the policemen left with a promise to follow up with her if they found anything. She watched them turn off her street and wrapped her arms around herself, trying to fight a chill that wouldn't seem to go away.

Grant, who'd stayed leaning against his truck like some silent sentinel, pushed to a stand and stepped in front of her, his hat pulled low over his eyes. Apparently noticing her goose bumps, he rubbed his palms along her chilled arms.

Somehow the little gesture of comfort had tears that had built up from the last twenty-four hours ready to burst free. But she wouldn't cry. She could handle this.

"You okay, freckles?" he asked.

"Freckles?" She looked up at him, trying to muster up some

I'm-totally-fine façade, even though having his hands on her had her thoughts fracturing and emotion trying to leak through. "Are you trying to get me back for calling you cowboy?"

"Just trying to make you smile," he said, concern underlying that twang.

She pushed a finger to his chest and tried to manage an intimidating expression. "I'd normally punch a guy for calling me that. You're lucky I'm too tired. And that you're so fucking big."

"Lucky, indeed." He smiled, but those blue eyes remained serious. He grabbed her hand before she could move it away from his chest. His palm closed over her fist, the hold firm. "Now are you going to tell me what really happened last night? You're shaking. And I know it's over more than stolen computer equipment."

She blinked at the change in subject and his grip on her hand. She stepped back, and he quickly let go of her. "What?"

His mouth dipped at the corners, and he eyed her in that knowing way he seemed to be so good at. "Fine. We can do this the easy way or the hard way. You can go on pretending that everything is sugar and sparkles to try to get me to go away and leave you to whatever mess you're in alone. Not going to happen, by the way. Or you can be honest with me so that maybe I can offer some help."

She groaned. "Look, I appreciate everything you've done. But I don't need help. I'm on a story that apparently has ruffled someone's feathers. I can handle it. After all this, I'm going to be on guard now and more aware."

The displeasure that crossed his face was strong enough to steal breath. He crossed his arms over his chest. "Someone ran you off the road last night. And don't lie and say I'm off base. You were yelling at them in your sleep."

She glanced away and took a sudden interest in a crack in her driveway. "It was probably just kids messing around."

"You don't strike me as a stupid woman, Charli. Don't talk like one."

She clenched her jaw, frustration building. Who was he to make demands on her? Being a Good Samaritan gave him the right to a thank-you but not some right to all her business. But before she could lash out and take out her stress from the last twenty-four hours on the man in front of her, another truck pulled into her driveway. A very familiar one.

"Son. Of. A. Bitch." Her simmering frustration boiled over into outright anger. She sent a fiery look Grant's way, as a ginger-headed man climbed out of the truck's cab.

Grant shrugged. "Sorry, darlin'. He would've done the same for me."

Suddenly, all the warm and fuzzy feelings she'd been harboring toward Grant earlier that morning dissipated into a red haze. She turned toward her uninvited guest, her fists curling, spoiling for a fight. "Max, what the hell are you doing here?"

Her brother's dark auburn brows dipped behind his aviators as he stepped around the back end of Grant's truck. "Well, hello to you, too, little sis. And I'm here to make sure you're all right. At least someone thought it was important to call me after you were in a goddamned car accident, Char."

He reached out and shook Grant's hand and nodded in that man-to-man way that seemed to say so much. She could read the words in the quick, silent exchange. *Thanks for calling me even though she told you not to. Thanks for handling my problematic, always-getting-herself-in-trouble sister. I'm here to save the day now.*

Her nails cut into her palms. "I'm fine. See?"

Max crossed his arms over his broad chest. "Yeah, you're fine. Someone ran you off the road, and your house has been broken into. You're just peachy."

Her lips parted. "How do you even know all that?"

"Grant called me while you were dealing with the police to update me."

She sent Grant a betrayed look. To think she'd actually found herself trusting the cowboy, even entertaining the fact that he kind of liked her. She should've known better. She'd spent too much time around dudes to not take into account the guy-code factor. Grant had spent his time being nice to her last night and today because she was Max's sister. A duty to take care of a friend.

"Max, you didn't need to rush out here. I don't even want to know how fast you had to drive to get here this quickly. I would've called you if I needed help. I can handle it."

"Last time you said that, you nearly broke your neck bungee jumping."

She rolled her eyes. "I got whiplash, drama queen. Big difference."

He shook his head, his stance softening. "You worry me, Char. You and Donovan are the only family I have left. It's hard enough knowing that you're this far away, but I need to be able to trust that you're not going to put yourself in danger. When Grant called me last night and told me about the accident, I thought . . ."

She frowned, some of the fight draining out of her. Max had taken it the hardest when her dad had died, and she knew he'd taken it upon himself to be the leader of their family now, the protector. The look in his eyes said his fear for her was real. But she also knew Max would storm in and take over if she gave him the smallest of openings. "I'm sorry I worried you. That wasn't my intention, but everything is under control. Really. The police are on it."

"Yeah, a report will be filed. They're not going to do anything to protect you in the meantime." He raked his fingers through hair that matched her own, his expression torn. He looked toward her house. "I know you think you're on the trail of some big story, Char. But apparently you're poking some dangerous lions. It's not worth it. I don't want you around it. I need you to come home with me until whatever this is blows over."

She looked at him as if horns had grown out of that ginger head. "The hell I am. I have a job. I'm working on getting a promotion. I can't just whisk away to Baton Rouge. And if I drop a story because someone tries to scare me, they win. Screw that."

"Someone tried to *run you off the road*, Char. This isn't about pride or work. You could've been fucking killed."

The thought made her shudder, but there was no way she could walk away from everything. She'd worked too hard to get to this point. "I can't leave."

"Char—"

"She can stay with me," a deep voice interrupted.

Both she and her brother turned to look at Grant, the unexpected statement silencing their argument.

"Do what?" She must've heard him wrong.

Grant tipped his hat up a bit. "You can stay in the cabin you were in last night. You'll be safe there. And when you're not on-site, you can check in with me by phone so that someone always knows where you are. You'll have a bit of a drive into work for a while, but at least you won't have to take time off."

"That's a great idea. Thanks, man," Max said, smiling and thumping Grant on the back. "Grant has top-notch security at his place. You'll be protected there."

Charli stared at Grant. He was serious? He didn't know her from a woman on the street, but he was going to give her a place to stay and play bodyguard. Just to be helpful? No, she corrected herself. This wasn't about being helpful. This was about debt. Max had saved Grant's life, and now there was an opportunity to pay him back. She was a transaction. Just like the time Max bribed his friend to ask her to the prom so she wouldn't be without a date. Then said friend had proceeded to tell everyone he was there with her as a favor. Total humiliation. Served up hot. "I appreciate the offer, but no, thank you," she said, smiling with forced politeness.

Max frowned. "Well, then I'll call in the last of my vacation time and move in with you for the next two weeks. I can keep watch until we get all your window locks replaced and install a high-tech alarm."

Oh, hell no. She loved her brother to pieces, but sharing her tiny place with him twenty-four-seven while she was trying to investigate her story would be a nightmare. She'd never be able to get away without him wanting to know where she was, who she was with, and what she was doing. Her brothers had always been protective, but since her father had died, Max had made it his personal mission to be the most annoyingly overbearing parental substitute ever. Two weeks of that and she'd be signing herself into the loony bin. Or jail—for choking her dear brother.

"I'll stay with Grant." At least there she could be alone in her own cabin without a babysitter. And though Grant had been the one to offer, he looked about as excited at the prospect as she did, so he probably wouldn't bother her much.

Max gave a triumphant smile and leaned over to kiss the top of her head. "My baby sister, always the voice of logic and reason."

"You're being paranoid."

"Better than underestimating the threat and having regrets later," Grant said quietly.

She glanced over at him, but he was staring off in the distance, hands in pockets, as if he had made the statement to someone else.

Something flickered over Max's face when he looked at Grant—sadness? Sympathy? But before she could pinpoint it, Max's attention was back on her. "Listen to what he says. He'll keep you safe." He touched the tip of her nose. "Now go get packed."

She gave him a narrow gaze.

He smiled. "Love you."

She gritted her teeth. She loved him, too. But at the moment she was having a hard time remembering why. She turned on her heel to head back toward the house.

What a way to cap off the most fantastic day and a half ever. All of her story research was gone, her car was trashed, and now she was going to have to figure out a way to live on the same grounds with a guy who made her thoughts run into each other when he got too close.

A guy who saw her as a job, a favor.

An A-plus day all around.

FOUR

"I really appreciate you doing this," Max said as Grant secured Charli's suitcase in the back of his truck. "I know it's a lot to take on, as busy as you are."

Grant climbed down from the truck bed and slammed the tailgate shut. Max had no idea how much this was costing him. He hadn't planned to make the offer, but he owed Max. And he knew Charli wasn't going to give in and go with her brother. But as soon as the words had fallen out of his mouth, he'd wanted to take them back.

Keeping an eye on Charli would be challenge enough, but keeping his hands off her in the process would be downright painful. He'd spent most of the morning forcing himself not to make a move. When she'd looked so forlorn there in the driveway, it'd taken everything he had not to pull her against him. "Not a problem. Your family is my family. I'll watch out for her."

Max's lip curled. "She's not gonna make it easy. You know that, right?"

"I'll manage." Grant glanced toward the house, making sure Charli hadn't come out yet.

"I know you will. I trust you." He sighed and shoved his hands in his pockets. "I love my sister, but sometimes her drive can get in the way of her good sense. She thinks she can take on anything and anyone."

Grant imagined Charli probably could hold her own more than most, but he wasn't about to test that theory and leave her unguarded. "I can keep my distance and still make sure she's safe. My property is locked down tight."

"Yeah, I'm sure, can't have anyone sneaking in and stealing the wine."

Right. Because the wine was what he was protecting behind The Ranch's gates. Not the sexual secrets of Dallas's elite. Not his own secrets.

Grant adjusted his hat but forced himself not to shift his gaze away from Max's—a trick he'd honed from years of having to lie bald-faced to enemies. "Gotta protect those grapes, my friend."

"Look, I've got to head back if I'm not going to take any vacation days. And I don't think I want to suffer Charli's wrath anymore today, anyway." He stuck his hand out to Grant. "Seriously, thank you, man. I don't think I'd be able to leave her with anyone else here and be able to sleep at night."

Grant shook Max's hand, guilt nipping at his boot heels. Max was trusting him with what he treasured most—his family. Now Grant had to figure out if he was worthy of that kind of endorsement. Though, with the way Charli had looked at him when she'd realized he'd called her brother, he may not have to worry about it. She wasn't exactly president of his fan club at the moment.

A few minutes after Max left, Charli stepped off her front porch with a bright red scratch on her cheek, her hair falling out of her bun, and a blue plastic carrier. She headed down the driveway and looked toward the end of her street. "So Mr. Save-the-Day is gone?"

Grant eyed the blue box warily. "Had to get back to work."

"Sure he does. The chicken." She handed him the carrier and it hissed. "Tom Brady doesn't like to travel. He may throw up by the time you get back to your place."

"Now, wait a second." The box jolted and the cat made some noise that sounded like it was in its death throes. "I invited *you* to stay, not . . . quarterback kitty."

"We're a package deal, cowboy. You should've listened when I told you not to call Max. Now he's thrown a kink into both of our worlds." She leaned against his truck, eyebrow cocked. "You know you can still back out. I won't tell him."

"Not a chance, freckles." Grant cringed when the carrier jolted again, and he yanked open the passenger door, setting the hissing beast inside the cab. "I know you're upset I called, but I would've wanted him to do the same thing for me if the roles were reversed. And I made him a promise. I don't make those unless I intend to keep them."

"Come on, you know this is ridiculous. I'm a grown woman. I've taken self-defense classes. Do I look like I need a babysitter?" She pushed off the truck, standing to her full height, which would probably be eye to eye or above most men. Too bad for her, he was six-seven and not afraid to use the advantage.

Before she could blink, he grabbed the crook of her elbow, spun her around, and hauled her against him, locking his arm around her waist and pressing his other thumb against her neck, mimicking a knife blade. She struggled, tried to stomp on his foot, but a few self-defense classes were no match for CIA training. "First rule of combat: hubris will bring you down every time."

"Let me go." She struggled for another second, but when she realized she wasn't going to escape, she stopped fighting him. Her muscles softened beneath his hold, her chest rising and falling with quick, choppy breaths—breaths that could indicate fear. But when he glanced down her body and saw the tight beads of her nipples pressing against her shirt, he realized her reaction was anything but. His cock stirred at the sight, and he quickly released Charli, stepping back before she could feel exactly how much she affected him.

She spun around, her cheeks flushed but her jaw clenched. "That was dirty fighting, cowboy."

"Only trying to show you that overconfidence can get you hurt." He hooked his thumbs in his belt loops, fighting the urge to touch her again. "Look, I get it. No one wants someone hovering over them. And I don't have time to be glued to your side, anyway. I have a business to run. I'm going to give you your space as long as you follow a few rules to keep safe." He saw her stiffen at the word *rules* but kept going. "We'll get through whatever this threat is and then you can get back to your normal life, and I'll get back to mine."

She stared at him for a second longer, then leaned over to pick up her purse, which had slipped off her shoulder when he'd grabbed her. She missed it on the first swipe, clearly flustered, and then yanked the strap upward on the second attempt. "I've got to go into work and take care of some things. I called my insurance company and got a rental car lined up. If you don't mind giving me a ride over to the car place, I can sneak Tom into work."

He took her lack of combative response as victory. And though the last thing he wanted to do was traipse around with a vomiting feline, he needed to offer an olive branch. "I can drive you over and keep the cat with me. I have a quick meeting with a supplier to pick up a few things, then I'll be headed back. I'll make sure he's not left alone in the car."

"Okay, well, thanks." She hooked her purse over her shoulder. "I'll head back to your place after work. You can enlighten me on these so-called rules of yours."

He smirked at her tone. "Look forward to it."

"I bet you do. You look like a guy who loves a rule."

Oh, you have no idea, freckles.

Charli gave up trying to keep her bun intact and secured her out-of-control hair into a ponytail before heading into the main offices of the Texas Sports Network. Even after the drive over, her hands were still shaky from the earlier moment with Grant. When he'd restrained her against him, she'd wanted to melt into the hold, give into it. But, of course, it had been a gesture meant to instill fear and prove a point, not to inspire images of a naked cowboy and sweaty sheets. Leave it to her to get turned on by a freaking choke hold. Her long stretch between relationships was apparently making her hormones light up over anything.

Luckily, Grant hadn't seemed to notice her body's instant reaction. When they'd broken apart, she'd been left a jittery mess, but he had looked cool as a November morning—all business and matter-of-fact.

She scoffed. Like he'd have any real interest in her anyway. She'd known men like him. They liked their women prim, yielding, and sweet. Those three words had never been used to describe her. If she was going to be hanging out at Grant's place, she needed to get her libido out of the clouds and steer clear of the cowboy. She'd only end up making a fool of herself if she kept entertaining illicit fantasies about him anytime a southern-soaked word slipped past his lips.

She shook the errant thoughts from her mind, trying to focus on work. Despite all the drama of the past two days, she did have one positive thing going for her—the potential for a monster story. She didn't have her fat file of notes since whoever had broken into her house had made off with that, but she still had the information from her investigative trip yesterday and the details she knew by memory. It wasn't enough to break a story yet, but it was a damn good foundation for a killer scoop. Her boss Trey was going to flip his shit when he saw how big this could be. The on-air position would be hers wrapped up with a bow.

This was going to be her moment. Finally, she could prove her mother wrong. This girl *was* meant to be on TV. Her dream wasn't something to laugh at.

Charli pushed open the doors to the main lobby and was greeted by the massive digital scoreboard that covered the back wall. All the scores of each Texas team's last game were displayed in bright blue numbers. She gave a little wave to the receptionist, then stepped into the elevator, her stomach flipping over for reasons other than the rush to the top floor.

The elevator dinged and the funeral-like hush of the executive floor greeted her. Two levels down, where Charli worked, there was constant noise—phones ringing, all the sports channels cued up on the television screens, chattering over the walls of the cubicles. She loved the energy of it, the adrenaline. All this peacefulness on the top floor would drive her crazy.

She made her way to the far end of the hall and rapped on Trey's partially ajar door. The door nudged open a bit farther from her knocking, and she could hear he wasn't alone. She probably should've called up first, but trying to catch Trey when he wasn't busy was like trying to find a break in traffic at rush hour.

"Yeah," he called out.

She pushed the door fully open and stepped in. "Sorry to interrupt, Tr—Mr. Winger." Though she'd known Trey since college and had dated him briefly back then, she did make an effort to address him formally in front of others. "I needed to talk to you about something. I was hoping you'd have a minute."

"Sure, Beaumonde, come on in," Trey said, his voice like a barking dog. "I was just finishing up with Stormy here."

The leggy blonde rose from her seat and flashed a toothpaste-ad smile Charli's way.

Trey came around his desk and pressed a palm to the small of Stormy's back as he guided her toward the door. "Let me know if you have any more questions, all right? I'm so happy this worked out."

"Absolutely, Mr. Winger," she said, her tone as perky as her Wonderbra. "And thank you. I know you'll be a great mentor."

Charli's eyebrows lifted. Was Trey *blushing*? She'd seen the former-football-player-turned-executive get red with rage before, but never a blush. She pressed her lips together to keep from smirking.

Trey walked the girl out without introducing her to Charli, then came back to sit behind his desk. Charli sat in the chair the blonde had vacated. "Is she the new intern or something?"

"Not exactly." Trey adjusted his suit jacket as if it had suddenly grown too small for his shoulders and frowned. "I called you earlier this morning, but you weren't at your desk."

"I had car trouble on the way back from an investigative trip. I sent you an e-mail about it."

He glanced at his computer screen, which was apparently in sleep mode, and grunted. "You're not supposed to be on investigative trips. I hired you to do lifestyle pieces."

"I know. And I'm sorry about being late, but I think you'll forgive me when you hear what I saw while on my trip. I drove out to take a look at Jensen Lerner's place. You should've seen the number of suits going in and out of his house."

"Beaumonde—"

She plowed on, too excited to share the information to pause for Trey's questions. But by the time she was done spilling all of the evidence she'd gathered, she could tell he was only half listening.

"Sounds interesting. And hard to prove."

She clenched her teeth, uninspired by Trey's lack of enthusiasm. "I understand that. I plan to get facts. But you know how big this could be if it's true? If they're cheating and boosters are really paying players, that could shut down the entire football program."

He waved his hand, a dismissive flip of the wrist that told her he was planning to ignore everything she'd said. "Keep me up to date with what you find. But make sure you don't lose focus on what I hired you for in the first place. Your notes on the elderly fantasy football league story lacked your usual enthusiasm and level of detail."

She resisted the urge to shake him. She'd been hired to research what most of the office considered fluff. Feel-good pieces that filled the space between the daily score updates and hard-hitting stories the network was known for. She enjoyed her job and believed those stories were just as important to tell, but she knew she'd need to bring in more breaking news–worthy pieces if she wanted to be seen as a serious on-air contender. She craved being in the action, there on camera sharing her passion in front of a live audience instead of from behind a desk. "I brought you the facts. You know I've never slacked. I don't plan to start now."

Trey's face softened and the vein that had begun throbbing at his temple smoothed. Suddenly, he looked like the kid quarterback she'd met her freshman year again—the guy with whom she'd attempted her first real relationship. "I know. You're a good reporter. But this is distracting you, and I don't want you spinning your wheels on something that will be near impossible to prove."

She could hear the underlying message in his words—*Don't fuck things up, Beaumonde.* He'd gone out on a limb to get her in this position, and his name was riding on her doing the job he'd hired her for. "Right. I won't let it interfere again."

She rose to leave.

"Hold up, Charli. There's something else I need to talk to you about."

She sat back down, a little stunned that he'd used her first name. He never did that—even when they'd dated, he'd called her Beaumonde. Maybe this was going to be it. The day she'd been dreaming about. Her heartbeat ticked upward. "Yes?"

"We didn't select you for the sideline reporter position."

A short, emotionless sentence—one that managed to hit her like a dump truck.

She blinked, words escaping her. She hadn't gotten it? They'd picked that smarmy-ass Pete over her?

Trey took a sudden interest in the pen he was rolling between his fingertips. "We just didn't think it was the right fit. We feel your strengths are in the behind-the-scenes work."

If the first revelation stole her breath, this one downright demolished her. Not only had she not gotten the position, but they didn't think she was *meant* for an on-camera job? Her heart climbed up her throat and lodged there. "I don't understand. You told me you thought I'd be a great candidate for it. And Pete froze up when we did our auditions. You think he's better suited for TV?"

Trey shifted in his seat, set the pen down, and folded his hands on his desk. "No, we didn't go with Pete either."

Thoughts raced through her mind, knocking into each other, and tumbling. "Then who?"

Trey's gaze flicked toward the door and he cleared his throat. "Uh, well . . ."

Oh, shit. She knew that look. He'd had the same one when he'd admitted he'd run up a gambling debt in college and had used money she'd lent him for rent to pay it off. It was the I-just-totally-screwed-you look. She followed his gaze, and realization clamored in her brain.

She gripped the arms of her chair to keep herself from leaping across the desk and choking Trey. "The *blonde*?"

He winced. "She's been really successful hosting a fashion show on the web."

"Fashion?" Her voice had gone too loud, but she couldn't help it. "You're going to put a fashion reporter on the sidelines? Does she even know what a touchdown is?"

"She was a baton twirler in college so she has been on the sidelines before."

"Oh, Trey, come *on*." Her head felt ready to explode. Being on the pep squad was now a *qualification*?

"She has good timing and a great speaking voice."

"And big tits and legs up to her ears," Charli countered.

His jaw twitched, though he was obviously trying hard to keep his impassive business face on. "When we showed audition tapes to a focus group and our sponsors, she got the best scores."

"No doubt that focus group was all dudes."

"Eighty-five percent of our viewing audience is men. And yes, men don't mind watching a pretty girl deliver their sports information. I didn't create that fact—it just is."

And she wasn't a pretty girl. He hadn't said it, but he might as well have. "So if I looked like her, then I'd be the one with the job?"

"No." Trey rubbed at the spot between his eyebrows, as if stalling to search for the right words. "Charli, I think you're great. Your sports knowledge is unparalleled. But the group didn't find you easy to watch. It's not about looks as much as vibe. Viewers want a guy with an air of authority or a real girly girl. Not . . ."

"Me." The tomboy. The girl who felt more comfortable in a locker room than a nail salon. The ugly-duckling daughter who wasn't worth sticking around for.

He met her eyes. "I'm sorry. Really sorry."

Trey did look like he felt like shit about it. And at least he hadn't pulled punches. She'd rather hear the truth than some manufactured attempt to make her feel better. Even if the truth had sliced and diced her.

She rubbed her lips together, willing herself to keep it together. "What about the weekend anchor position coming open next month?"

He sighed, tilting back in his chair. "Obviously, you have the right to apply for it. Pete already put his name in for it, too. But I can't see there being a different outcome. The same criteria are going to apply."

"I've got to get to my desk," she said, standing, smoothing the nonexistent wrinkles in her pants. She needed to get out of there before she cried like some loser.

Trey rose as well. "Beaumonde, don't let this get you down. There are behind-the-scenes positions that pay more than the on-air ones. With your skills, you're going to move right up the chain."

The gritted teeth smile she gave him made her face hurt. "Right."

"And—"

She raised her hand, cutting him off. "Stop. It's fine. *I'm* fine."

His shoulders sagged in relief. "Of course you are. You're the toughest woman I know."

And therein lay the problem.

She walked out of his office, the tattered threads of her childhood dream unraveling at the seams with each step.

Maybe her mother had been right to laugh at her.

FIVE

"Get down from there," Grant said, using his most authoritative tone. "Now."

Charli's cat licked a paw and gave him a glance from atop the cabinets that seemed to say, *I'm sorry, were you talking to me? Because I couldn't give a shit.* Grant grunted. The damn feline had gotten himself stuck up there and anytime Grant climbed up to get him out, Tom hissed and swatted at him. He didn't think he could find a Tom Brady he disliked more than the quarterback version, but this cat was moving up the charts.

This was ridiculous. Grant had horses that would approach at his subtlest signal. Had owned dogs he'd been able to train in a matter of hours. Hell, he could walk over to The Ranch, snap his fingers, and a line of subs would be kneeling at his feet in half a second. But this cat—this cat was topping him.

He picked up the food bowl he'd set out earlier and shook it in Tom's direction. "Come on. You must be hungry."

God knows the cat had emptied all the contents of his stomach in that carrier on the way over. Grant's truck was never going to smell the same.

The front door squeaked, and Grant peered through the pass-through to find Charli stepping inside. She closed the door behind her, set her bags down, and then sagged against the solid wood, shutting her eyes and running her hands over her face.

The simple despair of the move sent all his worry sensors going off. The cat forgotten, he headed out of the kitchen and into the lamp-lit living room. "Hey, you okay?"

She startled, her lids flying open and her hand going to her chest. "Grant."

"Sorry. Didn't mean to scare you." He crooked a thumb at the kitchen. "I had stopped in to check on the cat."

"Oh."

He took in her red-rimmed eyes, her pale cheeks, and moved closer. Tentatively. He wanted to touch her, to protect her from whatever it was that had put her in this state, but knew that would be a supremely unwise move. "Did something else happen?"

She pushed off the door and shook her head. "No, nothing like that. I'm fine."

"Well, obviously something's upset you."

"I appreciate your concern, but can we not talk about this?" She grabbed her bags, took a wide step around him, and made her way toward the kitchen.

His jaw flexed as he held back the demand to know more. He'd said he'd give her space and already he was itching to push her for information. He rolled his shoulders, trying to shake off his instinct to control the situation, and followed her into the kitchen. "I'm not trying to pry, but I need you to be an open book when it comes to any strange things happening, any threats, any information that may help us figure out who's after you. That's why you're here."

"I get it. But there's nothing to report. I've had a long day. I'm tired. My boss is a dick. End of story." She set her canvas grocery bags on the counter and started unloading things. "I want to have a glass of wine, watch some mindless TV, and go to bed."

"No television in here."

"What?" She sounded truly horrified but didn't turn around.

"People come here to relax and get away, not to watch Lifetime movies."

"Fabulous. Guess I'll be watching on my computer then."

He grabbed the bottle of the merlot she'd set on the counter and grimaced when he read the label. "Darlin', I can't let you drink this. It's crap."

She glanced back at him over her shoulder. "It's fine. It was on sale, and I've had it before."

He unscrewed the top and sniffed. God-awful as he expected. He tilted the bottle over the sink and poured. "You'd be better off drinking grape soda."

"Hey!" She turned around and made a grab for the bottle, but most of it was already swirling down the drain. "I spent ten bucks on that."

"They robbed you. I'll bring over a bottle of my own stock. I promise you it's worth more than ten bucks and will go down a lot smoother."

She slammed the bottle down on the counter and shot him a look that could wilt flowers. "Goddammit. You said you weren't going to hover, and already you're controlling my alcohol selections? Back off, cowboy. I've had enough of people telling me what I can and can't do today."

He knew he should listen. Clearly she was on edge. But she looked so decadent right then—color back in her cheeks, fire in her eyes, the small curves of her breasts rising and falling with her frustrated breaths. He could tell she wanted to lash out even more, that she wanted to take out her day on someone. She needed a release, and though he'd prefer to lift her up on that counter and show her a more fun way of letting go of all that energy, he knew that wasn't an option. So he was willing to field her wrath if it took that wrinkle out of her brow.

"So you had a bad day," he said, crossing his arms and leaning against the edge of the sink, purposely prodding her.

She narrowed her eyes, then turned back to her groceries, ignoring his statement. "Where's Tom?"

"Above you," Grant said, nodding at the ball of fur squeezed between the ceiling and tops of the cabinets. "I was trying to get him down when you came in, but he was less than cooperative."

She tilted her head back and looked up. "Oh, good Lord, Tommy. Get down from there."

She made some kissing and cooing sounds and in an instant, the cat slinked to the far end of the space, hopped to the top of the refrigerator, then down onto the counter to Charli's awaiting arms.

Grant shook his head. He'd been trying to do the same for half an hour and had been convinced the cat was stuck. Apparently, Tom was as strong-headed as his owner.

She set Tom on the floor, and Grant saw the flicker of sadness behind the stoic mask she'd put on after she'd realized he was in the cabin. But as quickly as it was there, it was gone. "I know we don't know each other very well, Charli, but I can be a pretty good ear if you need one. You don't have to put on a happy face on my account."

She glanced up at him, and for a moment, he thought he'd gotten through, but her expression went smooth as glass again. "Thanks, but I told you, I'm fine. Why don't you lay those rules on me? It's getting late."

So, she was going with the brush-off. Fine.

He'd let her get away with it . . . for now.

But if he was going to protect her, she needed to trust him.

Usually not a problem. Gaining a woman's trust was his stock and trade. Unfortunately, this time he was going to have to figure out how to do it without restraints and a firm spanking.

Charli kept her back to Grant, loading the few items she'd bought at the market into a cabinet and the refrigerator and trying to regain her composure. When Grant had looked at her, she'd had the uncanny sense that he was seeing to the root of her, seeing every ugly fear and vulnerability, every hurt and trauma. She didn't like it. At all.

She was too on edge after the disaster of a day to deal with someone like him. One errant word or look and she'd spill her guts on the floor like some damned therapy session. *Oh, poor me. Not only did I not get the job I've been dreaming of all my life, but oh, yeah, people find it hard to even watch me on television.* Talk about humiliating. Why not just put her in a prom dress and dump some pig's blood on her?

"Right, the rules," Grant said in that baritone that seemed to vibrate through her rib cage. "Pretty simple. You give me your schedule, where you're going to be. If you deviate from that, you call me and let me know ahead of time. You send me a text message letting me know when you arrive at work and when you're leaving. I'm putting a GPS tracking device on your rental car as a backup in case I can't get in touch with you and you need help."

She shuddered, flashbacks of her teen years rolling through her mind—the constant checking in and explaining herself to her dad and brothers. "Don't you think that's a little overboard?"

He frowned. "Hopefully, it is. I hope that none of this is necessary. But I'm not willing to take a chance."

She sighed. "Right."

"As for when you're here, feel free to explore the grounds, but stay on this side of the property. That long fence along the eastern edge divides the winery from the resort. Members only on the other side."

She glanced back at him, eyebrow lifted. "Seriously?"

"Is that a problem?"

"No, it's not like I'm here for a vacation. I just didn't realize it was exclusive with a capital *E*." She grabbed a bag of chips and opened them, her lack of dinner finally hitting her. "You're not housing the mob over there or something, are you?"

He pushed off the counter to rise to his full height and smiled. "No, nothing so sinister."

She eyed him, sensing he wasn't telling her everything, but his smile didn't falter. She held out the bag of chips. "Want some?"

Instead of taking a chip from the bag, he plucked the one from between her fingertips and popped it in his mouth. "The resort's room service is available on this side, too—twenty-four-seven. There's a menu in the desk drawer. Dial three on the phone and you can get anything delivered to your door, no charge."

"Oh, that's really generous, but I think I'm covered."

"A woman can't live by cheap wine and ham sandwiches alone. I'll make sure a bottle of wine and tonight's roast chicken make it over here within the half hour." He snagged his keys off the counter, spinning the loop around his finger and sauntered toward the side door, giving her an unimpeded view of broad shoulders and that lovely, jean-covered backside. "Give me a call if you need anything else or have any questions."

She smirked. "What? You're not sticking around to make sure I get tucked into bed all right?"

He halted his step and she had the urge to put her hands over her face. She'd meant the question as a joke, but once the words were out of her mouth, she'd realized how they'd sounded. Like a lame attempt at flirting.

And maybe it had been exactly that.

Maybe she wanted him to stay and help her forget her awful day.

But he kept his back to her and turned his head to the side, revealing only his profile. "I don't think that'd be a good idea, Charli."

"Right," she said softly, then added: "I was only kidding."

"Good night, freckles."

She sank back against the counter. *Good* was about the last thing tonight could be called.

The wine better make it over here quickly.

SIX

The night was filled with a harmony of frogs and crickets as Grant headed back to his house after checking on things at The Ranch. He had interviewed a potential trainee tonight—one who was having trouble letting go of control in her scenes with other doms. She'd been pretty and open to the type of play he enjoyed. She'd read through his contract and didn't have any major sticking points. But once he'd started talking to her, he figured out one thing rather quickly—he had no desire to tie her up and beat her. And that was a damn shame.

So instead, he'd thanked her for her time and had gone back to work. He'd ended up spending half an hour mediating a tiff between two longtime members over who had reserved what playroom when, then had worked the floor for the rest of the night. But instead of all that business clearing his mind, walking the play spaces had only inspired images of his new "neighbor" and how she would look naked and restrained on all that equipment—how she'd feel writhing beneath his hands and mouth.

In the end, he'd left with a hard-on and headache. Not exactly the kind of night he'd been craving.

He took a swig from the bottle of water he'd grabbed on his way out and made the last turn in the path toward his place. The glow of his porch light burned in the distance. Almost home. But snapping twigs and a muffled curse somewhere off to the left had him slowing his steps. He turned, squinting through the inky darkness and cluster of trees. "Hello?"

More unintelligible sounds, then a clear "goddammit."

Uh-oh. He took a step in the direction of the noise. "Charli? Is that you?"

"No."

But it was. Even having just met her, he would recognize that slight rasp in her voice anywhere. Despite his best efforts, the sound went straight to his groin every damn time. Something about that hint of hoarseness made him think of how she would sound when she cried out in pleasure. Or pain. He was a fan of both.

He adjusted the front of his jeans and made his way through the grove of trees, almost afraid of what he'd find. Once he got to the other side and the moon offered enough light to find her, he discovered Charli sitting in a puddle of mud with her hands above her head, holding something.

"What in the hell?"

She looked to the heavens and groaned. "Can you take this please? If it gets wet, they'll probably fire me."

He grabbed the device from her, an iPad from what he could tell, and offered her a hand. "Need some help?"

"I got it." She pushed herself up and then grimaced when she put weight on her right leg. "Ouch."

He had to hide his own grimace, but for a completely different reason. Since he'd left her earlier, she'd changed into boxers and a T-shirt—both of which were now soaked and covered in mud. If it had been anyone else, it would've been comical. But all he could focus on was how the garments now clung and outlined every naked part beneath—curves and dips and points. Mud wrestling had never sounded so tempting.

He cleared his throat, thankful for the dark night as his cock hardened behind the fly of his pants. "Are you all right?"

"I think I tripped over a root or something." She shifted her weight to her other foot and winced a bit. "Pissed off my ankle."

He frowned at the way her words stumbled into each other, hearing the slight slur in her voice for the first time. Apparently the wine had made it over to her cabin. "Let me help you get back to your place. Do you need me to carry you?"

She shook her head, swaying on her feet ever so slightly. "I can . . . manage. Just carry the tablet so I don't get any of this on it. Don't need another talk from the boss, now do I?"

She took a few hobbling steps and tilted to the left. He reached out and grabbed her elbow. "Enjoyed the wine, Charli?"

"It was soooo smooth," she said, flashing him an off-kilter smile and stumbling another step. "And potent."

"So I see." He tightened his grip, halting her. "Tell you what. This isn't working. Wait here and don't move."

Before she could protest, he left her standing there in the dark and jogged toward her cabin. She'd thankfully left the door unlocked, saving him the trouble of going to his place for the key. Once inside, he found the half-empty bottle of wine and a cupcake wrapper. The roasted chicken he'd sent over looked untouched. He set her computer tablet on the counter and grabbed a large towel from the bathroom.

He hustled back outside, finding she had followed his instruction, something that gave him more pleasure than it should have. He handed her the towel. "Clean off what you can, then I'm carrying you the rest of the way. You may have sprained your ankle."

"I don't need to be carried. I'm fine."

"This isn't a negotiation. You're injured and drunk."

She raised a finger to him. "I am n—"

He cocked his head, giving a pointed glance at her muddied state, and she clamped her mouth shut. With unsteady movements, she wiped off her bare legs and cleaned her arms and hands.

He looked over her shoulder toward the fields, trying to do anything but watch her spread that wet mud along that freckled skin. "What were you doing out here anyway?"

"The Internet signal sucks. Thought if I got close enough to your cabin, I could catch your wireless if you had it."

"You could've called me."

She gave him a warning glance, no doubt anticipating a hindsight lecture, but he kept quiet. Some things didn't need to be said.

Once she'd cleaned off what she could, Grant bent and put an arm beneath her knees and under her back, lifting her with one swift movement and catching her by surprise based on the hitch in her breath.

"You're going to throw out your back, you know?"

He gave her a wry look. "I've carried injured men on the battlefield. I can handle one little sports reporter."

"Little?" She snorted. "I'm almost six feet tall."

"You're small to me. Live with it."

She kept quiet the rest of the walk back to the cabin, though he wished she would've kept chattering—anything to take his mind off the fact that she was pressed up against him and that she clearly had no bra on under that wet T-shirt. Those pert nipples would fit so perfectly in his mouth, would look so pretty in clamps. He forced himself to keep his eyes forward.

"It's not good to stomp around here in the dark," he said, his voice coming out gruffer than he intended. "We're not in the city, freckles. A twig gotcha this time, but there are animals out here, too—coyotes, bobcats, snakes. They keep away from the lit areas of the resort, but you never know what you'll find over here in the shadows."

"I had only planned to be out for a minute." She rested her head against his shoulder, and he wondered if she even realized she was doing it or if the wine was softening her.

He bumped open the cabin door with the toe of his boot and turned sideways to fit them both through the door. "And look how much trouble you got yourself into with only a minute in your pocket."

"The half a bottle of wine didn't hurt," she said, the words sliding off her lips like lazy raindrops. "Made me forget about my shitty day for a little while, too."

He set her down gently in the slate-tiled bathroom and opened the door to the walk-in shower to turn on the spray. He wanted to ask her more about her day, but he'd already tried that earlier and she'd instantly shut down. He kept his back to her and adjusted the knobs. "The water takes a minute to heat, but it should help sober you up at least."

He started to turn around, but the sound of wet cloth smacking hard tile was like a sonic boom in his ears. His feet rooted to the spot as he caught the faint reflection in the shower glass of Charli bending and slipping off her shorts. Another plop as the boxers hit the floor. The steam fogged the glass before she straightened, but he had no doubt she was standing naked behind him. "Uh, Charli, I'm still in here."

"So," she said, sounding like a petulant teenager. "Didn't ya know? Guys don't think of me as a girl. So no harm."

"Guys don't wha—?" He must be having a dream. He'd really made it back to his cabin and he was in his bed now, having erotic dreams about Charli like the night before. That must be it.

"I'm *hard to watch*, cowboy" she said, her tone bitter. "They'd rather watch some blonde baton-twirling fashion reporter than me.

Because she's *pretty*. Even if she probably doesn't know a first down from first base."

Grant breathed in a deep gulp of steamy air, willing himself not to turn around and take the eyeful he so wanted. She was drunk. And apparently some idiot at her job had thrown a grenade at her today. He couldn't give in to the urge.

"Darlin', obviously you're working with some world-class imbeciles. But do you mind wrapping up with a towel? Otherwise, you're going to be real mad at yourself and me in the morning."

She sniffed. "Well, see, there you go. The thought of me naked is even too much for you to bear."

Oh, she had no idea. "Now you're just talking stupid."

"Great. So I'm not just ugly but stupid. Gee, thanks. You can go now."

"Enough." He spun around right as she was securing the towel, a towel that barely made it past the juncture of her legs. He wet his lips, the rest of his planned words sticking to his mouth like taffy.

"Just go."

He closed the distance between them with two strides, and up close he could see that even though her jaw was set, her eyes were glassy with unshed tears. "Look, I don't know what happened to you today or what you're trying to prove to yourself right now, but let's get one thing straight—you know nothing about what I think of you."

"So tell me then," she challenged. "Can't be any worse than what I've already heard today."

He moved into her personal space, backing her into the wall and bracing his hands on each side of her. "The truth? I think you've had a really shitty day and you're looking for a fight or a fuck to make you forget it."

Her eyes widened, her breath hitching.

"You want to yell at me, freckles? You want to pummel me to get all that anger out? Because go ahead. I'm right here."

She stared back at him, frozen for a moment, then she licked her lips nervously. "That's not what I want to do with you."

His breathing was loud in his own ears. He needed to walk away. Right. Now. But his mouth was acting on its own accord. "Tell me what you want, Charli."

Half of him hoped she wouldn't follow his command, that she'd push him away. Because this was about as bad an idea as he'd ever considered. But if she told him, if she asked, he didn't think he had it in him to deny her.

She couldn't seem to bring her gaze up to him, but he didn't miss the whispered plea. "I need to forget today. I need something good."

And with that, his desire knocked off his good sense. *Bang, bang.* Dead.

"Something good it is, then." He lifted Charli up and wound her legs around him, fitting the bare curve of her ass into his palms and dragging her against his straining erection. She tucked her face into the crook of his neck and made a soft, desperate sound that curled through him like hot smoke, filling his nerve endings.

But his raging libido was going to have to wait. He wasn't going to fuck her drunk, couldn't cross that line. But he could give her what she needed. He carried her over to the shower and pulled open the door, the steam spilling out into the room, then stepped in fully clothed, bringing them both under the hot stream of water. She lifted her head, surprise coloring her eyes as the water sluiced over her, soaking the towel and sloughing the dirt off her arms.

"Your clothes," she said, looking down at his now-saturated shirt.

"Don't worry about me, freckles. Just hold on to that towel bar behind you and let me make you feel good."

Her gaze went hazy with arousal and maybe a little fear, but she followed his instruction. He kept an arm banded around her to make sure she was steady on her feet, then he slipped his hand beneath the edge of the towel, brushing against the smoothness of her inner thighs and sliding upward to find the damp thatch of hair at their juncture. She closed her eyes and leaned her head back against the shower wall. God, he wanted to yank that towel off her, see her stretched out like this and totally bare, but he knew if he took it that far, he'd end up inside her, taking more than he had any right to. He brushed his finger along her cleft, and she bucked against him, the simple touch pulling a moan from her.

The sound was like a stroke to his cock, her sensitivity like waving a red flag in front of a bull. Oh, how he could torture someone so responsive, drag out her pleasure until she was begging for release. "Darlin', if you're that keyed up, this isn't going to take long."

"Please," she whispered, her hips tilting toward his touch.

He smiled, giving her what she sought, a firm slide over her clit. The nub seemed to swell beneath his fingers, her arousal coating his skin despite the shower water pounding down on them. He could smell her sexy scent, so sweet and tempting. He'd love to part those thighs and taste every bit of her, but instead he tucked two fingers inside her heat and kept his thumb against her clit.

"Oh, God." Her body clenched around his fingers and she rocked against his hand, shamelessly taking things to the pace she craved. Needy. Starved.

"That's right," he said against her ear as he pumped his fingers inside her. "Take what you need. Let yourself go."

As if she'd been waiting for the words, she let out a sharp cry and her fingers went bloodless against the towel bar. The tremor of orgasm seemed to go through every inch of her, her body quivering in front of him, going flushed and pink. Quick, breathy gasps slipped past her lips as she undulated against his touch, milking every bit of pleasure she could.

His cock pressed against his zipper, begging for relief, for her, but he clenched his jaw and willed the ache away. He knew how to hold back his own need for hours in a play session. He could handle this. At least that's what he kept repeating in his head as Charli drifted down from her quick-and-dirty orgasm.

He moved his hand away from her and resisted the urge to lick her arousal from his fingers, to let her watch how he would savor her taste. Or even better, to paint it over her nipples and then suck them clean. His cock flexed and he held back a groan. He was on the precipice of losing his control. This had been a bad idea. If she could push him to this point with him simply touching her, he was in trouble.

He reached out and turned off the shower. Her eyes fluttered open, the daze of orgasm still heavy in her expression. Her hands slipped off the bar and she pushed her sopping hair away from her face. "Wow, that was . . . I don't usually . . ."

He smiled, though the effort was strained from his own keyed-up state. "Feel better?"

"So much better. Thank you." She pushed off the wall and reached for the nape of his neck. He watched the play of desire move over her features, loving the way her fingers tightened against his skin. He found himself contemplating how easy it would be to loosen that towel, bind her arms with it, and take her right there against the shower wall. Her look said she would let him. But before he could truly lose all sense of right and wrong, she lifted up on her toes, her face moving toward him. Panic zipped through him like an electric bolt when he realized what she was going to do, and he instinctively moved his head to the left, dodging the kiss.

She blinked up at him, surprised by the quick movement, then she registered what he'd done. A cold mask crossed over her features.

"Charli, we can't, I can't—"

She grabbed the top of her towel, which was now sagging with the weight of all the water, and held it tight, not looking up. "Right. I get it."

"Charli," he repeated.

"No, really. It's fine. I got off, and that's what I asked for. Much obliged. You can go now."

He wanted to explain, to reach out and fix that wounded expression. But the damage was already done. And having her think he didn't want to take this anywhere was for the best. Max didn't send his sister here so that Grant could get her into his bed. And hell, he couldn't even remember the last time he'd had vanilla sex with anyone. This had been a mistake all around. She was everything he *didn't* look for in a woman.

Too bad his dick didn't give a damn about any of that.

He stepped out of the shower, his wet boots leaving puddles on the floor. "I'm sorry, Charli."

She turned her back to him. "Shut the door behind you."

He did exactly that, heading out of the house and leaving a wet trail behind him.

And the asshole award goes to . . .

The air outside had turned cooler and chilled his clothes against his skin as he made his way back to his cabin. Served him right for losing control like that. He should've walked straight out that door in the first place. If she had needed a release, she could've handled that herself. She didn't need him to come in and save the day. The move had been selfish on all levels.

By the time he reached his place he was cold, pissed, and tired. But unfortunately, the miserable walk back to his cabin and a heaping pile of guilt hadn't been enough to quell the hard-on from hell. He was now walking with a full hitch in his giddyup. The sound of Charli's sexy sighs as she came was burned into his brain.

He could head back to The Ranch and find someone to scene with for the night. But he'd never been a fan of fantasizing about one person while you fucked another. When he was with a submissive, he wanted it to be all about *that* woman. Otherwise, what was the point?

So as soon as he kicked his door shut behind him, he stripped out of his wet clothes and headed to his own shower. Charli would probably still be taking hers, sans towel—water running in rivulets down her freckled skin, soap sliding over her perfect handful breasts and along her belly, suds creeping down between her thighs where the lips of her sex would still be swollen and pink from orgasm. He imagined stepping in behind her, taking the soap, and washing her backside. She would yield to his touch, beg for it. He could cup her ass and press the ridge of his cock against her, tasting her neck.

The hot water hit him with a blast, and he let it envelop him for a moment as it chased away the chill, and he got lost in the fantasy. He leaned back against the tiled wall and reached for the soap, creating a lather that he wished he could rub on Charli. But instead, he moved his hand down and grasped his cock, coating himself in the slippery liquid and stroking. A hard shudder went through him as he imagined his own grip was really the hot clasp of Charli's body around him.

He moved up and down the length, sparing any finesse. He liked to give it rough, and he liked to get it the same way. His fist went on autopilot as his mind continued to weave images of Charli against him, around him . . . tied up for him, begging him, those green eyes drunk on pleasure instead of wine. The sound of soap against skin filled the shower, mixing with the steam and the pounding water. His knees tried to buckle beneath him as the pressure built low and fast.

He splayed his hand against the side wall, hanging on, and then sensation exploded through his system, shooting down his spine and radiating outward. Charli's name sat full on his lips as his hard, pulsing release splashed against his abdomen and the shower wall.

He leaned his forehead against the shower door, his breath rasping out of him as his cock went soft in his hand. The water turned cool long before he had the desire to open his eyes to his always-empty cabin.

SEVEN

Charli pulled her hair into a twist and kicked up the volume on the small radio in the cabin's bedroom. This place was too damn quiet, especially at night. And who would want to stay anywhere without a television?

Serenity made her antsy. She'd had better luck relaxing by riding roller coasters or learning to kickbox. Things that turned the adrenaline up and her mind off. Things like getting pressed up against a shower wall by a fully clothed cowboy and riding his hand until her brain exploded.

That had been a pretty big adrenaline rush—well, up until she'd realized she was the only one into it. That the mere thought of kissing her had made him recoil.

God, what had she been thinking? Talk about making a fool of herself. Nothing like coming across as desperate and sex-starved.

And drunk.

She couldn't forget that part.

Nice job, Beaumonde.

She sat on the edge of the bed, trying to shake off the memory, and booted up her iPad so that she could catch *SportsCenter* and her own station's end-of-the-day wrap-up show. The sports radio was not cutting it. And after her long day of purposely avoiding Grant and then an evening chasing down a lead that didn't pan out, she was ready to relax, watch the night's highlights, and get to bed. Plus, the network was going to introduce Blondie as the new sidelines reporter on-air and for some reason, Charli felt compelled to watch it.

The screen came to life, but when she tried to access the Internet, she got the no signal message. "You've got to be freaking kidding me."

When she'd done her morning check-in text with Grant, he'd let her know that he'd moved the router in his own cabin, which should give her access to his connection, but apparently it hadn't done the trick. She wasn't quite ready to chat with Grant in real time. She needed the mortification of the previous night to settle a little longer before she crossed that bridge, so she sent him another text. But after a few minutes, she hadn't heard back. She stared down at the absent signal icon on the tablet. "Damn."

She frowned at the screen. She should go to bed. What good would seeing it be anyway? Why torture herself? But the urge to have that closure was too strong. With a sigh, she got up and toed on her tennis shoes. If Grant wasn't answering a text, he probably wasn't home. She could probably sneak over to his yard and borrow his signal long enough to see the show.

Not ready to repeat the debacle from last night, she made sure she had a flashlight before heading out. The walk over wasn't very long and if she stayed on the gravel path this time, she'd be fine. Plus, being sober always helped. She grabbed her backpack and slipped the tablet inside, then locked up behind her. Grant had told her the grounds were secure and locking doors wasn't necessary, but frankly, at night the place looked ripe for a Friday the 13th installment. And she'd prefer to skip the ax murdering tonight.

She walked carefully along the path, making sure to keep an ear out for any animal sounds and holding the light out in front of her. But besides a rabbit that darted in front of her and inspired a near heart attack, she was alone on her trip over. Grant's porch light came into view and she let out a breath she hadn't realized she'd been holding. His truck was there.

She paused, suddenly panicked that he'd discover her out there. What if he wanted to discuss last night? Or had a woman over or something? She didn't know anything about his life really. Hell, maybe he had a girlfriend and that's why he'd left last night. She sniffed. *Yeah, keep telling yourself that, Charli.* She'd known exactly why he'd turned away. And it wasn't because of another woman. The way he'd reacted hadn't left much room for interpretation. It was simple. He was appalled by the thought of kissing her.

It was like high school and college all over again. She was the girl who was okay to fool around with on the sly for a fun night here or there, but not the girl guys actually wanted to date. She was a buddy fuck. Always had been and seemed always would be. She scanned the area for a somewhat safe place to sit and spotted a simple wooden bench beneath one of the large oaks at the edge of his yard. It was shrouded in the shadows and close enough to probably get the signal she'd come for in the first place, but far enough that Grant wouldn't see her if he happened to step outside. She headed over, parked on the bench, and pulled out her tablet.

The signal wasn't perfect, but it was there. She cued up her station's Internet feed and selected the most recent show. Most of today's scores she'd already heard, so she skimmed through that and made it to the part she'd been both looking for and dreading. The nightly anchors invited Stormy to sit at the desk with them and introduced her. Jack, head anchor, smiled an all-teeth smile at Stormy while he asked her questions and surreptitiously checked out her too-low-cut top. If he'd been a cartoon character, his tongue would've rolled out of his mouth and smacked the desk. And even worse were the Internet messages from viewers below the video. No one, of course, commented on whether or not Stormy had sports knowledge or experience. It was all talk of how hot the new sideline reporter was.

Charli's dinner churned in her stomach, and she clicked the off button. Well, apparently they'd nailed their target market. The market that had no interest in her. But before she could fall back into that lovely dark place of feeling sorry for herself, the front door of the cabin opened and Grant stepped out. She instinctively shrunk backward, making sure she stayed cloaked in the shadows of the oak. The last thing she needed was Grant finding her out here and adding creepy stalker to her list of attributes along with girl who throws herself at men whilst drunk.

He glanced around the yard, but not with intent, then shut the door behind him. He was still fully dressed in what she was beginning to think was his uniform—plaid shirt and worn jeans, but he'd taken his hat off, revealing that dark wavy hair of his beneath. Her fingers flexed, remembering what it felt like between her fingers, wondering how that shadow of a beard would feel against her skin.

Stop it. Even knowing he had no interest in her, she couldn't stop herself from the fantasies. It was as if his presence scrambled the signals in her brain—making her think things she never thought, want things she'd never considered. But after the humiliation of last night, she'd needed to get herself together and show him that she wasn't some desperate woman trying to get his attention. He couldn't know that he had any power over her. Not if they were going to exist together these next few weeks. They would need to agree to forget what happened last night and move on. Delete that episode altogether.

Just not tonight. She wasn't ready for that conversation quite yet.

She held her breath, though at this distance there was no way he'd be able to hear her breathe, and watched. She expected him to head to his truck, but instead he turned at the far corner of the house and walked away from her and toward the resort. Apparently, he was going to work, but what would a resort need the owner for this late at night? Wouldn't everyone be settling in or sleeping by now?

Once he was far enough away, she let her lungs empty and tucked her computer back into her knapsack. She'd be able to escape to her cabin without him ever knowing she was here if she left now. But as she watched Grant's sauntering gait disappear into the night, she found herself rising from the bench and heading away from her cabin instead of toward it, the draw of the unknown too tempting for her reporter instincts.

If he could install a tracking device on her car, then she could be nosy, too.

She tucked her bag behind a bush near the back side of his cabin, then picked up her pace so she wouldn't lose him. She kept a decent distance behind him. Grant had been in the military and so undoubtedly had finely tuned senses for people sneaking up on him. And the grounds were so damn quiet, one snapped twig and she'd reveal herself. But Grant never looked back, just continued to stride with that swagger of his. A man on a mission by the looks of it. Maybe something had gone wrong at the resort and he had been called over.

Grant opened the padlocked gate that led to the other side of the property, and Charli ducked behind a tree as he turned to swing the gate closed behind him. Some creepy-crawly thing landed on Charli's arm and it took everything she had not to yelp and shake it off. Grant snapped the lock closed, the sound echoing in the silence, and continued on his way. As soon as his back was to her again, she did a little shake and got the damn bug off her arm, shuddering. She'd rather face a coyote than bugs.

In order to follow Grant, she had to climb over the low post-

and-rail wooden fence, which made her glad she'd chosen sneakers tonight. She hopped down to the other side and glanced around, half-expecting a SWAT team to lower down from the surrounding trees. Grant had made everything sound so top secret over here.

But no one came to tackle her, and she was able to catch sight of Grant again in no time. There were paved paths on this side with solar-powered garden lights lining some portions of the trails. The wild Texas brush and trees were trimmed back and looked neater, more manicured. There really was no way to remain hidden, so instead she pushed her shoulders back and tried to pretend like she belonged there. If anyone but Grant saw her, maybe they'd assume she was another guest.

The main house loomed in the distance—a breathtakingly large building of cedar and river rock. Lights glittered around its perimeter but the few windows she could see were all dark. She had no idea if the main building had rentable rooms or if it was just the place for dining rooms and spas or whatever the hell rich people needed on their rustic vacation. Regardless, Grant seemed to be making a beeline in that direction.

As soon as she rounded the last bend though, something off to the right caught her eye. A flash of movement. She turned her head, taking her eyes off Grant, and almost tripped over her feet when she saw two men underneath a nearby tree. One of the men was shirtless and pressed up against the bark; his partner's forearm was pressed over his wrists, holding his arms taut above his head. Charli's gaze tracked down and she couldn't help but gasp when she saw where the man's other hand was. The fly of shirtless guy's pants was spread wide and the man's fist was wrapped around his partner's shaft in what looked to be a painfully tight grip.

The man against the tree shifted his gaze, catching sight of her. Their eyes locked.

Charli stopped, feet frozen in place. Not sure what to do. Was the guy being attacked? She couldn't imagine any man wanting to be gripped that tightly. Did he need help? But then he smiled at her—a lazy, drunk-on-pleasure smile, one that stirred something unfamiliar within Charli. His partner released his grip on the man's cock in an instant and smacked him audibly across the cheek.

Charli let out a little yelp.

"Eyes on me." Or at least that's what she thought she heard the man say after the slap.

She moved forward, not sure what she was going to do, but unable to stand there and watch someone get hurt. But the man against the tree shook his head at her and winked, then apologized to the guy who'd just hit him and lowered his head.

She halted her step. This was some kind of game.

A game he didn't want her interfering with.

She backed away, moving onto the path again and trying to get her legs to work correctly beneath her. She had no idea what was going on. How had Grant passed right by this couple and not seen what was happening? What if someone on a family vacation passed by with their kids?

She wrapped her arms around herself, somehow both hot and cold at the same time. Her body's odd reaction to seeing the couple was something she'd rather not think too hard on. She started walking up the path at a much faster pace than before. Now she was going to have to admit to Grant that she'd snuck onto the property. She didn't know what was allowed at his resort, but she couldn't imagine public sex was okay. He had a right to know what was going on.

She scanned the path in front of her and sighed. Of course, she'd lost sight of her cowboy during the diversion. Some stalker she was. Not sure what else to do, she made her way up to the main house and considered her options. The place had a number of doors and she had no idea which Grant had gone into or if they were locked or alarmed. And really, she no longer remembered why it had sounded like such a good idea to follow him in the first place. Maybe it was time to tuck tail and run.

"Do you need some help?"

The soft female voice startled Charli. She spun around to find a stunning blonde smiling back at her—a stunning blonde wearing what looked to be a red latex catsuit. "Uh . . ."

She tilted her head, assessing her. "You new here?"

"Yes." The word tumbled out automatically. "I'm a friend of Grant's."

"Oh, wow, that's great," she said with genuine warmth. "Just a friend or a trainee?"

"Huh?"

She laughed. "Sorry. You don't have to answer that if you don't want to. We're all just a little curious about our tight-lipped boss." She stuck out her hand. "I'm Kelsey, by the way. Or Lady K as most everyone knows me around here these days."

Pieces started to slide into place in Charli's brain. "Nice to meet you. I'm Charli."

"Are you only new here or are you new to this altogether?"

Oh, shit. "Altogether."

"Well, come on in, Charli. Boss man shouldn't have left you alone if you're brand-new. It's easy to get overwhelmed around here." She pulled open the nearest door. "I'm supposed to be assisting Colby with one of his training sessions. Feel free to come and watch. Or participate if the spirit moves you."

She walked through the door, her hips swaying on top of crazy-high-heeled boots with the ease of a pendulum. Charli followed her in, feeling like a schlub in comparison. How were some girls born with that vixen gene? Charli had no interest in other women, but even she couldn't help but be drawn in by Kelsey's magnetic sexuality.

Kelsey walked forward with long strides that belied her petite size. “So what side of the sandbox do you play in?”

Charli frowned. “I’m, um, not sure yet.”

Kelsey gave her a quick grin over her shoulder. “Oh, I know how that is. Sometimes you just have to give each role a shot and see what lights you up.”

“Right.”

The halls were quiet and decorated with deep maroons and dark wood. There were no windows but soft glowing sconces lit their way, giving the whole place a somehow comforting womblike vibe. Kelsey turned a corner and crooked a thumb toward the door on the left. “Here we are. Keep quiet when we go in. I’m a little late, so things have probably already gotten started. This is an open session, so if you want to join in at any time, go for it.”

Charli nodded, scared about what she was walking into but too damn curious to turn around and hustle back home. “Thanks.”

Kelsey turned the knob with nimble fingers and pushed the door open without a sound. On the other side was a small room. Charli peered over Kelsey’s shoulder, her lips parting when she saw the space was filled with half-dressed men and women on their knees. She pressed her fingers over her mouth, barely managing to choke down a gasp of surprise and avoid alerting everyone to her presence. Having a notion of what the place could be and actually seeing it were two different things. A ripple of nerves went through her.

Kelsey stepped inside, and Charli didn’t know what else to do but go in with her. Hell, at the very least, this was a whole lot more interesting than what was going on at her empty cabin. The man at the front of the room—the only person standing—nailed the two of them with his gaze. “Ah, I told you all we’d have a special treat. Lady K has generously offered to help tonight.”

One of the two men kneeling turned his head to see Kelsey and broke out into a wide, awed smile. Kelsey’s expression turned icy in an instant—from Snow White to evil queen in zero point five seconds. "Sub, I didn't give you permission to look at me."

The words were like the snap of a whip. The man instantly lowered his head as if he'd been struck. "So sorry, mistress. Forgive me. I was overwhelmed by your beauty."

She sniffed, a haughty tilt to her chin. "Flattery will get you nowhere. Master Colby must've not gotten to that part of your lesson yet."

The man at the front—Colby presumably—sent Kelsey a conspiratorial smile. "We've only started working on proper kneeling techniques. But I'll be sure Antoine earns your forgiveness later, Lady K." Colby looked to Charli as if noticing her for the first time, then back to Kelsey. "Have you brought us another trainee?"

"She's new and just observing tonight, trying to figure out her inclination," Kelsey said, her tone softening from the harsh one she used with the man.

Colby's dark eyebrows lowered, thunderclouds crossing his features, and he shook his head. "No observers for my trainings. Participate or leave."

Charli's throat seemed to shrivel, and she couldn't get a response out. Kelsey must've recognized the panicked look because she put a hand on Charli's elbow and leaned next to her ear. "Don't freak out. Nothing major happens in this session—it's all manners. Stay and see how you feel. Might help you with your decision."

More because her legs wanted to give out from under her than anything else, Charli let Kelsey guide her down into a kneel. So this is why Grant had been so guarded about the resort. Grant—the cowboy military guy turned vineyard owner—ran some sort of kinky S and M club? She couldn't even wrap her mind around the thought.

And if he ran it, did that mean he was into it, too?

Charli was dragged from her thoughts as Colby walked over to one of the younger women in the front—a dark-haired beauty who looked to be pulled from the pages of an old-fashioned pinup calendar. He cupped her chin and titled her face toward him. "Stella, would you please show the group what a nice stand and kneel you have?"

The girl kept her eyes down. "Yes, sir."

With one fluid movement, Stella rocked forward, tucked her toes under, and rose to a stand. It was a simple sequence of actions, but even Charli couldn't deny the utter elegance it conveyed—like a silk curtain lifting with a gust of wind.

Colby gazed down at her with pride. "Lovely, Stella." He looked to the group. "You see that, subs? None of this putting one leg up first or pushing yourself up with your hands. Unless you have some injury stopping you, your master or mistress deserves that kind of grace from you." He put a hand on Stella's shoulder. "Down."

"Yes, sir." As if the rewind button had been hit, Stella reversed her movements and rocked down into a kneel with the same fluidity. She ducked her head and placed her palms on her thighs. Beautiful. Subservient.

The idea should have rankled Charli. She'd spent her whole life making sure men saw her as an equal, showing no weakness, no softness. But there was such feminine beauty to Stella, Charli couldn't help but feel a tug of envy. What must it be like to draw that kind of rapt attention, to get that dripping-with-lust gaze from a man? Something low and deep within her stirred at the notion.

Colby crossed his arms over his broad chest, looking like a drill sergeant. "Now I want to see all of you follow Stella's example. Up."

The group instantly sprung to life, each person trying to emulate the graceful act. Charli hesitated for a moment but then snapped to it when she realized not following would only bring attention to herself. She attempted the movement, but her hand landed onto the floor when she overcorrected on her balance. She rose to her feet with the elegance of an offensive lineman suffering a concussion. Terrific.

"Down," Colby barked.

Everyone scrambled back to the floor. Some smoothly, some not so much.

Kelsey shook her head, *tsk*ing. "Pitiful."

Charli felt the heat of shame rising up from her chest. Shit, what had she gotten herself into? And why should she even care if she was a pretty kneeler or not?

Charli stared down at her hands, wondering how she could sneak out with anyone noticing. She needed to get out of here—stat. This was way out of her zip code. But right when she started to turn her head to venture a peek at the door, a heavy hand landed on her shoulder. "You seem to be lost, Ms. Beaumonde."

EIGHT

The voice behind Charli held barely restrained violence. She closed her eyes, wishing she could fall through the floor or wake up. This all had to be some bizarre nightmare, right? Dancing orangutans would twirl through the room anytime now. But of course when she opened her eyes again, Grant's hand was still on her shoulder. And she was still in the middle of some odd How to Be a Sex Slave class.

His breath was a hot tickle against her ear. "You have three seconds to stand up and come with me before I embarrass you and let everyone know you're an intruder here."

Her jaw clenched, but when she caught Kelsey's curious gaze, Charli tamped down her smart-ass reply. She didn't want to make Kelsey look bad. Plus, the thought of being exposed as an outsider suddenly seemed too much to stomach. She was in that role way too often in her life already. She rose to her feet—at least a little more smoothly than she had the first time.

Grant seemed huge next to her all of a sudden, as if being in this place somehow made him even taller. He grasped her upper arm and none too gently led her from the room. After shutting the door, he tugged her again like she was some disobedient puppy and guided her down the hallway. "Not a word until I get you behind a closed door."

The clipped command sent both a whisper of fear and some other unidentifiable emotion through her. She shivered beneath his grip, which apparently didn't go unnoticed by him. He gave her the side eye and the hard line of his mouth dipped into a full frown. But he stayed silent until they'd gone up an elevator, down another elegantly decked-out hallway, and into cozy sitting room, complete with a stone fireplace. Through another open door, she could see a bigger room with a desk and large plate-glass windows that looked out onto the black night. Grant's office.

He let go of her arm and shut the door they'd come through, then pinioned her beneath an iron gaze. "Sit."

"I'm not a dog."

"Charli, it's been a long night. You're trespassing after I explicitly told you not to, and you've taken me away from something important tonight. Do you really want to play word games right now?"

She sat, suddenly feeling the true extent of his anger. He was always a bossy son of a gun but here, at this place, she sensed that part of him had dialed up from low buzz to rattle-and-hum mode.

Then it hit her.

Grant was like Colby.

She remembered the way Grant had made her hold the bar in the shower, the way he'd taken control.

He was one of the men who made women kneel for him.

Charli thought of pretty, subservient Stella, and her stomach plummeted like she'd been thrown from a bridge. No wonder Grant had left last night. She was everything girls like Stella weren't.

She looked away from him, staring at the unlit fireplace. "I'm sorry. You're right. I shouldn't have come over here."

"Damn right, you shouldn't have," he replied, his angry voice hitting the wood floors and reverberating around her. "What the hell were you thinking? I told you I have security. You didn't think the staff would see someone hopping the fence?"

"I thought this was a swanky resort for rich families," she protested. "I didn't think I was going to stumble into some, some . . ."

"Some what, Charli? Say what you think this is."

She glanced up at him, meeting the challenge in his eyes. "Some, I don't know, sex club, brothel, God knows what."

He smirked. "You think I'm running a whorehouse?"

"Why else would you be training people how to kneel?"

He closed his eyes briefly, as if reining in the desire to shake her. "Because those people are submissives who want to learn how to please a dominant. This is a fantasy resort. BDSM being our speciality."

Her brows lifted. "BDSM? Is that the same as S and M?"

He blew out a breath, sinking onto the couch opposite her, the fight visibly draining from him. "That's the older term for it. But yeah, basically. Bondage, dominance, submission, and sadomasochism. And this is supposed to be a place where I guarantee people the highest level of privacy to practice it. If my members knew that I'd allowed some nosy reporter to sneak onto the property . . ." He leaned back in his seat. "It could ruin my entire reputation."

Her teeth had gnashed together at the nosy reporter comment, but she tamped down her response when she saw how weary he looked. This was obviously a very big deal here, and she had been the one to break the rules. She pushed back all the snarky things she wanted to say. "I'm sorry. Really, I am. I'm not going to pretend I understand all this, but I had no right to come over here. Sometimes my curiosity gets the better of me."

He eyed her. "You think?"

"Damn. Okay. I get it. I said I'm sorry. What do you want me to do? Grovel for forgiveness?" The words were out before she could snatch them back.

His head tilted, mischief in his eyes. "Not a totally unappealing idea. Maybe you learned more in that training class than I think."

Her neck burned, the heat traveling up like mercury in a thermometer.

"What *were* you doing kneeling in the intro class anyway?"

She studied the tops of her hands, his inquiring gaze suddenly too much to take head-on. "I sort of got persuaded by Kelsey."

A soft chuckle. "Ah, Kelsey. She's new to my staff, but a very promising domme. If she can persuade *you* to do something, maybe she deserves a raise."

Charli's head lifted, her eyes narrowing. "Right, of course, because I'm nothing like those women in that room."

He leaned forward, forearms braced on his thighs. "No. You're not."

For some reason, the words pierced her like barbed wire. She herself had been thinking in the session she was nothing like those women. But hearing him say it with such conviction lashed at the same battered spot her boss had created when he'd told her she hadn't gotten the on-air position. Not good enough. Not pretty enough.

She hauled herself up from the couch as if the furniture had caught on fire beneath her. The telltale stinging sensation of impending tears seared her throat. "I want to go back to my cabin."

He mouth dipped. "We're not done here. We need to talk about last night, and I need to know that you're not going to—"

But she was no longer listening as she moved toward the door. She had to get out of here. Right. Now. She wasn't exactly sure why she felt ready to fall apart. All she knew was she was not going to do it in front of Grant.

She reached for the doorknob but a large palm landed against the wood over her head, preventing the door from opening. "Charli, stop. Why are you running?"

She stared at the door, the polished wood blurring in her vision and Grant's body heat radiating against her back. He was so close. There was no way she was going to escape without him seeing her tears. She pressed her palms against the door. "Please. I need to go."

But the words were choked, cracked, revealing what she was trying so hard to hide.

"For God's sake, freckles. You're crying?" He put his hands on her shoulders and turned her around. "What's going on? Is this about last night? Because I am so sorry about that."

"Yes. No." She shook her head, staring at his boots because she was too mortified to look up at him.

"Tell me, Charli."

She didn't want to talk to him. Didn't want to lay her shame bare. But in that moment, she couldn't stuff it down any longer. She swiped at her ridiculous tears. "I've spent my whole life working hard, proving myself. And no matter what I do, everyone always wants what I'm not."

"What are you talking about? Is this about your job?"

"My job, my mother . . . you."

"Me?" he asked, sounding genuinely perplexed.

She raised her gaze to him and managed a *well-duh* smirk. "If I didn't make it embarrassingly clear last night in the bathroom, I'm attracted to you. And of course, you can't be a guy who would just want to have a quick fling with someone like me. No, you want the epitome of all that is stereotypically feminine. The gorgeous goddess on her knees."

The lines around his mouth deepened. "Charli."

She raised her palm. "Please. Don't. If you say some pitying comment, I'm going to punch you in the face."

His shoulders sagged with a heavy sigh. "That's not what I was going to do."

She stepped around him, walking to the window on the far side of the room and putting her back to him. "Right."

She heard his boots against the floor as he turned around, but he didn't come any closer. "Believe what you want, but let me say my piece. Since the night I found you out on the road, I haven't stopped imagining what it would be like to get you in my bed. Every time you talk back to me, I want to hush you up in all kinds of creative ways. And last night, it took every letter of my moral code to walk out and not take full advantage of the situation."

Her blood seemed to halt in her veins, her whole body pausing as if to make sure she'd heard him right. His footfalls sounded behind her, and then his scent was invading the air around her.

"Attraction is not the issue." His hands were on her shoulders again and she let him turn her around. His blue eyes found hers, the stark desire in them stripping her defenses. "But I don't have simple flings. I don't do simple anything. My tastes are intense and specific. And beyond the fact that I don't want to mess with my friend's sister, you're not a submissive. I don't do the vanilla thing."

Her heart was a hard, pounding knot in her throat. He was too close for her to get her thoughts in order. "Vanilla?"

"Regular sex and relationships. I'm not satisfied in that kind of dynamic."

She blinked, her tears forgotten. He didn't do normal sex at all? And . . . "Wait, you think I'm attractive?"

He laughed and lowered his hands to his sides. "Good grief, freckles. Is that your first question for me after my big I'm-a-kinky-bastard confession?"

She crossed her arms. "Yes. I need to hear what you think. The truth."

He looked to the heavens as if pleading for some divine patience. "The truth? You're hardheaded, you wear clothes too big for that body of yours, and you have awful taste in wine. But yes, I wanted you so badly last night that I could barely make it back to my cabin before wrapping my hand around my cock and jerking off to thoughts of you."

Even the tips of her ears went hot at that. “Well, there’s a backhanded compliment if I’ve ever heard one.”

He shrugged. “You wanted the truth. Would you rather I bullshit you?”

She glanced down at her comfy T-shirt and loose jeans, seeing her clothes through his eyes instead of hers for the first time. “No. I can take it.”

He tucked his hands in his pockets, his expression turning resigned. “Go back to your cabin, Charli. Don’t tell anyone about this place, and we’ll move on.”

“So that’s it?”

“We’ve got nothing left to discuss.” He turned around and headed through the side door that led to his office. He picked up the phone, keeping his back to her. “Marc, can you come to my office and make sure Ms. Beaumonde makes it back to her cabin safely? Thanks.”

And with that, she was dismissed.

So they were attracted to each other and it didn’t matter. Because she wasn’t some dainty, submissive girly girl.

If she were, then he’d probably have his mouth on her right now. And hell, she’d probably have her promotion, too.

The thought was like a match being struck. She peeked over at Grant again, a small smile forming on her lips.

Tonight, she’d let him be. But tomorrow . . . Tomorrow he’d find out just how hardheaded she could get.

Game, set, match, cowboy.

NINE

Grant grabbed the rag he'd thrown over his shoulder and wiped the sweat off his face. After the night he'd had, the only cure he could think of this morning was working his ass off in the fields. At least the grapes were doing well because everything else was going to shit. He'd had another failed interview with a potential trainee last night and then Charli had, once again, thrown a grenade into his evening.

Lord, seeing her kneeling there in that class had taken the floor right out from under him. For a moment, he hadn't been able to decide what action he wanted to take more—drag her to his office to yell at her or haul her off to his play space to discipline her in a much more inventive fashion. His body had wholeheartedly decided on the latter, but his brain had overruled.

This time.

He trudged through the last of the brush to get back to the main path, but muttered a curse when he saw Charli sitting on the fence near his cabin. Think of the devil and she shall appear. Charli had hooked her feet onto the cross post and that red mane of hair was blowing around her like wildfire. If trouble could be photographed, that's what it would look like.

She grinned and hopped off the fence when she saw him, a new light in her eyes. "Well, look at that. The cowboy actually does farm work?"

The shift to a lighthearted version of Charli surprised him. Huh, maybe they were actually going to be able to move on from the mess of the last few days. He closed the distance between them and tossed the rag back over his shoulder. "Have the calluses to prove it. How 'bout you? Aren't you supposed to be at your job, Ms. Beaumonde?"

She raised her palm to block her eyes from the glare and looked up at him. "Research day."

He reached up, took off his hat, and sat it on her head. "You need to get yourself a hat or some sunscreen. You're already starting to burn."

The hat tilted off-kilter, too big for her head. She tucked her hands in her pockets with a shrug. "Irish skin, what are you going to do?"

He could think of a number of things to do with it. Like lick it or bite it or turn it bright pink without any help from the sun. He pushed the images out of his head. *Focus, man.* "So, what are you doing here?"

"I need a favor."

Oh, Lord. "And I need a drink. Inside."

He walked past her and she followed him into the house, finding her way to one of his kitchen stools. He grabbed two bottles of water from the fridge, set one out for her, and then went about downing his in one long gulp.

He could feel her stare on him.

"You look like one of those Coke commercials with the sweaty construction worker," she mused. "Though he had his shirt off. That'd be better."

He tossed the empty bottle into the recycle bin and sent her a wary look. "Be careful, freckles. That sounds dangerously close to flirting."

"So?" she challenged, toying with the label on her water.

"So, I thought we settled that little situation last night." He leaned against the granite-topped island, feeling more than just physically tired. Resisting Charli was wearing him down like an iceberg grinding rock. "You said you needed a favor."

She straightened in her seat, and he couldn't help but notice how fucking cute she looked with his too-big hat on her. He wondered what she'd look like wearing *only* his hat.

"It's kind of a big favor."

Maybe he should have put bourbon in his water. "Okay . . ."

She rolled the plastic bottle between her palms, her hands belying her nerves despite her steady voice and gaze. "Is Colby available for private lessons?"

He damn near choked on his own spit. "What?"

"Well, I was thinking about those women last night and how . . . graceful and feminine they were. And if I could learn to capture even ten percent of that thing—whatever that thing is that those women have—I think I could turn things around at work." She peeked up at him from beneath the hat, but then trundled on, not giving him time for a response. "There's an anchor position coming open soon. Those positions are a big deal. There's no way they can pick someone who doesn't have rock-solid sports chops. I already have the knowledge and a big story brewing. And I know I've got what it takes to be on camera. I just need some, I don't know, refinement. Some softening."

Grant's thoughts were banging together in his head like cymbals. *Crash. Crash. Crash.* She wanted sub training? With *Colby*? "But you're not a submissive."

"Who says I can't learn? I can be a good student." She squared her shoulders. "I graduated salutatorian in high school, you know."

"It's not simply a skill, Charli," he said, his protest coming out more emphatic than he intended. "It's like a bone-deep thing, a part of who a person is. I've spent years in this world. I can sense it in people. And with you, I don't."

Her eyes narrowed dangerously, and he could feel her digging her heels in on the topic. "So what, you're like the Sorting Hat in *Harry Potter*? You're the be-all, end-all decision on which group I belong in?"

"No, I—" He stood, this whole conversation knocking him for a loop. "You don't even know what you're asking. That training is about more than kneeling and looking dainty. It's about being a *sexual* submissive. You ready to have Colby tie you up, spank you, and have you suck his dick in front of a room full of people?"

Her already sun-pink cheeks went full red, and he thought he'd succeeded in scaring her.

But then her nipples hardened beneath her T-shirt, and the pulse at her throat visibly quickened. Subtle signs, but ones that were his instinct to notice. He blinked at her, his own blood surging below his belt. *Fuck*. What he'd said had turned her on. She was having a submissive response.

At that realization, the need he was trying so hard to keep locked down jumped to the surface, uninvited but undeniable. All the urges he'd been failing to feel each time he interviewed a potential sub trainee flooded him like they'd just been lying there in wait for this moment, ready to yank him under. He stepped closer and braced his hands on the counter, inches from her. He needed to back away, to kick her out. Her response was probably a fluke, a reaction to the mention of sex. But he couldn't move.

She was holding her breath, but he didn't sense any fear. He sensed . . . want.

His voice was deadly calm when he finally managed words. And they weren't the words he'd intended to say. "Are you thinking about Colby doing those things to you, Charli? Is that why your body is coming to life?"

Her hands had stilled against the bottle and the hum of the refrigerator seemed deafening in the silence. She stared at the patch of counter in front of her, her normally defiant gaze not venturing upward. "No. Not him."

A slew of emotions came with her answer. Relief that she wasn't hot for Colby. Dread over who she *was* interested in. And fear about the swiftly dwindling control he had over his own desires. "Damn, you're bullheaded. Didn't you hear anything I said last night? I can be tough and mean, freckles. I don't just like to dominate a submissive; I like to *own* her while she's in training with me. You think I'm bossy now? You have no. Fucking. Idea."

She looked up at him, a glimmer of honest fear finally inching into the green depths of her eyes.

He took his hat off her head and tossed it to the side. "You need to go back to your cabin and forget about this plan. You're in over your head."

She stared at him with a go-to-hell in her eyes and a fuck-off hovering on her lips. He thought she was going to traipse off in a huff. But after a few pregnant beats, she tilted her chin up. "Try me."

The response didn't even compute in his head. "What?"

"Go ahead and dish it out, cowboy. I'm tougher than you think. If I can't handle it, I'll never bring it up again. If I can, you agree to train me."

She leaned back in her chair, sassy with courage now.

Which only made the crotch of his jeans go tighter, that haughtiness of hers taunting his most primal instincts. The sleeping tiger inside him stirred and lifted a dark eye, his prey in sight.

This was wrong in so many ways Grant had lost track. Charli was Max's sister. Non-submissive. Someone Grant was supposed to protect. They had no contract between them, no carefully negotiated limits. She was a D/s virgin, for God's sake. It was everything he was against.

But the switch had been flipped, the temptation too much.

He would have her.

"You think you can handle it, huh?" He crossed his arms and stared her down. "Stand up, Charli. And don't say another thing unless it's *yes, sir.*"

Charli's lips rolled inward as she watched the change come over Grant. There was almost a visible ripple over his skin, like he was shedding some costume he wore in public and showing her what really lay beneath.

She swallowed hard and rose to her feet. Knowing for sure that her mouth had gotten her into trouble this time. What the fuck was she doing?

But something about Grant's challenging tone and sun-and-sweat-glazed body had caused a coup in the decision-making part of her brain. Her hormones were now solidly in charge.

Grant walked with slow, measured steps around the counter, then stopped in front of her, peering down with a dark, almost clinical expression. "Your safe word is *Texas.* You know what that means, Charli?"

She tried to respond but her tongue had forgotten how to work. She shook her head.

"*No, sir* is the proper response. Say it."

She cleared her throat twice before managing a feeble "No, sir."

He grabbed her unopened bottle of water, twisted the cap off, and handed it to her. "Drink."

She did.

"In my world, *stop* and *no* are sometimes thrown around for effect. The only thing that makes everything stop is your safe word. Here that word is *Texas.* You say it and whatever is happening stops, no questions asked."

Everything stops. Meaning, if she said that word, he'd have proven she really couldn't handle him. Fat chance. Losing wasn't her style.

"Do you understand?"

"Yes . . . sir."

"Take off your clothes."

"What? Like here?" She knew the words sounded stupid even as she said them, but she couldn't help it.

He stalked forward, backing her into the counter. "Make me request something twice and I'll be sure and show you the punishment part of this dynamic. A favorite of mine."

The edge of the granite pushed into the small of her back. Her instinct was to rail against him. To tell him to fuck off. But her body wasn't on board with that plan, and she had agreed to try. So try she would. "Sorry."

She'd never stripped down for a guy in broad daylight like this. The blinds were open and anyone walking by would easily see inside. But bringing that up to Grant probably wasn't going to go over so well. With awkward fingers, she fumbled with the buttons on her shirt and peeled it off, revealing her plain cotton bra underneath. One that had gone an odd shade of gray when she'd accidentally washed it with the color load. Fabulous. Nothing said sexy like old Hanes.

She let the shirt fall to the floor, and Grant took a small step back, giving her room to continue. His hawk-like gaze watched her every move, every flinch. She took a steadying breath, toed off her sandals, and went to the button of her khakis. She closed her eyes and tugged them down, knowing that the comfy panties beneath were older and in worse shape than her bra. She stepped out of the puddle of clothing and stared down at her toes. Now she remembered why she always had sex in the dark.

"All of it," Grant said, his voice quiet but firm.

She glanced up at him, finding his expression maddeningly unreadable. "Grant, I feel—"

Awkward, embarrassed, freaking exposed.

"I didn't ask how you feel. This is about what I want. Not you. And right now, I want to see all of you. Go back to your cabin or get naked."

She gritted her teeth. So this was how it was going to be. Fine. Her brothers had learned a long time ago to never call her bluff. She never backed down from a dare. So if Grant thought he could scare her off of this by being an asshole, he had another thing coming.

"I'm waiting, freckles."

Here goes nothing.

She reached behind her, unhooked her bra, revealing her barely B-cup breasts, and then tugged her panties down and off. The warm air in the cabin suddenly felt ten times cooler against her bared skin. She shifted her weight, all too aware of the telltale moisture between her thighs. Damn. She almost didn't want to give him the satisfaction of knowing that simply seeing him walking in from the fields all glistening and dirty had gotten her body revving.

She stared at his boots, not wanting to see his reaction. Fearing she'd find disappointment there. Knowing that would make her call her safe word before anything else would.

His feet stepped forward until he was a breath away from her. "Look at me."

Her hands clenched, but she forced her face upward, bracing herself for whatever she was going to find there.

Blue fire raked over her as his eyes traced the planes of her face. "You do yourself a great disservice, Ms. Beaumonde, with those clothes you wear. What's beneath is even better than I imagined that night I stroked my cock thinking of you."

Oxygen forgot to move through her lungs.

He planted a hand on each side of her on the counter, caging her between his forearms, and leaned in. She closed her eyes, absorbing what he'd just told her, inhaling him. Clean sweat, grass, and man danced around her in a heady elixir. No aftershave or fancy cologne. Only the most erotic scent she could ever remember smelling in her life.

He nuzzled the spot behind her ear, drawing the tip of his tongue along her lobe. "Are you wet for me, Charli?"

The honeysuckle twang of his voice was like a hot lick to every one of her erogenous zones. She shuddered and he pressed against her, the soft denim of his worn jeans revealing the erection restrained behind that zipper.

"Shit, yes," she murmured.

He bit her earlobe, the sharp nip sending a zap through her. She gasped.

"Yes, what?"

"Sir," she corrected in a hurried rush. "Yes, sir."

Hell. What was he doing to her? She could barely grab on to her thoughts.

"Good girl." His hand found her waist, then traced down and over her hip bone in a slow, tortuous trail. His thumb brushed her mound. "You're so lovely here, Charli. Nothing sexier than a natural redhead."

She pressed her forehead into his shoulder, knowing that her skin was probably blotchy from a full-body blush. She was no virgin, but her encounters had mostly been casual, low-key romps. A little kissing, a little touching, and then the usually lackluster main event. She'd never felt so *observed* before. "Thank you."

His palm dipped lower, his finger parting her sex and finding her damp heat. The callused pad of his finger slid over her clit, causing her to arch against him.

"Mmm, good girl," he breathed against the side of her neck. "So wet and eager for me."

The dirty words were so different from the way he talked to her normally, so opposite the gentleman cowboy. But somehow that made it even more effective. Knowing that he was showing her this secret, darker side of himself had her insides fluttering. He stroked her with firm confidence, and a soft moan passed her lips.

"But no coming unless I say so," he added.

"Are you kidding?" She couldn't help it. Her mouth had a mind of its own.

He moved his hand away, stopping the decadent stimulation, and took a step back, leaving her there naked and aching. The disapproval on his face was like a lash to her skin. "Turn around, forearms on the counter."

Her heartbeat raced, her limbs tingling with a rush of fight-or-flight, but she turned around nonetheless and followed his instruction. The cool granite pressed against her arms and an overwhelming wave of vulnerability washed over her. His belt buckle clinked.

Whoa, was he going to take her right here, like this?

The idea shouldn't have been so damn appealing.

But instead of feeling his hands on her, she felt smooth, supple leather brush across the base of her spine. "Lace your fingers together and put your forehead against your hands."

"Grant, I—"

"Wrong answer." He planted a hand between her shoulder blades forcing her down into the position. Her blood was roaring in her ears and ribbons of dread curled in her stomach. It was like that moment before she'd bungeed the first time—fear and exhilaration twining together. She laced her fingers together, putting herself in a sort of praying position.

She probably needed to pray.

"Ready to press the escape hatch, Charli?" Grant asked, the question deceptively soft.

Escape. She could walk out right now. Go back to her safe, little existence where she had all the control, where everything was nice and predictable.

"No, sir." The answer was automatic but truthful. She shifted restlessly, both worried and desperate for whatever was to come.

"We'll see."

She heard the belt cut through the air before she felt the blazing sting as it landed across the fleshy part of her backside. The pain radiated like a line of fire over her skin. She cried out and her nails bit into the tops of her hands.

"Count, Charli."

Her mind took a second to process what he was telling her. Count what? *Oh, shit. The hits.* There were more coming? "One."

"One for questioning me."

The belt came down again, different spot, same wicked bite. She pressed her forehead hard into her hands. "Two."

"And two for failing to follow a directive after I warned you I don't like to repeat myself."

Anger sparked bright within her. Never in her life had she let anyone treat her like she was some misbehaving child. Her own father had never even raised a hand to her. As the only girl left in the household, she'd been treated with kid gloves. She wanted to turn around, rip that belt from his hands, and smack Grant in the head.

But then a low rumble of a noise came from him—something between a groan and a growl. His hands were on her in an instant, large palms massaging the throbbing stripes on her backside, activating a pleasant erotic burn that traveled over her nerve endings. "Oh, look how beautiful you are like this. Your skin gets so pretty and pink."

The tone and reverence of his voice shot straight to that needy part inside of her, dragging her focus away from any lingering sting and onto the pulsing ache between her legs.

"You ready for me, Charli? Or do you want to leave now that you have a taste of what I'm like?"

She could bail. Probably should. But her feet remained fastened to the floor. This was no longer about winning a challenge. Everything in her ached for him—to experience all of whatever he was. To fall under his dark spell. "I'm ready for you, sir."

He didn't say anything for a few seconds, then his low, commanding voice caressed her. "Push up onto your toes and hold that position, darlin'." She heard the rustle of clothing behind her as he moved. "Remember, no coming."

She found her bearings on the balls of her feet and gave herself over to the moment. Yes, she'd wandered into uncharted territory. Yes, there would be shit to deal with afterward, but right now all she wanted to do was be there for whatever happened next.

She didn't have to wait long to find out what he had in mind. Those roughened thumbs of his brushed against her folds and then spread her open from behind. A little noise of surprise eked out of her, and she almost dropped her heels back to the floor. But then his tongue, so hot and adept, was against her. Tasting her. Teasing.

Pleasure shuddered through her, lighting her up like a tree at Christmas. Every sensitive zone on her body perked to attention. Her nipples against the cold granite, the now strangely pleasant burn of the belt marks, the arches of her feet straining, the oh-so-tender skin he licked and nibbled at. Her heartbeat seemed to lodge right behind her clit, the throb becoming a desperate thing.

That urgency was so unfamiliar and unnerving. Guys didn't do this to her. Orgasms had always been such hard work. A battle. She thought the night in the shower had been a fluke, but he wasn't even inside her yet and she was ready to detonate.

"Please . . ." The pressure was building. She only needed the barest shift of his mouth and she would go over.

His tongue slid inside her channel and she moaned, losing her balance for a second. He held her in place, keeping her from slipping to the floor, and fucked her with his tongue. She clenched her threaded hands, the overwhelming need for release making her feel frantic, edgy. Starved.

Just when she thought she wouldn't be able to hold back anymore, he pulled away, planting a kiss on the back of her thigh. "Heels down."

She let her feet relax and melted against the counter, her heart pounding like she'd run miles on the treadmill. She didn't dare get up or look back though. She didn't want that belt again; she only wanted him.

She listened to him walk back into the living room, the pull of a drawer, then the sound of a crinkling foil as his steps got closer again. A condom. He palmed her hip. "Last chance to back out."

"Don't need it, sir." *I just need you. Right. Now.*

He slid two fingers inside her and her muscles clamped around them. He made a pleased sound under his breath. "Tell me what you want me to do to you, Charli."

She winced. Why couldn't he make this easy? Any other guy would see prone girl on counter, naked and willing, and would get right to it. But no. Not Grant. "Sir . . ."

"Beg me for it, freckles," he said, something dangerous and enticing in his voice, a pied piper's tune. "I'm not like other guys. I have no problem walking away unsatisfied to prove a point. So make me believe you don't want me to do that."

She bit her bottom lip, her inner feminist urging her to tell him just that—that she didn't need him. She could walk away, too. Hell, most of the guys she'd slept with had left her unsatisfied. She was used to it. But another deeper, quieter part of her whispered for her to let go and give in, to get her reward for surviving him. She swallowed hard and opened her eyes, staring hard at the fine pattern of the granite, wishing she could turn around and see his face. "Please, sir. I want you to take me. I need you to."

"Mmm, good girl." His body pressed against the backs of her thighs and she could tell he was still wearing his jeans. "Stretch out your arms."

She did as she was told and laid her cheek against the counter.

He grabbed her arms and guided them behind her back. The soft leather that he'd hit her with now looped around her wrists. He cinched the belt with a *clink*, binding her arms. Then, he kicked her heels apart with his booted foot.

She only had a second to realize how at his mercy she was before he was sliding inside her. Hot and thick and every bit as toe curling as she'd imagined. Every muscle in her body seemed to contract at the sweet invasion. A low moan drifted off her lips as he eased in, stretching her and taking his time burying himself inside her.

"Fuck," he murmured under his breath. His hand gripped her shoulder, as if he was trying to hold on to something within himself. "Am I hurting you? You're, God . . . you feel so . . ."

The fit was snug, her tissues tender, no doubt from her long bout of celibacy, but pain was definitely not how she would describe it. Fantastically intense was more like it. "No, sir. Feels . . . amazing."

At her words, she felt the tension in his grip ease a bit, and he canted his hips back, dragging himself almost all the way out then pushing deep again. Sensation went through her like ripples over the water. He groaned. "You're right about that."

She wiggled beneath him, an involuntary movement, her body craving more than the slow-and-sensual approach.

"Why so squirmy, beautiful?" he teased. "Not a fan of nice and easy?"

"Not right now . . . sir."

"Dirty girl. Hard and fast it is, then." His easy rhythm dialed up, and soon she was sliding back and forth across the counter, her skin slippery with sweat and highly sensitized, and the belt pressing into her tender wrists. The sound of his thighs hitting the back of hers and their shared moans supplied an erotic soundtrack she knew would haunt her fantasies.

His free hand wrapped around the front of her hip and found her swollen clit. She bucked against him, but he held her in place with ease. His fingers slid along the slick tissues and pinched gently, winding the tension inside her into a tight, glowing ball. Her breath caught in her throat.

"That's right. Give me your pleasure. Come for me, darlin'."

His pace turned NASCAR worthy, and his talented fingers did a move that made her nerves sing. Her body rocked against the counter, her back arching, and the glowing ball inside her burst into a hundred flecks of illuminated sensation. She lost conscious control of her body. Her head lifted and a sound unlike any that had ever come out of her filled the quiet cabin.

A deeper groan came from Grant, and his grip on her arms turned demanding as he reached his own release. Her name tumbled from his lips, and she couldn't ever remember her own name sounding so sexy. She closed her eyes and let herself fall into the afterglow with him.

Seconds—or maybe minutes—passed with both of them locked in that dreamy place of dwindling bliss, his body draped over her back. She wasn't sure she ever wanted to get up. But once the only noise in the cabin had returned to the droning fridge and the ticking clock, Grant freed her arms and slipped out of her. His voice was low. "Stay there. I'll be right back."

No problem. She wasn't sure she could move. Her muscles may have dissolved.

Before she knew it, he was back with a warm, wet cloth, attending to her. Then his palm was sliding over the spots where he'd hit her, rubbing in some sort of balm that cooled her skin. She knew when she looked back at this moment, she'd probably feel embarrassed, but right now she was buzzing too much from the orgasm to care.

"Can you stand up, Charli?" he asked, his voice all soft, rounded edges now.

She pushed herself onto her elbows then rose. He wrapped a robe around her from behind and rubbed her arms, making them tingle and bringing some feeling back into them.

"You okay?" he asked.

She turned around to find him looking like she'd left him. Fully dressed and wearing a frown. For the first time, she registered that he hadn't let her touch him or see him naked. He probably had only pushed down his pants and taken her. And he still hadn't kissed her. She'd let him hit her, restrain her, and fuck her, yet they hadn't had a first kiss.

The realization dampened her buzz. "I'm . . . fine."

He put his finger beneath her chin and studied her face, her eyes. "You're upset."

"I'm not." But the declaration sounded hollow even to her own ears. She didn't know what she was. Confused, mostly.

He deepened his frown, staring at her for another moment and apparently confirming whatever it was he was sensing. He lowered his hand and sighed. "I'm sorry, Charli. This was a bad idea."

The words sent a sharp snap of disappointment through her. She looked down and knotted the belt on the robe. "Always what a girl wants to hear after she's gotten naked with someone."

"I thought you would call the safe word from the get-go. Then I—" He paused, and she glanced up as he raked a hand through his hair.

"Then you what?"

"Then I couldn't resist taking you over." He shook his head and looked away, as if he was giving himself a firm lecture only he could hear. "Why didn't you stop me?"

Because she'd kind of loved it. Because it was thrilling in a way that no sex had ever been for her. Because for some odd reason, she'd trusted him not to go too far. But no way she was going to say any of *that* out loud. She crossed her arms and tilted her chin up. "Because I need this training and wanted to show you I can handle it. I'm not scared of you, Grant."

He glanced over at her, his expression darkening. "You should be."

She conjured up a practiced nothing-bothers-me smile, ignoring the fluttering anxiety in her belly, and claimed her victory—though now it felt like an empty one. "Guess I'm your new trainee, cowboy."

His lips parted, but she didn't give him time to respond. She picked up her clothes and ugly undergarments and traipsed out of his cabin, taking his robe and her shredded nerves with her.

TEN

He hated losing control.

This loss had at least come with a naked, spanked Charli splayed across his kitchen counter and sex that had damn near blown his head off.

But still, his jaw had yet to unclench.

She'd baited him, thrown a gauntlet down to test his own self-control. And he'd failed. Sure, he'd been the one giving the orders and the swats, but it had been driven by pure emotion—something he worked hard at keeping out of his sexual encounters. And dammit, he'd hit her with a fucking belt with no contract, without even knowing her hard and soft limits. He'd barely managed to stop himself before he'd completely gone off the reservation and taken her to his bedroom—a place he'd never taken any woman. Charli Beaumonde had unraveled him.

And hell if he could stop thinking about her. Since she'd walked out the door, he'd done little else than replay the scene and invent new ones, imagining how much further he wanted to take her. His claim-and-conquer gene was on a rampage, and he wasn't quite sure how to turn it off.

Plus, now Charli was apparently refusing to stick to his stay-safe rules until he agreed to his end of the bargain and took her on for training. Two days had passed since their encounter and she'd stopped checking in with him. He'd waited for her text this morning, knowing it wouldn't come, and turned on the GPS tracker. Luckily, Charli hadn't figured out where he'd installed it. Otherwise, he had no doubt that she would've disabled it.

Yesterday, she'd gone to the office and he'd been able to relax and get some work done. But today, she'd turned in the opposite direction, and he'd had to get in his truck and channel his old CIA persona to do a little surveillance. So now Grant found himself parked between two buildings across from a broken-down diner in some town he didn't know the name of watching Charli eat pancakes with a guy who talked with his hands. Grant adjusted the volume on his phone's earpiece, trying to stay focused on Charli while still listening in on the conference call with the Water's Edge department heads.

"If we switch to a screw top and a cheaper bottle, we can lower the price a bit," Lars, the head of sales, suggested. "We could get into some of the bigger stores."

The others began to debate.

"No screw top," Grant said, using his gavel-hit-the-desk tone. "I have no interest in going mass production. Our wines are an experience. As long as we keep producing the highest quality product, there will be a market for it."

"But in this economy . . ." Lars protested.

"Our numbers have only gone up," Grant said. "Next topic."

He knew his team meant well. They saw the sales at Water's Edge and knew the potential their wines had at becoming a mass-market brand, but Grant refused to sacrifice quality. His father had run a successful cattle ranch for decades using that philosophy, and

Grant didn't plan to veer from it in his own business. Plus, The Ranch now brought in enough money to fund him for as long as he needed. The wine business had turned into a mere bonus.

Lars moved on to another item in the agenda, but his voice faded into the background as Grant caught movement in his peripheral vision. Charli had parked her rental car in the alley between the diner and a pawnshop. The shiny rental was the only new model in sight and apparently, Grant hadn't been the only one to notice that. The pawnshop blocked most of the sunlight, but Grant hadn't missed the shift in the shadows behind Charli's car. Someone was in the mood for a little grand theft auto.

"Son of a bitch."

"Huh?" Lars asked.

Grant didn't have time to respond. He pulled out his earpiece and grabbed for his glove compartment, which was, of course, locked. "Dammit."

He yanked the keys out the ignition and unlocked the compartment, grabbing for his gun. He glanced back at the diner. Charli was stepping out, absently digging through her purse for something as she walked—her keys, probably. *Shit.* He definitely didn't need Charli surprising a thief.

Grant hopped out of truck, checked the safety, and tucked the gun into his waistband. "Charli! Hold up!"

Charli looked up from her bag and paused as if verifying she'd heard what she'd thought she heard, and then turned her head in his direction. He jogged toward her. Thank God he hadn't parked far away or he may have not been able to intercept her. When she realized it was him, she put her hands on her hips, her exasperation evident even from a distance.

"Go back inside," he called, pointing at the diner.

She glanced back at the restaurant. "What?"

He hustled past her toward the parking lot. "Inside. Now."

Whether she figured out there was danger or saw his gun, she listened. He turned the corner into the alley on full alert. Charli's car was third from the street, and besides an empty can rolling in the breeze, everything appeared to be still. He crept forward, his eyes and ears in full scanning mode. But after one step, the backside passenger door on the rental car jolted open and someone barreled out, dressed in all black and running full speed in the other direction.

Grant drew his gun and climbed over the hood of the first car, trying to catch up or at least get a description. But the thief had too much of a head start on him. The guy reached the end of the alley and disappeared into the greenbelt that stretched along the back of the buildings.

"Fuck." Grant ran to the edge of the trees but knew it would be pointless to go traipsing after him. No doubt the guy was a local and would know the landscape better than him. After one last fruitless search of the periphery for any kind of evidence, he headed back to Charli's car to see if there was any damage.

The rear passenger door was still wide open, and as Grant frowned down at it, a creeping feeling raised the hairs on his neck. What in the hell would a car thief be doing hiding in the backseat? If he had wanted to hot-wire it, he would've been fooling around the driver's side. Grant ventured closer and peered into the backseat. A shiny roll of masking tape sat on the floorboard. His grip on the frame of the door tightened, lividity burning a path through him. He looked back to the trees, ready to hunt the bastard down and show him all the torture techniques he'd perfected.

"Is everything okay?"

Grant backed away from the car, making sure not to touch anything else, and gave Charli, who'd poked her head around the corner of the building, a wary look. This was getting completely out of hand. This was more than someone trying to scare Charli. Someone was trying to *harm* her. And that shit was completely unacceptable. He wanted to grab her, put her in his car, and not let her out of his sight again until he could personally maim and dismember whoever the fucker was.

Even monitoring Charli this closely, he'd barely had time to step in before she'd gotten into the car with some kidnapping psychopath. Whispers of the night someone had broken into his and Rachel's home prodded at his mind. *No. Don't go there.* He swallowed past the panicky, choking feeling that always accompanied the memory. He didn't have time to have a freak-out. Charli needed him operating at a hundred percent.

Time for a new plan.

Charli wanted training? Well, she was about to get the session of a lifetime.

He tucked his gun back in his waistband. "We better call the cops, freckles. I thought someone wanted to steal your car, but it looks like someone wants to steal *you*."

Charli sat on Grant's couch, trying to rub the chill from her arms, but the too-cold feeling wouldn't go away. She stared out the front window, watching the rays of late-afternoon sun slant over the front yard. Someone had been hiding in the backseat of her car. If Grant hadn't been there . . . well, she couldn't stop thinking about the what-ifs. It had been stupid to go off on her own just to prove a point. She'd started to believe the threat wasn't real, that everyone had been overreacting. But now she was thanking the heavens that her brother had a paranoid streak and that Grant was so relentless in his mission.

"You sure the guy you were meeting with wasn't setting you up? Couldn't he have tipped off someone?" Grant asked as he walked out of the kitchen and handed her a steaming cup of coffee.

She took it from him, warming her hands against the mug. "I don't think so. Rodney was taking a big chance talking to me. He told me in not so many words that he was paid cash from boosters during his first two years at Dallas U. before he blew out his knee. If that came out and was proved to be true, the NCAA wouldn't just sanction the college, they'd do a full investigation on the current program. A program that is heading toward the national championship this year, by the way."

"So I've heard," he said dryly. "They beat my Longhorns to the ground a few weekends ago."

"Your defense sucks. They beat themselves."

Grant frowned at her, then apparently decided to wave off a football debate. Wise move. She'd win. "But this Rodney guy refused to give you an official statement. Seems kind of shady to me, like he was using that info as bait to get you out there."

She shook her head and tucked her legs beneath her. "That's not what my gut's telling me. I think he was being honest. But he's got kids now and putting his name out there as a snitch—well, it's dangerous. You know how people are about football around here."

Grant sat down on the couch across from her, his mouth set in that way that told her he was making plans without her input. "Yeah. I do know. It *is* dangerous. Which is why you're going to back off for a while."

She halted mid-sip. "The hell I am. Today proved how important it is to break this story. We just need to take extra precautions."

"Charli, this is not a negotiation," he said, his tone slipping into that dominant space he'd used with her the other day. "Your brother told me to keep you safe, and I intend to do that. But I can't keep doing it from a distance. This story isn't going anywhere. You need to cool your heels and let whoever is after you think that they were successful in scaring you off."

The chill she'd been trying so hard to chase off disappeared in a rush of angry heat. "*Cool my heels*? Grant, that's not how this works. I'm a reporter. This is what I do."

"And I'm former CIA. When your cover is blown, you have to

back off for a while or send someone else in. You're blinking bright red on someone's radar right now."

She groaned; of course he'd been a government operative. That explained a lot. "I'm not going to let them chase me off. I need this story."

"Why, Charli? Why do you *need* this story?" He leaned forward, bracing his forearms on his thighs. "What is so important about it that you'd be willing to risk your goddamn life to get it?"

She started to open her mouth to speak, to give the knee-jerk reaction that wanted to come out, but she knew nothing she said would be the real truth. Yes, she believed that what was happening was wrong. Yes, she believed cheaters should be punished. But that burning, desperate drive to get this story as soon as possible had nothing to do with some reporter champion-of-the-truth moral code. This was about proving something to herself, to the mother who had walked out on her, and to everyone who ever told her she couldn't do it. "You wouldn't understand."

"Oh, really? Try me," he said, leaning back and using the same words she'd thrown at him in the kitchen two days ago. Despite her frustration with him, her body's sensors perked at the memory.

She shifted on the couch and sighed. "I need to do more than I'm doing now. I didn't get into this field to sit behind a computer gathering research for some other reporter's piece. If I can land this story, there's no way they won't give me a promotion to an investigative reporter."

"Is that really the job you want?"

She stared down at her coffee. "No, I want the anchor position. But apparently I'm not good on camera."

"And those idiots who told you that must be touched in the head," he said, a thread of anger weaving through his tone. "You're a beautiful, intelligent woman. Yes, maybe you're a little rough around the edges with your approach, but that's something that can be refined. And if they can't see your potential, then I don't know if they deserve to have you anyway."

Charli looked up, startled by the conviction behind his words.

"I'll tell you what," he said, his drawl thickening as he got more fervent about whatever ideas were churning in his head. "You take some time off from chasing this story, try to do most of your other work from here for a while, and I'll take you on as my trainee. I usually require my trainees to stay here full-time for the month. But I know you can't take off that long, so give me two weeks. I'll make sure that when you walk in for that anchor audition, they won't be able to pick their jaws up off the floor. You'll be so damned polished they'll have to put on sunglasses to shield themselves from the glare."

She stared at him, then couldn't help it, she laughed. "You may be a little overconfident in your abilities there, cowboy. I'm a quick learner, but there's a lifetime of tomboy in here. Don't think two weeks is going to cure me of it."

The corner of his mouth tilted up, drawing his dimple out. "I don't want to cure you of it, freckles. But I also know that if you give me a little time, I'll show you how much woman is in there, too."

The promise in his statement and the look he gave her had her swallowing hard. "What exactly would I be signing up for? Obviously, the other day was a disappointment for you."

A crease formed between his brows. "You think I was disappointed in you? Darlin', I can't get you or that damn afternoon outta my head. I've barely gotten anything else done because you're so . . . distracting."

She looked down at her hands, trying to hide how much his words relieved her. After leaving his place, she'd been convinced she must have done something wrong.

"I was pissed at myself. I hammer into my members the rules of safe, sane, and consensual play. And here I am hitting a vanilla girl who's never played before with a belt, not even knowing anything about your limits."

She ran a finger around the rim of her coffee mug, not daring to look at him. "It was fine. You didn't hit me that hard."

"Yeah, but what if you'd had an abusive childhood where you were beaten with a belt and I had triggered that trauma for you? Or what if you had a former injury I needed to be aware of? It was irresponsible on my part, and I'm sorry."

She glanced up, surprised by the deep sincerity in his voice. "I didn't have an abusive childhood. And . . ." She attempted an it's-no-big-deal shrug. "I kind of liked the belt, for what it's worth."

"Is that right?" he asked, a devious smirk forming. "Duly noted. Maybe you're not as vanilla as I thought."

She didn't know what to do with that observation, wasn't sure what the hell was going on with her at this point. All she knew was that for the last two days, she hadn't been able to close her eyes without replaying the way Grant had handled her, the sharp way her body had reacted to his touch and words. She hadn't been able to go to sleep either night without sliding her hand beneath the band of her pajama bottoms, touching herself and imagining it was Grant's fingers and tongue instead. Her panties were damp already simply sharing the room with him.

She set her mug down and fiddled with the sleeve of her shirt, hoping her neck wasn't as pink as it felt. Damn redheaded complexion. "What do you suggest for training?"

"You sure you're serious about really trying this with me?" he asked. "Because I'm not good at doing anything halfway."

Boy howdy, had she learned that. "Yes. Lay it on me. What do you propose?"

He crossed his arms over his chest, looking resolute and foreboding. "For two weeks, when you're not working, you're all mine."

She wet her lips, her nerves starting to take root and bloom. "Meaning?"

"I'll *own* you, Charli."

ELEVEN

Charli had never been to a spa before. Her beauty regime usually consisted of a quick split-end trim in the salon at her gym with an occasional deep conditioner. For a rare treat, she'd spring for a pedicure. But today she had the feeling she was going to experience a whole other side of the rigors of beautification.

Kelsey was sitting in the zen-style waiting room when Charli walked in, looking vastly different than she had the first time Charli had seen her. The catsuit and expertly applied makeup had been replaced by jeans, a soft white sweater, and a bare face that was really unfairly beautiful. If not for the world-weary glint Charli had seen in her eyes the other night, Kelsey could pass for a college student.

Kelsey looked up from the magazine she'd been reading and broke into a smile. "Hey there. Guess you didn't get lost this time?"

Charli pulled the note Grant had left on her counter that morning from her pocket and held it up. "Grant gives good directions."

She cocked an eyebrow and her grin turned conspiratorial. "I bet he does."

Charli shoved the note back in her pocket, trying to cover up her instinctive, awkward reaction at Kelsey knowing exactly what she and Grant were doing. Being open about sex was going to take some getting used to. She'd grown up in a household where even the mention of her period had set her dad into a stuttering, bumbling mess. Any talk of sex would've probably made his poor head explode. An appointment card for the women's health center had just magically appeared on her bedside table the day after she'd turned sixteen. "No comment."

Kelsey laughed and tossed the magazine onto the coffee table as she stood. "So are you ready?"

She shrugged. "I guess so. Grant didn't exactly tell me anything more about this than to show up."

"Uh-oh," Kelsey said, pulling a note from the pocket of her jeans. She unfolded it and showed a very long list—all in Grant's precise handwriting. "Then you have a few surprises to look forward to. He's scheduled you for the works."

Charli leaned forward, trying to read what was on the list, but Kelsey folded it before she could read anything more than "wax." *Oh, shit.*

"No peeking. If he had wanted you to know, he would've already told you. But I promise you're going to look and feel fabulous by the end of it."

Kelsey linked arms with Charli like they were two little kids ready to skip down the hallway. The BFF vibe that rolled from Kelsey was foreign to Charli. She'd never really had that kind of thing with girls, even as a kid. While the other girls had been braiding each other's hair and talking about boy bands, Charli had been knocking down the guys in touch football. The one time she'd even been invited to a slumber party, the other girls had ended up teasing her about her unshaved legs and lack of training bra.

But she liked that things didn't feel fake or forced with Kelsey.

The woman's warmth and desire to help seemed genuine. So Charli took a deep breath, trying to relax even though she was completely out of her element. "If you say so."

Kelsey pushed open the main door to the spa area. "I do. This is going to be fun. And boy, are you going to break some hearts tonight. All those subs who were interviewing to be Grant's are going to be so jealous when they hear."

Charli's tennis shoe squeaked against the floor as her step faltered. "What do you mean?"

Kelsey peeked at her, a slight wince. "Shit. Big mouth. Sorry. Never mind."

Charli stopped and unlinked her arm from Kelsey's, her unease returning. "No, I want to know."

She bit her lip and peeked back down the hallway to make sure no one was around. "I thought you would've known. Training with Grant is highly coveted. Beyond getting a monthlong immersion with such a skilled dom, Grant also matches up the trainee with a new dom at the end of it. He has an uncanny ability to find the perfect match for his trainees, so everyone wants to be one of his girls. The waiting list is long and the interview process extensive. You jumped all those steps."

Waiting lists? Interviews? A bitter taste rolled over her tongue. "So he just uses some woman then turns her over to another guy when he's done with her?"

Kelsey's head tilted, as if Charli had spoken the question in Japanese. "It's not *using* anyone. It's an agreement. Both know what they're signing up for and both benefit. Grant's made it clear that he doesn't stay with any sub for longer than a month. He's not looking for more."

"More." The word was like a dry chunk of bread in her throat.

Kelsey shrugged. "You know, love, emotion, potential for marriage and kids. Grant's an amazing dom, but he likes to keep things businesslike. Contracts, clearly defined rules. I've heard he doesn't even let women come to his cabin. Everything happens here and then he goes home."

"Right," Charli murmured, trying to absorb it all.

"But, of course, that doesn't mean he's in any less demand. God knows most people aren't coming here for roses and love poems. Plus, who wouldn't be tempted to let a man like Grant take care of her for a little while?" She gave a rueful smile. "Grant's talked to so many women, but he hasn't chosen anyone for training in a while. And no one's even seen him do a scene in the last few months. I'm still pretty new here, but that apparent celibacy is odd for him. He used to be an active participant, not just the owner. So be prepared, people are going to be curious about you."

All the new information swam in Charli's head, not quite lining up. "Me? Why?"

"Because he picked you, silly," she said and poked her arm. "You're the *chosen one*."

Kelsey said the last two words with mock dramatics and spirit fingers, but Charli's breakfast had started to churn in her stomach. "This isn't really full training. I'm just uh, trying things out."

"Sure. You don't know until you've experienced it. Afterward, you'll either run like hell to get away from it, or you'll fall under its spell and never be able to shake it from your system." Her tone was bright, but there was a haunted look in her eye, as if she were trying to push out a memory she didn't want in there. "This place has been my saving grace."

There was a story there and Charli wanted to ask, but Kelsey turned and motioned at her. "Come on. We're wasting time and we can't get off schedule. Grant will be expecting you for dinner at seven sharp."

Charli hurried to catch up. "Seven? That's hours from now. We have lots of time."

"We're going to need every minute." Kelsey peeked over her shoulder with a sly smile. "Boss man has big plans for you."

Grant sipped his club soda and lime while relaxing in a corner booth of Vines, the only "proper attire required" dining room at The Ranch. The place was already half full, and groupings of every makeup spoke intimately over the candlelit tables. Soft piano music drifted from the other side of the room where Javier, one of the male submissives, played something mellow.

It could've been any high-end restaurant in Dallas at first glance. But if one looked harder, paid more attention, he would see the collars gracing the throats of many of the men and women. He would see that it wasn't just couples, but triads and foursomes sharing intimate conversations and promising looks. He would see same-sex couples being affectionate and relaxed with each other without fear of getting the side-eye from judgmental diners.

The sight gave Grant a deep sense of satisfaction—the kind of satisfaction that could only come from knowing that, for once, he'd done something right. He didn't have a lot of those things to add to his résumé. He'd let so many people down in his past, he could pave a hundred-mile sidewalk with those regrets and mistakes. But here—this place—he'd gotten that right. He'd built a haven for those who'd found themselves drifting outside the neat lines society had set up for them. And for that he was proud.

But now he was bringing an outsider into this space, and he was more than a little apprehensive about how Charli was going to react. This wasn't her world, and despite how well she'd handled the interlude in his kitchen, her mind had fought the submission hard. She may have a kinky streak hiding in there, but she definitely hadn't slipped into subspace at any point, hadn't truly let go. When he'd checked in with her afterward, her gaze and tongue had been as sharp as ever. She wasn't going to break easily, if at all.

Not that it was going to stop him from trying. That was for sure.

And though he was willing to do whatever it took to keep her on the property and safe, he knew agreeing to train her was pure selfishness on his part. He wanted to touch her again, to taste her, to make her let go and lose herself—if even for a few seconds. He could teach her ways to soften her image and approach, to act more feminine, without bringing her to his bed. He knew that. And he suspected she did, too.

But she'd agreed anyway. And once she had, he couldn't resist the opportunity to have her—even if it was for only two weeks. She was the first woman in as long as he could remember who had drummed up such an urgent need in him. And despite all that stockpiled bravado she carried around, he'd sensed a glimmer of relief in her when he'd held her down and taken her, that fleeting disappearance of will. And it'd been like a drug to his system.

A very dangerous drug.

Because now all he could think of was breaking that part of her open, of being the man to show her exactly who she could be if she gave into it. Of her fully surrendering to him during the next couple of weeks.

Something that was highly unlikely. Some women thrived on letting it all go, on being taken care of, on putting themselves into the hands of someone they trusted. But a woman like Charli, who prided herself on doing everything herself and in her own way, was going to rebel in the kind of arrangement he enjoyed. Even with the training being her idea in the first place, he knew she wasn't going to submit quietly.

But despite all his concerns, he relished the challenge ahead. Harnessing and redirecting that rebellion in Charli could prove to be a helluva good time. He'd get to enjoy her feisty, albeit reluctant, submission, and she'd get to learn how to be a lady. Win-win. Prizes for everyone.

He took another long drag from his soda, wishing it were some of his vineyard's Chardonnay instead but playing it safe in case he decided to initiate Charli tonight. He had no idea how pliant or pissed she'd be after all the treatments he'd set up for her today. He chuckled to himself, wondering what kind of hell she'd given the waxing technician. He doubted Charli had held back her opinion.

"Are you meeting someone?" The hostess's voice drifted across the room, pulling Grant's attention toward the main door.

His glass *thunked* onto the table as the muscles in his forearm forgot to work. He stared at the redheaded beauty murmuring to the hostess. *Well, I'll be damned.*

Charli peered into the dining room, her fingers worrying whatever she was holding in her hands. She looked lost. And unsure. And completely, jaw-hit-the-table gorgeous.

Grant rubbed the back of his neck, suddenly feeling hot all over. Damn. He'd known without a doubt that Charli would clean up well. Not many women could still look beautiful in relaxed-fit jeans and a ponytail like she did. But he hadn't expected her to channel a Hollywood starlet or something.

The hostess leaned over and pointed to Grant's booth. Somehow he managed to raise his hand in greeting and not smile like some goofy teenager who's realized he's landed a date with the prom queen. He straightened his shoulders, trying to regain his mental balance. He was supposed to be the cool and in control one here. Since when did he get like this over a pretty woman? He had beautiful subs offering themselves to him on a regular basis and it barely registered on his radar. This should be no different. *She* should be no different.

As Charli got closer, Grant saw what she was holding in her hands. Shoes. A pair of sexy black heels he'd picked out for her earlier today. A perfect complement, Kelsey had assured him, to the dark green strapless dress he'd chosen for Charli. His gaze went to her stocking feet, then slid up her long legs, to the hem of her short dress, and not stopping until he reached the column of her bare neck.

Not bare for long. The collar tucked into the inner pocket of his suit coat seemed to warm against his ribs at the thought. *Soon.*

He stood as Charli walked over to the booth. She set the shoes on the seat, put her hands on her hips, and arched a newly manicured brow at him. "Broken ankles or bare feet. Those are your choices."

He smiled down at her. "Already giving me orders, freckles? That's not how this works."

She released a breath and then leaned in, keeping her voice low. "Look, it's been a long day. I've been through what I think may be considered cruel and unusual under my constitutional rights as an American citizen. I've been waxed and plucked and exfoliated and . . . ironed, I think. Some woman whose name I can't pronounce has now seen more of me than my gynecologist ever has. And this dress is . . . drafty. You gotta give me something here."

He stared at her for a moment, a bit stunned by her rapid-fire speech, then laughed, loud and open, not caring that it drew the attention of the other guests. He raised his palms. "Fine. Point taken. Sit down. We'll save the shoes for later."

"Thank you." She took his offered hand and stepped up into the raised booth, obviously forgetting she had a dress on as she climbed in. He got a delicious glimpse of the bottom curve of her ass.

He palmed her waist and moved behind her to block anyone else's view. "Lesson one, freckles. When wearing a dress, you need to be more aware of yourself. Giving half the restaurant a *Basic Instincts* moment is not that big a deal here. But back in town that may be a bit embarrassing."

"Shit." She grabbed her hem, clamped her thighs together and hurriedly sat. "You shouldn't have made me wear such a short dress. I feel naked."

"You look beautiful," he corrected, then slid into the spot across from her. "And be thankful. As my sub, I could've requested you to come to dinner *only* wearing those shoes."

Panic flitted over her expression. "Seriously?"

He laced his fingers and leaned forward. "Yes. That's how it works, Charli. I need you to understand that before we go any further. This is a power exchange, it isn't 'let's play sexy times and get some plastic handcuffs and whipped cream so we feel kinky.'"

"I know that," she said in a huff. "I guess I'm just having a hard time grasping how . . . involved this all is."

"For some people, it's not that complicated. They may be perfectly happy with those plastic cuffs, and that's great. But this is a lifestyle for me, my way of being. It's not something I can punch in and out of. When I'm involved with a woman, even in a temporary capacity, the need to dominate is like a living, breathing thing."

She held his gaze for a moment, then looked down at her water glass as if needing a second to process what he'd said. "Right."

"Hey"—he reached across the table and laid a hand over hers—"no one said you have to do this. You can back out now or at any point. I'm not trying to scare you. I just need you to know what this is about, what I'm about."

She ventured a glance upward. "I'm not scared, not for my safety at least."

He nodded, pleased to hear that she at least trusted him on some level. He let go of her hand, giving her some space to speak whatever was on her mind.

"There isn't much that makes me nervous. Hell, ask Max. I'm sure I've taken years off his life with my thrill seeking. I've skydived, played tackle football with dudes twice my size, been on a roller-derby team. I've probably had more concussions and broken bones than many pro athletes." She gave him a wan smile. "But this is so far outside of my realm, it makes all that stuff look like cake. I look around at the women here, and I feel like I come from a different species."

"I assure you, you don't. I checked you out thoroughly the other day."

"Very funny. I'm just worried I'll spend these two weeks completely embarrassing myself." She looked down at her discarded shoes. "I can't even wear heels without tripping."

Her bottom lip jutted out in frustration, creating an unintentional pout. He had an urge to sink his teeth into that plump pink flesh. She was so damn cute when she was annoyed. "That only takes a little practice."

She gave him a *yeah, right* look. "I'm not even sure why you agreed to do this. There's obviously no shortage of women around here willing to, uh . . . service you or whatever. Every time I speak your name it's like I've mentioned some goddamned rock star."

He snorted.

Amusement lit her eyes. "What? I'm serious. I think some of the girls are planning to make I Heart Grant T-shirts."

She drew a heart shape in the air between them, while batting her eyelashes in an overexaggerated imitation of his so-called admirers.

He smirked, loving that she had no filter. Thought to mouth. He wondered if that's the real reason her bosses were reluctant to put her on the air. Nothing like live TV and someone who isn't afraid to say exactly what's on her mind. Could be disastrous.

It was going to get her in trouble as his sub as well, but he couldn't help looking forward to administering the fun consequences. "First of all, you wouldn't be servicing me, you'd be subbing for me. Different animal. This isn't prostitution. Both parties get equal benefit in this arrangement."

"Right. So I get the benefit of earning the right to service you?" she said, her sarcasm about as subtle as a tractor-trailer.

The waiter stopped by the booth and upon hearing Charli's words, simply laid down the escargot appetizer, gave Grant a new drink, and disappeared.

Grant took a sip of his club soda, amused. "That *is* a great benefit, but no. What you get is, well, that can be different for each person. Most subs would say they find freedom in the role."

She eyed the appetizer and frowned. "Freedom? By being someone else's slave?"

"Being a slave in this world is a bit different that what we're doing. Though I know slaves here who would say they've never felt free until they found their master." He grabbed one of the tiny forks and put a snail on a toast point, making sure to get lots of garlic butter sauce with it. He held it out to Charli, who took it reluctantly, then made a matching bite for himself. "But you never wonder what it'd be like to have a true break from everyday life? To not have to make any decisions or pretend to be something you're not? To wake up and know that all you have to do that day is let someone else take care of anything you may need?"

She sniffed the toast, examining it. "I'm thinking I could accomplish that with a trip to Barbados and an attentive waiter."

He laughed. "Yes, but could that waiter teach you how to wow those horseshit-for-brains bosses of yours with your feminine charm?"

She popped the escargot into her mouth and mumbled "no" whilst chewing.

"Don't talk with your mouth full." He took his own bite and watched the flare of rebellion flicker over her expression. He lifted an eyebrow, daring her to challenge him, but to her credit she held back her natural instinct to lash out.

Her eyes narrowed as she took a sip of water. "That wasn't a mushroom, was it?"

"Snail."

She winced. "Fabulous. Maybe a warning next time, cowboy."

"You could've asked me what it was. Did you like it?"

She grabbed another piece of bread and dipped it in the sauce, skipping the snail. "Yes, but they could probably pour this butter sauce on your boot and it would make leather taste good."

Hmm. Visions of Charli putting her lips to his shoe drifted through his mind. He smiled. Maybe she'd come to know exactly what leather tasted like before their two weeks were up. "That can be arranged if you'd like to test the theory."

She coughed, half-choking on her last bite of bread. "Shit. Everything I say around here is going to get me in trouble. You'll never catch me kissing any guy's shoe."

He leaned forward and put a finger to her lips. "No cursing. Unless we're in bed, then it's fair game. New, refined Charli is going to know how and when to speak like a lady."

Her lips pursed beneath his finger.

"In fact, any time you slip up, you'll earn a punishment of my choosing."

She tried to bite his finger, but he pulled away in time. "I have a feeling I'm going to be spending most of these two weeks in time-out."

"Oh, my punishments will be much more hands-on than putting you in a corner," he promised. "And much more effective. Though, based on how you reacted to the belt the other day, I have a feeling you may enjoy that part."

She didn't have a pithy response this time. Instead, she took a sudden, deep interest in her open menu. But he knew she wasn't deciding between steak or fish when a soft pink crept up her neck and found its way to her cheeks. My, my, maybe his little reporter had more of an appreciation for pain than he thought.

The sight had him wanting to skip dinner altogether. What exactly was she thinking about? Was her body warming at the thought of him disciplining her? Of him putting his hands on her? Because his temperature was certainly rising. Or was she simply embarrassed by the conversation?

She was such a puzzle. Coarse and hardheaded, beautiful and awkward, intelligent and driven. Anyone who met her would see right away she was a woman in charge of her life. But there, underneath all that, seemed to be something so vulnerable and innocent. Fragile, even.

And that had him both hungry for her and damn terrified.

Because if he could tear through all that other stuff, get to the core of where that glimmer was coming from, he was afraid he may not want to take her collar off when two weeks was up.

And there wasn't much he wouldn't try in this world.

But *permanent* wasn't in his vocabulary.

TWELVE

Charli could barely focus on chewing her fish. Why was she so damn jittery? It was as if her blood had been replaced with Red Bull. She'd thought she could hold her own with Grant. She'd even managed to banter with him at the beginning of dinner, despite him looking so damn hot in that suit of his.

But as the conversation had gone on, she'd felt the shift in their dynamic. Like tilting a water table, the power had rolled over to him. He corrected her posture, her bad language, the way she kept tugging at the low-cut bodice of her dress. He was subtle about it, but she didn't miss the significance. She had agreed to put herself in his hands. To be his . . . property.

The thought was still too much to wrap her head around. She'd spent half her life wiggling out from under her father's and brothers' crushing overprotectiveness, and now here she was giving the power over to a guy. Maybe all those concussions *had* caused some brain damage.

Grant glanced at her uneaten dinner, frowned. "Did you read through the contracts I sent you?"

Boy, had she. Some of the items listed in those papers had made her eyes pop . . . and others had made her body stir—even if the whole idea of a contract felt sort of clinical. She set her fork down and tried to drink some iced tea, hoping her voice wouldn't croak when it came out. "I did."

"Did you add any hard limits to mine?" he asked, his tone as casual as if they were discussing whether the Cowboys would make it to the playoffs this year. He took a sip of his drink, his eyes never leaving hers.

She'd looked closely at his limits. Most had been things related to The Ranch's rules and safety. He'd also included his medical test results and had her verify hers. The only one that had stood out was that his sub was not allowed to stay at his cabin. She would be provided her own space.

Even though she knew this wasn't a real relationship and hadn't been expecting overnight cuddling or whatever, seeing it in black and white had still stung a bit. She decided he needed a little poke as well. "Yes. I added one."

"Oh? Pray tell."

"No sex."

Mr. Cool Cowboy coughed, set his glass down. "Excuse me?"

She grinned, pleased that he looked so distressed. Maybe she still had some power in this dynamic after all. "Kidding. I'm so new to this, I'm still not sure what my hard limits could be. I didn't add anything to yours."

He didn't look at all amused by her little joke. He pulled his napkin from his lap and set it next to his plate. "Charli, I'm starting to wonder if we're making a big mistake here."

She paused, her fork hovering over her plate. "Wait, what? Come on, I was only messing with you. Don't be so uptight."

"This is not me being uptight. This is you trying to snatch back some control of the situation." He pushed his plate aside and set his elbows on the table, leaning forward. "Tell me why you're doing this."

She set her fork down and shifted in her seat, uncomfortable under his unyielding gaze. Had he answered when she'd asked him the same question? She couldn't remember what his response had been if he had. "You know why. I need to learn some things. Be more refined, as you put it."

His frown deepened. "You could learn that in one of those manners classes people give for debutantes. Why are you agreeing to give yourself to me?"

She fiddled with the edges of the napkin in her lap, wracking her brain for an answer. Why *was* she doing this? Yes, she wanted to learn to be more feminine. But he was right; she didn't need to be someone's submissive to do that. Was it simply because she was attracted to him and knew this was the only way he had relationships?

No, she may have not had a lover in a while, but she wasn't desperate. She'd long ago learned how to take care of her own sexual needs. She was better at it than any guy had ever been. Well, until the other day in the kitchen. She'd never get *that* kind of orgasm on a solo tour. But still . . .

Why this?

Grant reached out and put a knuckle beneath her chin, forcing her to look at him. "Charli, I need your honesty here. I don't want to take this any further until I know where you are with this."

She nodded, attempted a small smile, failed. Honesty, huh? Fine. What did she have to lose at this point. "I've had three relationships in my life. The first in high school with a cornerback who was happy to relieve me of my virginity, but not so keen on telling his friends he was sleeping with the team's 'chick kicker' instead of a cheerleader. Another early in college with the guy who is now my boss."

Grant frowned. "Your boss?"

"Yes, Trey barely counts because it was more a friends-with-benefits deal. And the benefit really wasn't that grand. I ended it a few months after it started. The last one was with a guy I met at the gym. It was . . . fine. He ended it to go back to his ex-wife." She blew out a breath, her dating history even more depressing when said aloud. But if they were going for honesty, she was going to give him all of it. "The number of times I've actually been able to enjoy sex with anyone? Maybe four."

Grant's brow wrinkled. "Meaning you only liked it four times? Or you only came four times?"

"Both. My mind doesn't stop racing. I get distracted at the littlest thing. The room's too cold. His cologne is too strong. Why is he making that face? Does he seriously think *that* is going to work? Am I doing this right? Does he realize having *SportsCenter* on in the background is only going to derail me?"

Grant's dimple appeared.

"Stop, I'm serious. It's a problem," she protested, unable to fight her own smile, feeling some weird relief at saying all of it out loud. "I have issues. Clearly."

"Maybe, maybe not." He leaned closer, his voice like a coaxing caress. "Tell me. When you touch yourself, can you come?"

She glanced over at the other tables, praying no one was listening to the conversation. How could this man turn her palms sweaty and her skin hot in one quick second? Never in her life had anyone asked her about something so personal. "Uh, sometimes. If I can stay focused on . . . you know, whatever fantasy I'm conjuring up."

"Then maybe it was the guys who had the issue, not you," he said simply. "You didn't seem to have a problem focusing the other day."

"Your humility is truly inspiring," she said with mock reverence.

He shrugged as if to say—take it or leave it. "Why do you think it was easier for you to enjoy it with me?"

"I don't know. I felt . . ." *Overtaken. Desired. Special.* All things that seemed to be running themes in those private fantasies she weaved late at night. She met his eyes. "I felt like I was able to be someone else. To take a break from everything I've always been, how people always see me."

"Is who you are so bad?"

"No," she said, turning the question over in her head. "But I'm the girl guys like to go out drinking with to watch a game. I'm the chick they tell about their wild sexual escapades. Not the one they actually want to have the escapades with. And sometimes it sucks to know that men are so comfortable around you, they don't even see you as a girl anymore."

"Did I mention yet that the guys you're hanging out with must be complete morons?"

The corner of her mouth hitched up. "But that's the thing. With you, I don't feel like that. I feel like you see *me*, the woman."

"How could I not?" His gaze stroked her face, then traced down her neck to her cleavage and back up. Everywhere his attention landed prickled with awareness.

"So maybe . . . maybe I want to get lost in that feeling for a little while." She swallowed hard but kept going, needing to get it all out there. "I know I can run circles around most of the guys at work. But I looked at my audition tape again, and I can see what they're seeing. It's like even when I'm not trying, I come across as if I'm daring someone to pick a fight with me. I'm tired of always being in battle mode, always being on guard." She lifted her head, her resolve crystallizing. "When you took control the other day, for the first time ever, I didn't want to fight anymore."

The blue in his eyes seemed to darken, and the scant slice of air between them charged with an energy that hadn't existed a few moments before. He laid his hand palm-up on the table. "Take my hand."

With only the slightest of hesitations, she obeyed.

He curled his fingers around hers, the grip possessive. "From this point on, here on the grounds you will go by your given name,

Charlotte. When I call you that, you are mine." His thumb caressed the backside of her hand. "My beautiful, obedient submissive."

Beautiful. Sure.

"You're not allowed to smirk at that, Charlotte. Every straight man in this room turned his head when you walked into the restaurant," he said, his accent getting thicker the more displeased he was. "And I damn near skipped dinner because I didn't know if I'd be able to spend an hour not touching you."

She blinked, a bit stunned by his swift reaction and apparent anger.

"Do you think I'm a stupid man, like those silly boys you surround yourself with? Someone who doesn't know what beautiful looks like?"

"What? No, I—" she said, stumbling over her words.

"Then don't insult me by discounting my compliments." His hold on her hand grew tighter. "Tell me you're beautiful."

She cringed and looked down. "Grant—er—sir, please."

"Say it, Charli."

She closed her eyes, her fight-or-flight response screaming at her. Why was this so hard? She didn't think she was horrible-looking. But memories assailed her—her mother standing her and her sister next to each other when her mom was still trying to get them both into pageants and modeling—comparing, contrasting, Charli never getting anything quite right. Wasn't her torso still a little too long, her smile too tilted, her figure too boyish?

She took a deep breath, trying to focus on the here and now. She wasn't that awkward kid anymore. Plus, Grant wasn't going to let this go. She managed to open her eyes and say, "I'm beautiful."

His eyes softened as he reached out and cupped her cheek. "Good girl. Now we have to work on getting you to believe it."

She rolled her shoulders, trying to release some of the tension that had gathered there. "I have a feeling you can be mighty convincing."

"There're a few terrorists in federal prison who would agree with you on that." He gave her a wry smile as he reached for his wallet and tossed a healthy tip on the table. "Come on, freckles."

He stood and held out a hand to her. She took it and let him guide her on the step down, this time very aware of keeping her dress in place. "Where are we going?"

Before she could take another step, he dragged her against him, his hot body pressing against hers in all the right places. His breath was warm against her ear. "It's been a real long while since I've acted like a true member here. I think it's time to fix that."

"Oh," she said, the word coming out in a gasp.

"You ready for that?" He skated his palm along her side. Then, in full view of the other diners, he slid his hand beneath the hem of her dress and up the curve of her outer thigh.

"Grant," she whispered urgently, trying to scoot away.

"Hush." He held her in place and his fingers found the waistband of her panty hose. He tugged. The pliable nylon gave easily, and despite her shocked intake of breath, he drew it down and over her hips, not stopping until he crouched in front of her and slid them completely off her legs.

She glanced around at the other people in the restaurant—almost all were now looking their way. Her cheeks burned and cool air drifted up her skirt, teasing her newly waxed skin.

Grant balled up the panty hose, rose, and tucked them in his suit pocket. He cupped her ass through the dress and molded her against him. "When you're with me, I don't want anything blocking my touch. No panty hose, no underwear. I don't even want your clothes in the way. Skirts, dresses, and lingerie only. Everything else is banned."

Normally, she would've protested, questioned. No underwear? No jeans? But the way his erection was dragging the soft material of her dress against her most sensitive spot was completely fragmenting her thoughts. She shuddered against him.

He pressed his nose into her hair. "That excites you, sweet Charlotte? Knowing that whenever I want you, wherever we may be, all I need to do is shove your skirt up and take you?"

Charlotte. Just hearing the name she'd never used sliding off his honeyed baritone helped her fall more deeply under his spell. And his words did excite her, more than she wanted to admit. She liked the idea that there could be times he wouldn't be able to resist her. That he'd have to have her right then and there. "Yes, sir."

"That's my girl." His fingertips caressed the bottom curve of her ass. "There's no room for shame or self-consciousness when you're with me. Let all of that go."

Just being this close to him had her body instinctively loosening, her muscles unwinding. Something about the combination of his easy touch, his illicit words, and that intoxicating masculine scent of his had her mind calming, her will quieting. What would it be like to do what he asked? To really let him take over?

No one knew her here. This was only temporary. Maybe she could slip into this foreign role for a little while—that of the yielding, cherished submissive. She'd never had a man look at her the way Grant was right now. Like there was no other woman who could possibly compete.

It was potent and erotic and so damn alluring.

Grant bent his head and brushed his lips against her jaw—a promise of kisses to come. "You ready, freckles?"

She wound her arms around his waist and pressed her forehead against his chest, feeling his steady heartbeat, feeling wanted. "I'm all yours."

And that was that. Before they stepped out of the restaurant, she'd done the impossible. She'd surrendered.

THIRTEEN

Grant wasn't sure what he wanted to do with Charli first. It'd been so long since he'd indulged in The Ranch's accommodations, and he'd never taken on someone who wasn't already part of the scene. Well, not since his wife. When he'd been with Rachel, he hadn't known such a lifestyle existed. They'd been young and had still been figuring out the basics of vanilla sex. Kink hadn't even hit their radar.

An edge of anxiety curled in his stomach at the thought of Rachel, but he shoved it to the back of his brain where he stored the bad shit. He wasn't going to ruin this night.

He couldn't decide if he should ease Charli in or drag her into the deep end with him. He didn't want to scare her or freak her out. But her tendency to overthink things and her penchant for thrill seeking made him wonder if going whole hog would actually be best. And hell, she hadn't checked one damn thing on her hard limits list, so he had no idea if she was simply unsure of her limits or if she was craving someone to push her. He'd need to try a few things and gauge her reaction before knowing the best path to lead her down. All he knew was that if she needed to be reminded how much of a woman she was, he was happy to make that happen.

He peeked over at her as they walked down the quiet hallway that led from the restaurant to the play areas. She gave him a wavering smile, and he squeezed her hand. "What's on your mind, freckles?"

"What's not on my mind?" she replied. "I'm going through a hundred scenarios of what may happen tonight. All those things in that contract, I . . . it's overwhelming. I have no idea what I'm doing."

He slowed his step and stopped, tugging her arm gently to square her to him. "Look at me, Charlotte."

Her shoulders rose and fell with a heavy breath, but she tilted her face toward him and met his gaze.

He pulled the leather collar from his suit's inside pocket and wound it around her neck, her pulse thumping against the delicate skin of her throat as he snapped the lock.

Seeing the simple strip of leather had his own heartbeat picking up speed. He cupped her face with his palms. "Now you're mine. All you need to do is focus on what I tell you. Try not to think when I give you a command, just do. I'm not here to embarrass or humiliate you. That's not my kink. I do enjoy giving some pain, but I gave you words to use if that is ever too much." He brushed his thumbs across her cheeks. "Anything I do with you or to you has a purpose and is for our mutual benefit. It may not always be clear how, but you're going to have to trust that I have a good reason."

She nodded, her shoulders straightening despite the obvious shadow of worry in her eyes. "Yes, Grant. I mean, sir."

He smiled and kissed the top of her head, a little swell of satisfaction going through him. A dangerous swell. *She's not really mine,* he reminded himself. He didn't have the right to feel that pride.

"It's okay. You can call me Grant or sir." He traced a finger over her bottom lip. "I like hearing you say my name with that hint of Cajun accent you keep trying to hide."

Her mouth curved under his touch. "Damn, I thought I'd lost that thing. And I can't believe *you* are teasing me about *my* accent."

"Watch it, freckles. And don't lose it. I like it." He put his arm around her waist and urged her down the hallway.

"Yeah, well, TV stations like their correspondents to sound non-regional."

He tightened his grip on her hip, her words niggling at him. Why would she want some job that was going to strip her of all her flavor? Did she really want to be some generic talking head—a woman who could be interchanged with any of the other ones on different stations?

He'd taken her on for training with the promise that he'd help her refine her image, but if she thought he was going to help her become some cookie-cutter, soulless version of herself, she had another think coming. The more he found out about this job of hers, the more he wanted to yank her from it and put her up at The Ranch. She wouldn't have to worry about her safety, her image, or anything in between. And she wouldn't need a salary because she would never go without. He could provide everything she needed.

The dark part of his mind laughed at him. Yeah, asshole. Everything except what she deserves.

He glanced down at Charli—she was so full of life and fire and ambition. Beyond her career aspirations, she no doubt wanted to get married one day and probably have a family. Be someone's soul mate. *That* was what she deserved. And that was the one thing he could never give.

All those years ago, when he'd knelt next to his wife's lifeless body, his soul had died there with her. And those things didn't grow back.

His fingers pressed against Charli's hip, halting her as they reached the door at the far end. Charli peeked over at him, frowning, her instincts too damn keen. "You all right? You've gone broody."

"I'm fine. Just deciding the best way to start your training." The lie rolled off his tongue, and though she didn't seem totally convinced, she gave a little nod of acceptance.

He needed to tamp down the ugly thoughts of the past. Charli deserved his full and undivided attention tonight. If he could slip fully into his dom role and do what he did best, he should be able to shake off all the riotous feelings Charli's presence seemed to kick up inside him. She was just a woman looking for some training and some fun. He had to keep that at the forefront of his mind.

He gave her rear a light swat. "Okay, darlin', ready to step into my world?"

Charli sent Grant a skeptical look. Something had darkened her cowboy's mood, but clearly he wasn't going to talk about it with her. His whole posture said trespassers will be shot on sight, so she fought her instinct to pry.

She reached out and grabbed his hand, lacing her fingers with his. "I'm ready if you are."

He lifted her hand to his mouth and planted a kiss on top of it, his eyes not leaving hers. "Born ready, beautiful."

A wash of heat went through her, radiating out from the simple touch. It was as if he knew some magic code that flipped her internal switch, lighting every erogenous zone in her body. Her nipples stiffened against the soft material of her dress, and a kernel of warmth gathered between her thighs. She shook her head, amazed at how instant her response was. "I bet you could walk into the grocery store and get a stranger to strip for you with that charm of yours."

He chuckled and tugged her close, trapping her hand between

them. "You have the urge to lose your clothes already, sweet Charlotte? I must really be on my game tonight."

Having his body pressed up against hers sent her ability for witty retorts short-circuiting. She took a shuddering breath, enveloping her senses in his natural, grass-and-sun scent.

He brushed her hair away from her forehead and tucked it behind her ear. "When we walk through this door, I expect you to become my submissive. I know this is all new to you, but look to me for your cues. Speak and act only with my permission. I'm looking forward to showing you off."

She swallowed hard. Showing her off? What exactly would that entail? Some weird combination of nerves and wild anticipation curled like vine around her stomach, but she found herself nodding. "Yes, Grant."

He pressed a kiss to her forehead, then turned her, tucking her arm into his elbow, and led her through the door.

Soft music met her ears and she blinked, adjusting to the low lighting of the room. People were milling around or sitting at small tables, all in various states of undress. Some were sporting suits and dresses like she and Grant. Others were in leather and lingerie. And a handful had nothing on at all. The mix of refined and conservative next to blatantly sexual scrambled her brain for a moment—two worlds crashing together.

As Charli was taking it all in, a man shuffled by wearing nothing but a collar and the leash his domme was tugging him by. Each time the woman yanked at the leash, the man grunted with pleasure. Unable to stop herself, Charli glanced downward and saw that his penis was trapped in what looked to be a painful contraption made of progressively smaller metal rings; something that had to prevent him from getting a full erection.

A little gasp escaped her, and she quickly looked away, feeling as if she'd intruded on the couple's privacy. She was no blushing virgin. But in this kind of environment, her sexual experiences were about the equivalent. There were probably more naked people in this room then she'd seen in her whole life. She actually had to fight the urge to put her hands over her eyes like some kid who knew she wasn't supposed to be watching an R-rated movie.

Grant moved his hand to the small of her back and put his lips next to her ear. "You're so damn sexy when you blush. But try to relax. No need to be embarrassed about anything here. You can look at what you want. Watching is half the fun."

She wet her lips, trying to tamp down the knee-jerk reaction. "It's just . . . a lot to take in. It feels awkward to look. And that seems . . . painful."

His fingers drew lazy circles at the small of her back as he guided her through the arrangement of tables. "It only feels awkward because you're seeing it through a preconceived filter, that shame response we're all taught. But if you can learn to push past that, you'll be able to see how beautiful all of this can be. Like how enthralled that male sub was with his wife."

She looked up at him in surprise. "They're married?"

He smiled. "For over ten years, I think."

She chewed on that information, and Grant stopped at a large booth. There was a small, gold plate fastened on the wall above the table that read *Master Grant*, but a lanky blond man had already taken up residence on one side of the booth.

When the man noticed them standing there, a smile appeared, a dazzling grin that somehow put Charli at ease in an instant—as if this stranger was someone she'd known her whole life. He stood and put out his hand to Grant. "Long time no see, my friend."

"And whose fault is that?" Grant pulled the man closer and clapped him on the back.

"Yeah, been busy. Wicked's Internet division needed a lot of work. Plus, ya know, I've got a lot to keep me occupied at home these days."

Grant laughed. "I just bet you do."

The two men exchanged a knowing look, and Charli realized she'd missed some private joke.

Grant put his arm around Charli again and urged her forward a tick. "Charlotte, this is Jace. He owns the store that supplies a lot of The Ranch's equipment, and he's also a good friend of mine."

"Nice to meet you," she said, automatically putting her hand out.

Jace's gaze dipped down to her collar, his eyebrow lifting a bit. He didn't reach for her hand but looked to Grant. "May I?"

Grant nodded, and Jace took her hand. "A pleasure."

The way Jace looked at her—not necessarily sexual, but appraising—clued her in that he was a dom, too. He released her hand and returned his attention to Grant. "She's lovely. Glad to see you taking a night off for a change. I thought with all the workshops on the schedule tonight, you'd be doing some demos."

Grant guided Charli into the booth as Jace returned to his seat on the other side. Grant slid in next to her and laid a hand on her thigh, idly rubbing his thumb along her bared skin. "No. It's so busy tonight because we have a group from an out-of-town club here for training. I put Colby in charge of coordinating everything though."

Jace leaned back in the booth, stretching his arm along the back of it. "That's too bad. I always learn something from your demos."

Charli looked back and forth between the two of them, having no idea what they were talking about. Her lips parted to ask, but Grant squeezed her thigh. A warning.

"I think that may have been too much for Charlotte's first time here."

Before Jace could respond, a couple stopped in front of their table. Jace turned his head and smiled at the petite dark-haired woman and the much taller Hispanic man. "Well, it's about damn time. I thought I was going to have to go back to the cabin and drag y'all out."

The woman rolled her eyes and crooked a thumb at her partner. "Not my fault. Andre got distracted by the new six-headed shower." She looked over at Grant. "Nice addition, by the way."

Grant nodded, an amused expression on his face. "Glad you enjoyed it, Evan."

Jace rose and wrapped his arm around the woman's waist, pulling her against him and laying a way-more-than-friendly kiss on her lips.

Charli watched them in confusion. She'd gotten the impression the two strangers were a couple. But the way the woman melted against Jace said otherwise.

When Jace released Evan, he moved around her and pressed a quick kiss to Andre's mouth as well. "Don't tell me she fell for the line—come and check out this new shower, baby?"

Andre's smile was like lazy sex on summer night. "I don't need lines, bro."

Charli could only stare. All three of them were together?

Evan glanced over, her blue eyes widening when she noticed Charli there. "Good Lord, how rude are we? Grant has a guest." She gently shoved Jace into the booth and slid in next to him. "I'm sorry. These two have a way of distracting me. I'm Evan. And this is Andre."

As Andre sank into the booth, flanking Evan's other side, Charli managed to introduce herself, her mind still absorbing the fact that this woman had managed to snag not just one but two freaking gorgeous men. And based on how Jace and Andre were looking at her, Evan hadn't only snagged them but had their utter devotion.

Maybe Charli should take training from this chick. Was she a submissive? Her gaze drifted to Evan's throat, but she saw no collar there.

Grant draped his arm along the back of the booth and idly played with a lock of Charli's hair. "Go ahead and ask your questions, freckles. I see them all over your face."

She shot a sharp look Grant's way. Was he trying to make her look like a complete novice? Embarrass her?

He sighed. "These are my friends, Charlotte. I planned for us to sit with them so that you could see that the people who are part of this scene are just regular folks. That you don't need to be intimidated or feel out of place."

Evan gave her an understanding smile. "I was totally freaked out the first time I visited. I had no idea what to expect. I definitely didn't expect to fall for these two." She raised her arms, showing matching bracelets on each wrist. The delicate circles were pewter and aged copper woven together in a pretty pattern.

Charli stared down at the jewelry, realizing the two metals probably represented her two lovers—fair and dark. No collar, but cuffs. So Evan was their submissive. A little spark of melancholy went through Charli as she remembered the band around her neck was only made of disposable leather.

Good Lord, what's wrong with me?

"Did you know that's what you wanted when you came here? To be a submissive?" Charli asked, her words coming out tentative even to her own ears.

Evan sniffed and nodded toward Grant. "Hardly. But Mr. See-Right-Through-Your-Bullshit here recognized it in me before we even finished my first tour."

Grant gave her an easy smile. "That's my job, darlin'."

Charli straightened, a little perturbed by Grant's obvious warmth toward Evan. Had he offered to train *her* when he'd figured out she was submissive? How close were all these "friends"?

The jealousy was ugly and totally uncalled for—as if she had any claim on Grant anyway. But there it was nonetheless, setting her teeth on edge. She tried to shrug off the tightness in her shoulders. Grant's fingers drifted from her hair to her neck and massaged.

"You're very tense, Charlotte. Come here." He spread his thighs and patted the spot in between his knees. "Sit."

Shyness threatened, but she remembered what he'd told her before they walked in—don't think, only do. So after a breath of hesitation, she scooted closer to him. His palms spanned her waist and he lifted her easily over his leg and settled her between his thighs, as if she were as petite as the woman sitting across from them. A beat of pleasure went through Charli, the feeling of being small and easily handled such a rarity for her.

Grant put his hands on her shoulders and began to work at the knots that had formed there with his thumbs. A soft sigh escaped her, as the muscles yielded to his commanding fingers. If this is what being submissive was about, she'd clearly been missing out. Wasn't she supposed to be the one serving him?

Though, honestly, massaging him wouldn't be a hardship either. Getting her hands on all those lean, honed muscles of his would be quite the treat.

The conversation continued around her, and Grant gave her permission to speak freely with his friends. Despite that first whip of jealousy, Charli found herself liking Evan. She seemed like a no-nonsense woman with a good head on her shoulders. Not at all what she would've imagined a submissive woman to be like. And Evan's two guys were like a comedy team with their easy volleys back and forth. Charli got the sense that the three of them probably created quite a cozy and loving household.

But just as Charli began to relax and mellow, the guy from the training class she'd crashed sidled up to the table. The dip in his brow said something was wrong before his mouth opened. "Hey, Boss."

Grant straightened a bit behind her. "Colby."

"I hate to bother you, but Elliot's sick as hell. He just called me to say he's going back to his cabin to get some sleep and won't be able to do his demonstration tonight."

Grant made a displeased noise under his breath. "What was he supposed to feature?"

"Shibari. It's one of the main things the Florida group wanted to see. And I've been working on it a little, but I'm definitely not in the position to demo it." Colby's attention diverted briefly to Charli, then back to Grant. "Nyla was scheduled to bottom for Elliot. She's still ready to go, but . . ."

Colby was speaking a different language as far as Charli was concerned, but could feel Grant release a long breath behind her, which didn't bode well. "Give me a minute, Colby."

Colby nodded. "No problem. I'll be in the staging room."

After Colby strode off, Grant scooted out of the booth, taking her along with him. She turned to face him, her recently loosened muscles starting to coil again. Grant put a hand to her cheek. "I'm sorry, darlin'. I planned for tonight to be about getting you acclimated, but I'm going to have to take care of this first. I promised my friend Stefan that we'd train his staff well for his club opening. We don't have anyone here besides me and Elliot who are trained in Shibari."

"What's that?"

"A Japanese rope bondage technique." He lowered his hand from her face and rubbed the back of his neck, looking more displeased than she'd ever seen him. "They're going to need me to do the demonstration tonight."

With some other woman. He didn't have to say it. She'd pieced together Colby's conversation. "Oh."

"I'm sorry." He tilted his head to look around her. "Would one of you guys mind walking Charlotte back to her cabin? She's staying in the one just west of my place."

"Whatever you need," Jace replied.

"Wait a second, you're sending me *home*?" Charli asked, yanking Grant's attention back her way. Anger began to simmer beneath the calm façade she was trying so hard to maintain.

"Yes, it's bad enough I have to end our evening early, but I'm certainly not going to make you watch me do this. You're still uncomfortable here, which is to be expected. I'm not going to make it worse."

She gritted her teeth. She'd been through the gauntlet of beauty treatments today, had been twisted up with nerves all evening, and now he was going to send her home so he could tie up some other naked woman? Oh, *hell* no. Her freshly polished nails dug into her palms as she tried to frame her retort to match her role. "Sir, *Grant*, you set up tonight as my opportunity to serve you, correct?"

His mouth thinned, no doubt noticing her words had come through clenched teeth. "Yes, Charlotte. But—"

"Then please let me do so. I know I'm new, but it can't be that hard to be the one being bound."

Either Jace or Andre coughed behind her, obviously covering up a laugh or a sound of surprise. She didn't bother to look back at them, her eyes fixated on Grant. He crossed his arms, staring down at her, his expression a mix of things she couldn't name. "Charlotte, you struggled standing naked in front of me the other day. You're not ready to do that in front of a room full of people."

Naked? In front of a crowd?

Her heart hammered against her ribs, her palms going sweaty at the thought. But she matched his posture and jutted out her chin. "Maybe you're underestimating me, *sir*."

He leaned closer, his voice going low and dangerous. "You're treading a fine line, freckles. I'm doing this to protect you from something you're not prepared for."

Red edged her vision.

"You know what I'm really tired of, sir? People telling me what I am and am not prepared for or capable of. Really. Fucking. Tired." Her mother. Her brothers. Her boss. And now Grant?

Screw that.

Without breaking eye contact, she lowered herself until she was kneeling on the cold floor at his feet. "I don't share, Grant. Add that to my hard limits. If you send me away, I won't need my cabin anymore."

The music and ambient conversation in the club seemed to fade as her challenge hung in the air between them. Grant stared down at her, the muscle in his jaw twitching. Power and anger seemed to drip off him, the impact of it splashing down over her like fat raindrops. She'd threatened him, and he didn't like it. Adrenaline leaked into her system, giving her that panicky rush that usually only preceded things like that slow climb on a roller coaster before the big drop.

He leaned forward, his evaluating gaze coming closer. She looked down at her lap, the response automatic. He grabbed her hair and forced her face back upward. "Don't play demure now. That's not going to get you out of trouble. Talking back *and* cursing? You're lucky this is your first night because otherwise I'd take you over my knee right this second in front of everyone."

Breath became hard to come by, and her limbs tingled as if blood had forgotten to flow. She managed a whispered "I'm sorry, sir."

"Now you want to apologize?" His gaze raked over her face and the pulse point at her neck, hovering there as if it held the answers to some question he hadn't asked. Then a sinister smile broke through that stubble of his. "Well, would you look at that?"

"At what, sir?" she said, her voice sounding soft and distant to her own ears.

His grip tightened against her scalp. "Oh, sweet Charlotte, this is going to be fun."

FOURTEEN

Grant led Charli to what he'd called the staging room. Her legs barely wanted to cooperate beneath her as she tried to keep up with his purposeful pace. She was really going to do this. She was going to let Grant get her naked and tie her up in front of an audience. She inhaled deeply through her nose, the combination of nerves and strange anticipation making her brain fuzzy.

Inside the staging room, Colby was standing with his back to them at a nearby table, laying out different lengths of rope, and a curvy, dark-skinned woman sat on the couch closest to him, her gaze down, her hands folded neatly in her lap—the picture of demure beauty. An inviting smile crossed the woman's lips when she peeked up and noticed Grant. Charli wanted to throw a right hook her way.

The door clicked shut behind them, and Colby turned. "Oh, hey, Boss. Nyla is rea—"

"She won't be necessary," Grand said, cutting him off. "Charlotte will handle the demonstration. Thank you, Nyla, but you can go now."

Colby's gaze went to Charli, a hint of surprise crossing his features. "Sure, you got it, Boss." He nodded at Nyla. "Go back to Master Elliot. I'm sure he would appreciate your comfort while he's sick. Tell him we appreciated his willingness to lend you to us tonight. And if his fever gets any higher, you call in the doctor even if he orders you not to."

Nyla's perfect posture sagged a bit, her relief evident. "Thank you, sir. And don't worry. I know how hardheaded he can be. I'll keep an eye on him."

Nyla peeked at Charli once more, obviously curious but too polite to stare, then headed out the back door.

Grant's hands landed on Charli's shoulders, causing her to jump. His breath tickled her ear. "Take off the dress."

Her attention slid toward Colby, who was winding another rope but watching her and Grant closely. Words stuttered and stumbled in her mouth, but none made it out.

Grant stepped around her and crossed his arms. "Scared of Colby seeing you naked? In a little while, he's going to be one of many."

She wet her lips, her heartbeat going staccato. She *was* scared, but that wasn't the only thing stirring inside her. Desire coiled low and hot in her belly.

"Back talk in front of my friends and now hesitation. I don't appreciate it, freckles," Grant said, his tone cool. "Lace your fingers behind your neck. Colby, please remove Charlotte's clothing since she can't seem to do it on her own."

"Wait, I can." She moved her hands to her dress, but Grant stepped forward and captured her wrists.

"Too late." He guided her arms behind her neck, waiting until she followed his earlier directive and intertwined her fingers. "You'll have to learn to follow a command when I give it. If you don't, the alternative will probably be less to your liking. Understand?"

She glared at him. "Yes, Grant."

He stepped back and released her arms, making room for Colby. Colby put his hands on her waist as he moved behind her, his touch surprisingly gentle for a man who looked like he could snap a two-by-four like a twig. His voice was low enough for only her to hear it. "You may want to drop the eat-shit-and-die look you're giving him, sweetheart. You're pushing his buttons, and there's a lot he can do to you once you're tied up and incapacitated."

Goose bumps prickled her skin at the warning. She lowered her gaze, and Colby went to work untying the corset-style fastening of her dress. The backs of his fingers grazed the sides of her breasts as he grabbed the soft fabric and drew it down her body. She closed her eyes, trying to quell her nerves and self-consciousness. Colby tapped her calf and she stepped out of the dress, leaving her completely exposed for the two of them.

Colby circled around and smiled as he openly peered at her nudity, somehow managing to convey warm appreciation instead of lewdness. "That full-body blush of yours is one of the sexiest damn things I've seen, sweetheart."

She dipped her head, her blush deepening no doubt. But the compliment made her feel more steady on her feet. A little sexy, even.

He turned to Grant. "I would say you're a lucky guy, Boss, but I have a feeling you're going to have your hands full with this one."

Grant didn't smile or even look at Colby. His focus was solely on her, his burning hot perusal turning her quivery and wet. His gaze tracked down to the juncture between her thighs, and she had the urge to shield herself. He'd ordered her to be waxed, and nothing but a trimmed triangle of hair at the top was left. There was no hiding how he was affecting her.

His eyes met hers. "I'm looking forward to the challenge."

Colby clapped him on the shoulder and chuckled, his easy nature a stark contrast next to Grant's stoicism. "I'll get these ropes set up. I'll let you know when the group is ready."

Grant waited until Colby left the room, then took a few steps closer. He palmed her waist, then tucked his other hand between her legs, finding her damp heat. He grazed her already throbbing clit. "You're so fucking gorgeous right now. I wish you could see yourself through my eyes. You would never doubt your feminine wiles again."

A harsh breath escaped her as he slipped two fingers inside her. She put a hand to his shoulder, steadying herself, his words knocking her off balance as much as his touch. "Thank you."

"Watch how nice I can make it when you remember your manners." He lowered his head and took her nipple between his lips, laving it with his tongue while continuing to pump his fingers inside of her. Her body clamped down around him, begging for more than his hand. She rocked her hips forward, bringing his callused thumb against her clit.

A few strokes and she'd be there.

But instead of continuing, he gave her nipple a soft bite and pulled his hand away. The corners of his mouth lifted into a sly grin. "Not so fast, darlin'."

He put his fingers in his mouth and sucked slowly, tasting her arousal and keeping his eyes on her. The satisfied sound he made in the back of his throat lit her body on fire. "*Mmm*, you're so tempting. But you haven't earned that orgasm yet. Not with that smart mouth you've been using tonight."

He took a step back, removing himself from her reach. She felt the loss of him immediately, cool, empty air replacing his scent and warmth. "I'm sorry, Grant. The thought of you tying up some other woman . . ."

She stopped, realizing she'd spoken her thought aloud, a thought that revealed how possessive she felt of him already.

His expression remained placid, but the flare in his eyes and the erection pushing at the fly of his perfectly tailored slacks said he was anything but. "Finish your sentence."

She cringed but forced her vocal cords to work. "The thought made me mad. And jealous."

He seemed to consider that for a moment, his head tilting ever so slightly. "Interesting. Kneel down."

She responded in an instant and attempted to rock down gracefully. Her knees hit the polished wood floors with barely a sound. *Yeah, buddy.* She fought back a proud smile.

He nodded in approval as he walked a slow circle around her, like an animal sizing up its prey. He stopped in front of her again. "Very nice. Get used to holding that kneel."

"Yes, sir."

He stepped back a few feet but continued to watch her as he slipped his suit coat off his shoulders—a slow, fluid motion of a man in no hurry. He folded the jacket and laid it neatly over the arm of the couch, smoothing out an errant wrinkle. Next, he pulled at the knot on his tie, the soft silk-against-silk sound the only noise in the room. His movements stayed methodical, deliberate—his stare unyielding. With each removed item, Charli found her heartbeat ticking up a notch. She moistened her lips. Was he going to take off everything? Was she finally going to get to see all of him, touch him?

He ran the silk tie over his palm with an oh-the-things-I-could-do look on his face, and she could almost feel its smoothness against her own skin. What would it feel like against her wrists, her ankles? But he laid it across his suit coat, leaving it unused. His long fingers went to his cuff links and he unfastened the buttons at his wrists. *Clink. Clink.* The cuff links hit the glass side table, startling Charli.

Grant gave her a wicked smile as he rolled the sleeves of his white dress shirt up his forearms. "Am I making you nervous, Charlotte?"

"Yes."

"Smart girl. Your instincts are better than your brother gives you credit for." He walked over to her, the tips of his shined shoes almost touching her knees. His hand cupped her chin, forcing her face upward. "Though I didn't appreciate your defiance earlier, your jealousy pleases me. I like that you want to be the only one serving me."

He ran the pad of this thumb over her mouth, and without pausing to think, she parted her lips and sucked. The dark blue in his eyes went almost black as he let her lick his salty skin. Seeing his response sent a hot rush through her, an ache. Knowing she could do that to him with such a simple act felt . . . invigorating.

In the past, she'd hated giving blow jobs. It'd always felt like a chore or a favor. Plus, Trey had always come too fast, then wouldn't be interested in sex for the rest of the night.

But right then, there was nothing she wanted more than to unzip Grant's slacks and take him in her mouth. The desire to give him that pleasure was as strong as her own need to be touched. *Let me please you.* The urge was entirely foreign, but her hormones were buzzing too strongly for her to examine it any deeper.

He brushed her hair away from her face with gentle fingers. "This is only supposed to be an intro training. But you're making it very hard for me to restrain myself, Charlotte, especially when you look at me like that."

She swallowed hard. This world, his world, scared her on some elemental level. But instead of making her want to run, the fear was like a heady elixir filtering through her blood, spiking it. She didn't want training wheels. She wanted Grant. The real Grant. "Please don't give me the watered-down version of yourself, sir. I'm a big girl and understand the safe word."

He shook his head as he twined her hair around his hand. Once. Twice. "I really did have you pegged all wrong, freckles. That's a first." His grip was snug, making her scalp sting. "The fear feeds you, doesn't it? That's why you're always chasing some edge."

She tried to shake her head, denying the accusation but not even fully processing what he was saying.

"Unbutton my pants. Let's see if you fuck as good with your mouth as you do with your eyes."

The sharp command was like a lightning strike to her system, sending her into some new dimension she was sure she hadn't visited before. She did as she was told, fumbling for a moment, before getting the button undone and the zipper down. His cock pushed through the opening in his boxers, hard and thick . . . and pretty, if cocks could be classified as such. *Oh, God, yes.* No longer thinking, just acting on her own impulses, she nuzzled her cheek against him, inhaling his scent, relishing the velvety skin of his shaft.

He groaned softly, his fingers flexing in her hair. "Open, Charlotte. I need to feel you around me."

The need spoken matched her own. She parted her lips, and he guided her into the position he wanted. His cock slid hot against her tongue, his masculine taste activating something wholly carnal inside her. She closed her eyes, savoring him for a moment, then moved forward to take more. But he held her fast.

"Open your eyes and look at me."

She lifted her gaze to him, her insides flipping over when their eyes met. The unfettered want in his expression was like a palpable blow to her body.

"I want you to watch what you do to me." He guided her, encouraging her to take him deeper. "And I'll set the pace. The crowd out there can wait. I'm not ready to share you yet."

Yet. The warning whispered through her and bloomed like a hothouse flower inside her. He was in control of her destiny here. Yes, he was going to share the sight of her with the audience, but she knew sharing could mean a lot more than that at The Ranch. She'd seen the limits checklist. Hadn't marked *no* on any of those boxes. Though some of those items had given her pause, she wasn't into half-assed. She'd agreed to give him the control, so she was going to let him use it.

She held the eye contact as she moved back and forth along his length. He took his time, the intense expression on his face a reward in and of itself. His sexuality was so raw, so close to the surface. Seeing it start to leak through that thin societal veneer fed something deep and dark within her, made her crave more. What was Grant like when he shed that layer completely?

He released the harsh hold on her hair and spanned his palms along the sides of her head, his tempo increasing. Every time his cock tapped the back of her throat, her sex clenched. But instead of feeling impatient for her own release, she was enjoying the slow burn that was overtaking her. It was like being enveloped by the sun-warmed ocean one agonizing inch at a time.

Grant's gaze never left hers, and she found herself falling into those blue depths, their surroundings blurring into the background. It was only the two of them and this one moment. Her eyelids fluttered closed.

Grant smacked her cheek, light but attention-getting. She blinked up at him—surprised that he'd hit her face, but more shocked that it'd sent a hot dart of need straight downward.

He rubbed a thumb over her cheekbone. "That's the risk and beauty of setting no limits, Charlotte. I get to find your edges. Dangerous game to play with me."

Dangerous, indeed. Especially when each time he pushed at those boundaries, she found herself wanting to vault over them, to see what was on the other side.

She shifted forward and took him as deep as she could, holding the eye contact and sliding the tip of her tongue along the base of his cock. He let out a groan and she slid back, oh-so-gently dragging her teeth along his tender skin, dishing out a little bit of his own medicine.

"Fuck." The word escaped on a harsh breath. He gripped her head again and all semblance of his cool control seemed to drain from him. She'd pushed him past his limit. His pace became a thundering gallop to the finish. He watched her eyes and fucked her mouth and said words that made her thighs damp with her own juices. Words like *beautiful* and *sexy* and *mine*.

The wildness in him broke through. The sight took her breath away and made every part of her throb. Her nipples brushed against the fabric of his pants with each thrust and she started to wonder if it was possible to come simply from that and the pressure of her thighs squeezing together. She moaned around him and that sent him over the cliff.

He shoved his cock deep to the back of her throat, and with a slew of swear words mixing with her name, his hot release pulsed into her. She took all he had to give, digging her nails into her thighs, and holding back her own orgasm.

After a few panted seconds, he slipped from her mouth and tucked himself back into his dress pants. His gaze skated down her body. She couldn't slow her breathing. Her skin felt so sensitized, and everything was throbbing in time with her heartbeat. How in the hell had he done this to her with a simple blow job?

There was a sharp rap on the door, drawing her focus to the other side of the room.

Colby stepped through the doorway, his gaze landing on Charli, then darting back to Grant. "Everything's all set up, Boss. Need anything else?"

When Grant didn't respond immediately, Charli looked back to him, finding her cowboy smiling darkly.

"Perhaps." Grant hooked a finger in her collar, guiding her upward. Her legs struggled to remember their function, and Grant had to grab her elbow to steady her. Once she'd regained her balance, he brushed the back of his hand along one of her nipples and she gasped at the sharp snap of sensation.

Fuck. She felt like a grenade with the pin stuck—ready to detonate, but unable to without that final pull.

"Do you need to come, Charlotte?"

God, yes. "Please."

"By whatever means I deem appropriate?"

"Yes, sir," she said quickly, too far gone to worry about details.

"Good girl."

He grabbed the tie he'd discarded earlier from the arm of the couch and stepped behind her, fastening her wrists at the small of her back. The move had her breasts jutting out and fully exposed to Colby, who'd stayed near the doorway. The wolfish grin that crossed Colby's face had her belly fluttering.

Grant slid a hot palm along her ass and sat his chin on her shoulder, his stubble sending goose bumps along her skin. "You know, Colby? Before I agreed to take her on myself, my lovely Charlotte asked to be trained by you."

Colby's eyebrow lifted. "Is that right? Well, color me flattered."

"And she probably thinks that I'm way too possessive to share her." Grant's finger traced the cleft where her butt met her thigh. "But she doesn't realize that one of the ultimate acts of ownership is having the say over who can and can't touch your sub."

Colby took a step toward them.

She forgot to breathe.

"I can't have her this squirmy when I'm tying her up for the demo." Grant traced his hand up her side and cupped her breast, plumping it. "Taste her, Colby. She's very sweet. And very, very responsive. I bet between the two of us, we can have her coming without ever touching her pussy."

Charli's heart hammered hard against her ribs. Grant was going to let another man touch her. She could stop it. She could use the safe word. But the thought of them both was only making her wetter. It was the stuff of fantasies, but no one really acted on those, right?

Grant had told her to put trust in him, that whatever he told her to do was for their mutual benefit. And for some reason, she felt compelled to listen. Plus, in her world, men didn't look at her like this. Having two potently handsome men treating her like she was some sort of siren was damn hot.

Colby's hazel eyes searched hers, obviously double-checking that she was on board with this. When she didn't say a word, he closed the distance between them and lowered his head. Moist heat wrapped around her nipple as Colby took her flesh into his mouth. She cried out at the sudden rush of sensation, her nerves humming like a power line ready to spark. Grant's hand continued to cradle her breast, holding her in place for Colby's attention, and he trailed kisses along the curve of her neck.

The sight of Colby's lips moving over her skin and Grant's long, tan fingers stroking her breast was erotic overload. Her clit pulsed between her thighs, blood pumping to all her most sensitive parts. Grant pressed his teeth into her shoulder until she felt the snap of pain race through her. "You're so goddamned responsive, freckles. You're getting me hard all over again."

He licked the spot he'd bitten, then stepped out from behind her. His gaze branded her as he took in the full frontal view of her naked and bound, another man sucking her nipple to a hard, aching point. Grant reached out and pinched her other nipple. She bit back another yelp.

He smiled and nudged Colby over a bit. "You have permission to come."

The hot cavern of Grant's mouth closed over the other aching bud, sucking and nibbling without pretense of gentleness. Whereas Colby was playful and teasing, Grant was unrelenting intensity. Her body bucked and her arms strained to reach out and grab the two men, but the tie didn't give.

Grant gripped her waist, steadying her. Moisture painted her thighs, her need for all of him turning her inside out. If he would just touch her clit, slide his fingers inside her, she'd be able to get there. She wriggled against his hand, trying to convey that message. But he smacked her thigh hard. Then, the two men bit down simultaneously, and every knotted part inside her came unraveled in one blissful moment.

She screamed, the combination of pain and wicked pleasure

launching her into orgasm. Her sex pulsed in time with her pounding heart, and her breath came in sharp bursts. The sensation was different than a normal climax, sharp and fast, a release that somehow satisfied and made her ache for more at the same time.

The men switched to gentle licks and her knees wobbled beneath her.

"Grant," she gasped, a plea.

"Don't worry. I've got you. I won't let you fall," he whispered.

Colby backed off, and Grant gathered her to him. Her head sagged against his chest, his words crashing over her.

I won't let you fall.

If only he could truly guarantee that. She already felt her world tilting, and it had nothing to do with her shaky legs.

FIFTEEN

Grant waited until Charli's breathing returned to normal, then wrapped a silk robe around her shoulders and kissed the crown of her head. She gave him a faint smile as she tucked her arms into the robe.

"What's that look for?" he asked.

She glanced at the doorway Colby had used to exit. "Nothing, really. I guess I just never would've pegged you as the sharing type."

"Is that right?"

She tied the robe's belt around her waist and sent him a sly look. "You have spoiled, only child written all over you."

He smirked, though the words niggled a sore spot inside him. "I'm the eldest of four actually. Two sisters and a brother. And though my momma tried, my daddy would've never let her get away with spoiling us."

She tilted her head, as if thrown by the revelation, and leaned against the wall. "Wow, one of four. Never would've guessed that. Are you close to your family?"

"Nope." He headed over to a large cabinet in the corner of the room to dig for a few things for the demo and to avoid her inquisitive look.

"Is it because of this?"

He grabbed a switchblade sharp enough to cut through rope and hooked it to belt. "Last I checked this isn't interview time, Ms. Reporter."

The little huff she made would've brought a smile to his face under any other circumstance, but her line of questioning was sending him to that guilty place he didn't like to visit.

"So you can strip me naked and tie me up, but I can't ask you a little bit about yourself?"

He turned around, pinning her with a fierce look. "Yes. That's how this works. We're not on a date, Charli. This isn't get-to-know-you time."

Her jaw flexed, a wounded expression flitting over her features before she covered it.

Ah, hell. Now he felt like a dick. This is why he avoided pillow talk at all costs. It never led anywhere good. But Charli hadn't earned his ire. "Fine. Yes, sometimes I like to share. Knowing someone is mine and I have the say on who can and can't touch her turns me on. But that's not to say I'm not possessive."

"Meaning?"

"When I'm with a sub, I expect her to be exclusive to me while we're involved. Me allowing someone else to touch her during play is different than her seeing other guys."

She nodded, a little I-told-you-so playing at the corners of her mouth. "So, I was right. You *are* selfish."

"Very." He stepped forward and set his hands on her shoulders. "And as for your other question, my family is happy and successful and better off without me as part of it. Can we leave it at that?"

The sympathy that crossed over her face dug through him like a trowel. She wrapped her arms around his waist and pressed her head to his chest. "I'm sorry. I shouldn't have pried."

He rubbed her back, enjoying holding her maybe a little too much. "You don't have to apologize. I should've expected it. You're nosy by nature."

"Hey." She shoved at his chest, a laugh on her lips as she made a feeble attempt at escape.

He grabbed her belt and pulled, opening her robe and pressing her against him. "Nosy. And naughty as all get out, I might add." He slipped his hands onto her bared waist. "Likes to be shared, gets off on a little fear, and has a body that responds like it was meant for this. You're a surprise at every corner, freckles."

"I've always been an overachiever," she said with mock seriousness. "And clearly, you're terrible at reading people."

He pinched her hip, earning him a delicious yelp. "Come on, smart-ass. Let's get this demo over with. If I have to wait much longer to get you in my dungeon, I'll end up fucking you in front of everyone out there."

There it was. That flare of heat and fear lighting her eyes. The desire in him swelled, feeding on it. It was a drug he could get used to imbibing.

She wet her lips, and he stared at her mouth, wanting to kiss her, to taste that need from her. The thought punched him in the sternum—the shock of that old, now-alien desire almost knocking him on his ass.

He didn't do kissing. Beyond the occasional friendly peck, it was off limits. The act always seemed too tender, too personal, a betrayal to the memory of the last woman he kissed.

He cupped Charli's cheek and brushed a thumb over her lips, but held back from putting his mouth on hers. What was it about this girl that made him want to break all his rules? He sighed and pressed a kiss to her forehead. "Time to get you trussed up, darlin'."

Grant led Charli out of the staging room and into one of the training rooms where a small audience waited for them. Charli tensed beneath his grip when she stepped into the spotlighted area.

He'd anticipated some fear and kept her close to his side. "Breathe, freckles. You look beautiful. These people are lucky that they get the privilege of seeing you."

She nodded, though he could feel the harried beat of her heart at her wrist. "Sorry. The last time I was paraded onstage like this was when I was eight and my mother forced me into a beauty pageant. I tripped, tore my dress, and all the other kids laughed at me."

Her tone was light, but the pain he could hear beneath it twisted something in his chest. He halted her at the center of the small platform and pulled the tie he'd used to bind her arms earlier from his pocket. He put his knuckle beneath her chin, keeping her attention on him and not on the people in the crowd. "Charlotte, I'm going to blindfold you."

Her eyes widened.

"Trust me. This will help you focus on my voice and the sensations, and let the fear go. Forget that the audience is here. It's just you and me up here, okay?"

He watched her throat work as she swallowed. "But what if I mess something up?"

He frowned. Her desire to do everything exactly right was damn endearing, but he hated to see the stress creasing her brow. "Relax, darlin'. Nothing you could do up here will disappoint me. No one is here to judge you or laugh at you. You could safe word the minute the rope touches your skin and everyone would understand. All right?"

She nodded, though doubt still lingered in her eyes. "Yes, Grant."

"Good girl." He stepped around her and tied the silk over her eyes, hoping the sooner he visibly blocked the audience out, the sooner she'd be able to forget they were there. After giving her a minute to adjust to the blindfold, he removed her robe.

She shivered, but to her credit, kept her posture proud.

He put a hand to her shoulder to ground her and guided her to a resting kneel. "If at any time something goes numb, becomes painful, or makes you feel panicked, use your words. *Yellow* means I'll back off and check in with you. Say *Texas* and I'm cutting the ropes off and kicking everyone out. There's no shame in using either."

She released a shaky breath. "Yes, sir. Thank you."

He kissed the spot on her shoulder where his hand had been, then straightened and stepped to the side to face the audience. He started off talking about the lengths of ropes, why hemp was usually preferred, how to soften the rope by boiling it. It was all relatively dry stuff, but having Charli naked and kneeling in his peripheral vision had his skin prickling with awareness. She looked so damn tempting, her color easing slowly from the pink flush of embarrassment back to her natural freckled alabaster. She was sinking into the zone he needed her in. Focused. Ready for whatever he needed from her. Submissive.

He ran the length of rope along his palm as he answered a few questions from the audience. What he wouldn't give to grab Charli and take her somewhere private. Though he liked a little exhibitionism and sharing every now and then, he preferred his D/s behind closed doors, enjoyed the sacred space it created between the dominant and submissive. And with Charli he was suddenly craving that more than ever.

He glanced over at his pretty sub. She'd lowered her head, shielding her face with that silky red curtain of hair. A wave of possessiveness went over him, and he found himself resenting the audience for being present. He wanted to tie her up for his eyes only. He wanted to run the rope along her soft skin, sensitize her, have her quivering and bound and begging for release. His cock pushed against his zipper as the images flitted through his head.

But he wouldn't give these strangers that gift. That would be his.

Deciding to cut the presentation as short as possible, he headed over to Charli and began to demonstrate a few of the basic tying techniques, binding her wrists and ankles in a few easy-for-beginners options. Then he tied her arms behind her with a series of double-coin knots, making a line down from her shoulders all the way to her wrists.

With each new knot, Grant could see Charli's breathing becoming more shallow, could feel her skin warming even though the room was cool. Some people panicked in rope bindings because it could feel more restrictive than cuffs, more claustrophobic, but Charli seemed to be having the opposite reaction. He could sense her sinking deeper into herself, any lingering anxiety draining from her.

Pride ballooned in his chest. His little trainee was quite the protégé. Despite her obvious issues with being exposed in front of others, she'd listened to his instructions and blocked everything out. She was only there with him, no one else. He finished the last knot and gave her shoulder a soft bite before whispering, "I can't even tell you how fucking perfect you look right now, sweet Charlotte. I'm the luckiest guy in the joint."

She flexed against her bindings, and her teeth dragged over her bottom lip.

"There's one more binding I want to do, but that one's going to be for my eyes only. I'm done sharing you tonight."

Hell, based on how he was feeling at this moment, he may not want to ever share her again.

Charli listened to Grant wrap up the demonstration with only half an ear. Her arms were still bound behind her, her breasts no doubt jutting forth for all to see, but she couldn't find it in herself to care. The audience's presence had melted away in her mind. Grant's steady voice, his sure hands as he tied the ropes, the feel of his callused fingers brushing over her skin, his scent . . . Those were the only things she could focus on. And with each passing minute, her body's awareness of him became more and more acute.

His slow footsteps sounded in her ears and she stretched her fingers, wishing she could reach out and touch him, explore. He stopped in front of her, his pant leg brushing her knee, then his voice was close enough for her to feel his breath on her cheeks. "We're all alone again, Charlotte."

He untied the blindfold and she blinked at him, the sudden light leaving spots in her vision. "They're gone?"

He was squatting in front of her, want in his eyes. "You didn't hear all that commotion as everyone left?"

She shook her head, still feeling a bit dazed.

He smiled and cupped her breast, circling his thumb around the tip and making her shiver. "So you *can* lose yourself to it." Deep satisfaction colored his tone. "You're getting a taste of subspace, freckles. I hope to bring you there often."

She didn't know what the term meant, but if he kept caressing her nipple like that, she wasn't going to be able to remember her name in a second.

He rose off his haunches and moved around behind her. "Let me get you out of this, then I'm taking you where I can have you all to myself."

"Sounds like an excellent plan."

After he removed all of the ropes, he slipped her robe back on her shoulders and tied the belt around her waist. "Be right back."

He left her there while he went into the staging room. When he returned a few minutes later, he was wearing jeans and boots and holding the bag he'd asked her to pack this morning. He held it out to her. "You're allowed to put on panties and shoes for now. My dungeon isn't in this building. We have to go outside."

She raised her eyebrows, but took the bag and followed his instructions, slipping on a pair of simple black panties beneath the robe and toeing on her ballet flats. "Okay."

He grabbed her hand and kissed the top of it. "Our chariot awaits, sweet Charlotte."

Chariot? She had no idea what he meant by that, but as he led her down a few hallways and out a side door, the last thing she'd expected was standing outside waiting for them—waiting and . . . chuffing. "Oh, you've got to be fucking kidding me."

Grant gave a hearty laugh. "Watch your mouth, freckles. Maggie here will be offended."

The horse turned a big eye on Charli, while Grant ran an affectionate hand down Maggie's blue-black flank. "Sorry, it's just I'm not exactly dressed for horseback riding."

Grant checked Maggie's saddle, then put out a hand to Charli. "You're fine. It's warm enough tonight and it will be quicker than walking. Plus, it's more fun than the golf cart."

With a sigh, she gave Grant her hand, and he helped her get her foot in the stirrup. He counted to three, then hoisted her up so she could mount the horse. Maggie stirred beneath her but otherwise seemed totally content with a half-naked stranger climbing on top of her. Charli snorted.

"What was that for?" Grant asked as he untied the horse from the hitching post.

"Nothing. Just realized Maggie and I have something in common tonight."

He shook his head. "Yeah, I'm not touching that one."

With the grace of a man who'd done it a thousand times before, Grant put his boot in the stirrup and swung his leg over, filling the space behind Charli. The heat of his chest seared through the thin silk of her robe, making every inch of her reignite with awareness. He reached around her and grabbed the reins, cocooning her with his scent. He nuzzled her ear, his voice low. "Hold on, freckles."

She grabbed onto the saddle horn, and Grant made a soft clicking sound to get Maggie moving. Charli gripped hard as the horse made its way down the slant in the path. "Whoa."

"Relax, darlin'. I'm not going to let you fall." His thighs pressed against the outside of hers, reminding her that he had her on all sides.

"Maybe I should mention I've never been on a horse."

He led Maggie away from the main building and toward the back of the property. Cabins dotted the area to the left, but Grant stayed off the walking paths and instead weaved along the fences protecting the vineyards. The rows of grapevines seemed to stretch out forever under the moonlight. "How is it Ms. Rough-and-Tumble has never been horseback riding?"

She adjusted her grip on the saddle horn, her fingers starting to hurt from grabbing it so hard. "I grew up in the suburbs. Riding four-wheelers was about as country as I got."

"I bet you were damn cute trying to keep up with those brothers of yours."

She sniffed. "*Cute* would probably not be the most accurate description. And I didn't get to do those things with my brothers. My dad was of the lock-daughter-up-until-she's-twenty mentality. I'd have to sneak out and play with the neighborhood boys and tell Dad I was playing with Barbies."

"What about your mom?"

What about her? was the first retort that jumped to her lips, but she bit it back, taking a long breath and staring out at the dark night in front of them. The last thing she wanted to do was talk about her mother, but she'd asked Grant some prying questions earlier, and it was only fair that she give him a little honesty, too. "My mom moved to Los Angeles when I was nine to help my older sister pursue her acting career. I wanted to go with them and be on TV, too, but mom told me the talent agent said I didn't have the right look."

The muscles in Grant's forearms twitched as he gripped the reins tighter, but he stayed silent.

She cleared her throat, trying to move past the lump that always lodged there when she thought about the day her mom walked out.

"It was supposed to be temporary—my mom living out her own failed dream through my sister. But my sister landed a part in a kid's show, and my mother landed a spot in the director's bed. They came home the next Thanksgiving, and Mom told Dad she was leaving him. Us. Neither she nor my sister ever came home again. It was like we didn't even exist for her anymore."

"Wow. That had to be tough for a little girl to understand," he said, sympathy in his voice.

"I survived. I'd spent my whole life trying to please her and live up to expectations I could never seem to reach. So in some ways, it was easier after she left. My dad was never the same though. She broke his heart, and that broke him. He did a good job raising us, but the light in him went out the day he found out she was leaving for good. He was never the same." She paused, tears threatening. Nothing could make her lose it quicker than thinking about her daddy. But she pressed her tongue to the roof of her mouth, an old method she'd learned to keep tears at bay.

"How is he now?"

"He died of cancer my junior year of high school. From diagnosis to gone in only six months." Tears did slip out this time. She brushed them away with the back of her hand. "She didn't even come home to see him. Me and my brothers took care of him, watched him fade. Part of me thinks he would've been able to fight it if he hadn't been so lost without her."

Grant kissed her shoulder. "I'm sorry, darlin'. I didn't mean to bring up something that would upset you."

She took a few seconds, waiting for the burning sensation of more impending tears to abate, then rolled her neck, trying to shake off the bad memories. "It's okay. It just makes me angry that he wasted the rest of his life loving someone who wasn't going to love him back. He was a great man. He could've found someone else and had another chance at being happy."

Grant turned quiet for a moment, and the only sound was

hooves hitting the packed dirt. She thought he'd ended the discussion, but finally he said, "Sounds like she was the love of his life. Sometimes there's no coming back from that."

She scoffed. "That's bullshit. Something doesn't work out, so you roll over and wait to die? Screw that."

"You think moving on is that easy?" Grant shifted in the saddle, and Maggie whinnied as if sensing the discussion had gone off course. "Have *you* ever been in love, Charli?"

Her jaw clenched—as if she needed a reminder of her piss-poor love life. "You know I haven't. But based on what I've seen, they can keep it."

"Oh, really?" She could hear the smile in his voice. The stiffness in his hold on the reins softened a bit. "You're too young to be so cynical, you know."

"Ha! Said the pot to the kettle."

"I'm not that young, freckles." He slowed Maggie down a bit and guided her to the right where a narrow path led to what looked to be a barn. Though it was hard to tell with only the moonlight. "I come by my cynicism honestly."

She frowned. She doubted Grant had even crossed into his forties yet, but she had a feeling he wasn't talking about his age in years. He'd seen a lot of hurt in his life; he wore it in his eyes. Part of her wanted to ask him if he'd ever been in love, but she had a feeling she already knew the answer. And it wouldn't be a happy story. She pushed away the melancholy thought and straightened her spine. "Well, good thing I'm only using you for your body and not trying to woo you then, Mr. Cynical."

"Oh, so that's what this is? I feel so cheap."

She laughed and poked him in the thigh.

He stopped Maggie in front of a fence and, after making sure Charli was still holding on, dismounted in one fluid motion. He tied the horse to the post, then helped her with her own awkward disembarkation. She landed with an unladylike *thunk* and almost toppled onto her butt. He grabbed her waist and held her steady. "Whoa, there."

"Thanks," she said, the near tumble and the look he was giving her enough to make her breathless. "Grace isn't my forte."

"Stop being so hard on yourself." He pushed her hair away from her face, looking down at her with a serious expression. "And yes, I'm cynical. But it hurts me to hear you be that way. You've got too much passion and too much life to live to be so jaded already."

"And you don't?"

His thumb brushed her lips, and a shade of sadness crossed his features. "I'm living the life that works for me. I have everything I need."

She looked back toward the main house, which was only a few squares of light from this distance. Of course he had everything he needed—a beautiful home and property, all the money he could want, and gorgeous women lining up to be with him. Most men would switch places with him in a second. But she sensed a deep loneliness behind his words.

She stepped closer and wound her arms around his waist, wishing she could peek inside her cowboy's brain. "But what about what you want?"

His lips curved a bit as he stared down at her. "Right now what I want is rubbing her body up against me and making me forget what we were talking about."

She laughed, loving that he could make her feel like a vixen with a few simple words. "I'm that distracting, huh?"

"You have no idea, freckles." He grabbed her by the backs of her thighs and hoisted her up, hooking her legs around his hips. "I've imagined getting you in my dungeon more times than I'd care to admit. Have imagined all the fun things I could do with this sexy body of yours."

She couldn't help the *yeah, right* snort that escaped her. "Sexy body? There are twelve-year-olds who have more curves than me."

His gaze turned lethal. "That just earned you a punishment, Charlotte. I'm getting real tired of you dismissing my compliments."

She winced. "I'm sorry. It's just . . ."

He set her down on her feet, cutting off her words, and grabbed her upper arm, the light mood from a moment before gone. "Let's go."

He led her away from Maggie and toward the wooden building looming against the dark skyline. "Where are you taking me?"

"My dungeon, Charlotte," he said, his words clipped. "I'm going to make sure you never doubt what I say about you again."

SIXTEEN

Charli's heart played a riotous beat as Grant guided her none too gently toward the barn. His jaw was set in a way that warned her to keep her mouth shut. She'd pissed him off. Again. She didn't know whether to run from him or throw herself at his mercy.

But for some reason, neither protest nor apology would form on her lips. She feared the unknown, of what lay behind those big barn doors, but she didn't fear *him*. Somehow being dragged into a barn in the middle of freaking nowhere by a guy she barely knew felt right. Part of her *wanted* his wrath, wanted to see him yank off that stoic mask.

Yep, she was officially certifiable.

He pulled up short before they reached the large doors and turned to her. With rough hands, he yanked off her robe and then took a pocketknife from his belt.

"Stay still," he said, his tone deadly calm. The blade grazed her skin as he slipped the knife under the waistband of her panties. She held her breath and squeezed her eyes shut, but instead of going cold with terror, her body heated, her sex dampening as the knife sliced through the cotton/silk. Good God, why would *that* turn her on?

He repeated the process on the other side, then tugged the panties off. He held the shredded material in his hand, no doubt feeling how wet they were. He cocked an eyebrow at her, but didn't comment on it. "Lose the shoes. You walk in with nothing."

"Yes, sir." She slipped out of her shoes and wrapped her arms around herself, not sure if she was shivering from the night air or the way Grant was eyeing her.

Finally, he reached in his pocket and pulled out a key to unlock the barn. The massive door swung open with a loud creak, piercing the silence around them. Was this really where his dungeon was? Was he going to make her lie in hay? Her skin itched at the thought.

But when they stepped in and he flipped on the lights, she realized hay was the last thing she needed to worry about. The space had been totally converted. Thick beams supported the impossibly high wood-planked ceiling, and large skylights let the moonlight in. There was also an open second level, presumably what used to be the storage portion of the barn, flanking both sides.

But what dominated her line of sight was the massive bed in the center of the room and the iron ring hanging over it. To a casual observer, the ring would look like a light fixture, some sort of medieval chandelier to hold candles. But as Charli's eyes trailed up the chain that went all the way to the apex of the pitched ceiling, she knew it had nothing to do with lighting.

Other equipment and cabinets filled different areas, but as his gaze traveled over the room, she found herself overwhelmed. It was like landing on another planet where she didn't quite speak the language. She wet her lips and looked to Grant, shutting everything else out.

He crossed his arms, his anger still simmering right below the surface. "Get onto the bed on your knees and face the right wall."

She glanced at the bed. Hesitated.

"Now," he said, his voice booming in the cavernous space.

She winced and hurried over the bed, scrambling into position. The mattress was firm beneath her knees, and the dark red sheets were the only adornment. No fluffy pillows, no comforter. This was not a place for sleeping.

Grant walked over in no hurry, his boots thudding against the tiled floor like the slow, steady beat of a bass drum. "Lift your arms above your head, Charlotte."

This time she knew not to hesitate. He disappeared from her line of sight as she raised her arms. The sound of metal grinding against metal skittered over her skin, raising her anxiety. She looked up and saw the iron ring moving downward. *Oh, shit.* She peeked over her shoulder to find Grant leaning against one of the supporting beams, his finger on a switch.

"Eyes forward."

She dragged her gaze back to the opposite wall and tried to steady her breathing. *In. Out. In* . . . The cranking noise stopped, and music with a heavy beat but no words replaced it. Grant walked over and stood against the edge of the bed, filling the space in front of her. He ran his hands along her lifted arms, leaving a trail of goose bumps in his wake, then circled soft rope around both her wrists. "Tonight I was planning to take my time and bind you in a beautiful pattern, was going to be gentle with you since you're new to this."

He threaded the other end of the ropes through holes in the contraption above her head and pulled, leaving hardly any slack. She rubbed her lips together, nervous words crawling up her throat. "I'm sorry, I—"

"I don't remember giving you permission to speak," he said, knotting the rope and giving her a quelling look.

She choked down her protest.

"It's too late for apologies, freckles." He checked the ropes and her wrists. "You're my sub. When you put yourself down, you're insulting me and my tastes." He grabbed her chin and brought his face close to hers. "And that pisses me the fuck off, you understand?"

She winced, his words as effective as that smack to her cheek earlier.

"Yes, sir," she said, her voice barely loud enough to be heard over the music.

He released her chin and made a frustrated noise. "You think your tits are too small?"

She looked down to the corner of the bed, shame burning through her. Wasn't this supposed to be fun? If he was going to enumerate her many flaws, she'd never be able to handle it. The word *Texas* hovered at the back of her throat.

"You know what I see when I look at them?" He cradled her left breast, then drew her nipple between his thumb and forefinger until it plumped. "I see pretty pink nipples that darken and harden at the slightest touch. I see breasts that are so beautifully sensitive that you have the rare talent to come from that stimulation alone."

Something cold and metallic touched her nipple. She glanced down right as Grant tightened the tiny clamp around her flesh. She gasped, the quick snap of pain and pleasure catching her off guard.

He gave the other breast the same treatment, and then tugged on the light chain connecting the two clamps. Her head tipped back, the dual sensations shooting straight downward as if the clamps were connected to her clit instead of her breasts. "Shit."

He gave her a dark smile as he cupped her sex and slid a finger in with ease. "Mmm, see what I mean? So hot and slick already. Responsiveness trumps cup size any day."

She whimpered, her body clenching around him, needing more. The safe word died on her lips.

He pulled his hand away and brought it to his mouth, sucking her arousal from his finger. "Responsive *and* sweet."

The iron rattled above her as she shifted her weight, her need for his touch making her restless.

He flicked her clamped nipple, causing her to yelp. "Calm down, Charlotte. Patience is a virtue."

She clenched her jaw at the sting and had to bite back a sharp retort.

He gave a low chuckle. "Keep looking at me like that, and I'll make you wait even longer. This is not about what you want. This is about taking the punishment that you've earned, about hearing what I'm trying to get through that hard head of yours."

Her wrists wriggled in the bindings. Even with him goading her, her body was getting hotter, wetter. She didn't understand the response. She dropped her focus to the sheets.

"Better," he said, approval coloring his tone. "Now spread your knees."

She did as she was told and fought hard to keep her eyes down and not peek at what he was doing. But curiosity won.

Grant turned to the large armoire that flanked the wall behind him and opened the doors. Charli had to hold back her gasp as the contents came into view. Shelves of items in boxes filled the interior, but the instruments hanging on the inside of the cabinet doors were what drew her attention. A coiled whip, lengths of rope, a riding crop, what looked to be a cane of some sort, and any number of other things she couldn't name.

Fear rippled over her. Fear and something else . . .

Grant turned back around, a small box in his hand. He gave her a wry smile as his gaze drifted over her body. "I see you like my collection."

Her brows knitted. Did she? Picking apart the difference between fright and anticipation was growing murkier and murkier.

"Stop trying to analyze your response, sweet Charlotte. I can hear your cogs grinding from here. That's not going to do you any good." He stepped closer and pulled something out of the box. "Maybe this will help you get out of your head."

She glanced down to see a flesh-colored dildo in his palm. The chains rattled again, her heart now pounding louder than the rock music filtering through the barn.

He tossed the empty box to the side and then tapped her inner thigh with his free hand. "Spread your legs wider."

She did, her body acting before her mind caught up. She flinched when he dragged the cool silicone along her folds, but her muscles trembled in anticipation. He tucked a finger inside her, readying her, then moved his hand away and inserted the dildo. She groaned, the fit tight, the sensation intense. Her fingers flexed against the ropes above as he slid it out a bit, then back in, nudging it deeper. God, was he going to be this slow and methodical about everything? He was going to drive her mad.

"Very nice, Charlotte. Now squeeze your thighs together. You're not allowed to let it slip out."

She shifted her legs back into position, her body clasping the invasion. Grant removed something from his pocket and pressed a button. Charli's body arched as the dildo hummed to life, vibrating inside her. "Oh . . ."

Her face tilted toward the ceiling as sensation radiated outward, crawling over her nerve endings.

"That's right, darlin'. Give over to it." Grant gave a little tug on the chain between her breasts and she jerked, the combination of pain and pleasure almost sending her right over into orgasm. She yanked at her bindings, desperate for that release, for that one little extra touch that would trigger it. But he didn't give it to her.

Grant brushed her cheek, his expression surprisingly tender. "You don't like your body. You think you're too tall, not soft and curvy enough." He stepped back toward his cabinet and selected a riding crop. He faced her, rolling the shaft of the crop between his fingers. "You know what I see?"

She shook her head, fighting to stay focused despite the throbbing need overtaking her body. "No, sir."

"I see an athlete, a woman who can endure more than most, a woman who I don't have to worry about crushing when she's beneath me." He walked forward and circled the tip of the crop around her navel. "A woman I can play rough with."

He snapped the crop against her mound, hitting right above her clit, and her control nearly shattered. She moaned and canted her hips forward. "Oh, God."

He smiled and walked around the bed, disappearing from view. But she could sense when he stopped behind her, feel his stare. "I see a woman who isn't afraid to bungee jump off a bridge or go after what she wants. A girl who likes to play at the edge."

Grant traced the tip of the crop down her spine, sliding it over her sweat-dampened skin. "And that, sweet Charlotte, is the most beautiful fucking thing I've ever seen."

She heard the riding crop slice through the air before it landed with a sharp smack against her ass. She reared up with a soft moan, the sensation foreign but somehow exactly what she craved—painful and sweet all at once. The vibrator shifted inside her and she clamped her thighs tight again, making sure not to let it slide out.

Grant hit her again on the back of her thigh, then on the other cheek. She writhed against the sting, somehow aching for more.

"That's right, darlin'. Look how perfectly you respond. Let go and I'll take you under."

He increased the speed, landing blow after blow along her ass, her thighs, her back and shoulders. *Smack. Smack. Smack.* The rhythm of his swats matched the driving beat of the music, sending her senses into a tumble. Adrenaline flooded her system and her brain began to buzz, a soft, pleasant hum she could get lost in. She sagged against the bindings, sweat glazing her skin and her body pulsing with need. Her sex throbbed around the vibrator, silently begging for the real thing.

Her fingers curled, her palms opening and closing, searching for a hold on something as everything inside her seemed to be breaking open. Her breath rasped out of her. "Grant, sir, please . . ."

The crop stilled, but the vibrating inside intensified as Grant apparently dialed up the strength. A groan rumbled out of her, and his boots came back into view. She closed her eyes, needing every ounce of focus to fight off her release. Her whole body began to tremble.

The smooth leather touched her folds. "Come for me, Charlotte."

Grant tapped the crop against her sex with a quick, smarting snap, and all semblance of her control fragmented into a million flecks of sensation. She screamed, her voice echoing through the cavernous space, as her orgasm flooded every nerve ending.

Grant continued to tap her with the crop, though with a softer hand, as her release rolled through her. Then, when she thought every ounce of energy had been wrung from her, he pulled off the nipple clamps, sending fiery pain spiraling in with the bliss. Another orgasm chased the first, short and intense. And she could do nothing but let it have her. The blinding sensations had stolen any control she had left over her own response. She was merely a blissed-out passenger on Grant's train.

"That's it, my girl," Grant soothed. "Let it take you down."

When her body finally quieted and the vibrator had been turned off, she melted against the bindings, the rope the only thing keeping her upright. Cool fingers touched the abraded skin at her wrists, and the tension gave way. Grant lowered her arms to her sides, rubbing the numbness from them, and then slowly eased the vibrator out of her. When he stepped back, she managed to raise her head and found him staring at her with the look of a man starved.

The sight stole her breath. Even though she knew she had to be a sight with streaked makeup and sweaty skin, she felt . . . beautiful.

He leaned forward and swiped moisture from her cheeks with his thumbs. "Are those good tears or bad ones, freckles?"

Confused, she reached up, touched her face. Had she been crying?

"I should give you a break," he said gruffly and moved to take a step back.

But with speed she wouldn't have thought herself capable of at the moment, she grabbed his forearm, halting him. "Please. Don't. I need . . ." His pulse beat hard and steady beneath her fingertips as she formed her thoughts.

Yes, part of her felt spent, like she'd been sliced right open and emptied, but something deep and indefinable yearned for more. Yearned for Grant. Inside her. On her. Invading her every cell. She wanted him to overtake her. To lose herself in him.

"I need you," she whispered.

His expression darkened, a sinister and wholly carnal desire flashing through his blue eyes. He pulled his arm from her grip. "Undress me."

Her blood surged at the words alone. She was going to be able to touch him, to see him. She scooted to the edge of the bed and stood on still shaky legs. "I'd love to."

She went to work on the buttons of his shirt, taking her time and enjoying the heat of his skin beneath her fingers. Without taking his eyes off her, he shrugged it off his shoulders, revealing a broad chest dusted with dark hair—sexy and masculine with a few scars from battles he'd probably never tell her about. She touched one smooth slash high on his shoulder, and he put his hand over hers, silently warning her.

She moved her hand away and went to the waistband of his jeans. Her fingertips traced over his hard belly, following the faint line of hair disappearing behind his jeans. She unbuttoned his fly and dragged the zipper down, finding no underwear beneath. His hard length sprang forth, and she dipped her hands into his open fly, unable to resist cupping and stroking him.

He grunted, a short, deep sound that told her he was more wound up than his expression revealed. "I didn't give you permission to touch."

Reluctantly, she pulled her hand back and dropped to her knees to pull off his boots. "I'm sorry, sir."

He asked her to remove his shoes and his jeans. Then when she stood again, he clamped a hand around her throat, pressing her collar into her skin in a possessive hold. "Apology accepted. On your back, sweet Charlotte."

She let him guide her down, his hand still on her neck as he climbed onto the bed with her. The sheets were cold against the sensitized skin of her backside, but all she could focus on was the man looming above her and the intoxicating feeling of being beneath his hand.

His hair fell across his forehead as he shifted his weight, planting his palms on each side of her and settling between her open thighs. He rubbed his cock along her still slick folds, sending sparks through her. "You look good with my collar and marks on you, freckles. You like wearing them?"

"I do." And it was the truth. She didn't want to study that fact at the moment, but knowing the welts on her back and rope burn on her wrists were his made her feel warm in all the right places—including squarely in her chest.

Fuck, she was in trouble.

Grant rose to his knees and turned, locking both of Charli's ankles into leather cuffs attached to the footboard, then positioned himself over her again. She tugged at the chains, but he knew there was only enough slack for her to bend her knees. Her body stiffened beneath him as a glimmer of fresh panic went through her.

"Breathe, darlin'."

She inhaled a few deep breaths, and as her instinctive response gave way, lovely surrender came to the surface. Her pupils dilated and her nipples, red and swollen from the clamps, hardened. God, she was perfect.

He could feel her wet heat pressing against his shaft and his balls tightened with want. She'd said she needed him. His gut had twisted at the plea. Had sent him entertaining the idea of extending this two-week training. She was everything he craved in a sub. Adventurous, feisty, and so fucking responsive it made his head spin. The things he could do with her, the edges they could find together. He could spend hours finding ways to draw that sexy whimper from her.

He glanced at the condom he'd placed on the bedside table, then discarded the thought. The urge to mark her, feel her against him without any barrier, gnawed at him. They'd both been tested and she'd put in her paperwork she was on birth control. "I don't want anything between us tonight, Charlotte. If that's not okay, tell me now."

"Screw condoms."

He smiled and pinned her arms above her, his palm flattening her forearms to the bed but avoiding her rope-abraded wrists. "You're so pink and swollen everywhere I could spend hours just nibbling and licking each part of you."

He bent down and circled the tip of his tongue over her abused nipple. She rewarded him with that sexy mewl of hers, and his cock stiffened to the point of no return. He had to have her. Right. Now. He lifted his head, then buried himself inside her without finesse. Another minute not inside her was a minute too long.

"Oh." She arched off the bed. The feel of her clenching around him, skin to skin, was almost too much pleasure for his body to compute. Her snug heat wrapped around him like a cashmere glove, drawing him deep. God, he'd forgotten how good that could feel.

He rocked back, sliding out, then sheathing himself again. The slow pace was insanity making, but he wanted to savor it, savor her.

He liked feeling her writhe beneath him when he pulled out, as if she couldn't bear to not have his cock filling her. She tilted her head back, eyes closed, and soft, begging words passed her lips.

He groaned and thrust into her again. Fuck, he loved having her beneath him, hearing her, feeling her. He kept one hand pressed down on her arms and moved his other hand back to her throat. Her eyelids snapped open, but her gaze was unfocused, enraptured. She liked him holding her like that. Her need for real surrender was palpable.

He increased his speed and put gentle pressure against her throat. Breath play was banned at The Ranch because he didn't want to take on the liability of untrained people using it on his property, but a firm neck hold could bring someone like Charli to a new edge. And he wanted to go there with her.

She moaned with every thrust and the chains rattled behind him as she tried to wrap her legs around him. Pressure built low and urgent in him, and he tilted his hips to grind his pelvis against her clit. "Go over with me, baby."

As if he'd flipped a switch, a cry ripped out of her, and her pussy spasmed around him. "Grant . . ."

"Fuck." He released her hands and neck, bracing his forearms on the side of her and pumping hard as pleasure shot down his spine and his cock swelled. His release exploded from him in pulses of pure, exquisite ecstasy.

Filling her. Marking her as his.

Mine, his mind whispered.

Mine.

When both their groans eased to soft panting, he let his head drop and ended up forehead to forehead with her, enjoying the quiet between them. Quivers continued to drift through them, gentle vibrations rolling over them as their bodies absorbed the aftershocks of their shared orgasm. They remained that way for a while, their heartbeats and breath slowing together, synchronizing . . . and then she reached up and touched his cheek.

He lifted his head to find her looking at him with soft eyes. She drew the pad of her thumb over his stubble. "Grant."

A simple word, but something cracked open inside him, her tenderness and his whispered name on her lips too much to bear. He no longer had the strength to stop himself—even when he knew it was the stupidest and cruelest move he could make.

He lowered his head, and he kissed her.

Kissed her like he meant it.

Because he did.

SEVENTEEN

Grant deepened the kiss as Charli's fingers threaded through his hair. Her lips were as soft as he'd imagined, her mouth hot and yielding. He wanted to lose himself in the kiss, to mold her against him and spend the rest of the night tangled up with her, idly exploring each other. But as he stroked his tongue along hers, images of the last woman he'd kissed filled his mind, pushing out the blissful moment of a second before. Raw emotion scraped at his insides, ugly guilt slashing at him. *No, no, no*. He broke off the kiss, pulling away as the massive barn seemed to close in around him.

Charli looked up at him with questions in her eyes. He pushed himself up and off of her, his heart thumping way too hard.

"Let me get you out of these." He turned abruptly to uncuff her legs, fumbling with the first one, his hands unsteady, his mind whirling.

Charli sat up on her elbows. "Is everything okay?"

He put his back to her and worked on the second cuff. *Run. Run. Run*. "It's fine. I'll get you out of these and then get the shower started so you can get cleaned up."

The cuff opened and the bed shifted as she pulled her legs toward her. He turned to find her hugging her knees to her chest and looking down at her toes. A little shiver went over her.

Fuck. He was being the world's worst dom. Her first big scene and instead of providing her with a cuddle and aftercare, he was in the middle of a goddamned panic attack. He took a deep breath, trying to get oxygen to his malfunctioning brain, and got up to grab robes from the drawer in the armoire and to shut off the music.

He donned one of the robes, then sat on the edge of the bed and wrapped the other one around her. He cupped her cheek, turning her face toward him, and forced his voice to sound calm. "You did beautifully, Charlotte. Perfect. Thank you for trusting me to take you that far."

She nodded and her eyes went shiny. She swiped at the tears with the back of her hand. "I'm sorry. I have no idea why I'm crying. I feel ridiculous."

"Don't apologize." He brushed a thumb over her cheek, then backed off when he saw his hands were still shaking. "Sometimes coming back down can do that. The whole thing can be overwhelming for a sub."

And the dom, he thought, anxiety rising in him like high tide. He lowered his hand to his side.

She tucked her arms into the sleeves of the robe and pulled it more tightly around herself, her entire posture closing to him. "That makes sense." She gave him a tight smile. "And a shower sounds great. That was a . . . thorough lesson."

Right, a lesson, that's what this was supposed to be. But if that were truly the case, he wouldn't feel so damn gutted right now. This had been a mistake. He should've known better than to take a chance with Charli. From the start, something about her had tested his control, had made him lose sight of his rules.

He'd fucking *kissed* her. He hadn't kissed anyone in over a decade. His throat felt like it had a fist closing around it. "I'll be right back."

He left her side, forcing himself to walk normally and not rush into the bathroom like he wanted to. When he reached it, he shut the door, pressed his back against it, and dragged his hands over his face. Sweat slicked his palms and his heart refused to slow down. *Calm the fuck down. It was just a kiss.*

He closed his eyes, expecting to see Rachel's face waiting there. But for the first time in as long as he could remember, he couldn't conjure up her image. Charli's worried expression dominated his vision instead. And that made him feel shittier than anything else could've. He'd screwed up everything tonight—breaking the vow he'd made to Rachel's memory and failing to provide Charli with the best experience she could have.

He needed to fix this. Now. He went to the sink, splashed some water on his face and got his breathing back to normal. Remembering what he was supposed to be doing in here, he turned on the shower to warm it up for Charli.

When he made his way back to the bed, Charli looked like she wanted to be anywhere but there. "You sure everything's okay? Did I do something wrong?"

"No, of course not." He sat on the edge of the bed with a heavy sigh. "It was me who did something wrong. I'm sorry I kissed you, Charli."

He didn't miss the wince she tried to hide. "Why are you sorry?" She attempted a smile. "Am I that horrible of a kisser?"

"No, of course not." He rubbed the back of his neck. "It's just, I got carried away. I shouldn't have done something . . . confusing."

She stared at him, her smile sinking, and the room seeming to chill around them.

"Confusing?" she asked, the word like a dagger. "Because what? I might get romantic notions?" She shook her head and scooted off the bed. "Don't worry, Grant. I'm far from confused. And I'm not stupid." She held her arms out to her sides. "I'm in a room you built specifically to fuck women. I'm not deluding myself into thinking that I'm special or that you have feelings for me or something. We had sex. We kissed. Big deal. Now, is the shower ready?"

Her speech had part of him wanting to grab her and tie her back down to the bed, show her that she wasn't some notch on his bedpost. But having her think that was better than her knowing about all the riotous emotions she kicked up in him, all the ugly stuff that kiss had brought to the surface. He needed to get through this night and find his bearings again. "Towels are in the bottom cabinet."

"Great." She turned on her heel and headed to the bathroom, closing the door none-too-gently behind her. The sound of the lock turning echoed through the barn.

She'd shut him out.

God, he was an asshole.

Charli walked outside through the main door of the barn, freshly showered and wearing the jeans and T-shirt she'd packed in her bag. She'd never been more ready in her life to be alone. The overwhelming sex had been enough to process, but Grant's kiss and subsequent retreat had her gray matter scrambled. She had so many clashing emotions going through her that her chest hurt more than the welts on her back.

She spied Grant sitting on a tree stump, staring out over the grounds, his forearms braced on his thighs. He somehow looked lost and right at home all at the same time—like being lost was his status quo. She took a deep breath, determined not to have another ridiculous emotional outburst in front of him, and headed his way.

He looked over at her when her shoe snapped a twig, his expression somber. "Hey."

She stuck her hands in her pockets, awkwardness filling the air around them. "Hey."

He turned his head, staring back out into the night. "I'm sorry I screwed things up tonight. I don't want you thinking that you're just another body to warm my bed. It's not like that."

She forced a casual shrug. "You told me upfront what this was. I wasn't expecting a fairy tale."

"Still doesn't excuse how I acted. It had nothing to do with you. Tonight was the best night I've had in a really long time."

She rolled a pebble under her shoe, contemplating his words. There was so much he wasn't telling her. She could feel whatever it was like a thick fog between them. When he'd pulled away from their kiss, he'd looked horrified. She should probably let it lie, but too many questions hung in the air. How was she supposed to go on with this ignoring that? "Grant, I need to know what happened in there."

He didn't look at her. "Nothing you need to worry about."

She pressed her lips together, counting to three before she spoke. "So all that shit about trust only applies to me? I'm supposed to trust you to tie me up, hit me, and put myself in your hands, but you can't even tell me why you freaked out over a simple kiss?"

He rubbed his palms on his jeans, staying quiet for a few long moments, then his shoulders dipped in resignation. "Have you ever made a promise to someone, Charli? Not something offhanded, but a real promise?"

"Yeah, I guess so." She'd promised her dad before he died that she'd go after her dream and not let anything stop her. That was going swimmingly. "Why?"

She thought he may have not heard her, but after a few moments, Grant finally looked at her, pain etching his features. "Well, that kiss broke a promise I've kept for a really long time."

The simple statement sucked all the wind out of her anger.

She knew then, recognized the grief, had seen it on her brothers' faces and in her own reflection when their dad has passed away. "You lost someone."

He stood, giving her a sad smile. "No, freckles, I lost everything. The wife I loved, an unborn son, and the life I thought I'd live."

Her heart fissured in her chest, the rawness in his admission making tears burn in her throat. A hundred questions popped into her head. What had happened? When had it happened? How? But those answers were inconsequential. All that mattered was the anguish she could see weighing down Grant's every limb. She stepped forward, wanting to touch him, wanting to do *something* to make it better, but unsure if he'd welcome her sympathy. "I'm so sorry. I shouldn't have pried."

He sighed as he reached out to grab her waist, tucking her against his chest and sitting his chin on top of her head. "It's okay. You deserved an explanation after I acted like a jackass tonight. Now you know."

I'm broken. He didn't say the words, but she heard them just the same.

"We don't have to continue this if it's bringing up bad stuff for you," she said, even though the thought of walking away from him already had regret strumming through her.

He angled back, looking down at her, a little smile trying to form on his lips even though the sadness still lingered in his eyes. "Oh, you're not getting off the hook that easily. You've got too much to learn. I'll be fine. I've lived with this a long time. Training will recommence tomorrow. I promise my past won't interfere again."

She returned his smile, but a gnawing worry settled in her stomach. She was going to have to get a hold of her emotions ASAP, because if she had any more nights like tonight, she was in deep shit. Grant was already seeping under her guards, and even if she was discovering she could appreciate a little physical pain, she wasn't up for emotional annihilation.

She could hold her own in a lot of competitions, but she'd never win against the dead love of his life.

EIGHTEEN

Grant leaned against the doorframe of Charli's cabin, fighting a chuckle as she teetered out from the bedroom on a pair of black heels. She looked smoking hot in the outfit he'd brought over. The snug gray pencil skirt hugged her hips just right and the tissue-thin silk blouse gave him a delicious glimpse of the lacy white bra she wore underneath. But the shoes, once again, were getting the best of her.

"Kelsey said those heels are an inch lower than the ones from last night," he offered, unable to hide his amusement.

"Praise God for that. The fall to the floor will be shorter."

He grinned. "You look fucking edible, though. So there's that."

She smirked, but he caught the flash of pleasure in her eyes at the compliment. She put a hand on the back of the couch to steady herself. "Thanks."

"Well, look at that, I gave you a compliment and you didn't shoot it down." He pushed off the doorframe. "You're learning. Two points to the pretty lady with no panties."

She rolled her eyes, and he made a mental note to pay her

back for that little nod of disrespect later. "So why am I dressed like this? I didn't see anyone else wearing this kind of thing at The Ranch."

He grabbed his Stetson, which he'd set on the entryway table when he'd come in, and secured it on his head. Then he put out a hand to her. "Oh, I never said we were going to The Ranch. Today I have an important business meeting with some distributors for the winery. And you, sweet Charlotte, are going to be my assistant."

Her eyes widened as she took a hesitant step forward and placed her hand in his. "What?"

"I gave my admin the day off, so I'll need someone to serve us the wine samples and cheese plates, to set up the slide projector, to take notes. That kind of thing." He drew her against him. "I'll need someone to dazzle them with hospitality."

"But—"

He slid his hands over her ass, loving the fact that she was bare underneath that tight little skirt. It took all he had not to lift it up and bend her right over the sofa. "You're going to do fine. And if you don't, you'll pay later. If you're rude to anyone, embarrass me in any way, or talk back to me in front of them, there will be a punishment."

She shuddered against him and he smiled inwardly. Charli would never admit it, but that little kernel of fear fed her. He could see it in the ways her pupils dilated the instant he mentioned possible punishment.

"Yes, sir. But what does this have to do with my training?"

He pressed a finger to her lips. "That's for me to determine and you not to worry about."

He'd figured out pretty quickly that Charli didn't have a femininity problem, she had a confidence problem. She expected people to be critical and steeled herself up for it, which inevitably came across as her being bristly and harsh. And he knew if he put her in a room of businessmen who were probably similar to that board of directors she was trying to impress, he could show her that she had everything she could possibly need to wow them.

He could honestly give a shit if she messed up in front of his colleagues, but he wanted to put the added pressure on her so she'd know how to pull it off when she had everything riding on her performance. Plus, a little role-playing would provide some much needed distance between the two of them. Things had gotten too raw last night. Too real. A fun little game was just what the doctor ordered.

He stepped back from Charli and removed something from the inner pocket of his jacket. "You look so prim and proper with your hair pinned up like that. I think these will be the perfect final touch."

He handed her the dark-rimmed glasses and her eyebrow arched. "Last I checked, I don't have a vision problem."

"The lenses aren't prescription. Put them on." She slid the glasses on, and he grinned. "Oh, what some of my members up at The Ranch would do to have you. Anyone with a naughty teacher or librarian fantasy would fall to his knees at your feet and beg."

She put her hand to her hip and tilted her head, batting her eyelashes in mock coyness. "What? You don't have one of those fantasies, cowboy?"

He grabbed her wrist and put her hand against his quickly hardening erection. "Not really. But maybe I have one about a hot little secretary."

Her fingers curled along the outline of his cock, stroked. "I'm not that kind of employee, Mr. Waters. Or that kind of girl."

Nice. Already she was slipping into character. "We'll see. I know how badly you need this job, Ms. Beaumonde."

He clasped her arm and moved her hand away before she pushed him past the point of self-control. "Let's go. If you make me late for my own business meeting, I'll be very unhappy."

And oh, what fun he'd have disciplining her for the tardiness.

Charli had to work hard to keep up with Grant's long strides as they headed over to the biggest building on the non-Ranch side of the property—home to Water's Edge Wines. Walking in heels along gravel was like learning to drive a stick shift on a steep hill; it took all of her concentration. While she worked on not face-planting, Grant explained that the main operation of Water's Edge and its employees worked out of a satellite office in Dallas, but that he liked to bring clients out here for meetings sometimes because they enjoyed seeing the vineyards.

Hearing him talk about his business, she could hear the pride in his voice, the dedication. This was no side business for him. It was a passion.

When they reached the building, he opened the door for her and let her walk inside first. The inside was rustic, not unlike the building at The Ranch, but there was a refined elegance present as well. The wall opposite the entrance was covered with smooth river rock, and a hidden spotlight projected the logo for Water's Edge Wines onto the stones. Water slid over the rocks, making the logo seem to ripple before falling into a fountain below.

To the right was a curved reception desk. A tall, gray-haired woman rose from behind the desk, greeting Charli and Grant with a warm smile. "Hello, Mr. Waters. Everyone is already here and set up in the conference room."

"Thank you, Madeleine. I should have everything covered from here. Charlotte is going to assist me in the meeting today. You can head back to your normal post."

Madeleine gave Charli a sly look, like they were sharing some unspoken secret, then nodded. "Very well."

Madeline glided from behind the desk with an elegance Charli could only dream of having. She walked with the confidence of royalty, the effect making her appear much younger than she probably was. Madeleine put a hand on Grant's biceps as she passed and gave him a little squeeze and a wink. "Good boy."

Charli watched her leave, a little stunned, then turned to Grant. "Why do I feel like I missed a joke?"

He shook his head, but seemed amused. "Maddy isn't just an employee, she's a good friend and one of the fiercest dommes you'll ever meet. She's been badgering me to take on a new sub for months. Told me celibacy will age me before my time."

"But how did she know what—who I was?"

Grant put his hand to the small of her back, guiding her forward. "Apparently, her radar for submissives is more finely tuned than mine."

Charli pressed her lips together to keep from smiling. That couldn't possibly have been Grant admitting he'd been wrong about her. That maybe his initial assessment of her had been a swing and a miss. She should buy a helmet—the sky might collapse.

"Gloating isn't becoming, Ms. Beaumonde," he said, his tone as cool as the air in the quiet hallway. "You just earned yourself a reprimand from the boss after this meeting is done."

The smile she'd been fighting broke through anyway. "Sorry, sir."

He stopped in front of pair of frosted glass doors. "Now don't embarrass me. I expect you to be professional. These people are important."

The warning had her grin sagging and her back straightening. Nerves settled around her like high-strung little birds, twittering all the what-ifs in her ear. She and Grant may be playing roles, but the people on the other side of that door were real. Grant's business and reputation weren't a game. She rubbed her lips together, smoothing her lipstick, and nodded her readiness.

He pushed open the doors and she followed behind him, focusing on putting one foot in front of the other. The last thing she needed was to trip and fall. The fearsome image of her doing a belly flop and exposing her lack of underwear to a room full of businessmen had her walking with the deliberateness of a gymnast on a balance beam.

The long conference table was filled with men in suits and one woman in a smart maroon blouse. Conversation was humming between them all, but quieted when they noticed Grant.

"Afternoon, everyone," Grant said, flashing one of his lazy cowboy smiles toward the room. "I appreciate y'all venturing out to the country to visit today."

Charli laced her fingers together in front of her, trying to blend into the background. The less she was noticed, the less chance she had of doing something wrong.

Greetings were exchanged, and Grant let everyone make introductions. Most everyone was involved with either a restaurant chain or a gourmet store—all places that could stock Grant's wine. Grant turned to her. "Charlotte, I have some brochures about the new line we're rolling out. They're in the bottom drawer of that file cabinet in the corner. Please retrieve them and make sure everyone has a copy."

"Yes, sir." She headed to the back corner of the room, happy to have a task as Grant flipped open a laptop and turned on the slide projector to begin his presentation. When she reached her destination, she realized the file cabinet was half blocked by a man with shaggy blond hair who'd pushed his chair back a bit so he could hook an ankle over his knee. He was making a note on the legal pad in his lap and didn't seem to notice he was in the way.

She leaned down, keeping her voice low "Excuse me, I'm sorry, but I need to get by."

He glanced up, his blue-eyed gaze colliding with hers. The smile he gave her could probably slay a cheerleading squad in one fell swoop. He was pretty in that way that was almost too perfect. She preferred the more rugged look, like Grant, but even she wasn't immune to this version of male beauty. He rocked forward in his seat, putting both feet on the ground, and rolled the chair to the side. "No problem."

Once he was out of the way, she moved toward the file cabinet, eyeing it warily. Grant had said the bottom drawer. Her pencil skirt wasn't overly short, but it was formfitting and there was no bending over easily. She peeked up at the front of the room and caught Grant watching her even though he was speaking easily about his new products. His lips tugged up at the corner, letting her know he was well aware of the predicament he'd put her in.

Dammit. She looked at the cabinet again, and noticed Grant wasn't the only one keeping an eye on her. Blondie gave her a sideward glance as he made more notes. Apparently, he had figured out her quandary, too. Not that he was offering any help or anything. With a huff, she attempted to get to her knees gracefully. Using the rocking motion she'd failed in the intro class, she managed to hit the floor without a sound and without exposing her ass to the world. Win!

She grinned and Blondie coughed, the noise sounding suspiciously like a muffled laugh, but she pretended to ignore him. The file drawer was full of materials, but she found the stack of brochures Grant had requested and grabbed them. Of course, now she had to get back up. She used her free hand to propel herself upward off the floor, but before she got to a full stand, her heel caught in the carpet and she had to reach out for the wall, dropping the papers all over the floor.

"Shit."

All heads turned toward her. She cringed, her cheeks going hot. So much for blending into the background. Blondie jumped up from his seat to help her.

Grant pinned her with a hard look, like an arrow shooting

across the room and fastening her to the wall. “Is there a problem, Charlotte?”

His words should have embarrassed her—he was admonishing her in front of all these people—but hell if she didn’t go wet from his authoritative tone. Her nipples went as hard as pebbles against the thin blouse. *Fuck.* “I’m sorry, sir. Just a little clumsy.”

He gave a put-upon sigh, letting her know she’d just earned a mark in the punishment column. “Kade, thank you for helping. Now back to what I was saying . . .”

Grant returned to his presentation, and Charli crouched down as best she could to help Kade. “Thank you, I’ve got it, really.”

“Clearly,” he said, his smile wry. He gathered the last of the brochures and handed them to her, then took her wrist to help her to her feet. His thumb brushed across the abrasion marks Grant’s rope had left. He shook his head, as if disappointed.

He bent close to her ear. “His?”

It was a simple word. A simple question. But the idea behind it had something strange welling up inside her. An ache that seemed to open up a fissure right down the center of her chest. She nodded even though it wasn’t true. She wasn’t Grant’s. Not really. Would never be.

“Lucky bastard,” Kade whispered before returning to his seat.

She stood there for too long. Kade’s interest was flattering. A week ago, a guy like him would’ve never given her a second glance. But for some reason, she wanted to cry. She stared at Grant, watching him captivate the room with his knowledge and his easy humor. He was so vibrant, so full of confidence. But she knew what lay beneath it, saw how lonely and lost he’d been last night.

She’d only seen that look on one other man—her father. And that grief over love lost had sucked the joy out of the last fifteen years of her dad’s life. A broken heart had killed him slowly and painfully.

And she'd be damned if she was going to stand by and let Grant do the same thing to himself. She may not be able to compete with the memory of his wife, but after that kiss last night, maybe she had a shot of reminding him he could feel *something*.

Because like it or not, she was starting to feel more than lust toward the cocky cowboy.

Maybe it was time for the trainee to turn trainer.

NINETEEN

Charli kept herself together for the rest of the meeting. She served cheese and samples of the wines, helped hand out more documents, and adjusted the slide projector when Grant asked. She was finally getting used to the heels and managed not to trip again. But as soon as she got a minute free, she scrawled a note on the back of one of the handouts and set it on top of Kade's legal pad.

She pretended to take a strong interest in the presentation, but she didn't miss the curious look or the barely concealed smile when Kade read her note. When she refilled his water glass a few minutes later, the slight nod from him was all she needed. The plan was a go.

Now the question was, could she actually pull it off?

Grant wrapped up the meeting, and everyone started to gather their things to head out. Many went toward the front of the room to shake hands and talk shop with Grant, and the room grew exponentially louder as people chatted amongst themselves. But after exchanging a few quick words with the man next to him, her recruited partner in crime made his way over to her.

Kade wasn't as tall as Grant, but he still had an inch or two on her, and he walked with the swagger of a guy who knew he didn't have to try too hard. When he got close enough, he put out his hand. "We weren't properly introduced. Kade Vandergriff."

His accent was refined twang—old Texas money, she'd guess. She gave him her hand. "Charlotte Beaumonde."

Instead of shaking her hand, he brought it to his mouth and laid a kiss on it. "A pleasure, Charlotte."

Her gaze shifted toward the front of the room, and she caught Grant peering in her direction. She looked back to Kade and put on her best attempt at a seductive smile. "Thank you so much for helping me, Mr. Vandergriff . . . with the brochures. I can't believe I was so clumsy."

"No problem. I can't resist a beautiful woman in distress." He leaned a shoulder against the wall, putting his back to Grant and the front of the room, caging her a bit in the corner. Amusement colored his features. "I have to say you must be a particularly brave sub or one who gets off on being bratty. Baiting your dom isn't usually wise, especially if you're dealing with someone like Grant."

She tilted her head and laughed a little, like he'd said something wildly charming. "I have my reasons."

"Wish I could stick around and see the ramifications. I have a feeling it will be quite entertaining to watch."

He said it with good humor, but her cheeks warmed anyway. They were putting on a show for someone else's benefit, but she could sense Kade was being genuine. He was flirting with her and helping her out because he found her attractive. The thought gave her a secret little thrill. Maybe this whole thing *was* transforming her. A week ago she would've never felt confident enough to even faux flirt with someone like Kade.

"He's watching us," she said, leaning a bit closer to Kade. "Maybe he doesn't mind."

"We'll see." Kade's voice had dropped to a conspiratorial level.

"Want the true test? I'm going to touch you, Charlotte. If he really sees you as his, that'll piss him off more than anything."

She bit her lip, attempting to look coquettish, and Kade reached out to push a hair that had escaped her French twist behind her ear. His fingers lingered at her nape a bit too long.

"You're quite enticing, Charlotte. I have a feeling you keep a dom on his toes. When your training ends with Grant, you should look me up."

"You're sweet." And he was—sexy even, but all she could think about was the man at the front of the room. Grant glanced over from his conversation when Kade's fingers were still against her skin. Grant's lips pressed into a hard line, but he turned back to the man he was talking with.

Her heart sunk. Damn. Maybe this wasn't going to work at all. Maybe what she'd thought had happened between them last night really wasn't anything more than sex. Maybe she was the only one developing a stupid attachment.

Epic fail, Beaumonde.

Grant couldn't even hear the words coming out of Chef Lane Donovan's mouth. Blood was roaring in Grant's ears, and his temperature was rising faster than the desert in summer. What the fuck was Kade Vandergriff doing with Charli?

Seducing her?

By the looks of it—yes. Charli couldn't seem to stop smiling, and the fucker had just touched her. Touched *his* sub.

Asshole.

Kade was a friend, a colleague, and a member at The Ranch. A good guy. But right now Grant had the urge to throttle him. Grant dragged his attention back to Lane. "Can I give you a call on Monday and we can discuss the details? I want to make sure we get you exactly what you need to complement your spring menu."

"No problem." Lane reached out for a handshake. "I've got some time before I need to confirm the wine list. We can get the details worked out next week."

Out of the corner of his eye, Grant saw Charli put a hand to Kade's chest in that oh-stop-it thing women did. He ground his teeth together. Well, Charli had certainly honed her flirting confidence in the last few days. With a quick good-bye to his friend, he freed himself from his conversation with Lane and headed toward the back of the room, forcing himself to be calm. This wasn't a playroom at The Ranch; the same rules didn't apply.

But Charli's eyes widened when she caught sight of him coming her way, so his expression must have been more charging bull than he'd intended. Grant laid a hand on Kade's shoulder, squeezed firmly enough to make a point. "Vandergriff, glad to see you could make it out here today."

Kade turned around, wearing an easy smile, and shook Grant's hand. "Of course. Your wines always do well in our locations, so I wanted to see what the new products were going to be."

"And I see you've already met Charlotte," Grant added.

Kade gave Charli a too-friendly look. "Yes, she was telling me her position with you is temporary, so I was letting her know that I'm in the market for a permanent . . . assistant if she was interested."

The words and the unspoken meaning behind them were like a fist to the jaw. Grant's fingers flexed, the urge to pull Charli to his side almost impossible to deny. But Vandergriff wasn't saying anything that wasn't true. Grant's agreement with Charli was a short one. If she discovered she liked the submissive role, she could move on to whichever dom she wanted. And Kade was a great one. Hell, if Charli had been a normal trainee, he'd already be looking for which dom to match her with at the end of training. And Kade would've probably hit the list.

But dammit if Grant didn't feel like punching out every one of

Kade's perfectly straight teeth at the thought. And that feeling was one of the most dangerous ones he'd had in a while. He couldn't feel territorial about Charli. She was going to walk away in a little over a week. Even if he offered to extend their arrangement, she'd never settle for what he was willing to give. She'd naturally gravitate to doms like Kade who were in the market for a relationship, who wouldn't flinch at the idea of a kiss or sleeping in the same bed, who'd be capable of truly loving her.

Something tightened in his chest. *Fuck*. What was going on with him? He wasn't this guy. He was possessive with his subs, but he didn't do jealousy. The feeling was so foreign he almost hadn't recognized it.

Whatever attachment he was forming to Charli needed to be broken now. She wasn't really his, and he needed to stop acting like she was going to be. This was training. And fucking. And fun. In a few days they were both going back to their own lives. He needed to get that through his thick skull.

He sucked in a deep breath, bracing himself for what he was about to do. "Charlotte, it is highly inappropriate to discuss *employment* with someone else while you're still working with me."

She looked down, the fake glasses sliding down her nose a bit. "Sorry, sir. I didn't think it was a big deal."

"This is going to require disciplinary action," he said, his voice sharp but low enough so that no one else in the room would hear.

Her head snapped up. "What? But—"

He raised a finger, quieting her protest. "Don't try to backpedal now. I need to discuss a few things with Kade, then you and I are going to have a chat."

Grant clapped Kade on the back. "You got a few minutes, Vandergriff? I'd like to iron out the details about the tastings you wanted to set up at your locations."

Kade's surprise was evident, but he recovered quickly, smoothing his expression. "I could probably stay for a bit."

"Great. Come with me." Grant nailed Charli with a hard glare. "Ms. Beaumonde, get this room back in order. Then I expect you in my office. Dawdle and you'll regret it. It's the door at the end of the hall."

Fear flared in her eyes, and he could see her pulse hopping against her throat, but she nodded. "Yes, sir."

He turned around and headed out of the conference room with Kade at his side. Grant was going to fix his little jealousy problem and make this good for Charli, but boy, was it going to take every ounce of his willpower to allow it to happen.

TWENTY

Charli stood in front of Grant's closed office door, trying to hold herself up on shaky resolve. Voices murmured on the other side. Kade was obviously still with Grant. And she had a feeling he may not be going anywhere anytime soon.

What the hell had she gotten herself into? She'd tried to reverse the rules on Grant, and it had completely backfired. Instead of stirring up his possessiveness, she'd managed to inspire him to bring in someone else.

Clearly, he didn't have any feelings for her. This was simply a game. Sex. Power play. An arrangement. Her insides twisted at the realization, but she knew it'd been a long shot anyway. How could she expect him to feel anything for her when they still hardly knew each other? She'd been ridiculous to think she could drag him out of the cave he'd locked himself in when his wife had died.

She needed to accept this fact and enjoy their arrangement for what it was worth—great sex. An adventure with a man who could coax her body to heights she hadn't known existed. She was going to have to tamp down her own misguided emotions and focus on the physical, on the way her body responded to him. Even with the emotional letdown, knowing what was on the other side of this door had her woefully turned on—albeit slightly terrified. She could do this. Keep it on the surface.

Men did it all the time. And if she knew anything about herself, it was that she could go toe-to-toe with any man on just about anything.

After one deep, cleansing breath, she knocked on the door.

"Come in." Grant's baritone cut through the door like the thing was made of rice paper instead of solid oak.

She turned the knob and slowly opened it, the creak of the hinges echoing through the now-empty building. When she stepped inside, she had to catch her breath. Sitting behind a massive wooden desk, Grant looked every bit the angry boss. He'd taken off his suit coat and hat, and his shirtsleeves were rolled to the elbows, a move she was starting to recognize as a harbinger. A hot shiver raced right down to her toes.

Kade sat in a chair on the other side of the desk, relaxed, his ankle resting on the opposite knee. He had his ever-present legal pad on his lap, notes scrawled across it. He gave her a quick glance, the deep blue of his eyes unreadable, then went back to his notes. She cleared her throat, feeling like she'd intruded on their business meeting. "You wanted to see me, sir?"

"I hired you to pour coffee and answer phones. I did not hire you to make a scene, curse in front of my colleagues, or flirt shamelessly with my clients," Grant said, his voice sterner than she'd ever heard it. "You put Mr. Vandergriff in quite an awkward position."

She bit the inside of her cheek. Even though she knew this was part of the game, the admonishment had her looking at a spot on the hardwood floor. "I apologize."

He gave a heavy sigh and leaned forward, forearms on the desk. "Charlotte, I'm starting to doubt your commitment to the position. Maybe this isn't the right job for you."

She lifted her face to him. Was he actually doubting her dedication to him and the training, or was this all part of a script she wasn't privy to? Either way she was ready to prove how wrong he was. "Please, Mr. Waters. I can do better. Give me another chance. I need this . . . job."

And as the words slipped past her lips she realized how true they were. This had gone beyond some fun training, some way to get her promotion. A part of her now needed this, craved it. Craved *him*. The thought of walking out and just . . . stopping and going back to her regular life gave her a panicky feeling.

Ah, hell, she was so screwed.

Grant gave her an up-and-down perusal, his eyes cool. "Lock that door behind you, Ms. Beaumonde. Perhaps we can work something out."

She kept her gaze locked with Grant's and reached behind her to turn the lock on the door. The grind of the metal was deafening in the heavy silence of the room.

Grant rose from behind the desk and stepped toward her, his footfalls echoing off the floor. She remained rooted to her spot as he circled around her like a tiger deciding which part of his prey to tear into first. Kade's gaze met hers, his interest evident, and Grant clamped a hand around the nape of her neck, startling her.

"Charlotte, verbal reprimands seem to be lost on you," he said, his grip tightening. "Maybe you need something a little more tangible to remind you to listen."

She swallowed hard as he nudged her forward toward the desk. He stopped along the edge, then pushed her flat against the surface, spreading her upper body across the top of the desk and removing her glasses. The angle and the high heels pushed her ass high, the position making her feel hopelessly vulnerable to him.

Hot palms cupped her ass through the thin fabric of her skirt, Grant's thumbs tracing the line between her cheeks. Warmth leaked through her system, making her nipples tighten against the desk's surface and wet need gather between her thighs. "Ah, will you look at that, Vandergriff. Apparently, Ms. Beaumonde is forgetful at home, too. Looks like she forgot to put on her panties today."

Charli watched as Kade got to his feet and then disappeared from her line of sight when he moved next to Grant. Fingers found their way beneath the hem of her skirt and tugged upward. A little cry of surprise passed her lips as one of them shoved the tight skirt all the way to her hips, exposing everything.

"Very nice." Kade's voice was soft, appreciative. A hand caressed her bare skin. Kade's. His fingertips didn't have the roughness of Grant's.

"She's sexy, isn't she?" Grant said, a tinge of pride in his words. His callused hand moved between her legs and found her slick folds. "I can barely look at her without getting hard."

She closed her eyes, trying to calm herself. Her body was revving like a race car engine. She didn't want to like this. Didn't want to think about the kind of girl this probably made her. The feminist in her was flailing about, but the protest was useless. Some part of her needed this. She couldn't ever remember feeling as wantonly female as she did right now. Two gorgeous men looking at her and touching her like she was some sort of prize.

Grant slid two fingers inside her, coaxing a quiet moan from her. "Well, well, Ms. Beaumonde, maybe I've underestimated your skill set. If you feel as good around my cock as you do around my fingers, I may have to reevaluate your daily duties."

She kept her eyes closed as he worked his magic, delving inside her, then sliding slippery fingers over her clit. "I'll do whatever you need me to, sir."

"Kade, I think she's having a little too much fun," Grant said. "This is supposed to be a reprimand first, and fun second. Why don't you remind her of that?"

"Happy to."

Before she could register what Grant had said, a hard slap rocked her backside. She cried out as the stinging rippled across her skin like a heat wave, waking up every receptor inside her. Kade clearly wasn't going to be tentative. She barely had time to suck in another breath before another smack hit her other cheek.

The pain may have been too much in isolation, but as Grant's hand continued to work her pussy, she felt the two ends of the pain/pleasure spectrum braiding together inside her, coalescing into that potent mix she was learning to feed on.

Kade didn't pause in his mission. The slap of palm on skin echoed in her ears mixing with her own breathy noises. The side of her face pressed into the smooth surface of the desk as she inadvertently braced herself for the blows. But instead of shrinking away from the spanking, she found her hips tilting upward of their own volition, her legs spreading to provide them both better access. Her thoughts began to blur at the edges, her brain drifting to that place it'd gone to the previous night where all that existed was sensation and the sound of Grant's voice. The tension began to leach out of her muscles.

She lost track of how long, but Kade's swats finally came to an end, and Grant's fingers slipped from her. Gentle kisses pressed against the tingling skin of her rear, both men simultaneously soothing her and dialing up her need. A hot tongue circled the entrance of her pussy, and her back curved as a hard shudder went through her.

"Your taste is so sexy, sweet Charlotte," Grant said, his words like chocolate melting over her. "I could spend all afternoon licking your pretty little cunt and making you beg for release. Kade, have a taste."

"It'd be my pleasure." She heard the shift of clothing as Kade adjusted his position, then his tongue was on her, teasing her throbbing clit. Grant's hands gripped her cheeks, spreading her wide, giving the other man complete access. His thumbs brushed across her back entrance, featherlight touches that seemed to increase the pleasure in her tenfold.

"Oh, God." She let out a whimper, her body going achy and desperate. "Please."

"Please what, Charlotte? Be careful what you're begging for," Grant warned, though there was something darkly enticing in his voice.

She dug her nails into the edges of the desk, trying to hold off orgasm as the two men pushed her closer and closer to the brink. "I'm going to come."

Both of them stopped touching her in an instant. Footsteps echoed in her ears, then a hand was twisting in her hair. Grant's voice was low and hot against her ear. "I decide when it's time for that, Charlotte. And right now, you've gone and gotten us both hard. Take care of that, and then you can have what you want."

She nodded as best she could with his grip so tight against her scalp. "Yes, sir."

"You think you can handle two of us, sweet Charlotte?"

She forced her eyes open, met his gaze as he stared down at her. There was desire there, need, but there was also something she couldn't read. Fear? Worry? But that wouldn't make any sense. "I can handle whatever you think I deserve, sir. I trust you."

He closed his eyes, his jaw flexing as he inhaled a deep breath. Then his grip gentled and traced a finger along the shell of her ear. His words were soft when he finally spoke, so low she doubted Kade could hear them. "I'm going to make this very good for you, Charli."

For some reason, his earnest tone and the way he'd said her real name had a knot forming in her throat. He'd slipped out of the role-play, and she could almost see a mental shift in him, some tide turning. He gave her one last, long look that seemed to say so much, though she had no idea what the words would be, then turned away.

"Vandergriff, secure her arms and feel free to make use of that lush mouth of hers. She won't need to do any more talking for a while." Grant's voice was gruff, almost as if the statement had been hard to make.

Charli's heart began to pound in her ears. She was really going to do this. Part of her was turned on by the idea of having Grant share her like he had the exclusive right to who did and didn't touch her, but anxiety curled in her stomach, invading the sexual energy humming through her. Something felt . . . off.

Grant scooted her forward on the desk, her silk blouse sliding along the polished wood, and Kade shoved the rolling desk chair out of the way. She could hear Grant walk to the other side of the room and open a cabinet while Kade filled the space in front of her, the hard ridge of his erection prominent against the front of his slacks. He grabbed Grant's desk phone and pulled the coiled cord from the base and the receiver.

"Put your hands behind your back, baby." She followed his instructions, and he leaned over her to bind her hands. His voice was quiet against her ear. "If you wanted to make him jealous, you've succeeded."

Her brow wrinkled, the statement not making sense to her. If Grant was so jealous, why was he sharing her? She peered up at Kade when he finished binding her. Shifting his eyes in Grant's direction, he touched a finger to her lips, warning her not to voice her thought.

He crouched down in front of her, making a show of pulling the pins from her hair. "Call your safe word, Charlotte."

"What?" she whispered.

"There's nothing I'd rather do right now than take advantage of that pretty mouth of yours, but Grant doesn't want this. I don't know why he's doing it—maybe because he thinks you want it—but he flinches every time I touch you."

The revelation tugged at her, making warmth of a different kind snake through her. Kade stood and went for the buckle of his pants, taking his time pulling the belt free. Grant took his place behind her again, his palms stroking along her hips. "You look delicious tied up like this, sweet Charlotte. You're about to make the two of us very happy."

Words seemed clogged in her throat, but when Kade dragged his zipper down, Charli found her voice. "Yellow!"

Grant's hands froze in place and Kade backed up a step.

"Charli, what's wrong?" Grant asked, his concern evident.

She tried to look behind her, a feat with her hands behind her back, but she managed to catch his eye. "Please, Grant. It's okay that Kade is here, but I don't want anyone inside me except you."

As soon as the words were out, she knew them to be true. She wasn't simply saying them for Grant's benefit.

He stared at her for a moment, the blue of his eyes swirling with an indecipherable concoction of emotions. Then his eyes crinkled at the corners, an invisible smile. "You got it, darlin'."

His lips hadn't curved, but she'd seen the pleasure there and couldn't help the ridiculous little leap of her heart.

Grant quickly unbound her hands and flipped her onto her back, his expression almost reverent. "It was brave to call your word. Thank you for letting me know. You sure you're okay with everything else?"

"Yes, sir."

"Good girl." He yanked at her shirt, pulling it open wide, the buttons plinking onto the desktop and floor, and unclasped her front-hook bra. "Then let's at least give our friend something to look at while he takes care of that hard-on you caused."

Kade moved to the side of her desk, looming over her on the left. She looked up at him, silently thanking him, but the concerned-friend expression had evaporated. His blue eyes darkened as his gaze raked over her with uninhibited male appreciation. The look alone raised goose bumps on her skin. Kade may be a nice guy and a friend to Grant, but there was no doubt an intense dominance ran right beneath that layer. Kade freed his cock from his boxers and stroked up the length, spreading the bead of moisture on the tip with his thumb and not taking his eyes off her.

Grant set something on the desk next to her and in front of Kade. Lube. Kade squirted some in his palm, then glossed his shaft until it was thick and pink. The sight riveted Charli. She'd never watched a guy jerk off before and hadn't imagined how freaking hot it could be to see a man taking his own pleasure. The fact that he was still wearing a full suit only added to the effect.

Grant's fingers spread her, finding her soaked. "I think she likes the show, Vandergriff. Dirty girl."

"The show ain't so bad from my perspective either," Kade said, his hand slowly working up and down, like he was taking his good, sweet time.

"It's about to get better." Grant flipped open the cap of the lube.

Charli's attention snapped toward Grant. Was he going to jerk off, too? Because even though she'd love to see that one day, she may fucking die if he wasn't inside her soon. Her body could only handle so much deprivation.

His smile was wicked, a dark promise. "Don't worry, darlin', I'm going to take good care of you. But I like seeing that panic in your eyes at the thought of me not fucking you."

He tugged off her shoes and pushed her heels onto the edge of the desk, spreading her fully, then brushed a teasing finger over her back entrance. An involuntary moan slipped past her lips.

"Yeah, that's what I thought," Grant said, his finger applying gentle pressure now. "You've ever been taken here, Ms. Beaumonde?"

"No," she said, gasping as his well-lubed finger slipped past the resistance. "Oh, God."

With slow, deliberate motion, he pumped his finger inside her ass, lighting up nerves she didn't even know she had. Edgy sensation made her squirm. She arched her hips, not sure if she needed less or more.

"Touch your clit, sweet girl," Grant directed in a pied-piper tone, daring her to trust his guidance. "The stimulation will chase away any discomfort and turn into something I think you'll thoroughly appreciate."

Don't think, just do. She brought her fingers to her sex, stroking herself the way she liked and brought her other hand to her breast, drawing her nipple between her fingers.

A soft groan sounded in her ears—Kade. "Fuck, she's sexy."

"That she is," Grant said, satisfaction underscoring his words. "Stay relaxed for me, Charlotte."

She hardly heard his instruction, the pleasure winding through her body and weighing her down, pulling her under. She touched herself without shame, not caring that two men were watching. She felt sensual and beautiful and more confident in her sexuality than she could ever remember feeling.

But right when she was sinking into the moment, something cool and unyielding pushed against her backside. She clenched automatically. But Grant's palm stroked her thigh. "Easy, relax your muscles. It's just a plug. You're not ready to take me yet, but this will be a good start."

Kade laid his free hand over the one she had against her pussy. "Keep going, Charlotte. You're driving me fucking wild. I love watching you."

She moved her fingers, dialing up the pleasure again, and Grant pushed the lubed plug past the tight ring of muscle, stretching her. She bucked against the bright burst of sensation. "Shit . . ."

Grant's expression turned ravenous, and he unfastened his pants. "Don't come yet. You've still got me to deal with."

Holy hell.

He grabbed her beneath her knees, pushing the backs of her thighs up and out, opening her for him. She had no idea how she was going to take him, too, but she yielded to his knowing hands, trusting that he wouldn't hurt her. His cock pressed against her soaked sex and, after a little bit of effort, slid in, filling her to the hilt. Every muscle in her body seemed to contract. The plug made everything tighter, fuller. It felt like he was everywhere.

"Oh, you feel good, darlin', so fucking good." He groaned as he moved all the way back then buried himself again, rocking her against the desk. "I can't wait until it's me in your ass, fucking you until you scream from release."

He pumped into her, his cock jostling the plug with every thrust, and her fingers pinched and stroked her clit as if under someone else's control. Her thoughts began to whirl into oblivion. She angled her head back, the onslaught of sensations making her body pulse with electricity. Orgasm waited impatiently in the wings, her mind holding it off until she heard the words she needed.

"Look at me, Charlotte. Just me," Grant demanded as he fucked into her harder. "I want to see your eyes when you come. Want you to know who's doing this to you."

Though it was near impossible to keep her eyes open, she locked onto Grant's gaze like a lifeline. But the intensity in his eyes was enough to knock what little control she had flat out of her. She was his in that moment. Whatever he said she would do. His pleasure was hers.

Sweat dotted his forehead and his hair was mussed, like he'd been running his hands through it. He looked like a beautiful beast, feral and determined, claiming his territory. And emotion danced through the blue of his eyes. He was in another place and was taking her there with him.

Moisture coated her fingers as she worked her clit, his pelvis hitting her knuckles with every thrust. Sensation climbed to a breaking point. Every tendon in her body seemed to coil, energy beating through her in colorful waves.

"Grant." The word was a mere gasp, a desperate plea.

"Come for me, Charlotte. Give me your pleasure."

The dam broke, and the rush of it all crashed over her. A scream tore from her throat as her every molecule seemed to crackle with sparks. Her body writhed, trying to handle it all.

Kade's groan mixed with their sounds of pleasure, and hot splashes landed against her skin—his release painting stripes across her breasts and belly.

"Ah, God." Grant came hard inside her, his body shuddering through his orgasm, her name tumbling from his lips over and over again.

She closed her eyes, absorbing the music of that sound, the feel of him surrendering to her as much as she was slave to him. She didn't think she could ever tire of hearing him call for her like she was the only woman that existed in the world.

She knew when they drifted back to earth, the outside world would push in, but in that moment, lying there beneath him, she was truly happy.

Maybe for the first time in her life.

And possibly for the last.

TWENTY-ONE

After Grant helped clean Charli up and gave her his dress shirt to wear, she curled up in a chair near his office door, looking a little unsure of herself all of a sudden.

He frowned over at her but was distracted when Kade returned from the restroom and touched Grant's arm. He turned to his friend, and Kade put a hand out to him. "I'm going to head out now, but thanks for inviting me in, Grant. She really is a lovely sub. You're lucky to have found her."

Grant shook his hand, weariness settling over him. "Thanks, man. I'm glad you had a good time. I wouldn't have trusted her with just anyone."

Kade smiled like he had some secret. "I know."

They exchanged good-byes and Kade walked toward the door, stopping next to Charli. He reached out and brushed a hand over her hair. "Thank you, Charlotte. It was a privilege."

She put her hand over his and gave him a warm smile. "You're a good guy, Kade Vandergriff."

"Don't let that get out, all right? It'd ruin my reputation." He leaned down and pressed a soft kiss to her lips.

Grant's chest seized with jealousy, the simple move kicking up a shit storm inside him. Kade may have not entered Charli's body, but he could give her something Grant couldn't, a tenderness that, by the looks of it, Charli craved.

Kade straightened and gave her shoulder a quick squeeze. "Later, gorgeous."

By the time Kade walked out, Grant's mood had tanked. *Later, gorgeous?* Guess Kade would be looking Charli up after Grant's time with her ended. He gritted his teeth and picked up the equipment he'd stocked his cabinet with this morning. "Let's get you back to the house. I'm sure you want a bath."

"Sounds good." She shifted in the chair and stood, unspoken questions all over her face. She looked so young standing there in his too-big shirt, her hair mussed and makeup smeared—like a college student after a long night out. Like Rachel used to look when they first moved into together. She'd always loved wearing his shirts.

The air whooshed from his lungs as if a sack of sand had been dropped on his chest. He turned away from Charli, bracing a hand on his desk.

"Hey, are you okay?"

"I'm fine," he snapped, his words coming out like broken glass.

"The hell you are," Charli said, her bare feet padding across the wood. "You've gone pale, like you've seen a ghost."

His shoulders hunched.

"Oh," she said softly.

He looked over at her, and she took a step back, as if she was suddenly afraid to touch him. "Charli."

She wrapped her arms around herself, acting chilled despite the warm room. "That's exactly what happened, isn't it? Something reminded you of your wife."

He forced himself to a stand, trying to regain control of his hammering heart. "I'm sorry. I'm okay." He closed his eyes, took a breath. "It's been happening a lot lately."

Ever since you stepped into my life. He didn't say it, but he knew it was Charli's presence that was knocking the dust off the memories he thought he'd packed away. He had no idea why. Charli didn't look like Rachel, and she damn sure didn't act like her. His wife had been quiet, almost fragile, and innocent to a lot of the world. She'd been sheltered her whole childhood by a very strict family, and Grant had felt the instinct to protect her from the start of their relationship. A job he'd failed in the worst way possible.

Charli's gaze shifted away from his, though she still held herself tightly. "I'm going to head back to the cabin, give you some space."

He frowned, turning fully toward her. He was doing it again—putting Charli through an intense scene and then leaving her on a limb by herself while he dealt with own shit. If they gave out membership cards to doms, his should be fucking revoked. He closed the space between them. "Come 'ere."

She lowered her arms but didn't make any other move. He drew her against him and tucked her against his chest. He wrapped his arms around her, feeling the tension she still held in her muscles. He was fucking things up with her. He could almost see the protective shell closing around her.

After the briefest of embraces, she pushed back, slipping from his arms and moving out of his reach. "I'm going to get going. I have an article I need to write."

"Charli, don't do that. I know that I keep screwing things up, but don't shut me out. This afternoon was fantastic."

She graced him with a small smile but sadness hung in her eyes. "It was, and I'm not shutting you out. I just need a breather to get myself back together."

Her eyes went a bit glassy, and she looked away. His heart lurched. "Charli."

She turned her back to him, swiping at the tears she didn't want him to see. "Ugh, I hate this. Am I going to cry every goddamned time? I'm supposed to be learning how to be more feminine, not how to turn into a crybaby."

He stepped behind her, putting his hands on her shoulders and massaging. "It's my fault. We should be sitting in that chair together right now, stroking each other, and coming down slowly after that scene. Instead, I'm acting like a fucking mental case."

The tension in her muscles unfurled beneath his fingers. Her head sagged forward. "It's okay. Grief is a bitch. Believe me, I know. I still can't go into a hospital without wanting to vomit. Even the scent of strong cleaners can yank me back to the day my dad died. And don't even try to talk to me on Father's Day."

He spun her to face him and swiped the tear tracks off her cheeks. How she could be so understanding was a wonder. She'd just put herself completely in his hands, taken risks she'd never taken before, and he'd brought another lover's memory into the room between them. Most women would've been insulted and strode out the door or pulled the saccharin oh-you-poor-thing routine.

But instead Charli was looking at him with gentle eyes—not pity, but empathy. He'd gotten used to the pity thing once people knew about Rachel. He hated it, which is why he rarely told anyone anymore. But the way Charli stared up at him only made him want to hold her tighter. To be open with her.

"You were beautiful today. Perfect," he said, pushing her hair behind her ears. "I'm sorry I ruined the afterglow."

She slid her hands up his still-bare chest to circle her arms around his neck. "You don't have to apologize. And you don't have to hide that part of yourself from me. I'd rather you be honest if you're dealing with something than putting on a happy face and pretending everything is hunky-dory. I don't need the unflappable master dom persona all the time. I can handle the human man beneath that."

Her words pried under that shield of armor he spent so much time honing and hit him right in the sternum. He was usually the one giving lectures to subs about letting down their defenses and being open and honest. Now his sub was turning the tables on him and calling him out on his own bullshit.

He turned her and lifted her, catching her by surprise, then carried her over to the chair she'd left. He adjusted her in his lap, fitting her against his chest.

"Grant, really, I'm okay. I don't need this."

He ignored her protest, afraid that if he responded, he wouldn't get what he needed to say out. He watched the second hand ticking on the clock over his desk, not really seeing it, but trying to decide how to start. How could he even explain? Finally, he began with the barest truth possible. "I loved her more than I ever thought was possible to love another person."

Charli stilled against him.

"I'd known Rachel since we were teenagers and had never planned to be with anyone else. The first time I kissed her I saw our whole future rolled out in front of us. Kids, house, the whole damn thing. I knew, just knew, she was the girl for me."

He paused, the sadness threatening to grip his throat and steal the rest of the story. He hadn't talked about Rachel aloud in so long. And certainly never to a woman he was with. But for some reason, he needed to get it out, to say it to Charli. He ran his hand up and down Charli's back, drawing strength from her warmth, from her willingness to listen.

He took a deep breath. "When she got pregnant, I thought things couldn't get any better. I remember wondering how I'd managed to get so lucky, to find the perfect life for me on the first try. And I thought I had it all figured out. She was naturally yielding, probably submissive if we'd been together long enough to figure out what that meant. She looked to me to be the man of the house, and I loved that, loved that sense of responsibility, that I was her rock, her protector. She'd had a pretty rough upbringing and I promised her I'd never let anyone hurt her again."

Charli's hand curled into his shirt, right over his now-pounding heart.

"But I failed her," he said softly, the familiar pain creeping into his chest, pressing on his lungs. "We had a break-in one night and instead of calling the police, I ran downstairs with my gun to go after the burglar. I left Rachel hiding in the bedroom, thinking she'd be safer there. The robber stabbed my shoulder, but I was able to shoot him. I thought I'd saved the fucking day. Big, brave husband to the rescue. But the guy hadn't been alone."

He shook his head, remembering the sick feeling when he'd heard Rachel's cry for help.

"The other guy came in and saw what I'd done to his brother, and he killed Rachel right in front of me."

Charli looked up at him, horror on her face.

"My wife and my unborn son died in my arms that night," he said, the words flat, like they were coming from someone else instead of from him.

Charli reached up and touched his face, tears filling her eyes. "Oh, Grant. I'm so sorry."

He looked away. "One phone call to the police and everything could've been different. I should've never left her side that night."

"You were doing what you thought was right. You didn't know—"

"Yeah, well, I should've," he said, cutting her off, unable to handle platitudes even though he knew she meant well. "I'm not telling you this to get your sympathy. I'm telling you because you deserve to know why I keep acting like a lunatic when things get too intense. And why what we're doing, us, can't go beyond what it is."

She looked as if she was going to push, to challenge him, but instead she simply nodded. "I understand. Thank you for telling me. I know you didn't have to do that."

He pushed her hair away from her face and smiled, trying to chase off the gut-wrenching memories he'd invited into the room.

"You made me want to tell. Maybe you missed your calling as a domme, pulling all my dark secrets from me."

She brushed at the tears she'd shed over his story and managed her own wavering attempt at a smile. "Maybe. Want to give me control of your whip, cowboy?"

He sniffed. "Hell, no. Your tongue is sharp enough. You'd be lethal with a weapon."

"Damn straight." She reached up and pressed a kiss to his stubbled chin, carefully avoiding his mouth. "Plus, I've always been the take-control girl in my life. I realize now that I don't want to have to do it in the bedroom, too."

"Well, I'll gladly take that responsibility off your hands," he said, turning her and wrapping her legs around his waist so he could see her face-to-face, see something good after all the ugliness of the rehashed memories.

She wiggled against his lap, obviously trying to distract him further.

He adored her in that moment. Any other woman would've wanted to talk about his feelings, would've wanted to coddle and *there-there* him. But not Charli. She'd recognized how much it had cost him to talk about Rachel, and she'd let him change topics without asking a bunch of questions or prodding for more. Somehow in a matter of minutes, she'd managed to lift his mood and ease the crushing pressure in his chest. Like it or not, this girl was getting to him.

And suddenly he wasn't sure if that was such a bad thing.

"Let's get you back to your cabin before I defile my desk a second time."

TWENTY-TWO

Charli sat in the break room at work, lost in thought as she unwrapped her sandwich. Coming into work after two weeks with Grant almost felt like waking up from some crazy-hot dream and realizing reality was still there waiting for you. It had been good to get back in the routine of things, to see some of her coworkers, but she'd missed Grant and the country as soon as she'd crossed the line into downtown.

The realization was sobering. She and Grant had definitely made strides in dropping the pretenses of their arrangement. They both knew they weren't doing this simply for training anymore and had agreed to another two weeks together. They enjoyed each other, had rocking chemistry and a taste for pushing boundaries. But every night after being together, she was painfully aware of the fact that he never kissed her, never stayed over at her cabin, and never invited her to his. This may not be training, but it was still a temporary dalliance. One that would be over soon.

Voices sounded to her left as her coworkers Pete and Steven pushed through the door of the break room. They were laughing and engrossed in conversation. Neither seemed to notice her sitting in the far corner of the room.

"Man, did you see how fucked up her report was at last week's game?" Pete said, pulling open the communal refrigerator. "She said the only way SMU could win was to get more points than the other team."

Steven barked a laugh. "Well, that *is* truly the only way to win. Though I didn't notice the gaffe. I was too busy looking elsewhere. Apparently, it was very cold out there on the sidelines, looked like she was smuggling Tic Tacs."

Pete grabbed a take-out container from the fridge. "Yeah, wouldn't mind having a little taste of that candy. Just wish the bitch wouldn't have stolen my promotion."

Anger, white hot and instant, flashed through Charli. Her soda can, which she'd been squeezing since the first off-color comment, clinked against the table, drawing both men's attention.

"Oh, crap," Steven said, having the nerve to look ashamed. "Didn't see you there, Charli. Sorry."

Pete sniffed and tossed his food in the microwave. "You don't need to apologize to Beaumonde about a little guy talk. She's one of us. Plus, I'm sure Stormy isn't her favorite person either. Beaumonde wanted the job, too."

Charli's can buckled beneath her death grip. "So because she got the job, you have the right to act like a goddamned pig, Pete?"

Steven hung back, sipping his soda and shifting from foot to foot like he had to pee. But Pete, undeterred, grabbed his food and perched on the edge of one of the tables near Charli. "Oh, chill out, Beaumonde. Every guy in this office is talking about her tits. If she cared, she wouldn't wear shirts that are two sizes too small. She likes the attention."

Charli's stomach turned. She pushed her sandwich away, muttering, "I think I've stepped back into 1970."

Pete brought a bite of his stir-fry noodles to his mouth, eyeing her, his brows rising as he took in the full view for the first time. He choked down the bite. "Well, fuck me. Look at you. You're taking a page from her book, aren't you?"

She stood, too disgusted to tolerate another second of this conversation. "I'm outta here. The average IQ level of the room has plummeted to prehistoric levels."

But he hopped off the table, sliding in front of her path. His gaze raked down her new silk blouse and the pencil skirt she'd worn as Grant's *assistant.* "I haven't seen you since your vacation. That's what you were up to, wasn't it? Redoing your image? You're worried you're going to get passed over again so you're going for the hot-piece-of-ass angle."

"Dude," Steven interrupted. "Shut the fuck up and get out of her way. You're just being a prick now."

She shuddered, feeling as if she needed to bathe in disinfectant after his perusal, but straightened to her full height, reminding him she had an inch or two on him. "I suggest you move or you'll be talking in soprano for your next audition."

"You're kind of cute when you get mad, Beaumonde."

As if acting on its own accord, her fist reared back and landed an uppercut square into Pete's stomach. He doubled over with an *oof.* She put her hand on his shoulder and bent next to his ear as he gasped for air. "You're lucky I'm wearing a skirt because otherwise your nuts would be in your throat right now. You say another disgusting thing about me or any other woman in this office, and I'll report you for sexual harassment."

She shoved past him and leveled a look at Steven, who raised his palms in surrender. "I really am sorry."

She simply shook her head and left the two of them in the break room. By the time she made it to the other end of the building, the nausea still hadn't abated. Pete was a dick, but what he'd said had rung a bell of truth inside her. Wasn't what she'd been doing these past two weeks exactly what he'd said? She was trying to mold herself into something that would please the guys who only wanted to ogle some girl's boobs on television.

She sagged in her desk chair, letting her head fall back. Was this the kind of thing she was signing up for? She wanted the on-air position more than anything, and knew her approach had needed some refining, but pretending to be something she wasn't suddenly felt way too similar to her failed pageant days. *Smile a little brighter, Charli. Flutter your lashes. Speak softly to the judges. Watch how your sister does it.*

Without thinking too much about it, she followed her first instinct. She picked up her office phone and dialed Grant's number.

After two rings, she almost chickened out, but then heard the click.

"Hey there, freckles," he said, his voice like warm ocean water over her skin, soothing her. "I didn't think I'd hear from you until you were done for the day. Everything okay?"

"I guess. Am I interrupting you?" she asked, feeling silly calling him in the middle of the day.

"You're never an interruption." She heard a squeak, as if he was leaning back in his desk chair. Even though she'd never seen the office he used in town, she could picture him there—tilted back, boot hitched over his knee. "How's your day going?"

She looked behind her to make sure no one was standing near her cubicle and lowered her voice. "I punched a guy in the stomach already. How's yours?"

Grant coughed. "You what?"

Somehow Grant managed to pronounce the *h* in *what*, his accent getting thicker when caught off guard. The simple little quirk managed to make the knot in her belly loosen a bit. "The guy I'm competing with for the job called me a hot piece of ass and then wouldn't get out of my way."

The chair squeaked again. "That motherfucker. I'm on the way over."

"No," she said, then realized she'd spoken too loudly. She took a breath. "I'm not calling you for help. I handled it. I just . . . I don't know. I'm starting to think morphing myself into something I'm not is the coward's way of getting this promotion."

He was quiet for a moment. "I see. And what do you think you're morphing yourself into, Charli?"

She twirled a lock of hair around her finger over and over again, a childhood habit that seemed to reappear when she was stressed. "I don't know. The sweet, pretty girl who acts submissive and yielding around guys. I'm becoming that girl my mother always wanted me to be."

Grant sniffed. "Darlin', you haven't changed into anything. You *are* sweet and you *are* pretty. Those things were there from the start even if you or your mother didn't realize it. As for the submissive part, the fact that you punched that guy today shows that you're still all tomboy. None of the training we've done has taken any of that from you."

She stared at her screen saver, contemplating his words. "So all this time, you've known training wasn't working?"

"I didn't want to train any of that out of you, freckles. We're only working on polishing what's already there for your audition. Your feistiness is what makes you so fucking sexy. Makes the fact that you submit to *me* and no one else so damn hot."

"Oh," she said, her blood beginning to pump a little harder, and not from anger this time.

"Honestly, I've got to tell you, the fact that you punched that asshole has got me hard as rock right now."

She bit her lip, holding back a smile. "Is that right?"

"Damn straight."

She leaned forward in her chair, shielding her face with her hair in case anyone walked by. "Maybe you should take care of that."

"Ah, naughty thing, you like the idea of me stroking myself to thoughts of you," he said, his voice dropping an octave. "Maybe I'll do just that. If you were close enough, I'd order you to come over here and climb onto my lap."

She crossed her legs beneath her desk, trying to fend off the dampness gathering there. "Too bad I already had lunch."

"Mmm." She could picture him spreading those muscular thighs of his and unzipping his pants, sliding his hand along his shaft. "That is a damn shame, freckles. My fist is a poor substitute for that sexy body of yours."

A thick file folder landed on her desk with a loud smack. She jumped, so engrossed in the conversation, she hadn't even heard anyone approach. "Hold on a sec."

She spun her chair to find Pete glaring at her. "Trey wants you to work on the Valley High School story. The information is in there."

"Fine," she spit out, hoping her cheeks weren't as flaming red as they felt.

He tilted his head, his gaze darting toward the phone and then down to her shirt. She glanced down. Of course, her nipples were standing at attention against the soft fabric of her shirt. He dragged his lips together, as if smoothing invisible Chap Stick. "He wants the story by the end of the week."

"Got it."

She feared he was going to linger, confront her about slugging him. But he turned around and was gone. She released the breath she'd been holding. Annoying ass. She put the phone back to her ear. "Sorry. Work stuff. Where were we?"

"Imagine those bastards expecting you to actually work," Grant mused. "And I'm about halfway to coming, where are you, sweet Charlotte?"

"Wishing I was there," she said wistfully. "Touching you."

"Are you wet for me?"

"Perhaps."

A soft groan slipped from him. "How much privacy does your office allow? Any security cameras?"

She peeked over her shoulder. "I'm in a back corner cubicle and my neighbor is at lunch. No cameras. The office is loud, but I have no door."

"Look in your purse, Charlotte. Inside pocket. I put a present in there for you," he said, mischief in his words.

"Uh-oh," she said, wary but intrigued. She reached into her bottom file drawer and pulled her purse out. Inside was what looked to be a tube of lipstick, but when she twisted the base, it started to quietly vibrate.

"Found it?"

"Yes," she said, her heart starting to hammer.

"I thought I'd be the one to call you one day this week and tempt you into some phone play, but lucky me, you called first."

"Grant, I can't—"

"Shh, you will because you want to," he said, his words like a stroke to her skin. "I'm taking a risk, too. My secretary is right outside, and my door isn't locked."

She rolled the lipstick tube between her fingers, so tempted, the sound of Grant's breath in her ears making her sex throb. Fuck it. With one last check over her shoulder, she quickly put her hand beneath her skirt and tucked the vibrator into her panties to hold it in place.

She gasped softly at the sensation, the vibration nestling right against her clit. "You're a bad, bad man."

"You love it," he said. "Now I can picture you there while I stroke my cock. All prim and proper in your little business outfit, your hips rocking ever so slightly to rub your pussy against the vibe, your scent filling that little cubicle. Ah . . ."

"Jesus." The dirty talk alone was going to put her over. She pressed her fingers into the edge of her desk, her knuckles going white, as she tried to keep still in her chair. "I'm not going to last long."

"Mmm, then let go with me. My cock is hard in my hand for you, the tip already slippery."

She wet her lips, wishing she was there to lick that salty taste off him. Her pussy clenched and she squeezed her thighs together, aligning the vibe to the sweet spot on the side of her clit. Sensation pinged through her, orgasm rushing toward her sharp and fast. *"Grant."*

"Ah, fuck yes . . ." he groaned on the other end, lost in his own release.

She closed her eyes, breathing fast, imagining his come spilling over his fist, and rode the wave of her orgasm. It took everything in her to not make a sound, to not call out his name.

Another flood of moisture coated the vibrator and soaked her panties as the last shudder went through her and she drifted down from the orgasm.

With lightning-fast movement, she pulled the vibrator from her panties, turned it off, and dropped it in her open purse. She clutched the phone to her ear, feeling a bit light-headed. "Whoa."

There was a click on the phone, and she thought she'd lost him, but then she heard him let out a satisfied sigh. "Ditto. Thanks for that, freckles."

"Believe me, the pleasure was mine."

She could feel his grin through the line. "Now get back to work, slacker. I'll pick you up at six, and I guarantee that won't be your last orgasm of the day."

With that, he hung up.

And as she walked to the restroom to get cleaned up, she came to terms with one foundation-rattling fact. She was addicted. Downright, no denying it, addicted. No matter how often she saw Grant, she couldn't get enough of him.

And that scared the ever-loving shit out of her.

Because this thing had an expiration date. And it was thundering toward them both.

TWENTY-THREE

Charli stepped out of the steam-filled bathroom, feeling refreshed after her long walk on the grounds this afternoon. In the heat of the shower, her muscles had loosened, but the remnants of last night's session with Grant remained. Phone sex had definitely only been the appetizer in his plans yesterday.

She unwrapped her towel and turned her back to the full-length mirror in the bedroom, peering over her shoulder. He'd used a whip on her for the first time. The angry welts had mostly faded, but a few bruises now colored her skin. For some odd reason, seeing those marks made her feel lighter, buoyant. She glanced down at her wrists and rubbed the faint pink rope burns, the brush of pain tightening something low in her belly.

"God, I must be freaking losing it."

The empty room had no response. With a sigh, she tucked the towel around herself again and headed toward the boxes on the bed. Grant had sent them over after she'd gotten home from work today with a terse note. *Charlotte, I'm taking you out to a business function tonight. This is what you will wear for me. No addi-*

tions or subtractions. Wear your hair down. Be at my cabin by six. Grant.

She shook her head but couldn't help smiling. He'd told her she was going as his date, not as his submissive. This was apparently something for the winery. But even on a supposedly "normal" date, the man couldn't help but be bossy.

She opened the first box and unfolded the tissue, finding a gorgeous plum-colored wrap dress. Wow, that hadn't been what she expected. She thought for sure he'd put her in something short and tight. But this had luxury and class written all over it.

She peeked into the smaller boxes. One had a lacy bra and panty set in the same shade of purple as the dress. She held up the thong. He'd said he'd let her wear underwear, but she wasn't sure if this little bit of material quite counted. Cheater.

The other small box had a pendant necklace and two cuff bracelets that would perfectly cover the marks on her wrists. The final package was a pair of buttery soft, knee-high leather boots. "Ooh."

A Post-it note was stuck to the left boot. *These should be a little more comfortable than those heels I always torture you with.*

She rubbed her thumb across Grant's neat handwriting, warmth whispering through her. Her cowboy had thought of everything.

She groaned. No. Not *her* cowboy. She had to stop thinking of him like that.

No doubt this wasn't the first or last time he bought an outfit for a woman to wear for him. This was all part of the game. She'd agreed to play sub to him for the month, and this was simply a part of that.

She let her towel fall to the floor and slipped on the panties and bra. If Grant ever decided to stay with someone longer than a month, did that mean he'd pick out her clothes every day? What if the woman wanted to wear jeans sometimes but he wanted her to wear a skirt? How would that work?

She frowned at her reflection in the mirror. The thought of

having Grant take care of her like that was simultaneously appealing and appalling. Knowing that she'd be wearing only things he'd selected for her tonight gave her a little thrill. It felt intimate and personal, having him choose things he thought would complement her body and coloring.

But someone doing that for her every day? She'd freaking lose it. Right?

She tilted her head back, staring at the ceiling. She needed to reel herself in. Over the last few weeks she'd had moments where she'd wondered what it'd be like to really be Grant's, secretly imagining how it would be to push things further than just a short experiment. But even if she was discovering that she had a submissive streak, Grant didn't want anything more than a month. He was already in a long-term relationship—with a memory. There was no room in his life for someone else.

And hell, it wasn't like Charli was Ms. 'Til-Death-Do-Us-Part either. Getting attached to someone was dangerous enough. She'd learned that the day her mother and sister had walked out of her life. But how much more intense would that loss be if she were in a D/s relationship and her dom left her? That kind of lifestyle and level of care could become addictive quickly, and having it end would surely make someone feel adrift.

She shuddered. She could never let herself become that dependent on anyone. Already Grant was becoming too important a part of her day.

Charli shrugged on the dress, wrapping it around herself and coming to a decision. Tonight, she'd be Grant's date, get some social practice in, but then they were going to have to talk about their situation afterward. She'd left herself too open with Grant. She'd wanted to help him see past his grief over his wife, but in the process, she'd forgotten to protect her own heart. The fact that she was even imagining the idea of giving herself to him for a moment proved she was sinking too deep, getting caught in the quicksand.

She took the cuff bracelets from their box and slipped them over her wrists, ignoring the hot shiver that went through her, and then bent to grab the necklace. But the sound of her cell phone vibrating on the bedside table had her veering in another direction.

Charli reached for the phone, the caller ID flashing *unknown number.* "Hello?"

"Ms. Beaumonde?"

"Yes, this is Charli."

There was a long pause, and Charli thought the call had dropped, but then the man cleared his throat. "This is Rodney Wilson. I'm sorry about the last time we met. I'm ready to talk now. For real."

Charli lost her ability to speak for a moment. And the first words that jumped to her lips were *holy shit*, but luckily she managed to choke those down. She gripped the bedpost, the reporter inside her jumping up and twirling. "On the record?"

"Yes. This whole thing is getting out of hand and needs to stop. They're trying to buy my silence now. I've sent my wife and kids to stay with her family for a few weeks. These assholes need to be outed. I can name names for you and give you some documents that may help."

"Pick the time and place. I'll be there," she said, searching the drawer in the bedside table for a pen.

"How about tomorrow morning around eight? You know where the Southern Pancake Hut is?"

"Yep. Perfect." She jotted down the time and place on the back of a napkin. "Thanks so much, Rodney."

"And, Ms. Beaumonde, watch your back. There are lots of powerful people who have their hands in this."

The warning sent a dart of anxiety down her spine, but not enough to outweigh the excitement of knowing she was finally going to get the truth and break this story. "Thank you. I'll be careful."

She ended the call and did a little spin for real this time, her dress swirling around her. This was it. Not only would she be able to expose some nasty cheaters, but she'd prove that she was capable of handling a big story.

With a smile on her face, she hurried to the bathroom to finish getting ready. A few days and she'd be able to go back to her normal life. No more worrying about someone trying to hurt her. No more hiding out.

And no more Grant.

Her smile faltered in the mirror.

Grant stared down at the scalloped-edge invitation he'd discovered in his mailbox. He read the words again, each sentence settling in his gut like heavy boulders.

Georgia Eleanor Waters and Barry Sparks request your presence at their wedding . . .

Grant sank onto one of his barstools, the combating emotions too much to process standing up. His mom was getting married again? To someone who wasn't his father. The notion seemed too preposterous to even comprehend.

And who the fuck was this Barry guy?

Did he treat his mother well? Did he make her happy? Did he have a job or was he just after the family's fortune?

You wouldn't know, asshole, his conscience whispered at him. *You never go home.*

Grant's front door swung open, banging the wall and startling him from his thoughts. "What the hell?"

Charli burst through the doorway like a cyclone, all smiles and flushed cheeks. "Oops, sorry, the wind took the door right from my hand."

She pranced inside and pushed the door closed behind her, her red mane whipping around in one final gust. She spun back around, a wide grin still on her face.

Fuck, she was gorgeous. The outfit he'd chosen for her looked even better hugging her body than he'd imagined. And knowing what she had on underneath had him almost forgetting what he was so upset about a moment before. He glanced at the clock over the fireplace. "You're early, freckles."

"I know," she said, a bit breathless. "But I couldn't wait to tell you my good news."

"Oh?"

"The guy I tried to get information from that day someone broke into the car is now ready to talk—on the record. He said he can name names in the cheating scandal." The words spilled out of her like a river overflowing its banks as she made her way across the living room toward the kitchen. "He's going to meet with me tomorrow morning. Isn't that great? I'm going to get my story."

Her excitement was contagious, and Grant couldn't help but return her smile. He tossed the invitation and accompanying note onto the counter and pulled her close when she reached him, caging her between his thighs. "That's awesome, darlin'. Congratulations."

Without warning, she wrapped her arms around him in an enthusiastic hug, almost knocking him off the stool. He closed his eyes, absorbing the scent of her shampoo and the feel of her body against his, a thread of regret knitting through him. If she landed her story, this would be one of the last nights she'd be here with him.

She pulled back from the hug but remained standing between his knees. "So I thought maybe tonight, I should stay at my house instead of coming back here. I have to meet him early, and it doesn't make sense to come all the way back out this way."

Grant frowned. "I'm not leaving you unprotected, Charlotte. Even for one night."

The little shiver she gave at the use of her full name, her sub name, brought Grant more pleasure than it should've. She shrugged. "So stay there with me."

The suggestion was a simple one on its surface, but the idea of sleeping next to her in her own house had tension gathering in his shoulders. He didn't sleep with anyone. And his nightmares wouldn't care if he was alone or otherwise. They'd come anyway. He rolled his shoulders, trying to loosen some of the tightness. There was always the couch, and he could pull an all-nighter, keeping guard. God knows he'd pulled enough of them in his military career.

"All right, we'll stay at your place." He slid his palms along her waist, then over the curve of her ass. "Hope your neighbors aren't too close. Having you on my arm all night, looking this edible, is going to have me ready to get you screaming the minute we're alone."

Her nipples hardened behind the soft material of her dress, her body instantly responding to his suggestions. She poked his chest. "Hey, you said this was going to be a normal date. Strictly business."

"What? Vanilla people have sex after dates, too," he teased. "Just with less . . . bells and whistles. Or ropes and violence, as the case may be. Poor bastards."

She rolled her eyes. "You're incorrigible."

"So I've been told, but we'll see how the night goes." He stood, pulling her fully against him, letting her feel how hard he was for her already. "And we'll see if I give good enough date to be asked in for a nightcap."

"Cocky cowboy." But the desire in her eyes belied her flippant response.

Reluctantly, he released her. "I need to get changed and pack an overnight back. Feel free to pour yourself a glass of wine. I shouldn't be long."

Before he realized what he was doing, he leaned over and kissed her on the corner of her mouth. Just a quick I'll-see-you-in-a-minute peck, but it was the kind of comfortable kiss lovers share when they've been together forever.

He froze for a second afterward, and Charli blinked at him, obviously surprised.

"Wineglasses are in the cabinet above the sink," he said gruffly, trying to cover his own shock, then turned on his heel and headed toward his bedroom.

Maybe it was for the best that Charli was about to walk out of his life. He liked his world steady and solid beneath his feet. And right now he was balancing on goddamned Jell-O.

TWENTY-FOUR

Charli fiddled with one of her bracelets as Grant drove along the two-lane highway. They'd made small talk about her story for a few minutes, but as dusk had settled in around them, cocooning the truck's cab in hazy blue-and-orange light, Grant had gone silent. Clearly, that little peck he'd given her had sent him retreating into his cave.

She shifted in her seat, the quiet becoming suffocating. It was a long ride into the city. Broody silence was only going to make her more nervous about the event tonight. She scrounged her mind for some neutral topic. "So who's getting married?"

He gave her a sidelong glance. "What are you talking about?"

"You had an invitation on your kitchen counter. I didn't read it, but I could tell what it was for."

That little muscle in his jaw twitched. "My mother, apparently."

"Oh," she said, sensing that she'd picked anything but a safe topic. "I didn't realize your parents weren't together."

He kept his eyes on the road, but his grip on the steering wheel seemed to tighten. "My dad passed away a few years back."

"I'm sorry," she said, knowing that was the pat response, but truly meaning it. Losing her father had been one of the hardest things she'd ever faced. She still had trouble thinking about him without getting teary. "Were you close?"

"Very. Talked every day until . . . well, until I lost my wife. I went into the army after that and didn't really want to talk to anyone," he said, regret tingeing his voice. "He died after I joined the CIA. My family owns a dairy farm, and Dad always insisted on being hands-on. He had a heart attack while checking on the herd one morning."

"I'm so sorry," she said again, wanting to reach out and give his hand a squeeze but sensing the sympathy wouldn't be welcome. "I didn't mean to bring up sad memories."

He shrugged, though the move seemed stiff. "It is what it is. The truth is, I should've been there. I should've been home running the farm so he could retire. But I was too caught up in my own shit to take on the responsibility."

She frowned. "You were serving our country. That isn't exactly shirking responsibility."

He glanced over at her, then back at the road. "Yeah, that's what I told myself, too. It sounds so brave and noble. But all I was doing was running—running fast and far. I let my family down."

"Grant—"

"Doesn't matter now," he said, cutting her off. "They've managed just fine without me. My younger brother and sister are running the farm these days."

Charli could tell he wanted to close the subject, but it took all she could not to press more. His guilt was so palpable it was like cigarette smoke filling the cab of the truck—acrid and invasive. She stared out the window, watching the sun sink below the horizon and the city lights come into view in the distance. "Are you going to the wedding?"

"No."

"Why?"

He groaned. "Are you always this relentless, freckles?"

"Yes," she said without apology.

He put the blinker on and merged onto the interstate. "Because I don't go home."

The stark statement was like a door slamming shut and locking. *You're not welcome here, Ms. Beaumonde.* She sighed and leaned against the seat, closing her eyes. It was going to be a long few miles before they made it to their destination.

After leaving the truck with a valet, Grant took Charli's elbow and gathered her close to his side. Somehow even in a tailored suit, he smelled like the country air. She had the urge to burrow against him and absorb his scent.

He nodded to a path that looped around the side of the events hall. "Looks like the party is out back. They like to have everything in the gardens when it's warm enough."

She nodded, her nerves starting to creep in. "Okay."

"I want you to relax and have a good time, but try to focus on the things we're working on. Pretend this is a dry run for your upcoming audition." He ran his fingers along her spine, sending chill bumps through her. "Be polite. But don't be afraid to talk or be yourself. You're a smart woman with a lot to say. Charm these stuffy bastards."

She laughed. "I'll do my best. Though it feels a little awkward posing as your date just so we can train."

He turned her toward him, cupping her shoulders and pinning her with his gaze. "Listen to me. You're not posing as anything. And you're not here as my submissive. You're my date—my smoking-hot, makes-me-hard-just-looking-at-her date. I wouldn't want anyone else by my side tonight."

Her neck went warm, and she glanced over at another couple

strolling a few feet away, hoping they couldn't overhear what Grant was saying.

"You walk into this party knowing that you look fantastic, that you're going to make my colleagues wish they were me, and that I'm probably not going to be the only one imagining you in just those boots."

She bit her lip, heat gathering much, much lower than her face now. Her panties went damp against her skin. "Yes, sir."

She put her hand to her mouth, surprised the response had rolled off her tongue so instinctively.

His eyes went almost black in the moonlight, and he smiled. "Oh, darlin', now you've really got me tempted to take you back to the truck and forget this whole plan." His arms slid from her shoulders down along her arms. "But I'm a man of my word, so let's get moving before my baser instincts veto my nobler ones."

She took a deep breath and nodded, trying to quell the surge of need rising in her. How was it that with a few simple words, this man could turn her sideways? She had every intention of telling Grant tonight that things were getting too intense, that they needed to back off. But right now, she was having an exceptionally hard time accepting that he'd never touch her that way again, never command her, that she would never visit that blissful place of surrender he'd brought her to.

Grant's hand closed around hers, and he turned them toward the path. "Come on, Charlotte. Let's go play nice."

Grant could barely concentrate on the conversations as he circulated around the gardens, introducing Charli and making small talk with friends and colleagues. He'd offered her a stiff drink when they'd first come in to help soften her nerves, and since then, she'd become downright effervescent. The girl could speak on almost any topic. Talking sports was her obvious favorite, but she was well schooled on current events, politics, and the city. The people he introduced her to seemed captivated and kept giving Grant approving looks. He'd even gotten a shoulder pat from the stodgy, retired CEO of a local restaurant chain and a whispered, "That one's a keeper, son."

The only time Charli had faltered was when a senator's wife asked her who had designed her dress. After a moment's hesitation, Charli had smiled and said she had no idea, that it was a gift and that she was fashion-challenged. The woman had laughed and confessed she'd found her own outfit at a consignment store.

As the night went on, Grant became more and more perplexed as to why Charli was having any issues at her job. Sure, he could tell that she was a little more deliberate in the heeled boots, a little more aware of the way her dress moved when she sat. But other than that, he didn't see any of the awkward tomboy image she was so worried she had. He'd been training her on a few things but knew that he hadn't provided some metamorphosis.

So why had she gotten passed over for that job? Did she panic on camera and lose the girl-next-door charm that seemed to glow from her tonight? Were her bosses unable to see the potential beneath her oversized clothes and clean-scrubbed face? Surely her company had makeup and wardrobe people. They had to see that Charli could be gussied up. No one on television wakes up looking like they do on camera.

Charli turned and smiled at him when the couple they'd been chatting with excused themselves. "You're going for the strong and silent image tonight, cowboy?"

He drained the last of his wine and set it on a nearby table. "Sorry, freckles. I thought I'd let you take center stage tonight. You're far more charming than I am."

She snorted. "Yeah and pigs have wings. All this chatting is exhausting, though."

"Come on. Break time." He grabbed her hand and tugged. He

needed a respite from the crowd as well. People milled around them as they weaved their way through the linen-covered tables that dotted the lawn and the strings of sparkle lights that had been draped from tree to tree swung gently above them, lighting their path.

"Where are we going?" she asked, her question barely audible as they passed near the string quartet.

"We have a few minutes before they start the awards presentation. And I know this quiet spot by the pond where we can take a breather." He guided her over a couple of stepping-stones that cut through a row of hedges. A small sign had been staked in the garden: *Private Property: No Visitors Beyond This Point.*

She glanced over at him with a conspiratorial smile as they made their way from the crowded lawn into a more secluded part of the property. "Breaking the rules, huh? You sure you're not just trying to get a girl alone, Mr. Waters? I've heard you've got a bit of a reputation."

"Oh, is that right?" he asked, releasing her hand once they were obviously alone and giving her ass a swift pinch.

She rewarded him with a little squeal and a flash of lust in her eyes. She picked up her pace and got a few steps out of his reach, peeking back over her shoulder at him.

"I wouldn't run from me," he warned. "That's like flashing a cape in front of a bull."

The eyebrow arch and head tilt she gave him were pure mischief. Before he could blink, she took off toward the water glimmering in the distance.

He launched into pursuit. "Oh, now that's your ass, freckles."

His dress shoes were slippery against the grass, but Charli wasn't exactly wearing sneakers either. So before long he was only a stride or two behind her. She dared a glance behind her, her smile wide, before she unexpectedly veered right and left him skidding past her. He grabbed onto a tree to slow himself, then changed direction.

Charli ran along the edge of the pond, but her steps faltered when she saw the thicket of trees on the far side of it. Grant grinned in triumph. She only had two choices—surrender or risk traipsing through the wilds surrounding the property in the dark. Before she could act, Grant reached her, capturing her by the waist and spinning her off her feet.

She shrieked and he dragged her to the ground, pulling her down on top of him in the grass. "Gotcha now, darlin'."

"You're going to get your suit dirty." She made a halfhearted attempt to escape, writhing against him and inadvertently making his cock stir to life. But when his arms didn't budge, she sighed and sagged against him, her forehead against his. "Man, I hate to lose."

He chuckled and slid his hands from her waist down to the curve of her butt, fitting her pelvis against his thickening erection. "Yes, but you make such a sexy little captive."

She groaned. "Down, boy. We're at a fancy-schmancy party, remember?"

"And those fancy-schmancy people are two hundred yards on the other side of those trees getting into their seats for a ceremony that starts in five minutes." He tucked his hand beneath the hem of her dress, dragging a finger along the lacy line of her thong. "But I can play nice. If you're not wet, I'll let you free right now."

"That's not fair," she protested.

"Ah, so you *are* ready for me then," he murmured as he slipped a finger beneath the lace. The silky heat of her arousal greeted him. *Fucking beautiful.* She wasn't just wet; she was soaked. "Well, well, someone likes being captured."

She made a soft sound and closed her eyes as he touched her. "I may or may not have entertained the idea before. How do you feel about pirate outfits?"

He laughed. "Not a chance." But maybe he'd have to play this cat-and-mouse game with her at The Ranch, where no one would blink an eye if he caught her, stripped her down, and tied her to a tree.

But right now, he didn't have the patience to wait until they were back at his place. He needed her now. Right here.

He traced his fingernail against her slit, and she quivered hard against him. "So responsive. You're protesting, but your body certainly appreciates that we're out in the open. I think you may have a bit of an exhibitionist streak in you, Ms. Beaumonde."

She dragged her teeth over her bottom lip, but no additional protest came.

"I love that you're so damn dirty," he said, sliding his hands along the backs of her thighs. "You could give me a run for my money."

"You're just a bad influence."

He gave her an unapologetic smile. "Sit up, sweet Charlotte, lift your skirt, and straddle me. Your only instruction is to not make a sound when you come for me. You understand?"

Even in the moonlight he could see her pupils go wide with desire, the risk of discovery clearly making her anxious but feeding her need for playing at the edge at the same time. "Grant, I don't know . . ."

But even as she made her lackluster objection, she was lifting off him, following his directive whether she knew it or not.

"You know how to make me stop, darlin'," he said, slowly bunching her dress up her thighs. "Say the word, and I'll take you back to the party."

Her breathing became more shallow with each inch of exposure. "What if I can't be quiet?"

"You will." He unfastened his pants and dragged his zipper down, releasing his erection. "Make a sound and I'll turn you over my knee and redden that pretty ass right here. I'll make sure you won't be able to sit when we get back to the party."

Her eyes went round, and her little hum of fear went straight to his cock, nourishing that dark desire inside him. He loved pushing her boundaries, making such a strong, put-together woman quiver.

"Spread your knees and pull those panties to the side before I rip them off of you."

She widened her legs, straddling him fully. The sight of her polished fingernails pulling aside the lace and revealing the pink, swollen lips of her sex was enough to have him let loose his own groan. "You have the sexiest fucking cunt I've ever seen. It's taking everything I have not to put you on your back and lick and nibble every tender bit of it."

Her cheeks darkened in the moonlight, but her eyes were pure want.

"I love that your whole body goes hot when I get crass," he said, brushing a finger over her cheekbone. "Hold your dress up with your other hand. I want to watch you take me inside you. Slow."

"Yes, sir," she whispered, the soft words mixing with the sound of the breeze rustling the trees.

He propped himself on his elbow and took his cock in his hand, positioning himself at her entrance. Damn, he was glad he'd decided to forgo condoms with her. Being bare inside Charli was the most decadent treat he could imagine. Her slick heat enveloped the sensitive head and sent a shock of pleasure marching up his spine. "Ah, baby, yes. You feel so good."

She lowered herself at a tortuous pace—teasing him but also teasing herself. He could feel her inner muscles clenching around him, trying to draw him deeper. He was glad he was the one lying down. His knees would've given out otherwise.

"That's right, take me in slow and easy." The visual alone was enough to have his balls tightening. The sensual slide of her taking each inch of him, the slight tremor in her thighs as she fought to hold herself still, the quick rise and fall of her belly as her breath hitched with each new sensation.

"I could come just looking at you like this." He reached out and stroked a thumb over her clit. She arched, her nipples going prominent against the material of the dress, but she managed to stay silent. "Ride me, Charlotte. Pull my orgasm from me. You can come when I do."

She sank down, burying him deep inside her heat, and he had to bite his own tongue not to moan. But the rapt expression on her face was worth it. She was no longer worrying that she was fucking him where someone could discover them. All she was focused on was the pleasure of it, her need for release, and her desire to please him. She'd gone into subspace without any restraints or pain play. She was all his right now. And he fucking loved it.

She raised herself and plunged back down, slowly at first and then faster, until she was riding him with a rhythm that had his own mind going fuzzy. The sound of skin meeting skin filtered through the night, and the intoxicating scent of sex enveloped them, mixing with the smell of the freshly cut grass. Grant's free hand curled into the sod as every nerve in his body seemed to vibrate.

Rarely did he give a woman free rein like this. He was so used to controlling the speed and execution of every little aspect of sex. But Charli was sending him down a track with no brakes, and all he wanted to do was enjoy the ride. No soft, romantic lovemaking for his girl. She wanted it hard and fast tonight, and he was happy to oblige her. He worked his fingers against her folds, teasing and pinching, then stroked her clit until he could feel she was on the brink.

"Grant," she whispered, the begging so gentle but the clench of her sex like a sweetly tortuous vise grip.

"I'm right there with you, darlin'. Go for it."

She fell forward, bracing her hands against his chest, and canted her hips even faster, fucking him with a desperation that turned his blood into rocket fuel. Her sharp pants hit his cheeks, but he couldn't tear his gaze away from her face—parted lips, closed eyes, the gorgeous glow of exertion. He loved how she let the passion engulf her.

He pressed his fingers along the sides of her clit, and her body tightened around him, her thighs squeezing his hips and her pussy contracting around his cock.

Liquid bliss shot through his veins and straight downward, his release hurtling forward. "Fuck, baby."

"Oh, God." Her head tipped back.

Orgasm crashed over both of them, pulling them under and drowning them. He grabbed her hips, driving deep, and stifling a moan as his release pulsed inside her. Her nails dug into his shirt, but the only sounds that escaped her were these little sharp catches in the back of her throat. It was the sexiest damn sound he'd ever heard.

When both their sounds of restraint had quieted, she finally opened her eyes and melted against him, pressing her cheek to her shoulder. "That was way more fun than an awards presentation."

"You got that right." He chuckled and kissed the top of her head, then froze. Was that the murmur of voices? The crunch of leaves? "Get up, freckles."

"What's wrong?" she asked, immediately raising herself up and off of him.

He hurriedly tucked himself back into his pants and pulled up his zipper. "I think I hear someone."

Panic lit her features. "Shit."

She scrambled to her feet, straightening her dress and checking to make sure she was covered. But there was no way she'd be able to hide that flushed, post-orgasm glow. He stood and dusted the grass off his backside. "Just take a deep breath. Someone's coming, but I doubt anyone saw us."

Soon, two men walked out from the bank of trees a few yards away and headed toward the edge of the pond. They were deep in conversation and didn't seem to even notice they weren't alone. Grant grabbed Charli's hand. "Come on. Let's pretend like we got lost and make our way back to the party."

She nodded and clasped his hand, but before they took a handful of steps, one of the men glanced over and saw them. The conversation halted.

"This part of the grounds is not open to guests," the man called.

Grant raised a palm. "No problem. We got a little off course. We're heading back now."

The white-haired man headed their way, and his companion turned and followed. As the two men approached, Charli went stiff next to Grant. She pulled her hand from his. "Crap. What the hell is he doing here?"

Grant was about to ask her what she meant, but then the elderly man's wide-shouldered friend squinted at Charli. *"Beaumonde?"*

Charli sighed. "Hi, Trey."

Trey. Grant searched his brain, trying to remember if Charli had ever mentioned that name.

The guy looked Charli up and down with evaluating eyes. "Wow, I barely recognized you all dressed up. What are you doing here?"

Grant gritted his teeth, the guy's tone and perusal of Charli pushing Grant's *mine* buttons.

Charli shifted from one boot to the other, then looked over to Grant as if deciding whether to come up with a story or tell the truth. "I'm on a date. This is Grant Waters. Grant, this is Trey Winger, my boss."

Her boss. And ex-lover. The guy who told her she wasn't good enough for an on-air position. Grant stuck out his hand and shook Trey's maybe a bit too firmly. Trey looked between Grant and Charli, openly curious.

"I didn't know you'd be here," Charli said.

Trey shrugged and put a hand on the older man's shoulder. "Mr. Brinkley invited me. He sits on the station's board of directors and owns this property."

More introductions were exchanged, and Grant could sense Charli's professional image rising like the tide. Her posture turned straighter, her voice firmer, despite the fact that her heart had to be hammering in her chest. Hell, his own knees were still a little weak from their interlude. Seeing Charli flip that switch so easily gave him a ridiculous sense of pride. His girl had her shit together.

His girl. Damn, he needed to tame those thoughts.

He grabbed her hand again anyway, ignoring the satisfaction he felt when she grabbed back.

Mine, his mind whispered.

TWENTY-FIVE

"So do you think your boss saw anything?" Grant asked as he turned the truck into Charli's neighborhood.

She shrugged, thinking back to the way Trey had looked at her when he'd realized who she was. That *wow* reaction had been more than a little satisfying, had made every wax and pluck of her make-over worth it. Nothing like a great how-ya-like-me-now moment. "I really don't think so. Trey's not smooth enough to cover up his reactions that well. He wouldn't have said anything, but he would've shown some sign."

"I thought when you two went off on your own for a few minutes that he was going to confess to having seen us."

"Nah, I just wanted to tell him about my big break in the story," she said, looking out the window at her sleepy neighborhood. "He was really excited. Offered to go with me in the morning."

"Is that right?" Grant said, his sarcasm evident.

She looked over at him, frowning. "It's going to be a huge story. Of course, he'd be interested in going."

"Uh-huh."

"What?"

Grant's gaze slid toward her, then back to the road. "You should know that boss of yours is still interested in you."

She snorted. "Oh, please. First of all, this is the guy who told me I wasn't pretty enough for TV. Second of all, I've been down that road with him and have no interest in going back. He knows that."

Plus, how could she go back to someone like Trey after experiencing what she had with Grant? It'd be like going back to canned ham after you've had Kobe beef.

"Freckles, I've spent a lot of time in my life observing people's behavior. And the way Trey acted with you tonight was like a dog on the hunt. His attention never left you when you moved around the party. And the guy looked at me with challenge in his eyes." Grant smirked at her. "Which proves he's not only interested in you but apparently has a death wish."

She laughed. "Ooh, jealousy. Looks kind of pretty on you, cowboy."

He sniffed.

"For the record, I told him he didn't need to come along. I don't want him spooking my source."

"Smart," Grant said. "Maybe you should be his boss instead of the other way around."

"I wish."

Grant made the turn onto her street and stared out at the road. "You know you could always stay at The Ranch and tell Trey and the rest of the guys who turned you down for the position to go fuck themselves. I could cover your expenses until you find something else."

His words sounded off the cuff, but the shift in his posture said otherwise. She stared at him, the suggestion stalling her ability to respond for a second. Was he seriously suggesting that she stay? The thought of having something longer term with him tugged at a longing deep within her bones, but she knew that it would eventually end badly. After all, he'd said she could stay at The Ranch, not *with* him. She had no interest in being some woman he kept around for occasional entertainment.

"I'm not going to quit my job," she said. "And I'm definitely not going to let you pay me for sex."

He shot her a come-on-now look. "You know that's not what I was suggesting. I just hate to see you working so hard for people who don't appreciate your skills. You're busting your ass, and they don't even pay you enough to afford a safe car to drive. I have the means to help you if you needed time to find something different."

"I appreciate the thought. But I can take care of things myself," she said, straightening in her seat.

"You don't always have to, though," he said quietly, almost more to himself than to her.

She didn't have an answer to that.

His truck rumbled up her driveway, and she couldn't help the little pang of sadness that hit her seeing her house so dark and lonely. Her home wasn't much, but it'd been her first real place after moving out of her family's house, so it always gave her a sense of pride knowing she'd gotten it on her own. And though Grant's guest cabin was great, nothing could replace having your own things around you.

Grant shut off the engine. "Give me your keys. I want to check inside and make sure everything's okay before you go in."

"I'm sure nothing else has happened. They took everything they could possibly want the first time."

He held out his palm. "Better to be safe, freckles."

She sighed and dropped her keys in his hand. He reached past her and unlocked the glove compartment, removing his handgun. Her first instinct was to protest, but if anything was wrong in the house, she'd want Grant to have protection. "Be careful, okay? I'd rather not end the evening with a dead date."

He smirked. "Aww, nice to know you care, freckles."

She rolled her eyes, but the move was forced. The truth was she *did* care. Too much probably. And the more they spent time together, the more her heart was digging roots into the slippery slope they were both residing on.

"Don't come in until I give you the all clear." He hopped out of the truck and headed toward her front door, scanning the area as he went.

He disappeared inside the house for a few long minutes, no doubt examining every nook and cranny, then finally stepped back onto the porch. He looked so big standing there in front of her dainty white house—like the big, bad wolf ready to blow it down. He leaned against a post and sent her a smile that promised sin.

Her stomach did a little flip. She pushed open the truck's door and climbed out. "Everything looks all right?"

"We've got the place all to ourselves," he said as she got closer. "And can I tell you how happy I am that you have a four-poster bed?"

She took the two steps up to the porch. "You didn't get enough by the pond, cowboy?"

He locked an arm around her waist and pulled her against him. "Not nearly. Never enough with you."

Her skin went goose bumpy as her chest pressed against his. "You know I have an early morning ahead of me?"

"Hmm," he said, backing them both through the open doorway, then kicking the front door shut. "Maybe we should skip sleep altogether, then."

"You're insatiable."

"Guilty as charged." He went for the tie on her wrap dress and pulled. "But you can always say no."

She knew she should stop him, knew that every time she let him touch her she became more ensnared in her fucked-up feelings for him, but she couldn't resist the siren song and the rush of having his hands against her again. "Why do I never want to?"

He shoved the dress off her and kissed and licked his way up her neck. "You're always so edible, Charlotte. I can taste the night air on you."

She tilted her head back, and he traced his tongue along the hollow of her throat. Like a burning match to wax, her insides went warm and liquid in an instant. "God, yes."

He chuckled against her jaw. "I'm not the only insatiable one here. Go to your bedroom and stand by the foot of the bed to wait for me. I want to take my time with you."

"Yes, Grant." There really was no other answer she could've given. Her body and mind craved him like nothing she'd experienced before. She needed this. Him.

He released her and she made her way through her small living room to her bedroom. The room was bathed in the warm glow of her bedside lamp, the scene so familiar but yet foreign. Never before had she walked into her room and viewed it through someone else's eyes. The thick posts of her bed now seemed a sensual choice, sinister in the best way possible. Her sheets—a high-thread-count gift to herself—now beckoned with promises of downy softness against bare skin. And oh, the things Grant could do with the small collection of vibrators she kept hidden in her panty drawer.

She left her undergarments on and faced the bed, keeping her back to the door, but her eyes fixed on the mirror above her dresser. Her heart hammered as she listened to Grant's heavy footsteps make their way around her home. She had no idea what he was doing but had no doubt he had more in store for her than a quick romp before bed.

A shadow crossed over the mirror and she sucked in a breath as Grant's wide frame filled her doorway. "What a pretty view."

He stepped behind her, his body heat radiating onto her skin, and ran a gentle hand over the curve of her ass, then traced along the crease. The pad of his finger pressed against her back entrance through the thin fabric of her panties. She shivered, the still-foreign sensation stoking the flames of need inside her.

"I need to take you here, sweet Charlotte," he said, his voice gruff. "I can't keep touching this beautiful ass of yours and not feel it around me."

She wet her lips, catching her own unsure eyes in the mirror's reflection even as the decadent sensation of him teasing her there had a new rush of moisture slicking her panties. She'd enjoyed the hell out of the plugs he'd used on her, but he was so much bigger than that. There was no way it wouldn't hurt. "I'm a little scared."

"Mmm," he said, taking a long, deep inhale as he continued to stroke her. It was as if he was breathing in her fear, feasting on it.

"You like that I'm scared," she said, more realization than accusation.

He kissed the slope of her shoulder, his teeth grazing her skin. "I could make you feel better and say it doesn't, but I'd be lying."

She closed her eyes, trying to reel in her runaway nerves. He was a sadist and had never apologized for that. Of course he didn't mind that she was scared.

"A little fear makes your pulse go fast and your skin turn flushed." He pulled her panties to the side, then slid a finger along her folds, sinking deep into her pussy. "And look how wet it makes you. I'm not the only one who gets off by the rush of adrenaline. There's a reason you seek out all those extreme sports and adventures. You're made for this, Charlotte. Your body and mind seek it."

Her leg muscles seemed to liquefy as he worked another finger inside her. She bowed forward, her palms hitting the mattress, saving her from falling face-first into the comforter. His words were like the sharp, quick stings of his riding crop—the accuracy behind them exposing all her vulnerable places.

"I bet if I lit candles and played soft music while gently introducing the possibility of anal sex to you over wine, you'd shut down. You're not that kind of girl."

She stiffened, the assumption—though screaming with truth in her ears—all too close to what she'd been dealing with all her life. *You're not like normal girls.* "So, what, I'm not worth the wining, dining, and romancing?"

His free hand came down hard on her ass, the sharp smack sending a jolt through her veins and a cry from her lips. "Don't do that, Charlotte. Don't turn my words around and use them as weapons."

Her fingers curled into the comforter, rebellion welling up inside her.

He pulled away, removing all contact. "Before you speak, I suggest you think long and hard about what you want. I'll give you one chance to make a request tonight. If that's candles and opera music, I'll make it happen. But whatever you request better be what you *really* want, not what you wish you wanted."

She stared at the tone-on-tone stripes of her comforter, her breathing rapid with a confusing combination of anger and desire. Grant's hard command had tempted a knee-jerk response, but she'd bit down on her tongue to keep it in. When she pictured the gentle, romantic evening he was offering her, it left her cold. Her other lovers had tried that route, and it'd never affected her the way she'd hoped it would. She craved genuine emotion with Grant, but not in that Hallmark-commercial kind of way, and definitely not in the bedroom.

The breath filling her lungs turned hot as reality coursed through her. Even if she wanted to be that sweet, flowers-and-hearts girl, she wasn't wired that way. And neither was he. She could either keep trying to convince herself she could be or accept what was. She shifted her weight from foot to foot. What she needed—wanted—

danced on her lips, the forbidden desire they'd playfully mentioned earlier tonight hovering in the silence between them. *Capture. Force.*

How often in the last few weeks had she wondered what it would be like to see Grant really let go? Despite everything they'd done together, she always sensed he was being careful with her, like he was afraid to show her too much darkness. But she craved that from him.

"Tell me what you want, Charlotte," Grant repeated, his voice like the far-off rumble of a thunderstorm. "And I'll do it."

She pushed herself upright, her resolve calming the disjointed emotions battling inside of her. She met his stoic gaze in the mirror, her own expression reflecting the confidence in her decision, but also the underlying trepidation inherent in it. She turned around to face him.

"Well?"

She swallowed past the kink in her vocal cords. "I want you to *make* me do it."

TWENTY-SIX

The flicker of surprise that crossed Grant's features at Charli's request was as quick as a blink, but she hadn't missed it. He unfurled his arms from their crossed position over his chest, his fingers flexing at his sides. "Tell me your safe word, Charlotte."

Her heart pounded so hard, she wondered if her ribs would have a permanent imprint. "Texas."

His eyes seemed to turn black in the soft light of the bedroom. He leaned over slowly, his mouth brushing the shell of her ear. Then one whispered word filled her mind. "Run."

Her body reacted before her mind kicked in, her bare feet squeaking against the wood floor as she juked around Grant and took off into the hallway. Her house wasn't big, but she had the advantage of knowing every hiding place and every room with a lock. He gave her a few seconds' head start, so she slammed her office door to make him think she was hiding in there and headed to the kitchen instead. The attached laundry room had a lock and had another door that led to the screened-in porch on the back of the house. That could work.

She hurried past the pantry and slipped inside the alcove. She locked the laundry room door, her fingers trembling, and pressed her back against the door to the porch. Even though she knew this was a game, an undeniable zip of fear buzzed through her. Grant wouldn't harm her in any kind of serious way, but she wasn't under the impression he'd go easy on her either. The thought only served to make the achy pulsing between her legs more unbearable.

She strained her ears, trying to listen for his heavy footfalls. She doubted the man could walk softly even if he tried. There was a distant squeak—probably the office door opening. He'd probably try the laundry room any second. She looked around for anything to use to distract him, but all that was in there was a basket full of unfolded laundry. She grabbed a T-shirt and a pair of running shorts off the top and slipped them on. He'd never expect her to go outside since she'd been half-naked, but this could give her the element of surprise.

She reached behind her and turned the knob on the door to the porch, keeping her eyes on the other door and doing her best to not make a peep. When the knob gave, she backed onto the porch, never taking her focus off the kitchen door. One, two, three steps and she'd be to the screen door that led to the backyard. She spun on her heel, ready to bolt, and slammed smack into the hard wall of Grant's chest.

Before the scream could even exit her throat, Grant turned her, clamping a hand over her mouth. The noise came out a pitiful, muffled sound.

"Going somewhere?" he said, his breath hot against her neck.

Not ready to lose so easily, she jammed her elbow into his ribs and tried to wriggle free. But he was too damn strong for her to even get an inch of space between them. He gripped her harder.

"Now you're just pissing me off, princess." He dragged her back into the laundry room and kicked the door shut behind him. "If you play nice, I won't have to get rough."

She grabbed for the hand he had locked over her mouth and dug her fingernail into his cuticle—a self-defense move her brother had taught her.

"Son of a bitch!"

His hand dropped, and the moment's distraction let her slip free. She vaulted back through the door to the kitchen, an angry cowboy hot on her heels. When she took the turn into the living room, she thought she had enough of a lead to make it back to the bedroom, but before she hit the hallway, he grabbed hold of her shirt and yanked her backward. He caught her before she landed on her ass, but soon she was on the floor anyway. He pinned her down on the rug, belly down, knee against her back.

"I should've known you wouldn't be cooperative." He yanked her shorts and panties off in one rough tug, then tore her T-shirt, a long rip down the back.

The sound of the tearing and his handling of her had every sensory system in her body firing. Her mind tumbled into that place where thoughts went quiet and sensation took over. She struggled beneath him. "Please, please don't do this. You can take whatever you want from the house."

His dark chuckle was almost unrecognizable as he unhooked her bra. "You think I'm in here for a fucking TV, princess?"

"I have money in my closet," she said on a whimper.

"I don't need your money." Something wound around one of her wrists, then he was shoving her knee under her, and the same scratchy material wrapped around her thigh—rope. "What I need is this tight, virgin ass of yours."

A hard tremor moved through her. She tried to move, but her wrist and thigh were now anchored to each other. He gave her the same treatment on the other side until she was left with her ass in the air, knees spread wide, and the side of her face pressed into the rug.

Breath rasped through her lungs as she fell into the moment, surrendering to him, her desire for him swallowing any lingering fear. Her clit throbbed from neglect, the soft rug caressing her nipples and only ratcheting up her desperation further. "Please."

He stood, his shoes coming into her peripheral vision. "Why do I get the feeling you're no longer begging for mercy but begging for me to fuck you?"

"Because I am. Please."

He crouched down and wrapped a hank of her hair around his fist, lifting her head ever so slightly. "You know how hot it makes me to hear you beg so nicely? I may even let you enjoy it now."

He released her hair and stood. The sound of his belt buckle raised goose bumps on her sweat-slicked skin. She peeked upward to find him peering down at her as he doubled the belt over and tucked the metal part in his hand. He smiled a smile that could simultaneously melt her insides and break her open, then he stepped out of view.

Even knowing it was coming couldn't prepare her for the blow. The belt landed across her ass, sending a rocket of stinging pleasure curling up her spine and down her legs. She cried out, her hands yanking at the ropes and inadvertently spreading her thighs wider.

Another swat came and grazed her exposed sex, jolting her and almost sending her into instant orgasm. Her back bowed, her head shaking back and forth like a restless horse trying to break loose. "Oh, God."

He hit her again and again, but she lost count of the lashes when the hot pain softened and blurred into the intoxicating rush of pure adrenaline and pleasure. Her pussy throbbed and her skin felt tight all over her, like she had too much sensation to hold in one body. She wanted to beg, to scream, to cry . . . to love him.

"I can't wait any longer for you, baby. You're driving me fucking crazy." The buckle hit the floor with a clang and the sound of a zipper filled in the space between her breaths. Then he was there behind her, his palms and mouth gentle and nurturing where he'd been brutal seconds before. "I need to be inside you."

Her verbal abilities had slipped into the part of her brain she didn't have access to at the moment, but nothing in the world sounded better than that. She tilted her hips upward, a silent appeal.

Cool liquid touched her backside, Grant's fingers massaging and spreading lube he'd apparently brought with him. "Just relax for me, princess. Let me in."

She didn't think she was capable of fighting the invasion even if she'd wanted to. His finger pushed inside her, one then another, and a moan spilled out of her. He worked her backside with one hand and moved the other to her clit. She squeezed her eyes shut, the pleasure almost too overwhelming to process. Methodically and with tortuous patience, he coaxed her body to cooperate, to open to him. As soon as she thought she'd explode with orgasm, he'd back off her clit and ease her down. If she could've formed the words, she would've begged—shamelessly and profusely.

But soon he'd hit his own limit and he shifted into position behind her, untying her hands so she could brace herself and then spreading her even wider. His cock pressed against her, the blunt head feeling impossibly huge in comparison to the fingers he'd been using. "Relax and push against me, baby. I'm not going to hurt you."

She breathed through one final whip of anxiety, then did as he said, mentally and physically accepting him. He moved through the last bit of resistance, and then he was gliding inside her, stretching her, setting off a circuit board of nerve endings that had her nails burying into the carpet and her body quivering with edgy need.

"Oh, Jesus, Charli," Grant said, his voice full of grit. "I want to take my time with you, but damn, you feel good."

She swallowed past her parched throat, her own words barely a whisper. "Please don't make me wait too long."

"Ah, hell," he said, draping himself over her back and hooking his arm around her hip. "That's a request I can definitely grant."

His fingers found her clit and stroked as his pelvis tapped her backside, his cock buried fully inside her. She reared up, and a strangled moan that she didn't even recognize as her own filled her ears. Grant sped up, his thrusts matching the urgency pulsing inside her. Her head sagged between her shoulders and she went down to her elbows, all her strength going toward holding back the dam of sensation threatening to overtake her.

"Please, please, please," she said, a mumbled string of unintelligible, desperate words pouring out of her.

He pinched her clit and switched from nice and easy to commanding—his dominance fully unleashed. "Come for me, Charlotte."

He fucked into her with long, spine-arching thrusts, rocking her against the floor and pushing her to a place she'd never visited before. Wretched sounds scraped past her throat as the need wound inside her, tighter and tighter, until she thought she'd die of sensory overload.

Then Grant moaned her name, and the erotic sound of his own loss of control pushed her over the cliff and sent her plummeting into orgasm. Tears pricked her eyes, and she screamed through the overwhelming surge of pleasure, the waves crashing against her over and over until she felt him empty inside her.

After a few panted moments and murmured words, he slipped out of her.

She melted into the floor, not sure she ever wanted to get up again. He kissed her shoulder, her hair, the top of her spine. "That was so, so perfect, Charlotte. I've never . . ." But he seemed to be struggling with intelligent speech as well. "Thank you, just thank you. You're amazing."

All she could do was sigh in response.

He laughed softly, his obvious affection rolling over her and wrapping around her. He laid his shirt over her quickly chilling skin. "Stay here, darlin'. There's a hot bath with your name on it. I'll be right back."

Charli lay there snuggled against Grant's chest, listening to the steady thrum of his heartbeat and enjoying the scent of her soap on him. Even after all that had transpired in her house tonight, it felt so normal, so right, lying there in her bed with him. Maybe she didn't crave candles and soft music, but this—this she ached for. She hadn't really had a chance to be like this with him yet, to simply cuddle and enjoy his presence.

For a moment, she let herself imagine that this was real, that he would sleep there beside her all night, that they were in a real relationship. But even with her system utterly exhausted, her logical brain wouldn't let her go there. *He'll never be yours.*

He traced his fingers along her spine with a languid motion. "What's on your mind, freckles? Your muscles have gone tense."

She frowned, staring at their intermingled shadows on the far wall. "It was nothing."

"No. Tell me."

She sighed. Did he always have to be so damn observant? She'd promised herself she wouldn't let herself fall deeper tonight. But her best intentions had been left somewhere between her bedroom and laundry room. Beyond the electric physical connection they'd shared tonight, when he'd put her in the bathtub afterward, his expression soft, his words tender, she'd plummeted into the abyss. He'd probably chalk it up to bottoming out after their intense scene, but she knew better. She needed to tell him the truth. Put it out there.

She closed her eyes, drumming up the nerve. There was only one thing she could say. "I don't think I can do this anymore."

"What?" The rise and fall of his breathing paused beneath her cheek. "Why?"

She pushed herself up on her elbow. It was hard to look at him, but she wasn't a coward. If she was going to be honest, she'd do it to his face, would jump off the cliff and suffer the consequences. She took one long, deep breath, then said what she'd been thinking for far too long. "Because I'm starting to wish this was real."

He winced.

Actually *fucking* winced.

The reaction, though not shocking, was like a rusty knife twisting into her chest. She managed a derisive smirk. "Exactly my point."

"Charli." He sat up on his elbows.

She rolled fully away from him, wrapping the sheet around her breasts. "Don't even bother, Grant. I don't need the speech. This is not your fault. It's mine. You never pretended this was anything different than what it is."

"That's not—"

"I'm falling in love with you and you can't even kiss me," she said, cutting him off. "How stupid am I? I knew better and did it anyway."

He reached out for her, turning her back toward him. "Charli."

She shrugged away from his touch, feeling as if her emotions were being held together with duct tape. One wrong move and she'd bust wide open. "Please don't. Don't coddle me. And don't pretend you weren't just going to lie here until I fell asleep so you can go sleep on the couch."

His gaze shifted sideways, confirming her suspicion.

"Look, I get it, okay? You're used to separating your emotions from this kind of arrangement. I'm just another woman who enjoys what you do in bed." She pulled in a deep breath, refusing to let any tears fall, refusing to crack in front of him. "But I don't have that kind of practice. Every time we're together, it breaks down another piece of me, strips away another row of fencing. And after tonight, the defenses are downright decimated. Nothing is left standing. Hell, I've even found myself entertaining thoughts of what it'd be like to be a real submissive to you. To not just play the game."

He lifted his eyes, his surprise evident. "You're not just another woman. And I would take you on as my submissive in a second, Charli. But you deserve more than what I'm capable of giving. You wouldn't be happy."

She shook her head, sadness filtering through her like oil spilling into the ocean, blackening everything, tainting it. "You know what? You're right, cowboy. I've spent my whole life being everyone's second best. I certainly don't intend to play that role in my love life as well."

"You wouldn't be . . ." But he clearly couldn't finish the sentence. He scrubbed a hand over his face.

"Go sleep on the couch, Grant," she said, resignation weighing down her words. "That's where you were going to end up tonight anyway."

She turned over in bed, putting her back to him and hiding the anguish that smothered her. Her bedroom door clicked shut a few seconds later, leaving her alone—a state she'd always been comfortable with.

Until now.

Somehow she had a feeing nothing would ever feel comfortable again.

TWENTY-SEVEN

Grant sipped his coffee, keeping his eyes on a booth on the other side of the Southern Pancake Hut. The place was hopping with customers, and the rattle of dishes and clinking forks was enough to block out any hope that he'd be able to hear Charli's conversation with her source. Not that he really needed to hear anything. He could see her face in profile from his perch and would be able to read her expression. If anything went wrong, she'd be able to alert him.

He set down his coffee mug, the smell of it mixing with the bacon and eggs he'd ordered. He shoved aside his untouched plate, the thought of food making his stomach revolt. Between the sick feeling his conversation with Charli had incited last night and the fact that he'd been unable to sleep, he felt as scrambled as the eggs on his plate.

She'd been like a stranger this morning. Her words had been polite, to the point, and all about the plan today. He was officially looking at her from outside the castle walls now. His visitor's pass had been revoked—and rightly so. She'd called herself his second best last night, and he hadn't even stood up and denied it.

He fingered the platinum wedding band he always wore on his right hand, the smooth metal suddenly feeling more like a shackle than a comfort. Why couldn't he just push past the fear and kiss her? Tell her that he had feelings for her, too?

He'd gotten off the couch a few times last night intending to do just that. But then reality would wallop him in the face. He could do that, but then what? Charli was fiercely independent and a dare-devil to boot. The first time she announced that she was going skydiving or something, he'd want to lock her in his cabin until he could convince her otherwise. And besides her risk taking, she could easily decide one day to simply walk away. The thought of loving and losing someone again . . .

He rubbed a palm over the back of his neck, sweat starting to gather there. He wouldn't survive it. No, this had to be the way it went. Ending things was best for both of them.

Movement near Charli's table caught his eye, yanking him from his morose thoughts. The man Charli had been interviewing shook her hand and stood. Charli was nodding, obviously thanking him, and then waved him off when he attempted to pay for breakfast. Her gaze shot Grant's way for a brief second. He could almost feel the energy vibrating off of her. She'd gotten her story. *Good girl.*

The guy left the restaurant, and Charli sat back down, making more notes. She glanced his way and discreetly gave him the signal for five minutes, disguising it as trying to get the waitress's attention for a refill. They had agreed not to interact in the restaurant on the off chance anyone was watching. They'd even taken separate vehi-cles as an added precaution.

He made one final visual sweep of the restaurant, making note of any patrons that seemed to be paying particular attention to Charli. But most customers had other people with them. The few loners seemed more interested in their laptops and cell phones than anything else. So Grant tossed a few bills on the table and swigged the last of his coffee. Then he slipped out the door to go scan the parking lot and make sure there was no one waiting for Charli to leave.

After quickly walking by her rental car and checking that nothing looked amiss, he made his way to his truck where he had a straight-shot view of the entrance of the restaurant. He kept the door unlocked in case he had to act quickly like the last time he'd watched her from afar. Hopefully, today wouldn't be a repeat of that nightmare. But at least this time, he'd be more prepared.

If he could get her past the next few days, she'd be able to relax a bit. Once her story broke, there'd be no reason for anyone to keep working so hard on keeping her quiet. At least that's what he hoped. Regardless, he wouldn't leave her unprotected anytime soon. Even if she no longer wanted him in her life, he had friends he could pay to keep guard for a while.

And he'd definitely get an alarm system installed for her.

An alarm. Before he could stop it from happening, the unwanted memories filled his head, like old friends you couldn't close the door on.

He'd made that promise to his wife, too, when they'd gotten their first house. They'd just moved off his family's property and into their new home in the suburbs to make room for the baby. The neighborhood had been new, quiet, well-to-do. In one of their discussions about things to add to the house, Rachel had asked if they could get an alarm system put in since she'd heard some news story about a rash of break-ins one town over.

Grant had thought she was being paranoid about living in the "big city" after country life, had playfully teased her about it. She'd always been the overly cautious type, and pregnancy had put that trait into hyperdrive. He'd assured her that they were safe. If anyone ever broke in, he had a gun and knew how to use it. He would always keep her safe. But a few weeks after they'd settled in, they'd become the next victims. He'd woken up in the middle of the night to the sound of breaking glass and had shoved Rachel into their closet—a fatal mistake. He'd been stupid and prideful. The fucking man of the house protecting his own.

When he'd reached the bottom floor, he'd caught the thief in the living room. Pulling the gun and thinking he had everything under control, Grant had confronted him. But the guy had been hopped up on drugs, fearless, and had launched himself at Grant, stabbing him in the shoulder right before Grant pulled the trigger.

The knife slash had been a nonfatal blow; the robber hadn't been as lucky. And Grant had thought everything was going to be okay. He'd won.

Only then had he heard Rachel's shriek and realized he'd failed to consider the most crucial thing of all—the thief may have not been alone.

Grant had propelled himself upward on adrenaline alone, but it'd been too late. The man's partner had dragged Rachel down the stairs after he'd heard the gunshot, had seen his brother dead on the floor of the living room. And had lost it.

Rachel's wide, terrified eyes had met Grant's a moment before the man had pressed a gun into her back and pulled his own trigger. Grant had fired back, getting the guy in the chest, but all had already been lost.

Grant had cradled his wife in his arms, telling her it was going to be okay, begging her not to leave him. But by the time the police had arrived, she'd lost too much blood. Rachel and their unborn son had died at the bottom of the staircase. Because Grant hadn't taken her seriously, hadn't protected her like he promised her he would.

If not for his mistake, they'd probably both still be here today.

Rachel would've opened her craft store by now. His son would be in school, playing sports, maybe learning how to ride horses with his daddy . . .

Grant pressed the heels of his hands to his eyes, the grief threatening to bust through every pore. He hadn't cried since the funeral. Part of him believed he'd cried so much when it'd happened that his lifetime allotment of tears had been used up. But as he sat there in his truck, moisture touched his cheeks. He swiped at the tears, gritting his teeth as he tried to reel in the waterfall of emotions pounding him.

He couldn't afford to lose it right now. He had a job to do. He forced his attention to the clock, trying to focus. Charli had said five minutes and it'd been ten. Her car still sat a few spots away, so he knew he hadn't missed her come out. She was probably caught up in finishing her notes. But Grant wasn't in the mood to take chances. Five more minutes. If she wasn't out, he was going back in.

He hadn't failed a mission since that night with his wife, and he didn't plan on doing so now.

Charli quickly jotted down a few more notes from her interview. Rodney had given her pay dirt. Not just an admission that he'd received cash payments while playing for the university but names of who he knew to be involved—including some pretty prominent businessmen and politicians in the area. But more important, he'd told her he suspected the university's dean had known the cheating was going on. The dean was well liked and a local celebrity. If those people could be implicated, the story was going to be huge. A career-making kind of scoop.

Finally. She was going to get her shot.

"Mind if I join you?"

Charli's head snapped up, the familiar voice startling her. "Pete? What the hell are you doing here?"

"I'll take that warm greeting as a yes." He gave her a cat-who-ate-the-mouse smirk and slid into the other side of the booth. He nodded toward her notebook. "Got some good stuff today?"

Instinctively, she dragged her notebook closer to her on the table, and glanced over to where Grant had been sitting. But of course, he wasn't there. She'd sent him the signal to go outside a few minutes earlier. "Just working on the piece about Valley High School."

"Bullshit," he said, leaning forward and putting his elbows on the table. "I saw Rodney walking out of here. You finally got him to talk, didn't you?"

Her stomach turned sideways, a sick feeling rolling over her. How would Pete even know what story she was investigating or why Rodney was important? Unless . . .

"You *fucking* prick."

"Always so crass, Beaumonde. Didn't your momma teach you any manners?"

It took everything she had not to jump across the table and throttle him. "Yours didn't teach you breaking and entering is a crime?"

He drummed his fingers on the table. "It's not breaking in when you leave a spare set of keys in your drawer at work. It was just . . . entering."

She grabbed her purse, her skin crawling being this close to the man who'd scared her out of her house, run her off the fucking road. He could've killed her. She moved to scoot out of the booth.

"I wouldn't leave so fast, Charli," he said, the humor fading from his voice. "I have something you may want."

He dropped a thumb drive onto the tabletop. She stared at it, the small thing seeming to loom between them. "What is it?"

He smiled, way too pleased with himself. "An audio file starring you."

Her brow knitted.

"Maybe this will refresh your memory." He pulled his cell phone from his jacket pocket and touched the screen.

Voices spilled from the small speaker. Very, very familiar voices.

I'm about halfway to coming, where are you, sweet Charlotte?

Wishing I was there. Touching you.

Charli gasped, reaching for Pete's phone, but he held it out of her reach. "Turn it off."

Are you wet for me?

Perhaps.

How much privacy does your office allow?

Charli looked around, mortified that anyone might hear, but luckily the restaurant was loud enough that they hadn't drawn anyone's attention yet.

Pete laughed and touched the screen, halting the embarrassing recording. "I have to admit, Beaumonde. Listening to you on that call was kind of hot. I didn't think you had it in you. But I knew you were up to something on the phone when I saw you were all flushed and breathless when I stopped by your office."

Anger rocketed through her, but she forced herself to stay calm, to not let him know how bad he'd gotten to her. "You're a sick bastard, Pete. I'm sure the jail psychologist will have a fucking field day."

"Oh, there will be no cops. You can't prove I broke into your house." He folded his hands on the tabletop, as if they were discussing next week's meeting agenda instead of criminal acts. "This can all be resolved quite neatly actually. You give me your interview notes, the signed statement Rodney gave you, and let me take credit for breaking the story. And . . . you step out of the running for the anchor position. Do those two things, and you get your recording back. I'll erase the copy on my phone and you can have the thumb drive."

"No fucking way. This is *my* story and that anchor job is mine."

He shrugged. "All right, well, I'm sure Trey and the board would love to hear what their reporter is doing at work on their dime. You won't have to worry about not getting the anchor position anymore because you'll be fired and have no references to find something else."

She balled her fists, ready to throw more punches at him, but as his words sunk in she realized he had her in a goddamned corner. What she'd done at work had been completely unprofessional. If they doubted how seriously she took her job now, she'd blow any shot at being seen as a professional if this came out.

But if she turned over her notes, Pete would get the glory. And the job.

The only chance she had at someone believing her was Trey. He'd known she was chasing this particular story. Maybe she could explain to him what had happened. They had a friendship. Surely he could keep the information about the phone sex to himself.

Charli took a deep breath and grabbed the thumb drive. "I want to watch you delete it off your phone."

Pete's expression lit with smug triumph. He hit a few buttons and the file was gone. She shoved her notebook across the table and stood. "Only a fucking coward would stalk and blackmail someone to get a promotion. It's really kind of pitiful. You know how much better I am than you are, and you don't have the balls to compete on an even playing field."

He scoffed. "The playing field is never even, Beaumonde. If it were, one of us would've had that sidelines position. You gotta do what you gotta do."

"Right. 'Cause almost killing me out on that road would've been worth a promotion. You're a goddamned psychopath."

A line formed between his brows. "Almost killing you?"

She shook her head. So now he was going to play innocent? "Come near me ever again, and I'll make that punch from the other day look mild."

She stalked out of the restaurant, her head about to explode. Fucking punk. He couldn't even man up and get his own damn story. If he'd put half as much energy into getting his own scoop as he had trying to hijack hers, he'd probably have a promotion already. All she could hope was that Trey would take her side and not accept Pete's story.

The sunshine blinded her as she stepped into the parking lot. She pulled her sunglasses from her purse and found Grant walking her way from the other side of the lot. He halted when he saw her, a glimmer of relief crossing his features. He must've been on the way to check on her since she'd taken longer than five minutes.

They had agreed not to interact in case anyone was watching, but now that Pete had outed himself, she had no reason to be covert. He turned to go back toward his truck, but she followed him over. "Wait, we don't have to play strangers anymore."

He spun to face her, frowning. "What?"

She gave him the quick version of what had just happened, venom dripping off her tone.

Grant's jaw flexed. "I see."

"So no more stalker, but no more story . . . or promotion for that matter unless Trey helps me out."

"Is that bastard still inside?" Grant asked, glancing toward the main door, a predatory glint in his eye.

She put a hand on his forearm. "Don't. You'll just get yourself in an unnecessary mess. Pete comes from a family of lawyers. We can't prove anything, and if you lay a hand on him, he'll press charges before you can blink. It's not worth it. Let me handle it."

He looked unmoved.

"I'm serious. Let it go."

He sighed. "That's not my strong suit, freckles, but I'll do my best."

She checked the time on her phone. "Look, I'm going to head into work and try to get to Trey before Pete does. You're relieved of bodyguard duty. Pete's got what he wants now."

"Charli—"

"I'll come by tonight and get my stuff from the cabin so I can move it back home." The words hurt coming out, but after last night she didn't see any other option. He'd had the chance to tell her that she was wrong, that he loved her back. But her house had remained silent last night, her bedroom empty.

He shifted his focus away from the diner and met her gaze, regret etching lines at the corners of his eyes. "We should talk."

"We already did." She went up on her tiptoes and kissed his cheek, closing her eyes and lingering for a second too long. This would be the last time she allowed herself to touch him. Tears lined her throat, but she forced them down. She pulled back and gave him her best attempt at a smile. "Thanks for everything, Grant. It's been . . . educational."

A pained expression shrouded his features. But he didn't say anything further.

What was there to say?

Only one thing. "Good-bye, Grant."

TWENTY-EIGHT

Charli was in the mood to break things by the time late afternoon rolled around. Or maybe *beat* things—like Pete's smarmy face. Trey hadn't been in the office, and no one seemed to know when he'd be coming back. She'd tried his cell number without any luck. Pete hadn't returned either. He was probably busy studying her notes so he could fake his way through owning her story.

She gripped the edge of her desk, letting out a groan of frustration.

Her phone beeped, indicating an internal call. She nearly pounced on the receiver. "Hello?"

"Beaumonde."

"Trey!" she said, relief zipping through her. "I've been trying to track you down all day."

"Sorry, it's been a crazy day. But I'm in my office now. We need to talk."

"Boy, do we."

Charli had never made it to her boss's office so quickly. She swung open the door, her story ready to burst from her lips, but Trey's grim expression halted her in her tracks.

He already knew. She could see it all over his face.

"Shut the door." He pointed to the chair in front of his desk. "And sit."

She clicked the door shut, then sank into the chair, her limbs half numb. "So Pete told you anyway."

He looked to the ceiling, as if counting to ten in his head to calm down. "I told you to back off that fucking story, Beaumonde. But you had to keep pushing. Always pushing."

She frowned. Wait, this wasn't about the audiotape? "What are you talking about?"

He leaned onto his forearms, his gaze trapping her. "Any sane person would've dropped a story if they'd been run off the road and threatened. But no, you're like a goddamned bulldog who keeps breaking its leash."

Her blood chilled beneath her skin, her muscles going taut.

"You know anything about the company you work for, Charli? In all that dogged research, did you ever look at what percentage of the board of directors graduated from Dallas U?"

"Why would I research that?" She couldn't wrap her thoughts around his question, her mind spinning, putting all the pieces in place.

"Because, those are the people who cut our fucking paychecks, Beaumonde," he barked, his cheeks going ruddy. "The people I answer to. Men who would do *anything* to make sure their good names aren't sullied and that their team keeps winning."

Her stomach lurched as her brain caught up with the conversation, rage welling up inside her. Her own company had tried to shut her up—hurt her.

Trey shook his head, resignation settling like dust in the creases of his face. "I've always liked you, Charli. May have even loved you once upon a time." He sighed. "I wanted to keep you out of it, tried to. But you couldn't leave well enough alone. You were never good at listening."

She wanted to yank him up by that collar of his and shake him. How dare he act like some martyr who'd tried to help her? "I was doing my *job*, Trey."

"It's not your job anymore, Charli. You're fired."

"*What?*" Red flooded her vision, his words like glass shattering in her brain. "You can't do that."

"I can and am." He grabbed a sheet of paper from his printer and slid it across the desk. "We had Pete destroy all of your notes and facts. So, you have no proof of your story anymore. Plus, he got us the added bonus of your phone interlude with your boyfriend. Legitimate grounds for termination anyway."

All she could do was stare at the notice of termination.

"Oh, and we talked to your source this morning, so don't bother going back to him again. He no longer has any memory of speaking to you."

She gasped, looking up from the document. "You hurt Rodney?"

He shrugged. "Hush money and a well-placed threat are much more effective than physical violence."

Well, now she knew where Trey had gotten the money for that new Mercedes he was driving around. But apparently she wasn't worth hush money. They were just getting rid of her. "So I'm just supposed to walk away?"

"If you don't cause a fuss, we'll just say you resigned. And believe me, Charli, you spill anything to anyone, you're taking your life in your hands." He rubbed a hand over his jawline, looking more weary than she ever remembered seeing him. "Their original plan was to get rid of you. They knew you didn't really have any family around. It would take a few days for anyone to even notice you were gone. That accident on the road was just their first try."

The cold wash of fear went all the way to her bones this time.

"If you hadn't hightailed it to your boyfriend's place, I'm not sure we'd be sitting here today." His eyes shifted downward, some glimmer of guilt surfacing. "I convinced them to give me a chance to get some dirt on you, a way to get you out of this without them hurting you."

She wrapped her arms around herself, wondering if she was going into some stage of shock. "Why are you doing this?"

He twisted his college ring round and round his finger. "I haven't changed that much since we dated. The stakes have just gotten higher."

She thought back to all the times she'd lent him a few bucks here and there, the time he needed rent money in their junior year but really spent it playing cards.

"I owed money to some dangerous people. I needed help." He met her eyes, having the nerve to wear a poor-me expression.

"Right. So my head instead of yours?" she said, disgusted. She signed the termination notice with a hard flourish and stood. "You're a pathetic excuse for a man. Rot in hell, Trey."

"Maybe I already am. But don't slip up, Charli," he said, his tone foreboding. "They're not going to stop watching you."

She stalked out of the office, her head held high despite the riotous emotions blending her insides. But before she reached her desk, she had to run into one of the bathrooms and vomit. The fear of what could've been overwhelmed her.

She'd lost her story, her job, and the childhood dream she'd set out for herself.

But she was alive.

And there was only one person to thank for that.

Grant's hand was slick against the steering wheel as he raced back toward town. *Please, God, please.* The chant was about the only cogent thought he could manage for the last ten minutes.

He tried to dial Charli's number again, but she wasn't answering at work or on her cell. He cursed, then hit another number on speed dial.

"Hey Grant, what's up?" Andre said, answering on the second ring.

"Are you on duty?"

"Yeah, why?"

"I need you to go over to where Charli—the sub you met the other night—works and find her. I'm on my way but still a while out and if you're in uniform, they'll cooperate quicker."

"What's going on?"

"I think her boss may be a danger to her," Grant said, his heart beating like an out-of-time marching band. "The GPS says her car is still there, but I can't get her to answer the phone and the secretary hasn't seen her."

"Give me the address."

Grant rattled off the location and clicked off the phone. He'd followed that scum Pete from the diner and around town until the guy had finally headed home. Grant hadn't wanted any witnesses for what he was planning to do. Charli had told him to leave the guy alone, but Grant knew how to extract information without leaving a mark. And nothing brought out the sadist in him more than an asshole who threatened women.

Grant had thought he was only going to get Charli's notes back, but that prick had sung like a man on death row when Grant had pinned him to the ground and threatened to show him all the fun torture techniques he knew. Fucking wimp.

But the information Pete had spilled and the names he'd named had sent fear exploding like mines inside Grant's head. Charli was with the enemy, and Grant had found himself on the other side of the city from her.

The thought of something happening to her, of never seeing her again or hearing her laugh . . . of their only kiss being the one where he left her feeling like shit—he wouldn't survive it. He should've known to look more closely at her boss. The guy had given Grant a weird vibe as soon as he'd met him. Grant had attributed that vibe to her ex-lover still having interest, but he shouldn't have let it go so easily. Everyone should've been labeled a suspect first. He'd made a crucial error . . . again.

He gripped the steering wheel tighter and yanked it to the right, taking the exit off the interstate at warp speed. Five more minutes if he didn't catch any lights. He passed through the first intersection without issue, but on the second one, he got caught behind a line of traffic. He slammed his fist against the dashboard, about ready to jump out and run the rest of the way to her office. Silent prayers ran through his head like ticker tape.

But unlike earlier, the painful flashbacks didn't invade his thoughts. Panic didn't overtake him. Instead, his focus had become laser sharp. He saw every break in traffic, every spot he could slide into to get to her more quickly. By the time his truck skidded into her building's parking lot, he was ready to dismantle anyone who tried to prevent him from getting to her.

But as soon as he hopped out of the truck, he saw a familiar cop walking out of the front of the building with his arm around a redhead. Grant's heart nearly jumped out of his chest to race ahead of him. He launched himself toward Andre and Charli, relief coursing through him like fingers of electricity. *She's okay, she's okay* . . .

Charli glanced up as he approached, her face white, her shoulders hunched. He couldn't ever remember seeing her look so frail, like a strong breeze would knock her over. Andre kept a firm hold around her shoulders until Grant reached them, then he handed her over to him. Despite her earlier standoffishness, Charli came to him willingly, sagging against him and curling her fingers into his shirt.

"Oh, thank God," he murmured, running his hands along her back, checking that she was all in one piece. "You're all right. Baby, what happened, are you okay?"

Andre frowned. "She said she doesn't want to talk here."

"Right. Of course." He kept Charli close and cocked his head toward his truck. "Andre, I have something I need to give you in my truck. Walk with us?"

"Yeah, no problem." Andre didn't hesitate or question why Grant had needed his help or what it involved.

The implicit trust hit Grant right in the gut. For so long, he'd kept everyone at arm's length. But Jace and Andre hadn't relented when they'd joined The Ranch. They'd somehow worked their way past his force field and for the first time in as long as he could remember, he had real friends. Ones who would drop everything to help him no questions asked if he needed it.

And as he wrapped his arm around Charli and guided her to his truck, he realized that Charli had done the same thing. With her hard head and take-no-bullshit attitude, she'd hurdled right over his defenses. But unlike Jace and Andre, Charli hadn't just worked her way into his circle of friends, but rather into every corner of his being. For the few minutes today that he'd thought he may never see her again, he'd felt the impact of just how deeply she'd burrowed into his psyche.

Once they got to his truck, he helped her into the passenger side, then grabbed the file box he'd set on his floorboard. He shut Charli's door with his hip, then handed the box to Andre. "Take this directly to the station. From what I understand, there are audio recordings and files that will implicate a number of government officials and business owners in a cheating scandal with Dallas University. My source also told me there are recordings of conversations where break-ins and attempted murder are discussed."

Andre gave him a you-gotta-be-shittin'-me look. "How the hell did you get this kind of information?"

"I have my methods. It's probably better you not know." He glanced over at Charli's building, making sure no one was heading their way. "Just don't turn it over to anyone you don't trust. I don't know how deep this goes within the city government."

"No worries." He nodded toward the truck. "You got everything covered with your girl?"

"Covered? Yes. Worked out? No."

Andre's expression was all too knowing. It wasn't that long ago that he was torn up about his own woman. "She went with you willingly. That's a start."

Grant clapped Andre on the shoulder as he passed him. "That's about all I've got right now. Thanks for your help, man."

"Anytime, brother. Good luck."

Grant headed to the driver's side. Luck. He was going to need more than that. Because what he knew he needed to do was going to make his days of facing down terrorists look like a day at kindergarten.

Here goes nothing.

TWENTY-NINE

Charli sat curled on the couch in her cabin, huddled around a cup of hot tea. Her stomach had finally settled, and a long shower had helped slough off some of the ugliness of the day, but she still couldn't settle her mind.

Grant had told her on the way what he'd done to Pete, what information he'd gotten out of him. Charli couldn't help the satisfaction the news had brought her. She almost wished she could've been there to see Pete's face when Grant, in all his six-foot-seven, pissed-off cowboy glory, had busted through his door. Grant hadn't given her details about what threats he'd laid down, but she had a feeling Pete was probably still hiding in a closet in his house.

Served the bastard right.

But finding out in the same day that Trey, a guy she'd trusted wholeheartedly, had put her life on the line had her questioning her judgment? How could she have been so stupid? At one time, she'd truly cared about Trey. Even if their relationship had dissolved, she'd always considered him one of her closest friends. Were her instincts that off?

Of course they were. Hell, she'd actually thought she could help Grant get over his wife. Her instincts were about as accurate as her ability to guess lottery numbers.

Grant sank onto the armchair opposite her. "Andre called, said they're putting together arrest warrants for at least seven people, including your boss and that Brinkley guy he was with last night at the fund-raiser. Apparently, Pete took 'cover your ass' to the *n*th degree. He secretly taped almost every conversation he had with anyone."

She sipped her tea. "Told you, lawyer family."

"Right." He took a pull from the beer he was holding and looked at her like he had a thousand things to say but couldn't put together one.

The short few feet between them seemed to grow wider as they sat there. Had it only been last night that they'd made love in the grass? "You don't have to babysit me. I'm fine."

"I don't want you going back to your place until everyone's been rounded up," he said, setting his beer on the coffee table. "Someone could come after you when they realize you were the one to turn them in."

"I know." She pulled the blanket more tightly around her shoulders, her skin prickling at the thought of always looking over her shoulder. "I talked to my brother a few minutes ago. I'm going to stay with him for a little while until I figure out what I'm going to do. I'm sure my employment will be reinstated after everything comes out, but as of right now I'm not even sure I want to go back to TSN."

Grant's stoicism fell away, revealing a shade of hurt beneath it. "So you're leaving?"

She looked down at the frayed ends of the blanket. "I can't stay here, Grant."

She knew if she hung around him long enough, she'd slip up. Her normal armor seemed to turn to gossamer anytime he was around.

She'd fall into bed with him in a weak moment and end up digging herself into a deeper hole. She was done settling. She wasn't going to play second best for anyone, and she wasn't going to stay in a job that wasn't challenging her anymore. Life was too short to give up and set up camp on the side of the mountain instead of reaching the summit.

Even if she was going to be sitting on that summit all by her damn self.

"When do you plan on leaving?" he asked quietly.

"Tomorrow."

He leaned forward, lacing his fingers between his knees. "Let me drive you to Baton Rouge."

She winced. Nine hours sharing that small truck cab with him? Listening to that voice, being surrounded by his scent, hearing him hum to his favorite country songs? It would kill her. "I don't think that's a good idea."

He looked up, the wear of the day showing on his face. "My wife lost her life because I slacked off on one little detail, assumed she was safe. If something were to happen to you because I didn't finish the job of protecting you, I . . . I would never forgive myself."

The naked honesty in his voice sliced right through her. He'd never forgive himself. He definitely hadn't forgiven himself for the first time. He wore that guilt like an extra layer of clothes. And though the chances of something actually happening to her between here and Max's place were slim, she couldn't bear the thought of adding anything else to Grant's burden. If she was a "job" to him, she'd let him finish it.

"Okay. We can ride together." She set her tea down and met his gaze. "But I wish you'd give yourself a break. It's not your job to protect the world, Grant. What happened to Rachel wasn't your fault; it was the fault of the man who murdered her. Sometimes bad things happen and there's nothing we could've done to stop it."

He stood, shoving his hands in his pockets and gracing her with a sad smile. "I don't want to protect the world. I just want to protect you, freckles."

And with that, he turned on his boot heel and walked out, leaving her sitting there staring after him.

Grant's internal military clock apparently hadn't eased up over time. The next morning they were on their way before the chickens had even cracked an eye open. Grant drove through town so she could retrieve her rental car and return it, then he stopped by her house so she could grab a few extra things.

She had no idea how long she'd be staying with her brother, so she wanted to be prepared. At this point, she didn't even know if she wanted to come back. Looking for work in Louisiana was starting to sound more and more appealing. What had Trey said to her? She was the kind of person who could disappear and no one would notice for a while? That basically summed up her years in Texas. Now that her job was gone, she had nothing tying her here.

She glanced over at Grant as they cruised down the mostly empty interstate between Dallas and Shreveport, her heart pinging at the realization that this was going to be the last day with him. They hadn't talked much so far. And she suspected the steady stream of music was by design. He was as uncomfortable with this arrangement as she was. Even in profile, she could sense his tension. That muscle in his jaw was flexing beneath the layer of stubble, and his hands were holding the steering wheel so hard she knew his fingers had to be aching.

The sunlight caught the metal in his wedding band, and the flash blinded her for moment, forcing her to turn away. Even in silence, she couldn't be spared a reminder of all that stood between them. She turned her gaze to the trees whizzing by her on the right side. Only what? Six hours to go? She tapped her head lightly against the glass.

“Hey, Charli?” Grant said a little while later, lowering the music and interrupting her brooding.

“Uh-huh,” she said, not bothering to look his way. She’d been counting the number of billboards with cows on them and didn’t want to lose her spot.

The truck slowed a bit. “You remember that little speech I gave you when we first went over The Ranch’s rules—the part about safe, sane, and consensual?”

That dragged her attention away from the road signs. “Uh, yeah.”

He sent her a don’t-hate-me look and veered right, sending them along the exit ramp. “Well, I promise this is going to be safe . . . and mostly sane. Hopefully you’ll forgive me on the consensual part.”

THIRTY

Charli had no idea what the hell had gotten into Grant. They'd exited the interstate twenty minutes earlier, and despite her questions, he hadn't let her in on where they were going or what was about to happen. If he thought they were going to go have some last wham-bam-thank-you-ma'am before they parted, he had another think coming.

But his demeanor was anything but sexual. The man who seemed to always be the epitome of cool control couldn't stop shifting in his seat or flexing his fingers. She wanted to reach out and touch him, soothe him in some way, but she feared he might actually leap off the seat.

"Grant, please tell me what's going on. You're starting to make me nervous."

But before he had the chance to answer, he turned the truck down a narrow side road. A ranch entrance gate framed the road, and a sign with a *W* hung from the overhead cross post. What the hell? She leaned over to get a better glimpse of the sign. But the minute they passed under it, Grant seemed to deflate like a tire rolling over a nail, as if he'd been holding his breath since they'd exited the interstate.

They passed a mailbox. Reflective letters on the side of it glinted in the sun—*Waters*.

Oh, shit. Anxiety welled up in Charli like a flash flood. This was his family's place.

Grant pulled to the side of the road, a large two-story farmhouse looming in the distance, and turned to her, his blue eyes pleading with her before his words did. "I know that I shouldn't have dragged you here with me without telling you. It isn't fair. This is something I should have the guts to do by myself."

"Grant . . ."

"I've done everything on my own for as long as I can remember. No fear, right? But"—he gave the house a long look, his hat blocking his face—"I think I need your help with this one, freckles."

The quiet desperation in his voice reached inside her and clamped around her heart. There was no way she could deny him what he asked, not when he sounded so damned lost. She reached out and put her hand over his clasped ones. "Tell me what you need me to do, cowboy."

He looked over at her then, every emotion coloring his eyes. "Just go in there with me. Be by my side. I know I've fucked this up. *I've* been fucked up. And maybe things can't be fixed." He lifted his hand and traced his thumb over her lips, stirring an ache deep in her bones. "But for the first time in years, I have the urge to try."

Her throat worked as she wrangled in her emotions and tucked them down. She didn't want to read too much into what he was saying. He wanted to face his family and had asked for her to help. That's it. Nothing had changed from two nights ago in her bedroom. She looked up the long driveway. "I'm here for whatever you need, Grant."

The drive up to the house was brief, but by the time they climbed out and stood facing the door, Charli had butterflies the size of buzzards flailing around inside her stomach. How was she supposed to do this? Grant hadn't seen his family in years and she was going to be some stranger tagging along with him. Talk about awkward.

But she'd seen how much it had cost him to even ask for her help. He was a man built on pride and control. This was uncharted territory for him, and no matter how uncomfortable this turned out to be, she wasn't going to let him traverse it alone.

Grant rang the bell, and soon the hollow sound of footsteps on wood broke through the country air. The door swung open and a woman with the same dark hair as Grant filled the doorway. Charli held her breath. In the space between seconds, Charli saw the recognition dawn, the relief in his mother's eyes, then the tears.

"Hey, Ma." Two words, but Charli heard the regret and apology heavy in Grant's voice.

Without a word, his mom stepped forward and wrapped her arms around her son, her hands pressing along his back as if checking to make sure Grant wasn't an apparition.

Charli moved back a little, not wanting to interfere with the reunion. Her own tears burned her eyes, the scene a potent reminder of what she no longer had in her own life now that her dad had passed, but she kept them at bay. This was Grant and his mother's moment.

Mrs. Waters pulled back from the hug after a long minute and looked up at her son with dewy but shrewd eyes. "Well, it's about damn time, you stubborn boy."

That actually pulled a quiet chuckle from Grant. "I'm sorry, Ma. Would it help if I told you you've gotten even prettier in the last few years?"

"Flattery didn't work when I caught you tipping cows when you were a teenager. It ain't any more effective now." She stepped back and straightened her checkered blouse, but her flip words couldn't mask the relief in her stance. "Tell me you're staying for a little while."

"Not sure yet." Grant put his hand out to Charli, and his mom's gaze slid her way, apparently noticing her for the first time.

Surprise flickered over her features. "And who's this?"

Grant's hand closed around Charli's, and he tugged her to his side. "Ma, this is Charli Beaumonde, the girl I love."

Charli's gasp was covered by his mother's own matching one. He gave Charli's hand a squeeze, hoping he hadn't just screwed everything up worse. The words hadn't been the ones he'd planned, but when his mother had asked who Charli was, the truth had tumbled out like a drunken confession.

And the internal backlash of guilt and grief he'd expected from such a declaration didn't knock his knees out from under him. Instead, a strange calmness seemed to overtake him, like being submerged in warm, still water. A smile grew in him, one that came from a place he hadn't accessed in a long while.

His mother recovered first, extending her hand to Charli. "Well, my goodness, Charli. I can't tell you how nice it is to meet you. I'm Georgia Waters."

"Thanks so much, nice to meet you, too." Charli shook his mother's hand, her words smooth and polite. But Grant could tell Charli had automatically fallen back into professional reporter mode—the place she went when she was off balance.

He was going to need to get her alone to explain himself, to tell her how he felt in the right way. But he knew his mother wasn't going to let them out of her sight anytime soon. Already, she was ushering them inside and rattling on about how she hadn't been expecting company and would've had food ready if she'd known. But of course, she had a lasagna in the fridge and was preheating the oven before he and Charli had settled onto the chairs in the large, eat-in kitchen. He suspected the scouts had stolen the *Be Prepared* motto from his mother.

Being in his childhood home after so many years had an onslaught of different emotions clattering through him. How many times had he sat in this kitchen while his mom prepared a meal, his dad stealing nibbles of stuff when he thought she wasn't looking. This had been a place of warmth in his life, a safe haven, the people in it had meant everything to him.

But it'd also been the place he'd courted his wife, where they'd lived before getting their own home. And it'd been the house everyone had gathered in after Rachel's funeral. The site of too many pitying looks, too many she's-in-a-better-place pats on the arm. So he'd let himself close the door to it, shut out the very people who maybe could've provided him comfort after the unthinkable happened.

For all these years since he'd left, he'd been surrounded by people but always alone. He'd thought it'd been the noble thing to do, a punishment for his sins, a way to save his family from dealing with the ugliness of his grief, his anger. But as he watched his mother piddle around the kitchen, casting surreptitious looks his way, as if to make sure he was still there, he realized how selfish his behaviors had been.

He hadn't been noble; he'd been a coward.

He peeked over at Charli as she answered a question his mom had asked. She hadn't looked at him since they'd entered the house. She'd kept up steady conversation with his mother, but her fingers were busy fiddling with the cloth napkin she'd grabbed off the table. If it'd been made of paper, the whole thing would've been shredded by now. She was freaking out. Elegantly. But freaking out nonetheless.

He'd handled things all wrong and needed to talk to her, but there was one more thing he had to do first. He picked his hat up off the table and stood. "Ma, you mind keeping Charli company for a little while? I need to take a walk."

His mother, who'd been digging through the pantry for Parmesan, peered over her shoulder. Her all-knowing eyes met his. "Sure, son. Take all the time you need. Lunch will be a while still."

He walked behind Charli's chair, giving her shoulder a gentle squeeze. He'd asked her to be by his side today, but this was the one last thing he needed to do all by himself. "Thanks, freckles."

She nodded, and he left her there in the kitchen, slipping out the side door and staring down the expanse of land behind his family's farmhouse.

He rubbed his thumb along his wedding band, secured his hat atop his head, and set off on the path that led to the back corner of the property.

Someone was waiting for him.

THIRTY-ONE

Charli stared out the kitchen window in the direction Grant had disappeared. He'd been gone for a while, and uneasiness had crawled under her skin and set up camp there. Maybe she'd fallen asleep on the drive to Baton Rouge and was in some alternate dream world. Had Grant really said he loved her out there on that porch? She couldn't even process that. Or the fact that somehow instead of being on the way to saying good-bye to Grant for the last time, she was sitting in his family's home, listening to his mother call up Grant's siblings to insist they come over.

Charli paced away from the window, walking over to the glass hutch in the corner of the room, trying to look like she was just browsing the knickknacks in the kitchen instead of running off nervous energy. She let her eyes drift over the family photos displayed on the shelves. Photos of children playing outside, family portraits, some old, some more recent. One that had to be Grant when he was a teen, basketball tucked under a gangly arm. Then her eyes hit one that definitely was Grant, his arm around a pretty blonde with a shy smile.

Without thinking, Charli picked up the framed photo, bringing it closer. Grant had laughter in his eyes and looked as if the ugliness of the world had never breathed on him. Innocent and happy—a couple with the whole world spread out before them, a lifetime to look forward to. The sight evaporated the air from Charli's lungs. She ran her thumb along the edge of the frame, grief for the people in the photo clogging her throat.

Georgia stepped up behind Charli, peering over her shoulder. "I'm sure Grant told you about Rachel," she said, her voice gentle.

Charli nodded, trying to swallow past the tightness in her chest. "She was beautiful."

Georgia sighed. "She was. I remember the day we took that picture of them, remember thinking how perfect everything was. My family was together, my husband was by my side, and my children were starting to build their own lives." She shook her head. "A year later, those murderers didn't just take Rachel and that baby-to-be away from us; they took everything. The light in my son's eyes, the tight bond we all had with each other, my ability to fix things for my children."

Charli turned to her, finding Georgia wearing a sad smile.

"It's a hard day when you realize you can't save your own child or take away their hurt." She took the photo from Charli and set it back on the shelf. "So, thank you."

Charli frowned. "For what?"

She walked over to the island and poured a glass of iced tea from the pitcher she'd set there. "For bringing him back."

Charli slid onto one of the stools flanking the island. "It was his idea to come."

She held a glass of tea out for Charli, her eyes crinkling at the corners. "That's not what I meant, hon."

Grant kneeled in the soft grass that blanketed the family cemetery. When he was a kid this area on the far side of the property used to scare him. He'd been convinced ghosts of his ancestors were hiding behind every headstone. Then when he'd buried Rachel here, this place had brought forth nightmares of a different sort. But today, with the sun shining and the bees buzzing around all the flowers, he simply felt the warm presence of family surrounding him.

He'd picked some wildflowers and placed them over his father's plot, saying a good-bye he'd never had the chance to make. Then he'd settled himself in front of Rachel's grave. The headstone had been simply stated—*Rachel Waters, wife and mother.* He brushed his fingers along the stone, feeling the engraved letters beneath his fingers, the finality of them. She wasn't coming back. He could punish himself, lock himself into a miserable existence, pay penance until the day he had a headstone himself, and it still wouldn't undo what had happened. He would just create another tragedy—his own slow death.

Is that what he would've wanted if the roles had been reversed? Would he have wanted Rachel to give up on being happy? Would he have expected her to shut herself off from real life and mourn him forever?

No. Of course not. He'd be pissed at her, actually.

Just like he couldn't imagine his dad being angry with his mom for finding someone after he passed. He'd want her to be happy, to not be alone.

He stared down at his wedding band, the metal gleaming under the noonday sun. For years, he thought he'd been wearing it for comfort, a little piece of what he'd lost against his skin. But he realized now it'd also been a crutch, a subtle way of torturing himself daily, an excuse not to let himself really live.

He slipped it off and got to his knees, the lawn soft beneath him. He held the ring up and brought it to his lips, remembering the day she'd slipped it on his finger. The sun had been shining just like this. "I'll always love you, Rach."

He lowered his hand and pressed the ring into the earth, pushing it into the dirt beneath the grass until it was fully covered. "But it's time I said good-bye."

The breeze swirled around him, ruffling his hair and drying the final tears he'd shed for the life that used to be. He closed his eyes, the scent of wildflowers surrounding him, so much like the fragrance Rachel used to wear. And in that moment, he sensed her there, and felt her forgiveness, her hope for him. He climbed to his feet and set his hat back on his head.

As he walked away, he knew the nightmares would never stalk him again.

Someone had finally chased them away.

And now he needed to thank her.

THIRTY-TWO

Charli sat on the wood plank swing that hung from the massive oak tree in the farmhouse's backyard, letting her feet dangle. The afternoon sun was sinking toward the horizon and voices drifted out of the house. Georgia had apparently called every family member in a thirty-mile radius to welcome Grant home.

Charli had snuck out to call her brother and let him know they weren't going to make it to Baton Rouge tonight.

"What's wrong?" Max asked, concern in his voice. "Car trouble or something?"

She wrapped her fingers around the rope of the swing. "Not exactly. We stopped at Grant's family's house to visit."

Her brother was quiet for a moment. "Char, why would he bring you to visit his family?"

The what-are-you-up-to tone was one she was all too familiar with. Her brother had the uncanny ability to sound just like her daddy. She ignored the question. "We'll probably get to your house sometime tomorrow."

"Ah, hell," he said. "You got involved with him, didn't you?"

God, how was it possible her brother could make her feel fourteen again with a few well-placed words. "Um, let's file that under things that are none of your business."

"Dammit, Char." She could picture his scowl. He'd probably started pacing, too. "Grant's my friend, a good guy, but he's got baggage. Like cargo-plane-sized baggage. I don't want you getting hurt."

Too late for that. And her brother's fears only underlined hers. Grant had told his mom he loved Charli, but what did that change? She'd known he had feelings for her already. Didn't mean he could act on them or that he wouldn't always be looking at her wishing she were someone else. The *L* word hadn't lightened that boulder in her stomach she'd been carrying around since she'd realized she'd fallen for him.

"I'll call you tomorrow, Max."

"Char—"

But she clicked off the phone before she could hear what else he had to say. She tucked her cell phone in her pocket and wrapped her other hand in the swing's rope, pumping her legs a bit to get a sway going. She closed her eyes and leaned back, trying to let her despair slough off her with each arc of the swing. Forward. Back. Forward. Back. The wind rushed past her ears and the swing creaked beneath her, the knotted rope grinding against the well-worn wood. If her feet didn't touch the ground, maybe she could push reality out for a little while.

"Enjoying my rope work again, Ms. Beaumonde?"

Charli's lids flew open as she swung past a black cowboy hat. Grant reached out and grabbed the rope when she passed again, slowing her. She held on tight so she wouldn't launch off the seat.

Grant continued talking as if she'd responded to his question. "I can't even believe these knots held up. I put this swing up for my sister when she was like ten." He ran his hand along the rope. "She used to stand on it to swing and then leap off. Would scare the shit out of Ma."

She smirked. "She and I probably would've gotten along as kids."

"No doubt." His smile was light, but the weight of the unspoken hung heavy between them. He stepped in front of her, grabbing both ropes, framing her. "I'm sorry I kidnapped you today. And I'm really sorry that I dropped a bomb on the porch. It just slipped out."

She looked away, toward the house, feeling as if she were constructed of stuff as fragile as the leaves falling off the tree. One more blow and she would scatter. "Of course, an accident."

"That's not what I—"

"No. Stop." She turned her head toward him, nailing him with her glare, all her frustration bubbling over. "What am I supposed to do with that, Grant? Tell me. You sleep with me, then shut down. You kiss me, then freak out. You admit you love me and then you disappear, leaving me with your mother who's talking to me like I'm your girl. Something I'm reminded over and over again that I can never be. That spot's already filled."

"Charli—"

But her tirade steamrolled right over his attempt to cut in. "I get it, okay. I *so freaking get it*. Your wife was amazing. Your life was perfect. And I'm sorry. I'm *so* sorry for what happened to you. No one deserves that kind of tragedy. My heart hurts thinking about it. But you can't keep doing this. You can't keep making me love you more, then yanking the rug out from under me. I'm tough, but I'm not the goddamned Terminator, Grant. I'm not—"

But his lips were on her before she could get the next word out, his hands sliding into her hair and cupping her head. She almost rocked right off the back of the swing, the shock jolting her, but he held her fast. Her eyes drifted shut, the feel of his mouth on hers like being dropped into some dream state where time slowed. Her fingers slipped from the ropes, her arms finding their way around his neck. His tongue twined with hers, his need and desire for her pouring into the kiss. She didn't want it to end, didn't want him to pull back, feared what would happen when he did.

But soon, the need for air trumped the wish to not break the spell. He pulled back, his hands cradling her face, caressing. "My turn to talk, freckles. Can you let me do that?"

Her heart was pounding so hard, she wondered if she'd be able to hear him over the thumping. She wet her lips. "Okay."

"You're right. You deserve someone who is going to love you without pretense, or caveats, or comparison. You deserve a guy who can look at you and know that he'd rather have no one else there next to him besides you. That no other girl could even come close to measuring up."

She looked down, bracing herself for the blow. But he grabbed her chin, not allowing her to look way.

"Listen, freckles. That guy is me. That's how I feel about you. I love you, Charlotte Beaumonde. Not second best, not as a consolation prize. You're the only woman I want in my life. Past, present, and future."

"But . . ." His image went wavy in front of her as tears clouded her vision, blocked her words.

"I'm done running, Charli." He held up his bare hand, the tan line the only remnant of the ring that used to be there. "And I know that being with me is complicated. I'll never be vanilla and my job is . . . interesting. And I'll probably freak out every time you go to chase some adrenaline rush because God knows you can get yourself into some predicaments. But I'll do whatever I need to if it means I get to have you. I'll even learn to like Tom Brady . . . the cat, not the quarterback—that'll never happen. I just—"

She pressed her fingers against his lips, laughing through her tears. "Stop."

He grinned beneath her touch. "Too much?"

"A dom should never beg, right?"

He grabbed her wrist and kissed her fingertips. "Darlin', if it means you'll be with me, I'll let you shackle me to the floor in front of everybody at The Ranch and beg like a dog."

"That won't be necessary." She shook her head, bliss seeping through her every pore, pushing out the melancholy that had claimed her minutes earlier. He loved her back. *Really* loved her back. She reached out and grabbed his hand. "Haven't you figured it out? You already have me, Grant. Even if you had dropped me off in Louisiana tonight, my heart would've left with you. I've been gone since the first time you kissed me. I'm the easiest sell in Texas right now."

He grinned, a boyish light she hadn't seen before filling his eyes. "You're going to be anything but easy, freckles. But I can't wait to get started."

She slid off the swing and wrapped her arms around his waist, pressing the top of her head to his chest. "Your place or mine?"

He nuzzled her ear, his breath a soft caress. "*Our* place, love. I don't want to sleep another night without you next to me."

The words were ones she never knew she needed but were exactly what she'd been waiting for her whole life. She raised her face to him and pressed her lips against his, relishing the feel of that once-forbidden territory. "Let's go home, cowboy."

EPILOGUE

Grant paced across his living room one more time, his boots creating a monotonous beat in the empty cabin. How could she not be answering her phone? Maybe the thing had died. Or, maybe she wanted to tell him the news in person. Or, maybe it hadn't worked out, and she was sobbing in her car and too upset to call him.

"Dammit." He checked his phone one more time to make sure it had a signal, then shoved it back in his pocket. "Come on, baby, toss me a crumb—a text, something."

He laced his fingers behind his neck, trying to massage some of the tension away. He'd offered to go with Charli this morning, but she'd given him that back-off-cowboy look that he'd learned to heed. She had no idea how that feistiness made him hard every time she directed it his way. If she thought she was getting away with being a bossy thing, so be it. She didn't need to know that all it did was add to the list of things he'd do to her later when he had her tied up and begging.

The sound of an engine had him hustling toward the front door.

He stepped outside, his blood pressure immediately lowering. She was home. Safe. However the audition went, she was here and they could deal with it. Charli climbed out of the car, and Grant scanned her expression trying to read the answer before she told him.

Her lips were tipped down as she headed up the driveway. "Hey there."

Her sad puppy tone and hang of her shoulders had his hopes tumbling. She hadn't gotten it. He pulled her up onto the porch as soon as she was within arm's reach and dragged her against him. "I'm sorry, freckles."

She circled her arms around his waist. "They said I was too quirky for an anchor position."

He pulled back, holding her at arm's length. "Quirky? What the fuck is wrong with them? It's called having a goddamned personality. I thought the new executives they hired couldn't be as idiotic as the others, but clearly I overestimated them."

She looked down, shaking her head. "It's my fault. I stumbled in my heels on the way to the desk, then tried to make a joke out of it by taking off my shoes and telling them I was the barefoot reporter. Then when they gave me a story about Tom Brady sustaining an injury, I mentioned in the report that I'd named my cat after him because they both had good hair."

Grant couldn't help the chuckle that escaped.

She hit him with a look equivalent to a kick to the balls. "You think this is funny? My dream just went to hell and you're laughing?"

She shrugged out of his grip and stomped into the house past him.

Well, shit. "Baby, I'm not laughing at you or your dream, I just . . ." He followed her into the house. "If those assholes can't appreciate your humor, the girl you are, then who the fuck needs them? There are other TV stations out there who'll appreciate you. We'll look . . ."

But as he babbled on like an imbecile, she spun around on her her heel and with her hands on her hips, her *how dare you* glare morphed into a broad *gotcha* grin.

His words halted and he narrowed his gaze, her shift in demeanor smacking him upside the head. "You little shit. You got the job, didn't you?"

She tipped her head to the side, her eyes all sunshine and mischief. "Not exactly."

"Spill it, freckles."

"So . . . all that stuff I told you was true. I did trip and talk about my cat. And they offered someone else the anchor job. But . . ." She rocked forward on her toes with every word, like she was barely restraining herself from bouncing up and down. "They offered me my own show."

"What?"

She made a sound he'd never heard come from her before—the *oh, my God* squeal that teenage girls seemed to have the patent on. Then her words poured out of her at a speed that could break the sound barrier. "They've been wanting to do a daytime show that features the kind of stories I research, feel-good stories about athletes and local organizations. Dig into the beyond-the-playing-field things. And they wanted someone the viewers could relate to—someone who would make them laugh but also who knew her sports. And they think that's me. They want it to be me!"

She did hop this time and then launched herself at him. If she'd known how very girly she looked in that moment, she'd never worry about being too tomboy again. He wrapped his arms around her and spun her off her feet, her elation contagious. "I'm so proud of you, baby. I knew someone would have to see how perfect you are for this."

He set her down on her feet and she grinned up at him. "I had you going there, didn't I? Mr. Dom who can read everybody got punked by my superior acting skills."

He attempted a stern look, though he was too thrilled for her to truly pull it off. "You had me worried out of my mind. Why didn't you answer your phone?"

"And miss out on this fun? Hell, no."

He gripped her hips and seated her against the growing bulge in his jeans. "You realize how much trouble you're in now, right, Charlotte? You didn't think tricking me would have consequences?"

Her tongue darted out, wetting her lips in a nervous tic that had anticipation tightening in his groin. "Maybe I don't mind consequences."

He pulled her down onto the couch with him, a soft yelp slipping past her lips. "Well, now I really have no choice. Purposely goading me. Reckless girl."

"Sorry, sir." The words were an apology, but he could hear the want in her voice, the ache.

God, he loved how playful she was. It made everything all the more fun. He turned her to the side, then draped her across his spread thighs. She squirmed against him for a moment, then softened, her muscles melting against him. He could already sense her slipping into subspace. She fell under so easily now it took his breath away. Beautiful.

He lifted her skirt and slid her lacy panties down her thighs. He ran a hand along the smooth skin of her ass, loving the quiver her body gave at his slightest touch. Her sexy scent drifted up to him and he had to take a few seconds to settle his own aching drive. Sometimes he wanted her so badly he feared he'd fire off like an inexperienced teenager.

"You think it was nice to make me worry about you, Charlotte?"

Her fingers curled into the couch cushion. "No, sir."

He rubbed a circular pattern along the globes of her ass with his palm, then drew back in a high arc and delivered a stinging smack on the right side. She arched her back and her breathy moan stoked the embers already burning hot in him. He gave her a matching swat on the other side, her fair skin going pink instantly. He relished seeing his handprint on her, his mark. His fingers traced the shape. Pity those marks faded so quickly.

"You made me pace the floors, love." He spanked her center, right above the soft, already damp folds of her sex. She let loose a more desperate sound as a shudder worked through her. Whether she realized it or not, her hips tilted higher, silently asking for more. He brushed his fingers along her wetness, dipping inside and feeling the clench of her pussy. "You know, if I was a betting man, I'd say that you tricked me knowing this would be the outcome. Am I not being hard enough on you, freckles? You need more discipline than I'm giving you?"

Since they'd moved into together, he'd been testing her limits, getting a feel for where she needed him to push and where he needed to pull back. But maybe he'd been too soft. Figuring out how to do this with love in the mix had been his own version of edge play—scary and thrilling but uncharted territory.

She turned her head, her cheek pressed to the couch but her hooded gaze on him. "All I need is you, Grant. You don't have to be careful with me or hold back. What pleases you is going to please me."

The words wrapped around his chest and squeezed, the gift of her true submission almost too heady to process. She was his. Honestly and without fine print. No contracts or carefully negotiated rules. Just he and Charli finding their way together.

He brushed the back of his hand over the line of her jaw. "Get up, Charlotte. Show me you know how to properly apologize for your inconsiderate behavior."

Charli pushed herself up and off his lap, her blood pumping and her head buzzing. Today had been one of the happiest she could remember, but nothing had felt complete until she'd walked into this cabin and told Grant about it. And he'd been right. She knew he'd make her pay for teasing him, but she'd needed nothing more at the end of this day then to give herself over to him, to surrender.

She'd never been able to stand the quiet before him, had always sought distraction. But now, this sacred space created between them in these moments was like balm for her psyche—the silence soothing. Contentment bled through her as she stood in front of Grant and slipped out of her clothes, keeping her eyes down and her movements slow. She could feel his gaze on her without looking up, could sense his overwhelming desire for her. If his goal in the beginning had been to make her feel beautiful, he'd succeeded. She never felt more confident than when she was stripped bare before him.

She knelt in front of him, placing her hands on her thighs.

He shifted forward on the couch, his hand drifting over her shoulder. "Darlin', I have to tell you, I've never been happier to have been so damn wrong about someone. You're more perfect in submission than anyone I've ever seen."

Her skin heated as if her blood had been turned to simmer, a slow rolling warmth starting at her chest and radiating outward. "Thank you, sir."

"Now, how do you think I should have you apologize?"

She dropped her focus to the floorboards, listening to the steady beat of her heart. The tips of his boots came into view. "I'll do whatever you'd like me to."

"Present your back to me, arms behind you."

She sat back on her legs and then hinged forward, chest to thighs. Her face ended up hovering inches above his boot. She'd joked with him early on that she'd never kiss a man's shoe—had scoffed at the idea. But as she stared at it in front of her now, she was suddenly mesmerized by the symbol of all that represented this man—tough, unpretentious, and scuffed in a way that made it more beautiful. And as if the desire had always been there, waiting until she was ready to accept it, she knew the perfect way to apologize. She lowered her head and pressed her lips to the warm leather.

For once, the sharp intake of breath wasn't her own. She closed her eyes, his approval falling over her like soft rain. She'd pleased him. And even if she still didn't fully understand why that affected her so deeply, she felt the stir inside her, the rightness. They both stayed there in a moment that seemed to stretch as wide as the land surrounding the cabin.

Finally, he shifted and she raised her head. His gaze hit her like a branding iron, a permanent sear to her system. He captured her face in his hands. "I'm going to take such good care of you, sweet Charlotte. I won't let a day pass where I don't show you how much you mean to me or how much I value the gift of your trust."

His words moved over her like soft strokes, his stripped-to-the-studs declaration smoothing any sharp places left inside her. She smiled, blinking through the hazy shield of unshed tears. "Just love me, Grant."

"I already do." He claimed her mouth, a slow languid dance, and she could feel everything in that kiss. The years of loss he'd been through, the ache for her in the moment, and the promise of all that was to come.

When he broke away from the kiss, there was fire in his eyes, a predatory flash. A ripple of delicious fear skated over her nerve endings. She loved his sweetness, the tender way he could make her melt. But that darkness that lay in wait for times like these fed something deep and primal inside her. She craved his control, his marks, the pain she knew would push her up and over the edge to pleasure.

She'd sensed him holding back with her since she'd moved in, as if he was afraid to really let her see the extent of that side of him. But the way he was looking at her now was anything but tentative.

"On your feet, Charlotte."

She climbed to a stand, and he grabbed her by the back of the neck, nudging her forward. "Kissing my boot is very much appreciated, but it's not going to get you out of what I have planned for you. Walk."

He led her into the bedroom and released his grip. "Strip the bed of all but the bottom sheet, then lie on your stomach."

"Yes, sir." She did as she was told, hurrying to yank the duvet and blankets from the bed and dumping them into a corner. Then she climbed onto the bed and lay down.

His hands were on her in an instant, wrapping rope around her wrists and ankles, stretching her into a facedown *X* position on the bed and knotting the rope at the far corners of the headboard and footboard. She tried to wriggle, testing the slack, but she was pressed tight to the bed with no give. A little wave of panic shimmered over her. He'd never bound her to where she couldn't move at all.

"Boy, you look pretty like this," Grant said, stalking around the bed and stepping out of her line of sight. She strained her ears, trying to determine exactly where he was but still flinched when he finally touched her. His palm cupped her sex from behind, spreading her and painting her with her own juices. "All spread and slick for me. Very nice."

She squeezed her eyes shut, the ache for him overtaking any lingering anxiety over her helpless position. She knew if he'd taken the time to tie her, he wasn't going to rush things. The thought was simultaneously enticing and maddening. He dipped his fingers inside her and grazed his thumb over her clit. *Yes*. She pressed her hips downward, seeking more pressure, but he moved his hand away.

"I'm thinking fair punishment is that you wait for me as long as I had to wait for you today. Which by my estimation was . . . an hour and ten minutes."

Oh, shit.

An hour of teasing? She wouldn't make it. She'd dissolve into desperation if he made her hold off that long. "Please. I'm so sorry, sir."

He scoffed. “I’m sure you are . . . now. Which, by the way, is an hour and eleven minutes too late.”

“I’m—”

“Hush.”

The ominous sound of him unzipping his “goody” bag had her breath quickening and her pulse hopping into her throat. Of course, he’d placed his stuff far out of her view so she had no idea what his evil plan may be. She turned her head, the one movement she could manage, but all she could see was his back reflected in the mirror over the dresser as he hunched over his bag.

He turned around, meeting her gaze in the mirror. “Worried, love?”

“Maybe.”

His grin bordered on sinister. “Smart girl.”

The bed dipped as he climbed behind her, making the sheet brush against her already sensitized skin. He placed a hand on her hip first and then slid it down her thigh. “Hold still.”

“Yes, sir.” As if she had a choice.

Cool silicon nudged her sex, then slid between her and the bed, pressing against her clit. He flipped on the switch, and the powerful hum of the vibrator filled the space.

“Oh, God, yes,” she murmured, sensation spreading from her center outward. Blessed relief.

But he wasn’t done with her. Without giving her a chance to adjust to the vibrator he slid something thick and flexible inside her channel—a dildo. *Whoa.* She arched but had nowhere to go, no escape from the rush of pleasure. Her body automatically tensed, trying to stave off the orgasm dancing at her nerve endings. She’d been revved up since she’d pulled into the driveway, and her body wasn’t in the mood for patience.

Grant traced the crack of her ass with his fingertip, the simple move sending a thread of need curling up her spine. “Denial can be a fun game, Charlotte. Forcing you to hold back for an hour could prove quite tortuous."

He smoothed cool gel over her back entrance, tucking a finger inside and sending her control system into near-meltdown stage. She pressed her face into the bed, the mattress absorbing her whimper, her pleas for mercy. *Hold on, hold on . . .*

"But the opposite can be fun, too," Grant said, his voice soft, lulling, and far too wicked to be trusted. He slipped his finger out of her and replaced it with what she knew had to be a plug, nudging it past her entrance and filling her to capacity.

"Oh, God." She raised her head, her neck arching, and sweat instantly slicked her body as her temperature seemed to increase tenfold. How could he expect her to hold anything back while being stimulated like this? The vibrator pulsed against her clit *slow-slow-fast*, *slow-slow-fast*, causing her muscles to clench around the dual invasions inside her. The sensation was overwhelming and relentless. Blissful torture. Even when she tried to shift her hips, there was no escaping the sure stroke of the vibe. Her fists clenched.

"Grant," she begged. "Please, I can't . . ."

"Shh . . ." He dipped his tongue into the dimples at the base of her spine, circling them with teasing strokes that somehow made her nipples tingle against the sheets. "I don't expect you to, sweet Charlotte. You can come as many times as you'd like."

"I can?"

But before she could even process what that meant, his teeth sunk into her ass cheek and it was like pulling the pin in a grenade. Her body rumbled against the mattress and sensation exploded through her, splintering her in all directions. Her muscles contracted around the foreign objects inside her, begging, needy. Her body wanted to writhe, to thrash, but the ropes bit into her, holding her taut.

"That's right, baby. Fight through it. You make the sexiest fucking noises. I could spend all night listening to you, watching you."

The slippery sound of lube against skin mixed in with her own moans, and she realized Grant was pleasuring himself behind her. Long, heavy strokes mixed with panted breaths. The image only served to push her orgasm higher, the idea of his big, firm hand sliding along his cock while she lay bound beneath him was one of the most erotic she could imagine.

"Ah, God," Grant groaned, the slippery sound of his hand getting faster, more urgent. "Give me another one, Charlotte. Come with me."

The vibrator shifted to the exact right spot and a second wave of bliss knocked the breath from her. A grinding scream left her throat, and Grant's moan joined hers. She trembled with the sharp intensity of the orgasm, this one almost unbearable in its power. "Grant!"

Hot spurts of his release landed on her back, marking her, owning her. She panted her way through the death throes of her orgasm as his seed dripped down her sides in a slow, sensual slide.

She sagged into the mattress, the vibrator still dancing against her oversensitive clit.

"So gorgeous, baby. I almost regret not setting up a camera and catching how perfect you look right now on film. But I'm not done with you yet." The mattress shifted and a wet towel touched her back as Grant cleaned her off.

Then the bed dipped again as Grant got up, and she waited for him to come around and remove the vibrator and dildos, but as seconds slipped, anxiety started to rise in her. "Grant?"

"Yes?" he said, the smile in his voice clear.

"The vibrator. I can't take . . ."

Then pain striped her back, slicing off the end of her sentence like a sharp knife. She cried out in surprise.

"We've still got a while to go. This will take your mind off the vibrator." The strips of leather hit the flesh of her backside, the sting raining down on her and crackling outward.

"Ah, Jesus." She gritted her teeth, the combination of pain coalescing with the continued stimulation and the remnants of her orgasm. She turned her head, catching sight of the cat-o'-nine-tails sailing through the air again. She braced. *Smack.*

She bit her lip, choking down another yelp. He'd never used that on her before, but son of a bitch, did it have a bite.

"Breathe through it, love," he said, his voice soothing though not apologetic. "Wait for it . . ."

He struck her across the back of her thighs, causing her body to shift hard against the vibrator. *Oh.*

Another lash.

Her skin was tingling, her muscles drawing tight, tighter.

Another.

The pain began to change, morph, drawing those lovely chemicals into her blood system, making her thoughts go fuzzy.

And another.

Wait for it, wait for it . . . His words drifted like a mantra in her head. So close . . .

He whipped a final time. Hard.

And there it was. Potent and without mercy, orgasm dragged her under, the agony and ecstasy mixing into that perfect cocktail to send her flying.

Tears stung her eyes as she cried out, shouted, calling Grant's name like a plea to God. For less, for more, she wasn't sure. But she no longer had control over the sounds she made or her body's reaction. As soon as she thought she was slipping from the peak, he'd rev her up again. Touching her, tasting her, knowing just what to do. All the while talking to her, praising her, loving her.

By the end of her hour, her mind had succumbed, the physical overtaking all executive functioning. He'd pulled so much from her, she wasn't sure she could form words or even move if she wasn't tied down. She wet her dry lips, her voice barely a whisper. "Grant, please."

He stepped to the side of the bed, pushing her sweat-slicked hair off her cheek. "What, baby, tell me what you need?"

She opened her eyes, meeting his gaze through her haze of pleasure. "I need you."

The smile that crossed his face nearly broke her open. He untied her wrists, rubbing the feeling back into her hands, but left her feet tied wide. Then he was behind her, slipping the toys from her and kissing the welts on her back. "You are so beautiful, Charlotte. So goddamned tough and beautiful."

Each kiss sent a shiver through her, the pain completely replaced with the sweet heat of adrenaline-laced bliss. She could barely lift her head. He draped himself over her back, supporting himself on his forearms, and pressed the head of his cock against her swollen entrance. "I'd turn you over to see that pretty face, but I don't want to put the pressure on your marks."

She angled her hips, pressing back against him, unable to bear another moment without him inside her. "Just take me like this. Please."

"You got it, love." He pushed forward, his cock hot and heavy inside her, and she let loose a sigh. She would've stayed tied up all night as long as she knew this was waiting for her at the end of it. He rocked his pelvis back then eased into her again, his breath spilling onto her neck. "God, you feel good, darlin'. Am I crushing you?"

"No, I like it." And she did. His body was heavy against hers, her lungs unable to fully inflate, but the feeling of being so completely overpowered by him had her drifting deep under the spell of the moment.

A low growl rumbled from him, and he canted his hips harder, claiming her with more ferocity, more speed. "You know what it does to me when you get like this, when I can actually feel your total surrender?"

Her breasts pressed into the bed, the rhythm of his motion scraping her nipples across the sheet and coiling her muscles again. Sparks seemed to light up every abused zone in her nervous system—sizzling and popping. Climax galloped toward her again.

She wasn't sure she'd survive this one.

Grant pumped into her, his own control slipping as his thighs slapped against the back of hers. "Come with me one more time, Charli."

That was all it took. She was sailing over again, gentle tremors rolling over her exhausted body, a quiet fall into oblivion. Her tears dampened the sheet, and Grant's own moan rattled out of him, his hot release jetting into her and his fingers lacing with hers.

Lost. Together. Perfect.

Finally, when she drifted back into the present, became aware of her surroundings again, Grant slipped out of her, untied her ankles, and carried her into the bathroom.

No words were exchanged as he drew her bath and then gently cleaned her—washing her hair and soothing her tender skin, combing out her knots and slipping her into a soft cotton nightgown. His quiet care allowed her mind to slowly pull itself back together, to ease to the surface again.

When they finally climbed into his bed—no, *their* bed—Grant gathered her against him and pressed a soft kiss to her mouth. "I love you, Charli Beaumonde. *Nothing* in my life has ever felt as right as you do."

She smiled, closing her eyes and snuggling against him. For the first time in as long as she could remember, she didn't have to worry about being second best. She was happy.

She was his.

Keep reading for a special preview of

NOT UNTIL YOU

a serial eBook

from Roni Loren, available Spring 2013

"Andre, this isn't a good time. Can I call you back?"

Marcela did her best not to let her cell phone slip from between her ear and shoulder. *Just don't drop the tequila*. She adjusted the enormous bottle her fellow classmate had given her as a graduation present from her right hand to beneath her left arm and tried to dig her keys out of her purse so she could open the main door to her apartment building.

"I'm so sorry I wasn't able to make it," her older brother said, his guilt obviously trumping her request to call him later. "I got caught at an investigation site. I thought I'd be able to get there in time, but we had a witness wanting to talk and . . ."

She cursed silently as her keys hit the pavement. She crouched down, doing her best not to flash her underwear to anyone who may be passing by. "Really, it's fine. They called my name. I walked across the stage and got a piece of paper and a sash for being *summa cum laude*. Dad yelled my name like he was at a baseball game instead of a ceremony. Not that interesting."

Her brother's heavy sigh said everything. She almost felt guilty that *he* felt so guilty. "Before you move back home next month, we're getting together to celebrate. My baby sister, the doctor. I'm so proud I could burst."

Cela smiled. She did like the sound of that. Dr. Marcela Medina, Doctor of Veterinary Medicine. Seven years of exams and studying and clinics, but it was finally done. Now it was time to leave Dallas and head back home to Verde Pass and take up the slack in her dad's practice.

That last part had her smile faltering a bit. She hooked her key ring with her finger and wobbled back to a stand. "That sounds great. But I really have to get going. I have my hands full and need to get through the door."

"Cela, you know better than to carry too much. Parking lots at night are one of the most dangerous places for women. Are you holding your mace?" he asked, his voice going into that bossy cop tone she was all too familiar with.

"It's in my hand," she lied, trying to remember where she'd stowed the last little canister he'd given her—probably in her junk drawer. "But I don't have a free hand to pull the door open."

"All right," he said, placated. "Congratulations again. I love you."

"Love you, too."

The phone call ended but she didn't have a way to take the phone off her ear, so she just shuffled forward in a sideways hunch, trying to juggle everything she was holding to get her key into the door. After two attempts, she got the lock turned and pressed her back against the glass door to push her way into the lobby.

As soon as she'd cleared the entrance and turned toward the stairs, male voices sounded behind her. Of course someone would show up right after she didn't need help anymore. She peeked back to see who it was, Andre's danger warnings still echoing in her head, but found something more distracting than criminals—her neighbors, Ian and Pike.

Ian stepped through the main door first and glanced her way. As usual, everything went melty inside her, his smile like a zap of heat to her system. "Need some help, neighbor?"

She straightened, but forgot about her phone in the process. Her brand-new iPhone went sliding off her shoulder.

"Crap!" She lurched forward, trying to save it from its imminent demise, dropping her plastic bag of Chinese takeout on the way.

"Whoa, there." Pike, Ian's roommate, was at her side in a second. His hand caught her elbow, saving her from losing the ginormous bottle of liquor along with her balance. But her phone clattered to the ground, the harsh sound mixing with the *splat* of her noodles hitting tile.

She winced, anticipating a broken screen. "Dammit."

Ian bent down, his tie brushing the ground as he swept her phone off the floor. He peered at the screen, dark brows lowering over pale eyes, then he turned the phone toward her—the happy puppy screen saver staring back at her intact. "All is well. Luckily these things are built to take a licking."

Her brain got snagged on the work *lick*, and the back of her neck went hot. Her lips parted, but words failed her.

Pike cleared his throat, easing the tequila from her arms, and then crouched down near the open bag at her feet. He grabbed a noodle from the spilled box of Chinese food, tipped his head back and dropped it into his mouth, his eyes watching hers. "The lo mein's a loss, though."

She swallowed hard, his gaze even more bad boy than the tattoos peeking out from his open collar. *Look away.* She forced her face upward, but then ended up focusing on Ian again. *Say something.* God, she was standing there like an idiot. This was why she always avoided these two like they were contagious. They made her go stupid.

Ian held out her phone, and she managed to take it, the slight brush of his fingers against her hitting the reset button on her brain. She managed a feeble, "Thank you."

Ian glanced at the mess on the floor. "I'm really sorry I said anything. I didn't mean to distract you from your intricate juggling act."

She shook her head. "No, it's my fault. I shouldn't have been trying to carry everything at once. It's been a long day, and I was hoping to save myself a second trip up the stairs."

"The joys of a walk-up." Pike grabbed a few napkins and started cleaning up the noodles at her feet like it was his mess to worry about.

"Oh, you don't have to do that." She lowered herself to her knees. "I'll take care of it."

He grinned over at her, the mirror opposite of his roommate. Ian was all suits and dark looks, whereas Pike was a drummer in some local band—jeans, a sex-on-the-rocks smile, and spiked, bleached hair his usual uniform. Not that Cela had studied either of them. Or listened to their escapades through the wall she shared with them. Not at all.

Keep telling yourself that, Cela.

Despite her protest, Pike helped her finish picking up the mess. "So what's the big-ass bottle of tequila for, doll? No one could've had that bad of a day."

She glanced over at the bottle he'd set on the floor, debated whether she could be trusted to have a normal conversation with these two without sounding like she had a speech impediment. "I, uh, graduated today. It was a gift."

"Oh, right on."

"Congratulations, Cela," Ian said, dragging her attention upward. Just the sound of him saying her name in that smooth Texas drawl had her stomach clenching.

Ay dios mio. Her body clamored to attention like an eager labrador ready to be petted. *Down, girl.* These guys were way above her pay grade. She'd seen the women who'd passed through their apartment door—women who looked like they'd earned their doctorates in the art of seduction.

Cela hadn't even reached the kindergarten level in that particular department.

"Thank you."

"You were going to vet school at Dallas U., right?" Ian had tucked his hands in the pockets of his slacks, and though the question was casual, she had the distinct impression he was tense beneath that suit jacket.

Pike handed her a napkin for her hands and stood to toss the food into a nearby trash can.

She wiped off her hands and pushed herself to her feet, trying to do it as gracefully as possible in her restrictive skirt. "Yes, how'd you know that?"

"The scrubs you wear have the school insignia on them," Ian said, as if it was totally normal that he'd looked at her that closely.

"Observant." Especially considering she usually only managed a head-down, mumbled *hey-how-are-ya* exchange when they passed each other in the hallway. Secretly listening to one of your hot neighbors having sex had a way of making eye contact a bit uncomfortable the next day—particularly if said eavesdropper had used the sound track to fuel her own interlude with her battery-operated boyfriend.

Pike sidled up next to Ian—a motley pair if there ever was one. "So, Doc, now that you've got no dinner and clearly too much liquor on your hands, why don't you join us? We already have pizza on the way and we can play a drinking game with the tequila. Do college kids still play Never Have I Ever? I was always good at that one."

Kid? Is that what they saw her as? She knew neither of them could be *that* much older than she was. Though in terms of life experience, she had no doubt they trumped her a few times over.

"Oh, no, that's okay." The refusal was automatic, long practiced. How many times had she turned down such offers—from guys, from friends? Her parents had been so strict regarding her whereabouts when she was younger that she almost didn't know how to say yes even after living on her own the last four years. Studies first, fun later. Yet there never seemed to be any time for fun after the first one was finished.

"You sure? I don't want you going to bed with no dinner because of us," Ian said, frown lines marring that perfect mouth of his.

Going to bed and *us* was about all she heard. Her father's stern voice whispered in her ears. *You don't know these men. You'll be all alone in their apartment. Medina women have more respect for themselves than that.*

"Really, I'm fine," she said, her smile brief, plastic. "But thanks."

"Oh, come on," Pike said, his tone cajoling. "We've been neighbors for what, two years? We should at least get to know a little about each other."

Get to know each other? She knew that Ian was loud when he came—even if he was alone. Knew that Pike liked to laugh during sex. Knew the two men shared women. And the other sounds she'd heard over the last two years . . . the smacks, the orders, the erotic screams. Her face went as hot as if she'd stuck her head in an oven.

"Y'all just want me for my tequila," she said, attempting to deflect her derailing thoughts.

The corner of Pike's mouth lifted. "Of course that's not all we want you for."

Oh, hell. Pictures flashed across her brain. Dirty, delicious pictures. She almost dropped her phone again. She had no idea what to do with her hands, her expression.

Ian put a hand on Pike's shoulder. "The lady said no. I think we should let her go celebrate her graduation however she wants."

"All right." Pike's face turned hangdog, but he handed the tequila bottle to her. "If you change your mind, we've got big plans. Supreme pizza and a *Star Wars*–themed porn marathon. *The Empire Sucks C—*"

Ian smacked the back of Pike's head, and Pike ducked and laughed.

"Kidding. I mean a Jane Austen marathon," Pike corrected, his green-gold eyes solemn. "*Pride and Pu—*"

Ian was behind Pike, his hand clamping over his friend's mouth in a flash. "I seriously can't take him out. He's like an untrained puppy. Maybe you can lend me a shock collar or something."

Pike waggled his eyebrows, all playful wickedness.

She laughed, putting her hand to her too-hot forehead, and turning toward the stairs. "Yeah, so, I'm going to go now."

"Cela," Ian said as she put her foot onto the first step.

She glanced back. "Yeah?"

His ice-melt eyes flicked downward, his gaze alighting along the length of her before tracing their way upward again. "Promise you won't go to bed hungry."

She wet her lips, her skin suddenly feeling too tight to accommodate the blood pumping beneath it, and nodded.

But it was a lie.

She always went to bed hungry.

And it had nothing to do with a spilled dinner.

ABOUT THE AUTHOR

Roni Loren wrote her first romance novel at age fifteen when she discovered writing about boys was way easier than actually talking to them. Since then, her flirting skills haven't improved, but she likes to think her storytelling ability has. Though she'll forever be a New Orleans girl at heart, she now lives in Dallas with her husband and son. If she's not working on her latest sexy story, you can find her reading, watching reality television, or indulging in her unhealthy addiction to rock stars, er, rock concerts. Yeah, that's it. Visit her website: www.roniloren.com.